Of
Lions
and
Unicorns

A Lifetime of Tales
from the
Master Storyteller

michael morpurgo

Of Lions and Unicorns

A Lifetime of Tales
from the
Master Storyteller

With illustrations by
Peter Bailey, Quentin Blake, Christian Birmingham,
Emma Chichester Clark and Michael Foreman

HarperCollins *Children's Books*

First published in Great Britain in hardback by HarperCollins *Children's Books* in 2013
HarperCollins *Children's Books* is a division of HarperCollins*Publishers* Ltd,
77-85 Fulham Palace Road, Hammersmith, London, W6 8JB.

The HarperCollins website address is: www.harpercollins.co.uk

1
Of Lions and Unicorns
For full copyright details, please see the back of this anthology.

HB ISBN 978-0-00-793726-4

Printed and bound in England by Clays Ltd, St Ives plc

For all our grandchildren.

CONTENTS

THE PITY AND THE SHAME

THE LONELY SEA AND THE SKY

TALES TOLD AND NEW

Only Remembered

Illustration by Peter Bailey

My Father is a Polar Bear

This story is a tissue of truth – mostly. As with many of my stories, I have woven truths together and made from them a truth stranger than fiction. My father was a polar bear – honestly.

Tracking down a polar bear shouldn't be that difficult. You just follow the pawprints – easy enough for any competent Innuit. My father is a polar bear. Now if you had a father who was a polar bear, you'd be curious, wouldn't you? You'd go looking for him. That's what I did, I went looking for him, and I'm telling you he wasn't at all easy to find.

In a way I was lucky, because I always had two fathers. I had a father who *was* there – I called him Douglas – and one who wasn't there, the one I'd never even met – the polar bear one. Yet in a way he was there. All the time I was growing up he was there inside my head. But he wasn't only in my head, he was at the bottom of our Start-Rite shoebox, our secret treasure box, with the rubber bands round it, which I kept hidden at the bottom of the cupboard in our bedroom. So how, you might ask, does a polar bear fit into a shoebox? I'll tell you.

My big brother Terry first showed me the magazine under the bedclothes, by torchlight, in 1948 when I was five years old. The magazine was called *Theatre World*. I couldn't read it at the time, but he could. (He was two years older than me, and already mad about acting and the theatre and all that – he still is.) He had saved up all his pocket money to buy it. I thought he was crazy. "A shilling! You can get about a hundred lemon sherbets for that down at the shop," I told him

Terry just ignored me and turned to page twenty-seven. He read it out: "The Snow Queen, a dramat—something or other – of Hans Andersen's famous story, by the Young Vic Company." And there was a large black and white photograph right across the page – a photograph of two fierce-looking polar bears baring their teeth and about to eat two children, a boy and a girl, who looked very frightened.

"Look at the polar bears," said Terry. "You see that one on the left, the fatter one? That's our dad, our real dad. It says his name and everything – Peter Van Diemen. But you're not to tell. Not Douglas, not even Mum, promise?"

"My dad's a polar bear?" I said. As you can imagine I was a little confused.

"Promise you won't tell," he went on, "or I'll give you a Chinese burn."

Of course I wasn't going to tell, Chinese burn or no Chinese burn. I was hardly going to go to school the next day and tell everyone that I had a polar bear for a father, was I? And I certainly couldn't tell my mother, because I knew she never liked it if I ever asked about my real father. She always insisted that Douglas was the only father I had. I knew he wasn't, not really. So did she, so did Terry, so did Douglas. But for some reason that was always a complete mystery to me, everyone in the house pretended that he was.

Some background might be useful here. I was born, I later found out, when my father was a soldier in Baghdad during the Second World War. (You didn't know there were polar bears in Baghdad, did you?) Sometime after that my mother met and fell in love with a dashing young officer in the Royal Marines called Douglas Macleish. All this time, evacuated to the Lake District away from the bombs, blissfully unaware of the war and Douglas, I was learning to walk and talk and do my business in the right place at the right time. So my father came home from the war to discover that his place in my mother's heart had been taken. He did all he could to win her back. He took her away on a week's cycling holiday in Suffolk to see if he could rekindle the light of their love. But it was hopeless. By the end of the week they had come to an amicable arrangement. My father would simply disappear, because he didn't want to "get in the way". They would get divorced quickly and quietly, so that Terry and I could be brought up as a new family with Douglas as our father. Douglas would adopt us and give us Macleish as our surname. All my father insisted upon was that Terry and I should keep Van Diemen as our middle name. That's what happened. They divorced. My father disappeared, and at the age of three I became Andrew Van Diemen Macleish. It was a mouthful then and it's a mouthful now.

So Terry and I had no actual memories of our father whatsoever. I do have vague recollections of standing on a railway bridge somewhere near Earls Court in London, where we lived, with Douglas's sister – Aunty Betty, as I came to know her – telling us that we had a brand new father who'd be looking after us from now on. I was really not that concerned, not at the time. I was much more interested in the train that was chuffing along under the bridge, wreathing us in a fog of smoke.

My first father, my real father, my missing father, became a taboo person, a big hush hush taboo person that no one ever mentioned, except for Terry and me. For us he soon became a sort of secret phantom father. We used to whisper about him under the blankets at night. Terry would sometimes go snooping in my mother's desk and he'd find things out about him. "He's an actor," Terry told me one night. "Our dad's an actor, just like Mum is, just like I'm going to be."

It was only a couple of weeks later that he brought the theatre magazine home. After that we'd take it out again and look at our polar bear father. It took some time, I remember, before the truth of it dawned on me – I don't think Terry can have explained it very well. If he had, I'd have understood it much sooner – I'm sure I would. The truth, of course – as I think you might have guessed by now – was that my father was both an actor *and* a polar bear at one and the same time.

Douglas went out to work a lot and when he was home he was a bit silent, so we didn't really get to know him. But we did get to know Aunty Betty. Aunty Betty simply adored us, and she loved giving us treats. She wanted to take us on a special Christmas treat, she said. Would we like to go to the zoo? Would we like to go to the pantomime? There was *Dick Whittington* or *Puss in Boots*. We could choose whatever we liked.

Quick as a flash, Terry said, "*The Snow Queen.* We want to go to *The Snow Queen.*"

So there we were a few days later, Christmas Eve 1948, sitting in the stalls at a matinee performance of *The Snow Queen* at the Young Vic theatre, waiting, waiting for the moment when the polar bears come on. We didn't have to wait for long. Terry nudged me and pointed, but I already knew which polar bear my father had to be. He was the best

19

one, the snarliest one, the growliest one, the scariest one. Whenever he came on he really looked as if he was going to eat someone, anyone. He looked mean and hungry and savage, just the way a polar bear should look.

I have no idea whatsoever what happened in *The Snow Queen*. I just could not take my eyes off my polar bear father's curling claws, his slavering tongue, his killer eyes. My father was without doubt the finest polar bear actor the world had ever seen. When the great red curtains closed at the end and opened again for the actors to take their bows, I clapped so hard that my hands hurt. Three more curtain calls and the curtains stayed closed. The safety curtain came down and my father was cut off from me, gone, gone for ever. I'd never see him again.

Terry had other ideas. Everyone was getting up, but Terry stayed sitting. He was staring at the safety curtain as if in some kind of trance. "I want to meet the polar bears," he said quietly.

Aunty Betty laughed. "They're not bears, dear, they're actors, just actors, people acting. And you can't meet them, it's not allowed."

"I want to meet the polar bears," Terry repeated. So did I, of course, so I joined in. "Please, Aunty Betty," I pleaded. "Please."

"Don't be silly. You two, you do get some silly notions sometimes. Have a Choc Ice instead. Get your coats on now." So we each got a Choc Ice. But that wasn't the end of it.

We were in the foyer caught in the crush of the crowd when Aunty Betty suddenly noticed that Terry was missing. She went loopy. Aunty Betty always wore a fox stole, heads still attached, round her shoulders. Those poor old foxes looked every bit as pop-eyed and frantic as she did, as she plunged through the crowd, dragging me along behind her and calling for Terry.

Gradually the theatre emptied. Still no Terry. There was quite a to-do, I can tell you. Policemen were called in off the street. All the programme sellers joined in the search, everyone did. Of course, I'd worked it out. I knew exactly where Terry had gone, and what he was up to. By now Aunty Betty was sitting down in the foyer and sobbing her heart out. Then, cool as a cucumber, Terry appeared from nowhere, just wandered into the foyer. Aunty Betty crushed him to her, in a great hug. Then she went loopy all over again, telling him what a naughty, naughty boy he was, going off like that. "Where were you? Where have you been?" she cried.

"Yes, young man," said one of the policemen. "That's something we'd all like to know as well."

I remember to this day exactly what Terry said, the very words: "Jimmy riddle. I just went for a jimmy riddle." For just a moment he even had me believing him. What an actor! Brilliant.

We were on the bus home, right at the front on the top deck where you can guide the bus round corners all by yourself – all you have to do is steer hard on the white bar in front of you. Aunty Betty was sitting a couple of rows behind us. Terry made quite sure she wasn't looking. Then, very surreptitiously, he took something out from under his coat and showed me. The programme. Signed right across it were these words, which Terry read out to me:

> *"To Terry and Andrew,*
> *With love from your polar bear father, Peter. Keep happy."*

Night after night I asked Terry about him, and night after night under the blankets he'd tell me the story again, about how he'd gone into the dressing-room and found our father sitting there in his polar bear costume with his head off (if you see what I mean), all hot and sweaty. Terry said he had a very round, very smiley face, and that he laughed just like a bear would laugh, a sort of deep bellow of a laugh – when he'd got over the surprise that is. Terry described him as looking like "a giant pixie in a bearskin".

For ever afterwards I always held it against Terry that he never took me with him that day down to the dressing-room to meet my polar bear father. I was so envious. Terry had a memory of him now, a real memory. And I didn't. All I had were a few words and a signature on a theatre programme from someone I'd never even met, someone who to me was part polar bear, part actor, part pixie – not at all easy to picture in my head as I grew up.

Picture another Christmas Eve fourteen years later. Upstairs, still at the bottom of my cupboard, my polar bear father in the magazine in the Start-Rite shoebox; and with him all our accumulated childhood treasures: the signed programme, a battered champion conker (a sixty-fiver!), six silver ball-bearings, four greenish silver threepenny bits (Christmas pudding treasure trove), a Red Devil throat pastille tin with three of my milk teeth cushioned in yellowy cotton wool, and my collection of twenty-seven cowrie shells gleaned from many summers from the beach on Samson in the Scilly Isles. Downstairs, the whole family were gathered in the sitting-room: my mother, Douglas, Terry and my two sisters (half-sisters, really, but of course no one ever called them that), Aunty Betty, now married, with twin daughters, my cousins, who were truly awful – I promise you. We were decorating the tree, or rather the twins were fighting over every single dingly-dangly glitter ball, every strand of tinsel. I was trying to fix up the Christmas tree lights, which, of course, wouldn't work – again – whilst Aunty Betty was doing her best to avert a war by bribing the dreadful cousins away from the tree with a Mars bar each. It took a while, but in the end she got both of them up on to her lap, and soon they were stuffing themselves contentedly with Mars bars. Blessed peace.

This was the very first Christmas we had had the television. Given half a chance we'd have had it on all the time. But, wisely enough I suppose, Douglas had rationed us to just one programme a day over Christmas. He didn't want the Christmas celebrations interfered with by "that thing in the corner", as he called it. By common consent, we had chosen the Christmas Eve film on the BBC at five o'clock.

Five o'clock was a very long time coming that day, and when at last Douglas got up and turned on the television, it seemed to take for ever to warm up. Then, there it was on the screen: *Great Expectations* by Charles Dickens. The half-mended lights were at once discarded, the decorating abandoned, as we all settled down to watch in rapt anticipation. Maybe you know the moment: Young Pip is making his way through the graveyard at dusk, mist swirling around him, an owl screeching, gravestones rearing out of the gloom, branches like ghoulish fingers whipping at him as he passes, reaching out to snatch him. He moves through the graveyard timorously, tentatively, like a frightened fawn. Every snap of a twig, every barking fox, every aarking heron sends shivers into our very souls.

Suddenly, a face! A hideous face, a monstrous face, looms up from behind a gravestone. Magwitch, the escaped convict, ancient, craggy and crooked, with long white hair and a straggly beard. A wild man with wild eyes, the eyes of a wolf.

The cousins screamed in unison, long and loud, which broke the tension for all of us and made us laugh. All except my mother.

"Oh my God," she breathed, grasping my arm. "That's your father! It's him. It's Peter."

All the years of pretence, the whole long conspiracy of silence were undone in that one moment. The drama on the television paled into sudden insignificance. The hush in the room was palpable.

Douglas coughed. "I think I'll fetch some more logs," he said. And my two half-sisters went out with him, in solidarity I think. So did Aunty Betty and the twins; and that left my mother, Terry and me alone together.

I could not take my eyes off the screen. After a while I said to Terry, "He doesn't look much like a pixie to me."

"Doesn't look much like a polar bear either," Terry replied. At Magwitch's every appearance I tried to see through his make-up (I just hoped it *was* make-up!) to discover how my father really looked. It was impossible. My polar bear father, my pixie father had become my convict father.

Until the credits came up at the end my mother never said a word. Then all she said was, "Well, the potatoes won't peel themselves, and I've got the Brussels sprouts to do as well." Christmas was a very subdued affair that year, I can tell you.

They say you can't put a genie back in the bottle. Not true. No one in the family ever spoke of the incident afterwards – except Terry and me of course. Everyone behaved as if it had never happened. Enough was enough. Terry and I decided it was time to broach the whole forbidden subject with our mother, in private. We waited until the furore of Christmas was over, and caught her alone in the kitchen one evening. We asked her point blank to tell us about him, our 'first' father, our 'missing' father.

"I don't want to talk about him," she said. She wouldn't even look at us. "All I know is that he lives somewhere in Canada now. It was another life. I was another person then. It's not important." We tried to press her, but that was all she would tell us.

Soon after this I became very busy with my own life, and for some years I thought very little about my convict father, my polar bear father. By the time I was thirty I was married with two sons, and was a teacher trying to become a writer, something I had never dreamt I could be.

Terry had become an actor, something he had always been quite sure he would be. He rang me very late one night in a high state of excitement. "You'll never guess," he said. "He's here! Peter! Our dad. He's here, in England. He's playing in *Henry IV, Part II* in Chichester. I've just read a rave review. He's Falstaff. Why don't we go down there and give him the surprise of his life?"

So we did. The next weekend we went down to Chichester together. I took my family with me. I wanted them to be there for this. He was a wonderful Falstaff, big and boomy, rumbustious and raunchy, yet full of pathos. My two boys (ten and eight) kept whispering at me every time he came on. "Is that him? Is that him?" Afterwards we went round to see him in his dressing-room. Terry said I should go in first, and on my own. "I had my turn a long time ago, if you remember," he said. "Best if he sees just one of us to start with, I reckon."

My heart was in my mouth. I had to take a very deep breath before I knocked on that door. "Enter." He sounded still jovial, still Falstaffian. I went in.

He was sitting at his dressing-table in his vest and braces, boots and britches, and humming to himself as he rubbed off his make-up. We looked at each other in the mirror. He stopped humming, and swivelled round to face me. For some moments I just stood there looking at him. Then I said, "Were you a polar bear once, a long time ago in London?"

"Yes."

"And were you once the convict in *Great Expectations* on the television?"

"Yes."

"Then I think I'm your son," I told him.

There was a lot of hugging in his dressing-room that night, not enough to make up for all those missing years, maybe. But it was a start.

My mother's dead now, bless her heart, but I still have two fathers. I get on well enough with Douglas, I always have done in a detached sort of way. He's done his best by me, I know that; but in all the years I've known him he's never once mentioned my other father. It doesn't matter now. It's history best left crusted over I think.

We see my polar bear father – I still think of him as that – every year or so, whenever he's over from Canada. He's well past eighty now, still acting for six months of the year – a real trouper. My children and my grandchildren always call him Grandpa Bear because of his great bushy beard (the same one he grew for Falstaff!), and because they all know the story of their grandfather, I suppose.

Recently I wrote a story about a polar bear. I can't imagine why. He's upstairs now reading it to my smallest granddaughter. I can hear him a-snarling and a-growling just as proper polar bears do. Takes him back, I should think. Takes me back, that's for sure.

MEETING CÉZANNE

I don't remember why my mother had to go into hospital. I'm not sure she ever told me. She did explain that after the operation she would be needing a month of complete rest. This is why she had had to arrange for me to go and stay with Aunt Mathilde, my mother's older sister, in her house down in the south, in Provence.

I'd never been to Provence, but I had met my Aunt Mathilde a few times when she'd come to see us in our little apartment in Paris. I remembered her being big and bustling, filling the place with her bulk and forever hugging and kissing me, which I never much cared for. She'd pinch my cheek and tell me I was a "beautiful little man". But she'd always bring us lots of crystallised fruits, so I could forgive her everything else.

I was ten years old and had never been parted from my mother. I'd only been out of Paris once for a holiday by the sea in Brittany. I told her I didn't want to be sent away. I told her time and time again, but it was no use.

"You'll be fine, Yannick," she insisted. "You like Aunt Mathilde, don't you? And Uncle Bruno is very funny. He has a moustache that prickles like a hedgehog. And you've never even met your cousin Amandine. You'll have a lovely time. Spring in Provence. It'll be a paradise for you, I promise. Crystallised fruit every day!"

She did all she could to convince me. More than once she read me Jean Giono's story "The Man Who Planted Trees", the story of an old shepherd set in the high hills of Provence. She showed me a book of paintings by Paul Cézanne, paintings, she told me, of the countryside outside Aix-en-Provence, very close to Aunt Mathilde's home. "Isn't it beautiful, Yannick?" she breathed as she turned the pages. "Cézanne loved it there, and he's the greatest painter in the world. Remember that."

A city boy all my life, the paintings really did look like the paradise my mother had promised me. So by the time she put me on the train at the Gare de Lyon I was really looking forward to it. Blowing kisses to her for the last time out of the train window, I think the only reason I didn't cry was because I was quite sure by now that I was indeed going to the most wonderful place in the world, the place where Cézanne, the greatest painter in the world, painted his pictures, where Jean Giono's old shepherd walked the high hills planting his acorns to make a forest.

Aunt Mathilde met me off the train and enveloped me in a great bear hug and pinched my cheek. It wasn't a good start. She introduced me to my cousin Amandine, who barely acknowledged my existence, but who was very beautiful. On the way to the car, following behind Aunt Mathilde, Amandine told me at once that she was fourteen and much older than I was and that I had to do what she said. I loved her at once. She wore a blue and white gingham dress, and she had a ponytail of chestnut hair that shone in the sunshine. She had the greenest eyes I'd ever seen. She didn't smile at me, though. I so hoped that one day she would.

We drove out of town to Vauvenargues, Aunt Mathilde talking all the way. I was in the back seat of the Deux Chevaux and couldn't hear everything, but I did pick up enough to understand that Uncle Bruno ran the village inn. He did the cooking and everyone helped. "And you'll have to help too," Amandine added without even turning to look at me. Everywhere about me were the gentle hills and folding valleys, the little houses and dark pointing trees I'd seen in Cézanne's paintings. Uncle Bruno greeted me wrapped in his white apron. Mother was right. He did have a huge hedgehog of a moustache that prickled when he kissed me. I liked him at once.

I had my own little room above the restaurant, looking out over a small back garden. An almond tree grew there, the pink blossoms brushing against my window pane. Beyond the tree were the hills, Cézanne's hills. And after supper they gave me a crystallised fruit, apricot, my favourite. All that and Amandine too. I could not have been happier.

It became clear to me very quickly that whilst I was made to feel very welcome and part of the family – Aunt Mathilde was always showing me off proudly to her customers as her nephew, "her beautiful little man from Paris" – I was indeed expected to do what everyone else did, to do my share of the work in the inn. Uncle Bruno was almost always busy in the kitchen. He clanked his pots and sang his songs, and would waggle his moustache at me whenever I went in, which always made me giggle. He was happiest in his kitchen, I could tell that. Aunt Mathilde bustled and hustled; she liked things to be just so. She greeted every customer like a long-lost friend. She was the heart and soul of the place. As for Amandine, she took me in hand at once, and explained that I'd be working with her, that she'd been asked to look after me. She did not mince her words. I could not expect to spend my summer with them, she said, and not earn my keep.

She put me to work at once in the restaurant, laying tables, clearing tables, cutting bread, filling up breadbaskets, filling carafes of water, making sure there was enough wood on the fire in the evenings, and washing up, of course. After just one day I was exhausted. Amandine told me I had to learn to work harder and faster, but she did kiss me goodnight before I went upstairs, which was why I did not wash my face for days afterwards.

At least I had the mornings to myself. I made the best

of the time I had, exploring the hills, stomping through the woods, climbing trees. Amandine never came with me. She had lots of friends in the village, bigger boys who stood about with their thumbs hooked into the pockets of their blue jeans, and roared around on motor scooters with Amandine clinging on behind, her hair flying. These were the boys she smiled at, the boys she laughed with. I was more sad than jealous, I think; I simply loved her more than ever.

There was a routine to the restaurant work. As soon as customers had left, Amandine would take away the wine glasses and the bottles and the carafes. The coffee cups and cutlery were my job. She would deal with the ashtrays, whilst I scrunched up the paper tablecloths and threw them on the fire. Then we'd lay the table again as quickly as possible for the next guests. I worked hard because I wanted to please Amandine, and to make her smile at me. She never did.

She laughed at me, though. She was in the village street one morning, her motor-scooter friends gathered adoringly all around her, when she turned and saw me. They all did. Then she was laughing and they were too. I walked away knowing I should be hating her, but I couldn't. I longed all the more for her smile. I longed for her just to notice me. With every day she didn't I became more and more miserable, sometimes so wretched I would cry myself to sleep at nights. I lived for my mother's letters and for my mornings walking the hills that Cézanne had painted, gathering acorns from the trees Jean Giono's old shepherd had planted. Here, away from Amandine's indifference, I could be happy for a while and dream my dreams. I thought that one day I might like to live in these hills myself, and be a painter like Cézanne, the greatest painter in the world, or maybe a wonderful writer like Jean Giono.

I think Uncle Bruno sensed my unhappiness, because he began to take me more and more under his wing. He'd often invite me into his kitchen and let me help him cook his *soupe au pistou* or his *poulet romarin* with *pommes dauphinoises* and wild leeks. He taught me to make chocolate mousse and *crème brûlée*, and before I left he'd always waggle his moustache for me and give me a crystallised apricot. But I dreaded the restaurant now, dreaded having to face Amandine again and endure the silence between us. I dreaded it, but would not have missed it for the world. I loved her that much.

Then one day a few weeks later I had a letter from my mother saying she was much better now, that Aunt Mathilde would put me on the train home in a few days' time. I was torn. Of course I yearned to be home again, to see my mother, but at the same time I did not want to leave Amandine.

That evening Amandine told me I had to do everything

just right because their best customer was coming to dine with some friends. He lived in the chateau in the village, she said, and was very famous; but when I asked what he was famous for, she didn't seem interested in telling me.

"Questions, always questions," she tutted. "Go and fetch in the logs."

Whoever he was, he looked ordinary enough to me, just an old man with not much hair. But he ate one of the *crème brûlées* I'd made and I felt very pleased a famous man had eaten one of my *crème brûlées*. As soon as he and his friends had gone we began to clear the table. I pulled the paper tablecloth off as usual, and as usual scrunched it up and threw it on the fire. Suddenly Amandine was rushing past me. For some reason I could not understand at all she grabbed the tongs and tried to pull the remnants of the burning paper tablecloth out of the flames, but it was already too late. Then she turned on me.

"You fool!" she shouted. "You little fool!"

"What?" I said.

"That man who just left. If he likes his meal he does a drawing on the tablecloth for Papa as a tip, and you've only gone and thrown it on the fire. He's only the most famous painter in the world. Idiot! Imbecile!" She was in tears now. Everyone in the restaurant had stopped eating and gone quite silent.

Then Uncle Bruno was striding towards us, not his

jolly self at all. "What is it?" he asked Amandine. "What's the matter?"

"It was Yannick, Papa," she cried. "He threw it on the fire, the tablecloth, the drawing."

"Had you told him about it, Amandine?" Uncle Bruno asked. "Did Yannick know about how sometimes he sketches something on the tablecloth, and how he leaves it behind for us?"

Amandine looked at me, her cheeks wet with tears. I thought she was going to lie. But she didn't.

"No, Papa," she said, lowering her head.

"Then you shouldn't be blaming him, should you, for something that was your fault. Say sorry to Yannick now." She mumbled it but she never raised her eyes. Uncle Bruno put his arm round me and walked me away. "Never mind, Yannick," he said. "He said he particularly liked his *crème brûlée*. That's probably why he left the drawing. You made the *crème brûlée*, didn't you? So it was for you really he did it. Always look on the bright side. For a moment you had in your hands a drawing done for you and your *crème brûlée* by the greatest painter in the world. That's something you'll never forget."

Later on as I came out of the bathroom I heard Amandine crying in her room. I hated to hear her crying, so I knocked on the door and went in. She was lying curled up on her bed hugging her pillow.

"I'm sorry," I said. "I didn't mean to upset you." She had stopped crying by now.

"It wasn't your fault, Yannick," she said, still sniffing a bit. "It's just that I hate it when Papa's cross with me. He hardly ever is, only when I've done something really bad. I shouldn't have blamed you. I'm sorry."

And then she smiled at me. Amandine smiled at me!

I lay awake all night, my mind racing. Somehow I was going to put it all right again. I was going to make Amandine happy. By morning I had worked out exactly what I had to do and how to do it, even what I was going to say when the time came.

That morning, I didn't go for my walk in the hills. Instead I made my way down through the village towards the chateau. I'd often wondered what it was like behind those closed gates. Now I was going to find out. I waited till there was no one about, no cars coming. I climbed the gates easily enough, then ran down through the trees. And there it was, immense and forbidding, surrounded by forest on all sides. And there he was, the old man with very little hair I had seen the night before. He was sitting alone in the sunshine at the foot of the steps in front of the chateau, and he was sketching. I approached as silently as I could across the grass, but somehow I must have disturbed him. He looked up, shading his eyes against the sun. "Hello, young man," he said. Now that I was this close to him I could see he was indeed old, very old, but his eyes were young and bright and searching.

"Are you Monsieur Cézanne?" I asked him. "Are you the famous painter?" He seemed a little puzzled at this, so I went on. "My mother says you are the greatest painter in the world."

He was smiling now, then laughing. "I think your mother's probably right," he said. "You clearly have a wise mother, but what I'd like to know is why she let a young lad like you come wandering here on his own?"

As I explained everything and told him why I'd come and what I wanted, he looked at me very intently, his brow furrowing. "I remember you now, from last night," he said, when I'd finished. "Of course I'll draw another picture for Bruno. What would he like? No. Better still, what would you like?"

"I like sailing boats," I told him. "Can you do boats?"

"I'll try," he replied with a smile.

It didn't take him long. He drew fast, never once looking up. But he did ask me questions as he worked, about where I'd seen sailing boats, about where I lived in Paris. He loved Paris, he said, and he loved sailing boats too.

"There," he said, tearing the sheet from his sketchbook and showing me. "What do you think?" Four sailing boats were racing over the sea out beyond a lighthouse, just as I'd seen them in Brittany. But I saw he'd signed it *Picasso*.

"I thought your name was Cézanne," I said.

He smiled up at me. "How I wish it was," he said sadly. "How I wish it was. Off you go now."

I ran all the way back to the village, wishing all the time I'd told him that I was the one who had made the *crème brûlée* he'd liked so much. I found Amandine by the washing line, a clothes peg in her mouth. "I did it!" I cried breathlessly, waving the drawing at her. "I did it! To make up for the one I burned."

Amandine took the peg out of her mouth and looked down at the drawing.

"That's really sweet of you to try, Yannick," she said. "But the thing is, it's got to be done by him, by Picasso himself. It's no good you drawing a picture and then just signing his name. It's got to be by him or it's not worth the money."

I was speechless. Then as she turned away to hang up one of Uncle Bruno's aprons, Aunt Mathilde came out into the garden with a basket of washing under her arm.

"Yannick's been very kind, *Maman*," Amandine said. "He's done me a drawing. After what happened last night. It's really good too."

Aunt Mathilde had put down her washing and was looking at the drawing. "Bruno!" she called. "Bruno, come out here!" And Uncle Bruno appeared, his hands white with flour. "Look at this," said Aunt Mathilde. "Look what Yannick did, and all by himself too."

Bruno peered at it closely for a moment, then started to roar with laughter. "I don't think so," he said. "Yannick may be a genius with *crème brûlée*, but this is by Picasso, the great man himself. I promise you. Isn't it, Yannick?"

So I told them the whole story. When I'd finished, Amandine came over and hugged me. She had tears in her eyes. I was in seventh heaven, and Uncle Bruno waggled his moustache and gave me six crystallised apricots. Unfortunately Aunt Mathilde hugged me too and pinched my cheek especially hard. I was the talk of the inn that night, and felt very proud of myself. But best of all Amandine came on my walk in the hills the next day and climbed trees with me and collected acorns, and held my hand all the way back down the village street, where everyone could see us, even the motor-scooter boys in their blue jeans.

They still have the boat drawing by Picasso hanging in the inn. Amandine runs the place now. It's as good as ever. She married someone else, as cousins usually do. So did I. I'm a writer still trying to follow in Jean Giono's footsteps. As for Cézanne, was my mother right? Is he the greatest painter in the world? Or is it Picasso? Who knows? Who cares? They're both wonderful and I've met both of them – if you see what I'm saying.

Muck and Magic

Some years ago, we got to know Elisabeth Frink, a wonderful sculptor, particularly of horses, and a kind and generous person too. She became a great friend and ally in life. Sadly, she died all too young. Her very last work now hangs above the west door of Liverpool Cathedral. It is a Risen Christ.

I am sometimes asked these days how I got started. I should love to be able to say that it was all because I had some dream, some vision, or maybe that I just studied very hard. None of this would really be true. I owe what I am, what I have become, what I do each day of my life, to a bicycle ride I took a long time ago now, when I was twelve years old – and also to a pile of muck, horse muck.

The bike was new that Christmas. It was maroon, and I remember it was called a Raleigh Wayfarer. It had all you could ever dream of in a bike – in those days. It had a bell, a dynamo lamp front and rear, five gears and a silver pump. I loved it instantly and spent every hour I could out riding it. And when I wasn't riding it, I was polishing it.

We lived on the edge of town, so it was easy to ride off down Mill Lane past the estate, along the back of the soap factory where my father worked, and then out into the countryside beyond. How I loved it. In a car, you zoomed past so fast that the cows and the trees were only ever brief, blurred memories. On my bike I was close to everything for the first time. I felt the cold and the rain on my face. I mooed at the cows, and they looked up and blinked at me lazily. I shouted at the crows and watched them lift off cawing and croaking into the wind. But best of all, no one knew where I was – and that included me sometimes. I was always getting myself lost and coming back at dusk, late. I would brace myself for all the sighing and tutting and ticking off that inevitably followed. I bore it all stoically because they didn't really mean it, and anyway it had all been worth it. I'd had a taste of real freedom and I wanted more of it.

After a while I discovered a circuit that seemed to be just about ideal. It was a two-hour run, not too many hills going up, plenty going down, a winding country lane that criss-crossed a river past narrow cottages where hardly anyone seemed to live, under the shadow of a church where sometimes I stopped and put flowers on the graves that everyone else seemed to have forgotten, and then along the three-barred iron fence where the horses always galloped over to see me, their tails and heads high, their ears pricked.

There were three of them: a massive bay hunter that looked down on me from a great height, a chubby little pony with a face like a chipmunk, and a fine-boned grey that flowed and floated over the ground with such grace and ease that I felt like clapping every time I saw her move. She made me laugh too because she often made rude, farty noises as she came trotting over to see me. I called her Peg after a flying horse called Pegasus that I'd read about in a book. The small one I called Chip, and the great bay, Big Boy. I'd cuddle them all, give each of them a sugar lump – two for Peg because she wasn't as pushy as the other two – told them my troubles, cuddled them a little more and went on my way, always reluctantly.

I hated to leave them because I was on my way back home after that, back to homework, and the sameness of the house, and my mother's harassed scurrying and my little brother's endless tantrums. I lay in my room and dreamed of those horses, of Peg in particular. I pictured myself riding her bareback through flowery meadows, up rutty mountain passes, fording rushing streams where she'd stop to drink. I'd go to sleep at nights lying down on the straw with her, my head resting on her warm belly. But when I woke, her belly was always my pillow, and my father was in the bathroom next door, gargling and spitting into the sink, and there was school to face, again. But after school I'd be off on my bike and that was all that mattered to me. I gave up ballet lessons on Tuesdays. I gave up cello lessons on Fridays. I never missed a single day, no matter what the weather – rain, sleet, hail – I simply rode through it all, living for the moment when Peg would rest her heavy head on my shoulder and I'd hear that sugar lump crunching inside her great grinding jaw.

It was spring. I know that because there were daffodils all along the grass verge by the fence, and there was nowhere to lie my bike down on the ground without squashing them. So I leant it up against the fence and fished in my pocket for the sugar lumps. Chip came scampering over as he always did, and Big Boy wandered lazily up behind him, his tail flicking nonchalantly. But I saw no sign of Peg. When Big Boy had finished his sugar lump, he started chewing at the saddle of my bike and knocked it over. I was just picking it up when I saw her coming across the field towards me. She wore long green boots and a jersey covered in plants and stars, gold against the dark, deep blue of space. But what struck me most was her hair, the wild white curly mop of it, around her face that was somehow both old and young at the same time.

"Who are you?" she asked. It was just a straight question, not a challenge.

"Bonnie," I replied.

"She's not here," said the woman.

"Where is she?"

"It's the spring grass. I have to keep her inside from now on."

"Why?"

"Laminitis. She's fine all through the winter, eats all the grass she likes no trouble. But she's only got to sniff the spring grass and it comes back. It heats the hoof, makes her lame." She waved away the two horses and came closer, scrutinising me. "I've seen you before, haven't I? You like horses, don't you?" I smiled. "Me too," she went on. "But they're a lot of work."

"Work?" I didn't understand.

"Bring them in, put them out, groom them, pick out their feet, feed them, muck them out. I'm not as young as I was, Bonnie. You don't want a job do you, in the stables? Be a big help. The grey needs a good long walk every day, and a good mucking out. Three pounds an hour, what do you say?"

Just like that. I said yes, of course. I could come evenings and weekends.

"I'll see you tomorrow then," she said. "You'll need wellies. I've got some that should fit. You be careful on the roads now." And she turned and walked away.

I cycled home that day singing my heart out and high as a kite. It was my first paying job, and I'd be looking after Peg. It really was a dream come true.

I didn't tell anyone at home, nor at school. Where I

went on my bike, what I did, was my own business, no one else's. Besides there was always the chance that Father would stop me – you never knew with him. And I certainly didn't want any of my school friends oaring in on this. At least two of them knew all about horses, or they said they did, and I knew they would never stop telling me the right way to do this or that. Best just to keep everything to myself.

To get to the house the next day – you couldn't see it from the road – I cycled up a long drive through high trees that whispered at me. I had to weave around the pot-holes, bump over sleeping policemen, but then came out on to a smooth tarmac lane where I could freewheel downhill and hear the comforting tic-a-tic of my wheels beneath me.

I nearly came off when I first saw them. Everywhere in amongst the trees there were animals, but none of them moved. They just looked at me. There were wild boar, dogs, horses and gigantic men running through trees like hunters. But all were as still as statues. They *were* statues. Then I saw the stables on my right, Peg looking out at me, ears pricked and shaking her mane. Beyond the stables was a long house of flint and brick with a tiled roof, and a clock tower with doves fluttering around it.

The stable block was deserted. I didn't like to call out, so I opened the gate and went over to Peg and stroked her nose. That was when I noticed a pair of wellies waiting by the door, and slipped into one of them was a piece of paper. I took it out and read:

Hope these fit. Take her for a walk down the tracks, not in the fields. She can nibble the grass, but not too much. Then muck out the stables. Save what dry straw you can – it's expensive. When you've done, shake out half a bale in her stable – you'll find straw and hay in the barn. She has two slices of hay in her rack. Don't forget to fill up the water buckets.

It was not signed.

Until then I had not given it a single thought, but I had never led a horse or ridden a horse in all my life. Come to that, I hadn't mucked out a stable either. Peg had a halter on her already, and a rope hung from a hook beside the stable. I put the wellies on – they were only a little too big – clipped on the rope, opened the stable door and led her out, hoping, praying she would behave. I need not have worried. It was Peg that took me for a walk. I simply stopped whenever she did, let her nibble for a while, and then asked her gently if it wasn't time to move on. She knew the way, up the track through the woods, past the running men and the wild boar, then forking off down past the ponds where a bronze water buffalo drank without ever moving his lips. White fish glided ghostly under the shadow of his nose. The path led upwards from there, past a hen house where a solitary goose stretched his neck, flapped his wings and honked at us. Peg stopped for a moment, lifted her nose and wrinkled it at the goose who began preening himself busily. After a while I found myself coming back to the stable-yard gate and Peg led me in. I tied her up in the yard and set about mucking out the stables.

I was emptying the wheelbarrow on to the muck heap when I felt someone behind me. I turned round. She was older than I remembered her, greyer in the face, and more frail. She was dressed in jeans and a rough sweater this time, and seemed to be covered in white powder, as if someone had thrown flour at her. Even her cheeks were smudged with it. She glowed when she smiled.

"Where's there's muck there's money, that's what they say," she laughed; and then she shook her head. "Not true, I'm afraid, Bonnie. Where there's muck, there's magic. Now that's true." I wasn't sure what she meant by that. "Horse muck," she went on by way of explanation. "Best magic in the world for vegetables. I've got leeks in my garden longer than, longer than…" She looked around her. "Twice as long as your bicycle pump. All the soil asks is that we feed it with that stuff, and it'll do anything we want it to. It's like anything, Bonnie, you have to put in more than you take out. You want some tea when you've finished?"

"Yes please."

"Come up to the house then. You can have your money." She laughed at that. "Maybe there is money in muck after all."

As I watched her walk away, a small yappy dog came bustling across the lawn, ran at her and sprang into her arms. She cradled him, put him over her shoulder and disappeared into the house.

I finished mucking out the stable as quickly as I could, shook out some fresh straw, filled up the water buckets and led Peg back in. I gave her a goodbye kiss on the nose and rode my bike up to the house.

I found her in the kitchen, cutting bread.

"I've got peanut butter or honey," she said. I didn't like either, but I didn't say so.

"Honey," I said. She carried the mugs of tea, and I carried the plate of sandwiches. I followed her out across a cobbled courtyard, accompanied by the yappy dog, down some steps and into a great glass building where there stood a gigantic white horse. The floor was covered in newspaper, and everywhere was crunchy underfoot with plaster. The shelves all around were full of sculpted heads and arms and legs and hands. A white sculpture of a dog stood guard over the plate of sandwiches and never even sniffed them. She sipped her tea between her hands and looked up at the giant horse. The horse looked just like

Peg, only a lot bigger.

"It's no good," she sighed. "She needs a rider." She turned to me suddenly. "You wouldn't be the rider, would you?" she asked.

"I can't ride."

"You wouldn't have to, not really. You'd just sit there, that's all, and I'd sketch you."

"What, now?"

"Why not? After tea be all right?"

And so I found myself sitting astride Peg that same afternoon in the stable yard. She was tied up by her rope, pulling contentedly at her hay net and paying no attention to us whatsoever. It felt strange up there, with Peg shifting warm underneath me. There was no saddle, and she asked me to hold the reins one-handed, loosely, to feel "I was part of the horse". The worst of it was that I was hot, stifling hot, because she had dressed me up as an Arab. I had great swathes of cloth over and around my head and I was draped to my feet with a long heavy robe so that nothing could be seen of my jeans or sweater or wellies.

"I never told you my name, did I?" said the lady, sketching furiously on a huge pad. "That was rude of me. I'm Liza. When you come tomorrow, you can give me a hand making you if you like. I'm not as strong as I was, and I'm in a hurry to get on with this. You can mix the plaster for me. Would you like that?" Peg snorted and pawed the ground. "I'll take that as a yes, shall I?" She laughed, and walked round behind the horse, turning the page of her sketch pad. "I want to do one more from this side and one from the front, then you can go home."

Half an hour later when she let me down and unwrapped me, my bottom was stiff and sore.

"Can I see?" I asked her.

"I'll show you tomorrow," she said. "You will come, won't you?" She knew I would, and I did.

I came every day after that to muck out the stables and to walk Peg, but what I looked forward to most – even more than being with Peg – was mixing up Liza's plaster for her in the bucket, climbing the stepladder with it, watching her lay the strips of cloth dunked in the wet plaster over the frame of the rider, building me up from the iron skeleton of wire, to what looked at first like an Egyptian mummy, then a riding Arab at one with his horse, his robes shrouding him with mystery. I knew all the while it was me in that skeleton, me inside that mummy. I was the Arab sitting astride his horse looking out over the desert. She worked ceaselessly, and with such a fierce determination that I didn't like to interrupt. We were joined together by a common, comfortable silence.

At the end of a month or so we stood back, the two of us, and looked up at the horse and rider, finished.

"Well," said Liza, her hands on her hips. "What do you

OF LIONS AND UNICORNS

think, Bonnie?"

"I wish," I whispered, touching the tail of the horse, "I just wish I could do it."

"But you did do it, Bonnie," she said and I felt her hand on my shoulder. "We did it together. I couldn't have done it without you." She was a little breathless as she spoke. "Without you, that horse would never have had a rider. I'd never have thought of it. Without you mixing my plaster, holding the bucket, I couldn't have done it." Her hand gripped me tighter. "Do you want to do one of your own?"

"I can't."

"Of course you can. But you have to look around you first, not just glance, but really look. You have to breathe it in, become a part of it, feel that you're a part of it. You draw what you see, what you feel. Then you make what you've drawn. Use clay if you like, or do what I do and build up plaster over a wire frame. Then set to work with your chisel, just like I do, until it's how you want it. If I can do it, you can do it. I tell you what. You can have a corner of my studio if you like, just so long as you don't talk when I'm working. How's that?"

So my joyous spring blossomed into a wonderful summer. After a while, I even dared to ride Peg bareback sometimes on the way back to the stable yard; and I never forgot what Liza told me. I looked about me. I listened. And the more I listened and the more I looked, the more I felt at home in this new world. I became a creature of the place. I belonged there as much as the wren that sang at me high on the vegetable garden wall, as much as the green dragonfly hovering over the pool by the water buffalo. I sketched Peg. I sketched Big Boy (I couldn't sketch Chip – he just came out round). I bent my wire frames into shape and I began to build my first horse sculpture, layer on layer of strips of cloth dunked in plaster just like Liza did. I moulded them into shape on the frame, and when they dried I chipped away and sanded. But I was never happy with what I'd done.

All this time, Liza worked on beside me in the studio, and harder, faster, more intensely than ever. I helped her whenever she asked me too, mixing, holding the bucket for her, just as I had done before.

It was a Rising Christ, she said, Christ rising from the dead, his face strong, yet gentle too, immortal it seemed; but his body, vulnerable and mortal. From time to time she'd come over and look at my stumpy effort that looked as much like a dog as a horse to me, and she would walk round it nodding her approval. "Coming on, coming on," she'd say. "Maybe just a little bit off here perhaps." And she'd chisel away for a minute or two, and a neck or leg would come to sudden life.

I told her once, "It's like magic."

She thought for a moment, and said, "That's exactly

what it is, Bonnie. It's a God-given thing, a God-given magic, and it's not to be wasted. Don't waste it, Bonnie. Don't ever waste it."

The horse and rider came back from the foundry, bronze now and magnificent. I marvelled at it. It stood outside her studio, and when it caught the red of the evening sun, I could scarcely take my eyes off it. But these days Liza seemed to tire more easily, and she would sit longer over her tea, gazing out at her horse and rider.

"I am so pleased with that, Bonnie," she said, "so pleased we did it together."

The Christ figure was finished and went off to the foundry a few weeks before I had to go on my summer holiday. "By the time you come back again," said Liza, "it should be back. It's going to hang above the door of the village church. Isn't that nice? It'll be there for ever. Well, not for ever. Nothing is for ever."

The holiday was in Cornwall. We stayed where we always did, in Cadgwith, and I drew every day. I drew boats and gulls and lobster pots. I made sculptures with wet sand – sleeping giants, turtles, whales – and everyone thought I was mad not to go swimming and boating. The sun shone for fourteen days. I never had such a perfect holiday, even though I didn't have my bike, or Peg or Liza with me.

My first day back, the day before school began, I

cycled out to Liza's place with my best boat drawing in a stiff envelope under my sweater. The stable yard was deserted. There were no horses in the fields. Peg wasn't in her stable and I could find no one up at the house, no Liza, no yappy dog. I stopped in the village to ask but there was no one about. It was like a ghost village. Then the church bell began to ring. I leant my bike up against the churchyard wall and ran up the path. There was Liza's Rising Christ glowing in the sun above the doorway, and inside they were singing hymns.

I crept in, lifting the latch carefully so that I wouldn't be noticed. The hymn was just finishing. Everyone was sitting down and coughing. I managed to squeeze myself in at the end of a pew and sat down too. The church was packed. A choir in red robes and white surplices sat on either side of the altar. The vicar was taking off his glasses and putting them away. I looked everywhere for Liza's wild white curls, but could not find her. It was difficult for me to see much over everyone's heads. Besides, some people were wearing hats, so I presumed she was too and stopped looking for her. She'd be there somewhere.

The vicar began. "Today was to be a great day, a happy day for all of us. Liza was to unveil her Rising Christ above the south door. It was her gift to us, to all of us who live here, and to everyone who will come here to our church in the centuries to come. Well, as we all now know, there was no unveiling, because she wasn't here to do it. On Monday evening last she watched her Rising Christ winched into place. She died the next day."

I didn't hear anything else he said. It was only then that I saw the coffin resting on trestles between the pulpit and the lectern, with a single wreath of white flowers laid on it, only then that I took in the awful truth.

I didn't cry as the coffin passed right by me on its way out of the church. I suppose I was still trying to believe it. I stood and listened to the last prayers over the grave, numb inside, grieving as I had never grieved before, or since, but still not crying. I waited until almost everyone had gone and went over to the grave. A man was taking off his jacket and hanging it on the branch of a tree. He spat on his hands, rubbed them and picked up his spade. He saw me. "You family?" he said.

"Sort of," I replied. I reached inside my sweater and pulled out the boat drawing from Cadgwith. "Can you put it in?" I asked. "It's a drawing. It's for Liza."

"Course," he said, and he took it from me. "She'd like that. Fine lady, she was. The things she did with her hands. Magic, pure magic."

It was just before Christmas the same year that a cardboard tube arrived in the post, addressed to me. I opened it in the secrecy of my room. A rolled letter fell out, typed and very short.

Dear Miss Mallet,

In her will, the late Liza Bonallack instructed us, her solicitors, to send you this drawing. We would ask you to keep us informed of any future changes of address.

With best wishes.

I unrolled it and spread it out. It was of me sitting on Peg, swathed in Arab clothes. Underneath was written:

For dearest Bonnie,

I never paid you for all that mucking out, did I? You shall have this instead, and when you are twenty-one you shall have the artist's copy of our horse and rider sculpture. But by then you will be doing your own sculptures. I know you will.

God bless,

Liza.

So here I am, nearly thirty now. And as I look out at the settling snow from my studio, I see Liza's horse and rider standing in my back garden, and all around, my own sculptures gathered in silent homage.

HOMECOMING

I was near by anyway, so I had every excuse to do it, to ignore the old adage and do something I'd been thinking of doing for many years. "Never go back. Never go back." Those warning words kept repeating themselves in my head as I turned right at the crossroads outside Tillingham and began to walk the few miles along the road back to my childhood home in Bradwell, a place I'd last seen nearly fifty years before. I'd thought of it since, and often. I'd been there in my dreams, seen it so clearly in my mind, but of course I had always remembered it as it had been then. Fifty years would have changed things a great deal, I knew that. But that was part of the reason for my going back that day, to discover how intact was the landscape of my memories.

I wondered if any of the people I had known then might still be there; the three Stebbing sisters perhaps, who lived together in the big house with honeysuckle over the porch, very proper people so Mother always wanted me to be on my best behaviour. It was no more than a stone's throw from the sea and there always seemed to be a gull perched on their chimney pot. I remembered how

I'd fallen ignominiously into their goldfish pond and had to be dragged out and dried off by the stove in the kitchen with everyone looking askance at me, and my mother so ashamed. Would I meet Bennie, the village thug who had knocked me off my bike once because I stupidly wouldn't let him have one of my precious lemon sherbets? Would he still be living there? Would we recognise one another if we met?

The whole silly confrontation came back to me as I walked. If I'd had the wit to surrender just one lemon sherbet he probably wouldn't have pushed me, and I wouldn't have fallen into a bramble hedge and had to sit there humiliated and helpless as he collected up my entire bagful of scattered lemon sherbets, shook them triumphantly in my face, and then swaggered off with his cronies, all of them scoffing at me, and scoffing my sweets too. I touched my cheek then as I remembered the huge thorn I had found sticking into it, the point protruding inside my mouth. I could almost feel it again with my tongue, taste the blood. A lot would never have happened if I'd handed over a lemon sherbet that day.

That was when I thought of Mrs Pettigrew and her railway carriage and her dogs and her donkey, and the whole extraordinary story came flooding back crisp and clear, every detail of it, from the moment she found me sitting in the ditch holding my bleeding face and crying my heart out.

She helped me up on to my feet. She would take me to her home. "It isn't far," she said. "I call it Dusit. It is a Thai word which means 'halfway to heaven'." She had been a nurse in Thailand, she said, a long time ago when she was younger. She'd soon have that nasty thorn out. She'd soon stop it hurting. And she did.

The more I walked the more vivid it all became: the people, the faces, the whole life of the place where I'd grown up. Everyone in Bradwell seemed to me to have had a very particular character and reputation, unsurprising in a small village, I suppose: Colonel Burton with his clipped moustache, who had a wife called Valerie, if I remembered right, with black pencilled eyebrows that gave her the look of someone permanently outraged – which she usually was. Neither the colonel nor his wife was to be argued with. They ruled the roost. They would shout at you if you dropped sweet papers in the village street or rode your bike on the pavement.

Mrs Parsons, whose voice chimed like the bell in her shop when you opened the door, liked to talk a lot. She was a gossip, Mother said, but she was always very kind. She would often drop an extra lemon sherbet into your paper bag after she had poured your quarter pound from the big glass jar on the counter. I had once thought of stealing that jar, of snatching it and running off out of the shop, making my getaway like a bank robber in the films. But I knew the police would come after me in their shiny black cars with their bells ringing, and then I'd have to go to prison and Mother would be cross. So I never did steal Mrs Parsons's lemon sherbet jar.

Then there was Mad Jack, as we called him, who clipped hedges and dug ditches and swept the village street. We'd often see him sitting on the churchyard wall by the mounting block eating his lunch. He'd be humming and swinging his legs. Mother said he'd been fine before he went off to the war, but he'd come back with some shrapnel from a shell in his head and never been right since, and we shouldn't call him Mad Jack, but we did. I'm ashamed to say we baited him sometimes too, perching alongside him on the wall, mimicking his humming and swinging our legs in time with his.

But Mrs Pettigrew remained a mystery to everyone. This was partly because she lived some distance from the village and was inclined to keep herself to herself. She only came into the village to go to church on Sundays, and then she'd sit at the back, always on her own. I used to sing in the church choir, mostly because Mother made me, but I did like dressing up in the black cassock and white surplice and we did have a choir outing once a year to the cinema in Southminster – that's where I first saw *Snow White* and

Bambi and *Reach for the Sky*. I liked swinging the incense too, and sometimes I got to carry the cross, which made me feel very holy and very important. I'd caught Mrs Pettigrew's eye once or twice as we processed by, but I'd always looked away. I'd never spoken to her. She smiled at people, but she rarely spoke to anyone; so no one spoke to her – not that I ever saw anyway. But there were reasons for this.

Mrs Pettigrew was different. For a start she didn't live in a house at all. She lived in a railway carriage, down by the sea wall with the great wide marsh all around her. Everyone called it Mrs Pettigrew's Marsh. I could see it best when I rode my bicycle along the sea wall. The railway carriage was painted brown and cream and the word PULLMAN was printed in big letters all along both sides above the windows. There were wooden steps up to the front door at one end, and a chimney at the other. The carriage was surrounded by trees and gardens, so I could only catch occasional glimpses of her and her dogs and her donkey, bees and hens. Tiny under her wide hat, she could often be seen planting out in her vegetable garden, or digging the dyke that ran around the garden like a moat, collecting honey from her beehives perhaps or feeding her hens. She was always outside somewhere, always busy. She walked or stood or sat very upright, I noticed, very neatly, and there was a serenity about her that made her unlike anyone else, and ageless too.

But she was different in another way. Mrs Pettigrew was not like the rest of us to look at, because Mrs Pettigrew was "foreign", from somewhere near China, I had been told. She did not dress like anyone else either. Apart from the wide-brimmed hat, she always wore a long black dress buttoned to the neck. And everything about her, her face and her hands, her feet, everything was tidy and tiny and trim, even her voice. She spoke softly to me as she helped me to my feet that day, every word precisely articulated. She had no noticeable accent at all, but spoke English far too well, too meticulously, to have come from England.

So we walked side by side, her arm round me, a soothing silence between us, until we turned off the road on to the track that led across the marsh towards the sea wall in the distance. I could see smoke rising straight into the sky from the chimney of the railway carriage.

"There we are: Dusit," she said. "And look who is coming out to greet us."

Three greyhounds were bounding towards us followed by a donkey trotting purposefully but slowly behind them, wheezing at us rather than braying. Then they were gambolling all about us, and nudging us for attention. They were big and bustling, but I wasn't afraid because they had nothing in their eyes but welcome.

"I call the dogs Fast, Faster and Fastest," she told me.

"But the donkey doesn't like names. She thinks names are for silly creatures like people and dogs who can't recognise one another without them. So I call her simply Donkey." Mrs Pettigrew lowered her voice to a whisper. "She can't bray properly – tries all the time but she can't. She's very sensitive too; takes offence very easily." Mrs Pettigrew took me up the steps into her railway carriage home. "Sit down there by the window, in the light, so I can make your face better."

I was so distracted and absorbed by all I saw about me that I felt no pain as she cleaned my face, not even when she pulled out the thorn. She held it out to show me. It was truly a monster of a thorn. "The biggest and nastiest I have ever seen," she said, smiling at me. Without her hat on she was scarcely taller than I was. She made me wash out my mouth and bathed the hole in my cheek with antiseptic. Then she gave me some tea which tasted very strange but warmed me to the roots of my hair. "Jasmine tea," she said. "It is very healing, I find, very comforting. My sister sends it to me from Thailand."

The carriage was as neat and tidy as she was: a simple sitting room at the far end with just a couple of wicker chairs and a small table by the stove. And behind a half-drawn curtain I glimpsed a bed very low on the ground. There was no clutter, no pictures, no hangings, only a shelf of books that ran all the way round the carriage from end to end. From where I was sitting I could see out over the garden, then through the trees to the open marsh beyond.

"Do you like my house, Michael?" She did not give me time to reply. "I read many books, as you see," she said. I was wondering how it was that she knew my name, when she told me. "I see you in the village sometimes, don't I? You're in the choir, aren't you?" She leant forward. "And I expect you're wondering why Mrs Pettigrew lives in a railway carriage."

"Yes," I said.

The dogs had come in by now and were settling down at our feet, their eyes never leaving her, not for a moment, as if they were waiting for an old story they knew and loved.

"Then I'll tell you, shall I?" she began. "It was because we met on a train, Arthur and I – not this one, you understand, but one very much like it. We were in Thailand. I was returning from my grandmother's house to the city where I lived. Arthur was a botanist. He was travelling through Thailand collecting plants and studying them. He painted them and wrote books about them. He wrote three books; I have them all up there on my shelf. I will show you one day – would you like that? I never knew about plants until I met him, nor insects, nor all the wild creatures and birds around us, nor the stars in the sky. Arthur showed me all these things. He opened my eyes. For me it was all so exciting and new. He had such a knowledge of this wonderful world we live in, such a love for it too. He gave me that, and he gave me much more: he gave me his love too.

"Soon after we were married he brought me here to England on a great ship – this ship had three big funnels and a dance band – and he made me so happy. He said to me one day on board that ship, 'Mrs Pettigrew –' he always liked to call me this – 'Mrs Pettigrew, I want to live with you down on the marsh where I grew up as a boy.' The marsh was part of his father's farm, you see. 'It is a wild and wonderful place,' he told me, 'where on calm days you can hear the sea breathing gently beyond the sea wall, or on stormy days roaring like a dragon, where larks rise and sing on warm summer afternoons, where stars cascade on August nights.'

"'But where shall we live?' I asked him.

"'I have already thought of that, Mrs Pettigrew,' he said. 'Because we first met on a train, I shall buy a fine railway carriage for us to live in, a carriage fit for a princess. And all around it we shall make a perfect paradise and we shall live as we were meant to live, amongst our fellow creatures, as close to them as we can be. And we shall be happy there.'

"'So we were, Michael. So we were. But only for seventeen short months, until one day there was an accident. We had a generator to make our electricity; Arthur was repairing it when the accident happened. He was very young. That was nearly twenty years ago now. I have been here ever since and I shall always be here. It is just as Arthur told me: a perfect paradise."

Donkey came in just then, clomping up the steps into the railway carriage, her ears going this way and that. She must have felt she was being ignored or ostracised, probably both. Mrs Pettigrew shooed her out, but not before there was a terrific kerfuffle of wheezing and growling, of tumbling chairs and crashing crockery.

When I got home I told Mother everything that had happened. She took me to the doctor at once for a tetanus injection, which hurt much more than the thorn had, then put me to bed and went out – to sort out Bennie, she said. I told her not to, told her it would only make things worse. But she wouldn't listen. When she came back she brought me a bag of lemon sherbets. Bennie, she told me, had been marched down to Mrs Parsons's shop by his father and my mother, and they had made him buy me a bag of lemon sherbets with his own pocket money to replace the ones he'd pinched off me.

Mother had also cycled out to see Mrs Pettigrew to thank her. From that day on the two of them became the best of friends, which was wonderful for me because I was allowed to go cycling out to see Mrs Pettigrew as often as I liked. Sometimes Mother came with me, but mostly I went alone. I preferred it on my own.

I rode Donkey all over the marsh. She needed no halter, no reins. She went where she wanted and I went with her, followed always by Fast, Faster and Fastest, who would chase rabbits and hares wherever they found them. I was always muddled as to which dog was which, because they all ran unbelievably fast – standing start to full throttle in a few seconds. They rarely caught anything, but they loved the chase.

With Mrs Pettigrew I learnt how to puff the bees to sleep before taking out the honeycomb. I collected eggs warm from the hens, dug up potatoes, pulled carrots, bottled plums and damsons in Kilner jars. (Ever since, whenever I see the blush on a plum I always think of Mrs Pettigrew.) And always Mrs Pettigrew would send me home afterwards with a present for Mother and me, a pot of honey perhaps or some sweetcorn from her garden.

Sometimes Mrs Pettigrew would take me along the sea wall all the way to St Peter's Chapel and back, the oldest chapel in England, she said. Once we stopped to watch a lark rising and rising, singing and singing so high in the blue we could see it no more. But the singing went on, and she said, "I remember a time – we were standing almost on this very same spot – when Arthur and I heard a lark singing just like that. I have never forgotten his words.

'I think it's singing for you,' he said, 'singing for Mrs Pettigrew.'"

Then there was the night in August when Mother and Mrs Pettigrew and I lay out on the grass in the garden gazing up at the shooting stars cascading across the sky above us, just as she had with Arthur, she said. How I wondered at the glory of it, and the sheer immensity of the universe. I was so glad then that Bennie had pushed me off my bike that day, so glad I had met Mrs Pettigrew, so glad I was alive. But soon after came the rumours and the meetings and the anger, and all the gladness was suddenly gone.

I don't remember how I heard about it first. It could have been in the playground at school, or Mother might have told me or even Mrs Pettigrew. It could have been Mrs Parsons in the shop. It doesn't matter. One way or another, everyone in the village and for miles around got to hear about it. Soon it was all anyone talked about. I didn't really understand what it meant to start with. It was that first meeting in the village hall that brought it home to me. There were pictures and plans of a giant building pinned up on the wall for everyone to see. There was a model of it too, with the marsh all around and the sea wall running along behind it, and the blue sea beyond with models of fishing boats and yachts sailing by. That, I think, was when I truly began to comprehend the implication of what was going on, of what was actually being proposed. The men in suits sitting behind the table on the platform that evening made it quite clear.

They wanted to build a power station, but not just an ordinary power station, a huge new-fangled atomic power station, the most modern design in the whole world, they said. They had decided to build it out on the marsh – and everyone knew by now they meant Mrs Pettigrew's Marsh. It was the best place, they said. It was the safest place, they said, far enough outside the village and far enough away from London. I didn't understand then who the men in suits were, of course, but I did understand what they were telling us: that this atomic power station was necessary because it would provide cheaper electricity for all of us; that London, which was only fifty or so miles away, was growing fast and needed more electricity. Bradwell had been chosen because it was the perfect site, near the sea so the water could be used for cooling, and near to London, but not too near.

"If it's for Londoners, and if it's so safe, what's wrong with it being right in London then?" the colonel asked.

"They've got water there too, haven't they?" said Miss Blackwell, my teacher.

Mrs Parsons stood up then, beside herself with fury. "Well, I think they want to build it out here miles away from London because it might blow up like that bomb in

Hiroshima. That's what I think. I think it's wicked, wicked. And anyway, what about Mrs Pettigrew? She lives out there on the marsh. Where's she going to live?"

Beside me Mother was holding Mrs Pettigrew's hand and patting it as the argument raged on. There'd be any number of new jobs, said one side. There are plenty of jobs anyway, said the other side. It would be a great concrete monstrosity; it would blight the whole landscape. It would be well screened by trees, well landscaped; you'd hardly notice it; and anyway you'd get used to it soon enough once it was there. It would be clean too, no chimneys, no smoke. But what if there was an accident, if the radiation leaked out? What then?

Suddenly Mrs Pettigrew was on her feet. Maybe it was because she didn't speak for a while that everyone fell silent around her. When she did speak at last, her voice trembled. It trembled because she was trembling, her knuckles bone-white as she clutched Mother's hand. I can still remember what she said, almost word for word.

"Since I first heard about this I have read many books. From these books I have learnt many important things. At the heart of an atomic power station there is a radioactive core. The energy this makes produces electricity. But this energy has to be used and controlled with very great care. Any mistake or any accident could cause this radioactive core to become unstable. This could lead to an explosion, which would be catastrophic, or there could be a leak of radiation into the atmosphere. Either of these would cause the greatest destruction to all forms of life, human beings, animals, birds, sea life and plants, for miles and miles around. But I am sure those who wish to build this power station have thought of all this and will make it as safe as possible. I am sure those who will operate it will be careful. But Arthur, my late husband, was careful too. He installed a simple generator for our home. He thought it was safe, but it killed him.

"So I ask you, gentlemen, to think again. Machines are not perfect. Science is not perfect. Mistakes can easily be made. Accidents can happen. I am sure you understand this. And there is something else I would like you to understand. For me the place where you would build your atomic power station is home. You may have decided it is an uninteresting place and unimportant, just home to one strange lady who lives there on the marsh with her donkey and her dogs and her hens. But it is not uninteresting and it is not unimportant. It is not just my home either, but home also for curlews and gulls and wild geese and teal and redshanks and barn owls and kestrels. There are herons, and larks. The otter lives here and the fox comes to visit, the badger too, even sometimes the deer. And amongst the marsh grass and reeds and the bulrushes live a thousand different insects, and a thousand different plants.

"My home is their home too and you have no right to destroy it. Arthur called the marsh a perfect paradise. But if you build your atomic power station there, then this paradise will be destroyed for ever. You will make a hell of paradise."

Her voice gained ever greater strength as she spoke. Never before or since have I heard anyone speak with greater conviction.

"And I do mean for ever," she went on. "Do not imagine that in fifty years, or a hundred maybe, when this power station will have served its purpose, when they find a new and better way to make electricity – which I am quite sure they will – do not imagine that they will be able to knock it down and clear it away and the marsh will be once again as it is now. From my books I know that no building as poisonous with radiation as this will be will ever be knocked down. To stop the poison leaking it will, I promise you, have to be enclosed in a tomb of concrete for hundreds of years to come. This they do not want to tell you, but it is true, believe me. Do not, I beg you, let them build this power station. Let us keep this marsh as it is. Let us keep our perfect paradise."

As she sat down there was a ripple of applause, which swiftly became tumultuous. And as the hall rang loud with cheering and whistling and stamping I joined in more enthusiastically than any. At that moment I felt the entire village was united in defiance behind her. But the applause ended, as – all too soon – did both the defiance and the unity.

The decision to build or not to build seemed to take for ever: more public meetings, endless campaigning for and against; but right from the start it was clear to me that those for it were always in the ascendant. Mother stood firm alongside Mrs Pettigrew, so did the colonel and Mrs Parsons; but Miss Blackwell soon changed sides, as did lots of others. The arguments became ever more bitter. People who had been perfectly friendly until now would not even speak to one another. At school Bennie led an ever growing gang who would storm about at playtime punching their fists in the air and chanting slogans. "Down with the Pettigrew weeds!" they cried. "Down with the Pettigrew weeds!" To my shame I slunk away and avoided them all I could.

But in the face of this angry opposition Mother did not flinch and neither did Mrs Pettigrew. They sat side by side at every meeting, stood outside the village hall in the rain with their ever dwindling band of supporters, holding up their placards, SAY NO TO THE POWER STATION they read. Sometimes after school I stood there with her, but when people began to swear at us out of their car windows as they passed by, Mother said I had to stay away. I wasn't sorry. It was boring to stand there, and cold too, in spite of the warmth of the brazier. And I was always terrified whenever Bennie saw me there, because I knew I'd be his special target in the playground the next day.

Eventually there were just the two of them left, Mother and Mrs Pettigrew. Mad Jack would join them sometimes, because he liked the company and he liked warming his hands over the brazier too. Things became even nastier towards the end. I came out of the house one morning to fin red paint daubed on our front door and on our Bramley apple tree, the one I used to climb; and someone – I always thought it must have been Bennie – threw a stone through one of Mrs Pettigrew's windows in the middle of the night. Mother and Mrs Pettigrew did what they could to keep one another's spirits up, but they could see the way it was going, so it must have been hard.

Then one day it was in the newspapers. The plans for the atomic power station had been approved. Building would begin in a few months. Mother cried a lot about it at home and I expect Mrs Pettigrew did too, but whenever I saw them together they always tried to be cheerful. Even after Mrs Pettigrew received the order that her beloved marsh was being compulsorily purchased and that she would have to move out, she refused to be downhearted. We'd go over there even more often towards the end to be with her, to help her in her garden with her bees and her hens and her vegetables. She was going to keep the place just as Arthur had liked it, she said, for as long as she possibly could.

Then Donkey died. We arrived one day to find Mrs Pettigrew sitting on the steps of her carriage, Donkey lying near her. We helped her dig the grave. It took hours. When Donkey had been buried we all sat on the steps in the half-dark, the dogs lying by Donkey's grave. The sea sighed behind the sea wall, perfectly reflecting our spirits. I was lost in sadness.

"There's a time to die," said Mrs Pettigrew. "Perhaps she knew it was her time." I never saw Mrs Pettigrew smile again.

I was there too on the day of the auction. Mrs Pettigrew didn't have much to sell, but a lot of people came along all the same, out of curiosity or even a sense of malicious triumph, perhaps. The carriage had been emptied of everything – I'd carried some of it out myself – so that the whole garden was strewn with all her bits and pieces. It took just a couple of hours for the auctioneer to dispose of everything: all the garden tools, all the furniture, all the crockery, the generator, the stove, the pots and pans, the hens and the hen house and the beehives. She kept only her books and her dogs, and the railway carriage too. Several buyers wanted to make a bid for it, but she refused. She stood stony-faced throughout, Mother at her side, whilst I sat watching everything from the steps of the carriage, the dogs at my feet.

Neither Mother nor I had any idea what she was about to do. Evening was darkening around us, I remember. Just the three of us were left there. Everyone else had gone. Mother was leading Mrs Pettigrew away, a comforting arm round her, telling her again that she could stay with us in the village as long as she liked, as long as it took to find somewhere else to live. But Mrs Pettigrew didn't appear to be listening at all. Suddenly she stopped, turned and walked away from us back towards the carriage.

"I won't be long," she said. And when the dogs tried to follow her she told them to sit where they were and stay.

She disappeared inside and I thought she was just saying goodbye to her home, but she wasn't. She came out a few moments later, shutting the door behind her and locking it.

I imagined at first it was the reflection of the last of the setting sun glowing in the windows. Then I saw the flicker of flames and realised what she had done. We stood there together and watched as the carriage caught fire, as it blazed and roared and crackled, the flames running along under the roof, leaping out of the windows, as the sparks flurried and flew. The fire engines came, but too late. The villagers came, but too late. How long we stood there I do not know, but I know that I ached with crying.

Mrs Pettigrew came and lived with us at home for a

few months. She hardly spoke in all that time. In the end she left us her dogs and her books to look after and went back to Thailand to live with her sister. We had a few letters from her after that, then a long silence, then the worst possible news from her sister.

Mrs Pettigrew had died, of sadness, of a broken heart, she said.

Mother and I moved out of the village a year or so later, as the power station was being built. I remember the lorries rumbling through, and the Irish labourers who had come to build it sitting on the church wall with Mad Jack and teaching him their songs.

Mother didn't feel it was the same place any more, she told me. She didn't feel it was safe. But I knew she was escaping from sadness. We both were. I didn't mind moving, not one bit.

As I walked into the village I could see now the great grey hulk of the power station across the fields. The village was much as I remembered it, only smarter, more manicured. I made straight for my childhood home. The house looked smaller, prettier, and tidier too, the garden hedge neatly clipped; the garden itself, from what I could see from the road, looked too well groomed, not a nettle in sight. But the Bramley apple tree was still there, still leaning sideways as if it was about to fall over. I thought of knocking on the door, of asking if I might have a look inside at my old bedroom where I'd slept as a child. But a certain timidity and a growing uneasiness that coming back had not been such a good idea prevented me from doing it. I was beginning to feel that by being there I was tampering with memories, yet now I was there I could not bring myself to leave.

I spoke to a postman emptying the postbox and enquired about some of the people I'd known. He was a good age, in his fifties, I thought, but he knew no one I asked him about. Mad Jack wasn't on his wall. Mrs Parsons's shop was still there but now sold antiques and bric-a-brac. I went to the churchyard and found the graves of the colonel and his wife with the black pencilled eyebrows, but I'd remembered her name wrong. She was Veronica, not Valerie. They had died within six months of each other. I got chatting to the man who had just finished mowing the grass in the graveyard and asked him about the atomic power station and whether people minded living alongside it.

"Course I mind," he replied. He took off his flat cap and wiped his brow with his forearm. "Whoever put that ruddy thing up should be ashamed of themselves. Never worked properly all the time it was going anyway."

"It's not going any more then?" I asked.

"Been shut down, I don't know, maybe eight or nine

years," he said, waxing even more vehement. "Out of date. Clapped out. Useless. And do you know what they had to do? They had to wrap the whole place under a blanket of concrete, and it's got to stay there like that for a couple of hundred years at least so's it doesn't leak out and kill the lot of us. Madness, that's what it was, if you ask me. And when you think what it must have been like before they put it up. Miles and miles of wild marshland as far as the eye could see. All gone. Must've been wonderful. Some funny old lady lived out there in a railway carriage. Chinese lady, they say. And she had a donkey. True. I've seen photos of her and some kid sitting on a donkey outside her railway carriage. Last person to live out there, she was. Then they went and kicked her out and built that ugly great wart of a place. And for what? For a few years of electricity that's all been used up and gone. Price of progress, I suppose they'd call it. I call it a crying shame."

I bought a card in the post office and wrote a letter to Mother. I knew she'd love to hear I'd been back to Bradwell. Then I made my way past the Cricketers' Inn and the school, where I stopped to watch the children playing where I'd played; then on towards St Peter's, the old chapel by the sea wall, the favourite haunt of my youth, where Mrs Pettigrew had taken me all those years before, remote and bleak from the outside, and inside filled with quiet and peace. Some new houses had been built along the road since my time. I hurried past trying not to notice them, longing now to leave the village behind me. I felt my memories had been trampled enough.

One house name on a white-painted gate to a new bungalow caught my eye: New Clear View. I saw the joke, but didn't feel like smiling. And beyond the bungalow, there it was again, the power station, massive now because I was closer, a monstrous complex of buildings rising from the marsh, malign and immovable. It offended my eye. It hurt my heart. I looked away and walked on.

When I reached the chapel, no one was there. I had the place to myself, which was how I had always liked it. After I had been inside, I came out and sat down with my back against the sun-warmed brick and rested. The sea murmured. I remembered again my childhood thoughts, how the Romans had been here, the Saxons, the Normans, and now me. A lark rose then from the grass below the sea wall, rising, rising, singing, singing. I watched it disappear into the blue, still singing, singing for Mrs Pettigrew.

My One and Only Great Escape

I still think of the house on the Essex coast where I grew up as my childhood home. But in fact it was my home for just four months of every year. The rest of the time I spent at my boarding school a whole world away, deep in the Sussex countryside. In my home by the sea they called me Michael. In my boarding school I was Morpurgo (or Pongo to my friends), and I became another person. I had two distinctively different lives, and so, in order to survive both, I had to become two very different people. Three times a year I had to make the changeover from home boy to schoolboy. Going back to school was always an agony of misery, a wretched ritual, a ritual I endured simply because I had to.

Then one evening at the beginning of the autumn term of 1953 I made up my mind that I would not endure it any longer, that I would run away, that I would not stay at my school and be Morpurgo or Pongo any more. I simply wanted to go home where I belonged and be Michael for ever.

The agony began, as it always began, about ten days before the end of the holidays – in this case, the summer holidays. For eight blessed weeks I had been at home. We lived in a large and rambling old house in the centre of a village called Bradwell-juxta-mare (near the sea). The house was called New Hall – *new* being mostly seventeenth century, with lots of beams and red bricks. It had a handsome Georgian front, with great sash windows, and one or two windows that weren't real windows at all but painted on – to save the window tax, I was told. House and garden lay hidden and protected behind a big brick wall.

Cycling out of the gate, as I often did, I turned left on to the village street towards Bradwell Quay and the sea, right towards the church, and the American airbase, and then out over the marshes towards the ancient Saxon chapel of St Peter's near the sea wall itself. Climb the sea wall and there was the great brown soupy North Sea and always a wild wet wind blowing. I felt always that this place was a part of me, that I belonged here.

My stepfather worked at his writing in his study, wreathed in a fog of tobacco smoke, with a bust of Napoleon and a Confederate flag on his leather-topped desk, whilst my mother tried her very best to tame the house and the garden and us, mostly on her own. We children were never as much help as we should have been, I'm ashamed to say. There were great inglenook fireplaces that devoured logs. So there were always logs for us to fetch in. Then there were the Bramley apples to pick and lay out in the old Nissen huts in the orchard. And if there was nothing that had to be harvested, or dug over or weeded, then there was the jungle of nettles and brambles that had to be beaten back before it overwhelmed us completely. Above all we had not to disturb our stepfather. When he emerged, his work done for the day, we would play cricket on the front lawn, an apple box for a wicket – it was six if you hit it over the wall into the village street. If it rained, we moved into the big vaulted barn where owls and bats and rats and spiders lived, and played fast and furious ping-pong till suppertime.

I slept up in the attic with my elder brother. We had a candle factory up there, melting down the ends of used-up candles on top of a paraffin stove and pouring the wax into jelly moulds. At night we could climb out of our dormer windows and sit and listen to the owls screeching over the marshes, and to the sound of the surging sea beyond. There always seemed to be butterflies in and out of the house – red admirals, peacocks. I collected dead ones in a biscuit tin, laid them out on cotton wool. I kept a wren's nest by my bed, so soft with moss, so beautifully crafted.

My days and nights were filled with the familiarity of the place and its people and of my family. This isn't to say I loved it all. The house was numbingly cold at times. My stepfather could be irritable, rigid and harsh; my mother anxious, tired and sad; my younger siblings intrusive and quarrelsome; and the villagers sometimes very aggressive. What haunted me most, though, were stories of a house ghost, told for fun, I'm sure; but nonetheless, the ghost terrified me so much that I dreaded going upstairs at night on my own. But all this was home. Haunted or not, this was my place. I belonged.

The day and the moment always came as a shock. So absorbing was this home life of mine, that I'd quite forgotten the existence of my other life. Suddenly I'd find my mother dragging out my school trunk from under the stairs. From that moment on, my stomach started to churn. As my trunk filled, I was counting the days, the hours. The process of packing was relentless. Ironing, mending, counting, marking: eight pairs of grey socks, three pairs of blue rugby shorts, two green rugby shirts, two red rugby shirts, green tie, best blazer – red, green and white striped. Evenings were spent watching my mother and my two spinster aunts sewing on name tapes. Every one they sewed on seemed to be cementing the inevitability of my impending expulsion from home. The name tapes read: *M. A. B. Morpurgo*. Soon, very soon now, I would be Morpurgo again. Once everything was checked and stitched and darned, the checklist finally ticked off and the trunk ready to go, we drove it to the station to be sent on ahead – luggage in advance, they called it. Where that trunk was going, I would surely follow. The next time I'd see it would be only a few days away now, and I'd be back at school. I'd be Morpurgo again.

Those last days hurried by so fast. A last cycle ride to St Peter's, a last walk along the sea wall, the endless goodbyes in the village. "Cheer up, Michael, you'll be home soon." A last supper, shepherd's pie, my favourite. But by this time the condemned boy was not eating at all heartily. A last night of fitful sleep, dreading to wake and face the day ahead. I could not look up at my aunts when I said goodbye for fear they would notice the tears and tell me I was "a big boy and should have grown out of all this by now". I braved their whiskery embraces and suddenly my mother and I were driving out of the gates, the last chimneys of home disappearing from me behind the trees.

We drove to the station at Southminster. Then we were in London and on the way to Victoria Station on the Underground. She held my hand now, as we sat silently side by side. We'd done this so many times before. She knew better than to talk to me. My mouth was dry and I felt sick to my stomach. My school uniform, fresh on that morning, was itchy everywhere and constricting. My stepfather had tightened my tie too tight before he said his stiff goodbye, and pulled my cap down so hard that it made my ears stick out even more than they usually did.

Going up the escalator into the bustling smoky concourse of Victoria Station was as I imagined it might be going up the steps on to the scaffold to face my executioner. I never wanted to reach the top, because I knew only too well what would be waiting for me. And sure enough, there it was, the first green, white and red cap, the first familiar face. It was Sim, Simpson, my best friend, but I still didn't want to see him. "Hello, Pongo," he said cheerily. And then to his mother as they walked away: "That's Morpurgo. I told you about him, remember, Mum? He's in my form."

"There," my mother said, in a last desperate effort to console me. "That's your friend. That's Sim, isn't it? It's not so bad, is it?"

What she couldn't know was that it was just about as bad as it could be. Sim was like the others, full of the same hearty cheeriness that would, I knew, soon reduce me to tears in the railway carriage.

The caps and the faces multiplied as we neared the platform. There was the master, ticking the names off his list, Mr Stevens (maths, geography and woodwork), who rarely smiled at all at school, but did so now as he greeted me. I knew even then that the smile was not for me, but rather for the benefit of my mother. "Good to see you back, Morpurgo. He's grown, Mrs Morpurgo. What've you been feeding him?" And they laughed together over my head. The train stood waiting, breathing, hissing, longing – it seemed – to be gone, longing to take me away.

My mother did not wait, as other mothers did, to wave me off. She knew that to do so would simply be prolonging my agony. Maybe it prolonged hers too. She kissed me all too briefly, and left me with her face powder on my cheek and the lingering smell of her. I watched her walk away until I could not see her any more through my tears. I hoped she would turn around and wave one last time, but she didn't. I had a sudden surging impulse to go after her and cling to her and beg her to take me home. But I hadn't the courage to do it.

"Still the dreamer, Morpurgo, I see," said Mr Stevens. "You'd better get on, or the train'll go without you."

Hauling my suitcase after me, I walked along the corridor searching for a window seat that was still empty. Above everything now I needed a window seat so that I could turn away, so they couldn't see my face. Luckily I found something even better, a completely empty carriage. I had it all to myself for just a few precious moments before they arrived. They came all at once, in a pack, piling in on top of one another, "bagging" seats, throwing suitcases, full of boisterous jollity. Simpson was there, and Gibbins, Murphy, Sanchez, Webster, Swan, Colman. I did my best to smile at them, but had to look away quickly. They weren't fooled. They'd spotted it. "Aren't you pleased to see us, Morpurgo?" "Don't blub, Pongo." "It's only school." "He wants his mummy wummy." Then Simpson said, "Leave him alone." One thing I had learnt was never to rise to the bait. They would stop in time, when they tired of it. And so they did.

As the train pulled out of the station, chuffing and clanking, the talk was all of what they'd done in the "hols", where they'd been, what new Hornby train set someone had been given on his birthday. By East Croydon, it was all the old jokes: "Why did the submarine blush?" "Because it saw *Queen Mary*'s bottom!" "Why did the chicken cross the road?" "For some *fowl* reason!" And the carriage rocked with raucous laughter. I looked hard out of my rain-streaked window at the grey green of the Sussex countryside, and cried, silently so that no one would know. But soon enough they did know. "God, Morpurgo, you go on like that and you'll flood the carriage." All pretence now abandoned, I ran to the toilet where I could grieve privately and loudly.

At East Grinstead Station there was the green Southdown coach waiting to take us to school, barely half an hour away. It went by in a minute. Suddenly we were turning in through the great iron gateway and down the gravel drive towards the school. And there it was, looming out of the trees, the dark and forbidding Victorian mansion that would be my prison for fourteen long weeks. With the light on in the front porch it looked as if the school was some great dark monster with a gaping orange mouth that would swallow me up for ever. The headmaster and his wife were there to greet us, both smiling like crocodiles.

Up in my dormitory I found my bed, my name written on it on a sticking plaster – *Morpurgo*. I was back. I sat down, feeling its sagging squeakiness for the first time. That was the moment the idea first came into my head that I should run away. I began unpacking my suitcase, contemplating all the while the dreadful prospect of fourteen weeks away from home. It seemed like I had a life sentence stretching ahead of me with no prospect of remission. Downstairs, outside the dining hall, as we lined up for supper and for the prefects' hand inspection, I felt suddenly overcome by the claustrophobic smell of the place – floor polish and boiled cabbage. Even then I was still only thinking of running away. I had no real intention of doing it, not yet.

It was the rice pudding that made me do it. Major Philips (Latin and rugby) sitting at the end of my table told me I had to finish the slimy rice pudding skin I'd hidden under my spoon. To swallow while I was crying was almost impossible, but somehow I managed it, only to retch it up almost at once. Major Philips told me not to be "childish". I swallowed again and this time kept it down. This was the moment I made up my mind that I'd had enough, that I was going to run away, that nothing and no one would stop me.

"Please, sir," I asked. "Can I go to the toilet, successful?" (Successful, in this context, was school code for number twos. If you declared it before you went, you were allowed longer in the toilet and so were not expected back as soon.) But I didn't go to the toilet, successful or otherwise. Once out of the dining hall, I ran for it. Down the brown-painted corridor between the framed team photos on both walls, past the banter and clatter and clanging of the kitchens, and out of the back door into the courtyard. It was raining hard under a darkening sky as I sprinted down the gravel drive and out through the great iron gates. I had done it! I was free!

I was thinking out my escape plan as I was running, and trying to control my sobbing at the same time. I would run the two or three miles to Forest Row, hitch a lift or catch a bus to East Grinstead, and then catch the train home. I still had my term's pocket money with me, a ten-shilling note. I could be home in a few hours. I'd just walk in and tell everyone I was never ever going back to that school, that I would never be Morpurgo ever again.

I had gone a mile or so, still running, still sobbing, when a car came by. I had been so busy planning in my head that I hadn't heard the car until it was almost alongside me. My first instinct was to dash off into the fields, for I was sure some master must have seen me escaping and had come after me. I knew full well what would happen if I was caught. It would mean a visit to the headmaster's study and a caning, six strokes at least; but worse still it would mean capture, back to prison, to rice pudding skin and cabbage, and squeaky beds and maths and cross-country runs. One glance at the car, though, told me this was not a master in hot pursuit after all, but a silver-haired old lady in a little black car. She slowed down in front of me and stopped. So I did too. She wound down her window.

"Are you all right, dear?"

"No," I sobbed.

"You're soaking wet! You'll catch your death!" And then: "You're from that school up the road, aren't you? You're running away, aren't you?"

"Yes."

"Where to?"

"Home."

"Where's home, dear?"

"Essex. By the sea."

"But that's a hundred miles away. Why don't you get in the car, dear? I'll take you home with me. Would you like a sticky bun and some nice hot tea?" And she opened the door for me. There was something about her I trusted at once, the gentleness of her smile perhaps, the softness of her voice. That was why I got in, I think. Or maybe it was for the sticky bun. The truth was that I'd suddenly lost heart, suddenly had enough of my great escape. I was cold and wet, and home seemed as far away as the moon, and just as inaccessible.

The car was warm inside, and smelt of leather and dog.

"It's not far, dear. Half a mile, that's all. Just in the village. Oh, and this is Jack. He's perfectly friendly." And by way of introducing himself, the dog in the back began to snuffle the back of my neck. He was a spaniel with long dangly ears and sad bloodshot eyes. And he dribbled a lot.

All the way back to the village, the old lady talked on, about Jack mostly. Jack was ten, in dog years, she told me. If you multiplied by seven, exactly the same age as she was. "One of the windscreen wipers," she said, "only works when it feels like it, and it never feels like it when it's raining."

I sat and listened and had my neck washed from ear to ear by Jack. It tickled and made me smile. "That's better, dear," she said. "Happier now?"

She gave me more than she'd promised – a whole plate of sticky buns and several cups of tea. She put my soaking wet shoes in the oven to dry and hung my blazer on the clothes horse by the stove, and she talked all the time, telling me all about herself, how she lived alone these days, how she missed company. Her husband had been killed on the Somme in 1916, in the First World War. "Jimmy was a Grenadier Guardsman," she said proudly. "Six foot three in his socks." She showed me his photo on the mantelpiece.

He had a moustache and lots of medals. "Loved his fishing," she went on. "Loved the sea. We went to the sea whenever we could. Brighton. Lovely place." On and on she rambled, talking me through her life with Jimmy, and how she'd stayed on in the village after he'd been killed because it was the place they'd known together, how she'd taught in the village school for years before she retired. When the sticky buns were all finished and my shoes were out of the oven and dry at last, she sat back, clapped her hands on her knees, and said:

"Now, dear, what *are* we going to do with you?"

"I don't know," I replied.

"Shall I telephone your father and mother?"

"No!" I cried. The thought appalled me. They'd be so disappointed in me, so ashamed to know that I'd tried to run away.

"Well then, shall I ring the headmaster?"

"No! Please don't." That would be worse still. I'd be up the red-carpeted stairs into his study. I'd been there before all too often. I'd bent over the leather armchair and watched him pull out the cane from behind his desk. I'd waited for the swish and whack, felt the hot searing pain, the stinging eyes, and counted to six. I'd stood up, trembling, to shake his hand and murmured, "Thank you, sir," through my weeping mouth. No, not that. Please, not that.

"Maybe," said the old lady. "Maybe there's a way round this. You can't have been gone long, an hour or so at most. What if I take you back and drop you off at the top of the school drive? It's nearly dark now. No one would see you, not if you were careful. And with a bit of luck no one would have missed you just yet. You could sneak in and no one would ever know you've run away at all. What d'you think?"

I could have hugged her.

Jack came in the car with us in the back seat, licking my neck and my ears all the way. The old lady was unusually silent for a while. Then she said: "There's something Jimmy once told me not long before he was killed, when he was home on leave for the last time. He never talked much about the war and the trenches, but he did tell me once how scared he was all the time, how scared they all were. So I asked him what made him go on, why he didn't just run away. And he said: 'Because of my pals. We're in this together. We look after each other.' You've got pals, haven't you, dear?"

"Yes," I replied, "but they *like* coming back to school. They *love* it."

"I wonder if they really do," she said. "Maybe they just pretend better than you."

I was still thinking about that when the car came to a stop.

"I won't go any nearer than this, dear. It wouldn't do for anyone to see you getting out, would it now? Off you go then. And chin up, like my Jimmy."

Jack gave me a goodbye lick as I turned to him, on my nose.

"Thanks for the sticky buns," I said.

She smiled at me and I got out. I watched her drive away into the gloom and vanish. To this day I have no idea who she was. I never saw her again.

I ran down through the rhododendrons and out into the deserted courtyard at the back of the school. The lights were on all over the building, and the place was alive with the sound of children. I knew I needed time to compose myself before I met anyone, so I opened the chapel door and slipped into its enveloping darkness. There I sat and prayed, prayed that I hadn't been found out, that I wouldn't have to face the red-carpeted stairs and the headmaster's study and the leather chair. I hadn't been in there for more than a few minutes when the door opened and the lights went on.

"Ah, there you are, Morpurgo." It was Mr Morgan (French and music, and the choirmaster too). "We've been looking all over for you." As he came up the aisle towards me, I knew my prayers had been answered. Mr Morgan was much liked by all of us, because he was invariably kind, and always thought the best of us – rare in that school.

"Bit homesick, are you, Morpurgo?"

"Yes, sir."

"It'll pass. You'll see." He put his hand on my shoulder. "You'd better get yourself upstairs with the others. If you don't get your trunk unpacked by lights out, Matron will eat you alive, and we don't want that, do we?"

"No, sir."

And so I left Mr Morgan and the chapel and went upstairs to my dormitory.

"Where've you been? I thought you'd scarpered, run away," said Simpson, unpacking his truck on the bed next to mine.

"I just felt a bit sick," I said. Then I opened my trunk. On the top of my clothes was a note and three bars of Cadbury's chocolate. The note read: *Have a good term. Love Mum.*

Simpson spotted the chocolate, and pounced. Suddenly everyone in the dormitory was around me, and at my chocolate, like gannets. I managed to keep a little back for myself, which I hid under my pillow, and ate late that night as I listened to the bell in the clock tower chiming midnight. As it finished I heard Simpson crying to himself, as silently as he could.

"You all right, Sim?" I whispered.

"Fine," he sniffed. And then: "Pongo, did you scarper?"

"Yes," I said.

"Next time you go, take me with you. Promise?"

"Promise," I replied.

But I never did scarper again. Perhaps I never again plucked up the courage; perhaps I listened to the old lady's advice. I've certainly never forgotten it. It was my one and only great escape.

A Medal for Leroy

Michael doesn't remember his father, an RAF pilot lost in the war. But his Auntie Snowdrop gives him a medal, and then a photograph, and a story begins to unfold...

It wasn't until I felt the glass that I knew it for what it was. There, looking up at me, was Papa's face. The frame was not polished, I noticed, as it always had been before on the mantelpiece in their sitting room in Folkestone. I felt Maman's hand on my shoulder.

"He looks pleased to see you, *chéri*," she said.

When Auntie Pish fell asleep soon after, we crept out of her room and drove home. I sat in the car with the parcel on my lap all the way back to London, opening up the wrapping from time to time to look at Papa.

"I'll polish that frame when we get home," Maman said.

"I'll do it," I told her.

In the end Maman and I did it together, on the kitchen table, with Jasper up on a chair beside us, watching. Maman did the hard work, putting the polish on, and rubbing the tarnish off. It took some doing. Then I had the satisfaction of shining it up, breathing and polishing till it gleamed. Once it was done I took it up to my bedroom and stood it up on my desk. I sat there and stared at Papa. That was when Auntie Snowdrop's words came back to me – I hadn't thought about them in a long while. "Always remember, Michael, it's not the face that matters, not the skin, not the hair, it's what lies beneath. You have to look deeper, Michael, behind. Look through the glass, through the photo, and you'll find out who your Papa really was."

I looked hard into Papa's face, into his eyes, trying all I could to know the man behind the glass, behind the photo, behind the eyes.

Jasper was with me, snuffling around my feet. I wasn't paying him any attention, which was why, I suppose, he decided to jump up on to my desk and shove his nose into my face, knocking the photograph over as he did so. I heard the glass shatter as it fell.

"Get off, Jasper," I shouted, pushing him aside angrily. I'd never been so angry with him before. As I was standing the frame up again the glass fell out on to my desk in several pieces. I've often thought since that Jasper might have done it on purpose, because he knew, because he was trying to tell me, because Auntie Snowdrop had told him all about it, and he knew that's what Auntie Snowdrop wanted him to do. He wanted me to find it, and so did Auntie Snowdrop. That's why he broke it. That's what I think, anyway.

It was the first time I'd seen Papa's face not through glass. He was already somehow more real to me, closer and more alive without the glass in between us. The photo was loose in the frame now, and had slipped down. I noticed there was one small piece of broken glass still trapped there in the bottom corner of the frame. I tried to prise it out with the point of my pencil, but I couldn't do it. I'd have to open up the frame at the back if I was going to get it out.

I hadn't really noticed, not until now, but the back of the frame was nothing but a piece of cardboard, held in place by a few rusty-looking pins. All I had to do was to pull these out one by one and the cardboard came away easily enough. I had expected to see simply the back of the photograph, but there was something else there, a writing pad about the same size as the photo. On the front it said, 'Basildon Bond', in fancy printing, and below it, written in pencil, in large capital letters:

"WHO I AM, WHAT I'VE DONE,
AND WHO YOU ARE"
BY
MARTHA MAHONEY

(AUNTIE SNOWDROP)
FOR MICHAEL, SO HE'LL KNOW
FOR HIS EYES ONLY

WRITTEN IN MAY 1950

It took me a little while to cast my mind back, to work it out. This must have been written then about a month or so before she died, because I knew that was in June of 1950. (I checked later in my diary and I was right about that.)

She'd hidden it behind the photo for me to find. Behind the photo! Behind the photo!

Maman called up from downstairs. "*Chéri*, I've got to go down to the shops. Have you got that dog up there? I'd better take him with me. He hasn't had his walk yet. You'll be all right on your own?"

"I'll be fine," I told her. I opened the door to let Jasper out. He didn't seem to want to go even when Maman whistled for him. She had to shout for him more than once. Even then he went only because I pushed him out – I was still cross with him. He gave me a long last look before he left. *Read it*, his eyes were telling me. *Read it*. Then he was gone, scuttling down the stairs. I heard the front door close after them.

I was alone. I went back to my desk, picked up Auntie

Snowdrop's writing pad, sat on my bed, pillows piled behind me, rested the pad on my knees, and opened it. My heart was pounding. I knew even as I began to read – and I have no idea how I knew – that my life would be changed for ever, that after I'd read this I would never be the same person again.

Who I am, What I've done, and Who you are

I'm tell you this, writing it down for you, Michael, because we all have a right to know who we are. I should have told you myself, face to face a long time ago. Early on, when you were little, I always thought you were too young – or that was my excuse. And then as you grew up, I didn't know how to tell you. I never had the courage, that's the truth of it. I should have told your Maman too, but I could never quite bring myself to do that either.

Now that I've been told in the hospital that time is running out for me, that I have only a few months left, I thought this was the one last thing I had to do. Somehow I had to tell you, and there seemed to me only one way to do it. I would put it all down on paper, and arrange things, if I could, so that one day you would find it and read it for yourself. I did try to point you in the right direction. I did tell you where to look, didn't I? Look behind the face. Remember?

I could have given it to your Auntie Mary for her to give to you, but I don't want her to know I'm doing this – I don't like to upset her. And anyway, as you'll soon discover, this is between you and me. Your Auntie Mary knows the truth of everything that's written here – she was so much part of the whole story – but she's always told me it was best to keep it as a secret between her and me, just the two of us, and so it always has been. That way, she thinks, no one comes to any harm.

Until just recently, until my last visit to the hospital, when they told me, I suppose I always used to believe she was right. But not any more. I think there are some things that are so much part of who we are, that we should know about them, that we have a right to know about them.

If you're reading this at all, Michael, then it means you've found my little writing pad behind the photo of your Papa, just as I intended you to. Please don't be too upset. Read it again from time to time as you get older. I think it will be easier to understand as you get older. It's not so much that wisdom comes with age – as we older people rather like to believe. It doesn't. But I am sure that as we grow up we do become more able to understand ourselves and other people a little better. We are more able to deal with difficulty, and to forgive perhaps. If you are anything like me, Michael – and I think you probably are – I am sure you will become more understanding and forgiving as the years pass. I hope so, because I'm sure that it's only in forgiving that we find real peace of mind.

I'm writing this as well, because I want you to feel proud of who you are, and proud of the people who made you. Believe you me, you have much to feel proud about. Perhaps my problem has always been that I have never been proud enough of who I am. I am a bit muddle-headed, simple-minded perhaps, and foolish, certainly foolish. I have always allowed my sister, whom I love dearly, to do most of my thinking for me. It's just how we are and always have been. She's been the strong one all my life, my rock you might say. I know she can seem a bit of a know-all, a bit overbearing; but as you'll soon discover, she has looked after me, stood by me when no one else would. There's a lot more to Mary than meets the eye – that's true of everyone, I think. I should have been quite lost in this life without her. So here's our story, hers and mine – and most importantly, yours.

THE AMAZING STORY OF ADOLPHUS TIPS

In 1943, Lily Tregenza was living in a sleepy seaside village, scarcely touched by the war. But all that was soon to change. This is how I began to learn of her story...

Ever since I could remember I'd been coming down to Slapton for my holidays, mostly on my own. Grandma's bungalow was more of a home to me than anywhere, because we'd moved house often – too often for my liking. I'd just get used to things, settle down, make a new set of friends and then we'd be off, on the move again. Slapton summers with Grandma were regular and reliable and I loved the sameness of them, and Harley in particular.

Grandma used to take me out in secret on Grandpa's beloved motorbike, his pride and joy, an old Harley-Davidson. We called it Harley. Before Grandpa became ill they would go out on Harley whenever they could, which wasn't often. She told me once those were the happiest times they'd had together. Now that he was too ill to take her out on Harley, she'd take me instead. We'd tell Grandpa all about it, of course, and he liked to hear exactly where we'd been, what field we'd stopped in for our picnic and how fast we'd gone. I'd relive it for him and he loved that. But we never told my family. It was to be our secret, Grandma said, because if anyone back home ever got to know she took me out on Harley they'd never let me come to stay again. She was right too. I had the impression that neither my father (her own son) nor my mother really saw eye to eye with Grandma. They always thought she was a bit stubborn, eccentric, irresponsible even. They'd be sure to think that my going out on Harley with her was far too dangerous. But it wasn't. I never felt unsafe on Harley, no matter how fast we went. The faster the better. When we got back, breathless with excitement, our faces numb from the wind, she'd always say the same thing: "Supreme, Boowie! Wasn't that just supreme?"

When we weren't out on Harley, we'd go on long walks down to the beach and fly kites, and on the way back we'd watch the moorhens and coots and herons on Slapton Ley. We saw a bittern once. "Isn't that supreme?" Grandma whispered in my ear. Supreme was always her favourite word for anything she loved: for motorbikes or birds or lavender. The house always smelt of lavender. Grandma adored the smell of it, the colour of it. Her soap was always lavender, and there was a sachet in every wardrobe and chest of drawers – to keep moths away, she said.

Best of all, even better than clinging on to Grandma as we whizzed down the deep lanes on Harley, were the wild and windy days when the two of us would stomp noisily along the pebble beach of Slapton Sands, clutching on to one another so we didn't get blown away. We could never be gone for long though, because of Grandpa. He was happy enough to be left on his own for a while, but only if there was sport on the television. So we would generally go off for our ride on Harley or on one of our walks when there was a cricket match on, or rugby. He liked rugby best. He had been good at it himself when he was younger, very good, Grandma said proudly. He'd even played for Devon from time to time – whenever he could get away from the farm, that is.

Grandma told me a little about the busy life they'd had before I was born, up on the farm – she'd taken me up there to show me. So I knew how they'd milked a herd of sixty South Devon cows and that Grandpa had gone on working as long as he could. In the end, his illness took hold and he couldn't go up and down stairs any more, they'd had to sell up the farm and the animals and move into the bungalow down in Slapton village. Mostly, though, she'd want to talk about me, ask about me, and she really wanted to know too. Maybe it was because I was her only grandson. She never seemed to judge me either. So there was nothing I didn't tell her about my life at home or my friends or my worries. She never gave advice, she just listened.

Once, I remember, she told me that whenever I came to stay it made her feel younger. "The older I get," she said, "the more I want to be young. That's why I love going out on Harley. And I'm going to go on being young till I drop, no matter what."

I understood well enough what she meant by "no matter what". Each time I'd gone down in the last couple of years before Grandpa died she had looked more grey and weary. I would often hear my father pleading with her to have Grandpa put into a nursing home, that she couldn't go on looking after him on her own any longer. Sometimes the pleading sounded more like bullying to me, and I wished he'd stop. Anyway, Grandma wouldn't hear of it. She did have a nurse who came in to bath Grandpa each day now, but Grandma had to do the rest all by herself, and she was becoming exhausted. More and more of my walks along the beach were alone nowadays. We couldn't go out on Harley at all. She couldn't leave Grandpa even for ten minutes without him fretting, without her worrying about him. But after Grandpa was in bed we would either play Scrabble, which she would let me win sometimes, or we'd talk on late into the night – or rather I would talk and she would listen. Over the years I reckon I must have given Grandma a running commentary on just about my entire life, from the first moment I could speak, all the way through my childhood.

But now, after Grandpa's funeral, as we walked together down the road to the pub with everyone following behind us, it was her turn to do the talking, and she was talking about herself, talking nineteen to the dozen, as she'd never talked before. Suddenly I was the listener.

The wake in the pub was crowded, and of course everyone wanted to speak to Grandma, so we didn't get a chance to talk again that day, not alone. I was playing waiter with the tea and coffee, and plates of quiches and cakes. When we left for home that evening Grandma hugged me especially tight, and afterwards she touched my cheek as she'd always done when she was saying goodnight to me before she switched off the light. She wasn't crying, not quite. She whispered to me as she held me. "Don't you worry about me, Boowie dear," she said. "There's times it's good to be on your own. I'll go for rides on Harley – Harley will help me feel better. I'll be fine." So we drove away and left her with the silence of her empty house all around her.

A few weeks later she came to us for Christmas, but she seemed very distant, almost as if she were lost inside herself: there, but not there somehow. I thought she must still be grieving and I knew that was private, so I left her alone and we didn't talk much. Yet, strangely, she didn't seem too sad. In fact she looked serene, very calm and still, a dreamy smile on her face, as if she was happy enough to be there, just so long as she didn't have to join in too much. I'd often find her sitting and gazing into space, remembering a Christmas with Grandpa perhaps, I thought, or maybe a Christmas down on the farm when she was growing up.

On Christmas Day itself, after lunch, she said she wanted to go for a walk. So we went off to the park, just the two of us. We were sitting watching the ducks on the pond when she told me. "I'm going away, Boowie," she said. "It'll be in the New Year, just for a while."

"Where to?" I asked her.

"I'll tell you when I get there," she replied. "Promise. I'll send you a letter."

She wouldn't tell me any more no matter how much I badgered her. We took her to the station a couple of days later and waved her off. Then there was silence. No letter, no postcard, no phone call. A week went by. A fortnight. No one else seemed to be that concerned about her, but I was. We all knew she'd gone travelling, she'd made no secret of it, although she'd told no one where she was going. But she had promised to write to me and nothing had come. Grandma never broke her promises. Never. Something had gone wrong, I was sure of it.

Then one Saturday morning I picked up the post from the front door mat. There was one for me. I recognised her handwriting at once. The envelope was quite heavy too. Everyone else was soon busy reading their own post, but I wanted to open Grandma's envelope in private. So I ran upstairs to my room, sat on my bed and opened it. I pulled out what looked more like a manuscript than a letter, about thirty or forty pages long at least, closely typed. On the cover page she had sellotaped a black and white photograph (more brown and white really) of a small girl who looked a lot like me, smiling toothily into the camera and cradling a large black and white cat in her arms. There was a title: *The Amazing Story of Adolphus Tips*, with her name underneath, Lily Tregenza. Attached to the manuscript by a large multi-coloured paperclip was this letter.

Dearest Boowie,

This is the only way I could think of to explain to you properly why I've done what I've done. I'll have told you some of this already over the years, but now I want you to know the whole story. Some people will think I'm mad, perhaps most people – I don't mind that. But you won't think I'm mad, not when you've read this. You'll understand, I know you will. That's why I particularly wanted you to read it first. You can show it to everyone else afterwards. I'll phone soon… when you're over the surprise.

When I was about your age – and by the way that's me

on the front cover with Tips – I used to keep a diary. I was an only child, so I'd talk to myself in my diary. It was company for me, almost like a friend. So what you'll be reading is the story of my life as it happened, beginning in the autumn of 1943, during the Second World War, when I was growing up on the family farm. I'll be honest with you, I've done quite a lot of editing. I've left bits out here and there because some of it was too private or too boring or too long. I used to write pages and pages sometimes, just talking to myself, rambling on.

The surprise comes right at the very end. So don't cheat, Boowie. Don't look at the end. Let it be a surprise for you – as it still is for me.

Lots of love,

Grandma

PS Harley must be feeling very lonely all on his own in the garage. We'll go for a ride as soon as I get back; as soon as you come to visit. Promise.

BILLY THE KID

Billy the Kid was Chelsea football club's champion striker,
but that was before war broke out. His love of the beautiful
game sees Billy through the lowest of times, when he is
made a prisoner of war…

I used to have this dream that I was back home and the
crowd was doing their chanting: "Billy, Billy the Kid!
Billy, Billy the Kid!" And I'd score a goal and Joe would
come running on to the pitch from the Shed End and clap
me on the back and I could see in his face that he was so
proud of me. Then I'd wake and I'd know I was in the hut.
I knew it by the smell of it: wet clothes, wood smoke and
unwashed men. I'd lie there in the dark of the hut, and
think of home, of Joe, of football.

Once the letters came I felt much better, for a while.
Lots of them came at once – we never knew why. But it was
good just to hear that Mum and Ossie and Emmy were all
right, that they were still there, and I wasn't alone in the
world. There'd been some bombing in London, so they'd
sent Emmy down to Aunty Mary's in Broadstairs for a
while. She sounded very different in her letter, very grown

up somehow. She told me how she wanted to go back home, but that Mum wouldn't let her, how Aunty Mary fussed over her and how she was fed up with her. She told me she had decided she was going to be a nurse when she was older. I read the letters over and over again, and wrote home whenever I could. Those letters were my lifeline. The next best thing in the world were the Red Cross parcels. How I looked forward to them – marmalade, chocolate, biscuits, cigarettes. We did a lot of swapping and bartering after they came. I'd swap my cigarettes for Robbie's chocolate – never did like smoking, just not my vice – I did my best to end up with mostly chocolate. It lasted longer, if I didn't get too greedy.

As for the Italians guarding us – there were two sorts. You had the kind ones, and that was most of them, who'd pass the time of day, have a joke with you; and then the others, the nasty ones, the real fascists who strutted about the place like peacocks and treated us like dirt. But what really got me down was the boredom, the sameness of every day. I had so much time to think and it was thinking that always dragged me down, and then I wouldn't feel like doing anything. I wouldn't even kick a football about.

It was partly to perk me up, I reckon, that Robbie came up with the idea of an FA Cup competition. He organised the whole thing. Soon we had a dozen league sides – all mad keen supporters only too willing to turn out for 'their' club back home. I trained the Chelsea team, and played centre forward. Robbie was at left back, solid as a rock. For weeks on end the camp was a buzz of excitement. Everyone trained like crazy. Suddenly we all had something to do, something to work for. What some of us might have been lacking in skill and fitness, we made up for in enthusiasm. The Italians laughed at us a bit to start with, but as we all got better they began to take a real interest in it. In the end they even volunteered to provide the referees.

I was a marked man of course, but I was used to that. I got up to all my old tricks, and the crowd loved it. Robbie was thunderous in his tackling. Chelsea got through the final, against Newcastle.

So in April 1943, under Italian sunshine and behind the barbed wire, we had our very own FA Cup Final. The whole camp was there to watch, over two thousand men, and hundreds of Italians too, including the Commandatore himself. It was quite a match. They were all over us to start with, and had me marked so close I could hardly move. Paulo – one of the Italian guards we all liked – turned out to be a lousy ref, or maybe he was a secret Newcastle supporter, because every decision went against us. At half time we were a goal down. Luckily they ran out of puff in the second half and I squeezed in a couple of cheeky goals. Half the crowd went wild when I scored the winner, and when it was all over someone started singing 'Abide With

Me'. We fairly belted it out, and when we'd finished we all clapped and cheered, and to be fair, the Italians did too. They were all right – most of them.

Next day came the big surprise. Paulo came up to me as I was sitting outside the hut writing a letter. "Before the war I see England play against Italia in Roma," he said. "Why we not play Italia against England, here, in this camp?"

So there we were a couple of weeks later on the camp football field facing each other, the best of us against the best of them. We all had white shirts and they had blue – like the real thing. Paulo captained them, I captained us. They were good too, tricky and quick. They ran circles round us. I found myself defending with the back four, marshalling the middle and trying to score goals all at the same time. It didn't work. They went one goal up soon after half time and were well on top too for most of the second half. We really had our backs to the wall. The crowd had all gone very quiet. We were all bunched – when the ball landed at my feet. I was exhausted. All I wanted to do was boot it up the field, just to get it clear. But I had four Italians coming at me and that fired me up. I beat one and another, then another, and leaving Paulo sprawling, made for their goal. I had just the goalie to beat. I feinted this way, that way and stroked it in. It was the best goal I ever scored. The whistle blew for full time. I was hoisted up and carried in triumph round the camp. We hadn't won, but we hadn't lost. Honours even. Just as well, I've always thought. Both sides could laugh about it afterwards. Important that.

THE WRECK OF THE ZANZIBAR

Michael remembers his childhood visits to Great Aunt Laura on the Scilly Isles. He always loved the stories she would tell. As a parting gift, Great Aunt Laura leaves him the most special story of all…

My Great-aunt Laura died a few months ago. She was a hundred years old. She had her cocoa last thing at night, as she usually did, put the cat out, went to sleep and never woke up. There's not a better way to die.

I took the boat across to Scilly for the funeral – almost everyone in the family did. I met again cousins and aunts and uncles I hardly recognised, and who hardly recognised me. The little church on Bryher was packed, standing room only. Everyone on Bryher was there, and they came from all over the Scilly Isles, from St Mary's, St Martin's, St Agnes and Tresco.

We sang the hymns lustily because we knew Great-aunt Laura would enjoy a rousing send-off. Afterwards we had a family gathering in her tiny cottage overlooking Stinking Porth Bay. There was tea and crusty brown bread and honey. I took one mouthful and I was a child again.

Wanting to be on my own, I went up the narrow stairs to the room that had been mine when I came every summer for my holidays. The same oil lamp was by the bed, the same peeling wallpaper, the same faded curtains with the red sailing boats dipping through the waves.

I sat down on the bed and closed my eyes. I was eight years old again and ahead of me were two weeks of sand and sea and boats and shrimping, and oystercatchers and gannets, and Great-aunt Laura's stories every night before she drew the curtains against the moon and left me alone in my bed.

Someone called from downstairs and I was back to now.

Everyone was crowded into her sitting room. There was a cardboard box open in the middle of the floor.

"Ah, there you are, Michael," said Uncle Will. He was a little irritated, I thought.

"We'll begin then."

And a hush fell around the room. He dipped into the box and held up a parcel.

"It looks as if she's left us one each," said Uncle Will. Every parcel was wrapped in old newspaper and tied with string, and there was a large brown label attached to each one. Uncle Will read out the names. I had to wait some minutes for mine. There was nothing I particularly wanted, except Zanzibar of course, but then everyone wanted Zanzibar. Uncle Will was waving a parcel at me.

"Michael," he said, "here's yours."

I took it upstairs and unwrapped it sitting on the bed. It felt like a book of some sort, and so it was, but not a printed book. It was handmade, handwritten in pencil, the pages sewn together. The title on the cover read *The Diary of Laura Perryman* and there was a watercolour painting on the cover of a four-masted ship keeling over in a storm and heading for the rocks. With the book there was an envelope.

I opened it and read.

Dear Michael

When you were little I told you lots and lots of stories about Bryher, about the Isles of Scilly. You know about the ghosts on Samson, about the bell that rings under the sea off St Martin's, about King Arthur still waiting in his cave under the Eastern Isles.

You remember? Well, here is my story, the story of me and my twin brother Billy whom you never knew. How I wish you had. It is a true story and I did not want it to die with me.

When I was young I kept a diary, not an everyday diary. I didn't write in it very often, just whenever I felt like it. Most of it isn't worth the reading and I've already thrown it away – I've lived an ordinary sort of life. But for a few months a long, long time ago, my life was not ordinary at all. This is the diary of those few months.

Do you remember you always used to ask where Zanzibar came from? (You called him "Marzipan" when you were small.) I never told you, did I? I never told anyone. Well, now you'll find out at last.

Goodbye, dear Michael, and God bless you.

Your Great-aunt Laura

PS I hope you like my little sketches. I'm a better artist than I am a writer, I think. When I come back in my next life – and I shall – I shall be a great artist. I've promised myself.

Farm Boy
Grandpa's Story

I love Grandpa's farm. When I was younger I'd go down there whenever I could; but I didn't just go for the farm. I went for Grandpa and his stories too…

When I was a littleun Mayday up in Iddesleigh village was always the best day of the year. There was the march around the village behind the Hatherleigh Silver Band all the menfolk following the Friendly Society banner blue ribbons on their jackets and Father standing a head higher than any of the others.

There were swing boats up around the village green and a carousel and pasties and toffee apples and lemonade and then in the afternoon we had games down on West Park Farm. We did all sorts of egg and spoon races and sack races three legged races skipping races. You name it we did it. But best of all was chicken chasing. They let some poor old fowl loose in the middle of the field and old Farmer Northley waved his flag and off we went after him, the fowl not old Farmer Northley. And if you caught him well then he was yours to keep. We had some fun and games I can tell you. You could see more bloomers and petticoats on Mayday up in Iddesleigh than was good for a chap. Every year I went after that cockerel just like everyone else but I never caught him.

I can mind it was the year that Father caught him that it happened. I were maybe seven or eight perhaps. He flew at Fathers face and Father had him and hung on spite of all the flapping and squawking.

We would have a good supper out of that and we were pleased as punch I can tell you. Father and me stayed up in the village and Mother went off home with the fowl. There were a whole crowd of folk in the Duke of York and as usual there was some that had too much of the beer or cider. It were rowdy in there and I was sat outside with the horses waiting for Father. It was the drink that started the whole thing. Mother always said so after.

Harry Medlicott he had West Park in them days. Biggest farm in the parish it was. Harry Medlicott comes out of the Duke drunk as a lord, he was knowed for it. He was a puffed up sort of chap a bit full of himself. Had the first car in the parish the first tractor too. Anyway Father and me we were mounting up to leave. Father was on Joey and I was up on Zoey and this Harry Medlicott comes up and says. Look here Corporal he says you got to get yourself up to date you have.

What do you mean says Father.

Those two old nags of yours. You should go and get yourself a proper new-fangled modern tractor like me.

What for says Father.

What for. What for. I'll tell you what for corporal says he. My Fordson can plough a field five times as fast as your two old bag of boneses. Thats what for.

Bag of bones is it says Father. Now everyone knows what Father thinks of his Joey how he won't hear a word against him. Common knowledge it was at the time. Well for a moment or two Father just looks down at Harry Medlicott from on top of Joey. Then he leans forward and talks into Joeys ear.

Do you hear that Joey says he. Joey whips his tail and paws the ground like he wants to be off. A bit of a crowd was gathering now most of them as drunk as Harry Medlicott and laughing at us just like he was. He dont much like what youre saying Mr Medlicott says Father. And whats more neither do I.

Like it or not Corporal, Harry Medlicott is still swigging down his cider. Like it or not the days of horses is over. Look at them two. Fit for nothing but the knackers yard if you ask me.

Tis true that Father had drunk a beer or two. I am not saying he hadn't else I am certain sure he would have just rode away. I don't think he was ever angry in all his life but he was as upset then as I ever saw him. I could see that in his eyes. Any rate he pats Joeys neck and tries to smile it off. I reckon theyre good enough for a few years yet Mr Medlicott says he.

Good for nothing I say Corporal. And Harry Medlicott is laughing like a drain all the while. I say a man without a tractor these days can't call himself a proper farmer. Thats what I say.

Father straightens himself up in his saddle and everyones waiting to hear what hes got to say just like I was. All right Mr Medlicott says he. We will see shall us. We will see if your tractor is all you say it is. Come ploughing time in November. I will put my two horses against your tractor and we will just see who comes off best shall us.

Well of course by now Harry Medlicott was splitting himself laughing, and so were half the crowd. Whats that Corporal he says. They two old nags against my new Fordson. I got a two furrow plough reversible. You got an old single furrow. You wouldn't stand a dogs chance. I told you I can do five acres a day easy. More maybe. You havent got a hope Corporal.

Havent I now says Father and theres a steely look in his eye now. You sure of that are you.

Course I am says Harry Medlicott.

Right then. And Father says it out loud so everyone can hear. Heres what we'll do then. We'll plough as many furrows as we can from half past six in the morning to half past three in the afternoon. Hour off for lunch. We'll have Farmer Northley to do the judging at the end of the day. Furrows got to be good and straight like they should be. And another thing Mr Medlicott since youre so sure youll win we'll have a little bet on it shall us. If I win I drive away the tractor. If you win theres a hundred bales of my best meadow hay for you. What do you say.

But my Fordsons worth a lot more than that says Harry Medlicott.

Course it is says Father. But then your not going to lose are you so it don't matter do it. And he holds out his hand. Harry Medlicott thinks for a while but then he shakes Fathers hand and that was that. We rode off home and Father hardly spoke a single word the whole way. We was unsaddling by the stables when he sighs deep and he says. Your mothers going to be awful vexed at me. I shouldnt have done it. I know I shouldnt. Dont know what came over me.

He was right. Mother was as angry as I ever saw her. She told him just what she thought of him and how could we afford to go giving away a hundred good bales and how he was bound to lose and how no horse in the world could plough as fast as a tractor. Everyone with any sense knew that she says. Father kept his peace and never argued with her. He just said he couldnt go back on it now. What was done was done and he would have to make the best of it.

But I tell you something Maisie he says to her. That Harry Medlicott with his fancy car and his fancy waistcoat and his fancy tractor hes going to be worrying himself silly from now on till November you see if he wont.

But you'll be the silly one when you lose wont you says Mother.

Maybe I will maybe I wont Father says back. And he gives her a little smile. Be something if I win though wont it.

Not Just a Shaggy Dog Story

Illustration by Christian Birmingham

THE SILVER SWAN

The silver swan, who living had no note,
When death approached, unlocked her silent throat:
Leaning her breast against the reedy shore
Thus sung her first and last, and sung no more.
Orlando Gibbons

A swan came to my loch one day, a silver swan. I was fishing for trout in the moonlight. She came flying in above me, her wings singing in the air. She circled the loch twice, and then landed, silver, silver in the moonlight.

I stood and watched her as she arranged her wings behind her and sailed out over the loch, making it entirely her own. I stayed as late as I could, quite unable to leave her.

I went down to the loch every day after that, but not to fish for trout, simply to watch my silver swan.

In those early days I took great care not to frighten her away, keeping myself still and hidden in the shadow of the alders. But even so, she knew I was there – I was sure of it.

Within a week I would find her cruising along the lochside, waiting for me when I arrived in the early mornings. I took to bringing some bread crusts with me. She would look sideways at them at first, rather disdainfully. Then, after a while, she reached out her neck, snatched them out of the water, and made off with them in triumph.

One day I dared to dunk the bread crusts for her, dared to try to feed her by hand. She took all I offered her and came back for more. She was coming close enough now for me to be able to touch her neck. I would talk to her as I stroked her. She really listened, I know she did.

I never saw the cob arrive. He was just there swimming beside her one morning out on the loch. You could see the love between them even then. The princess of the loch had found her prince. When they drank they dipped their necks together, as one. When they flew, their wings beat together, as one.

She knew I was there, I think, still watching. But she did not come to see me again, nor to have her bread crusts. I tried to be more glad for her than sad for me, but it was hard.

As winter tried, and failed, to turn to spring, they began to make a home on the small island, way out in the middle of the loch. I could watch them now only through my binoculars. I was there every day I could be – no matter what the weather.

Things were happening. They were no longer busy just

preening themselves, or feeding, or simply gliding out over the loch taking their reflections with them. Between them they were building a nest – a clumsy messy excuse for a nest it seemed to me – set on a reedy knoll near the shore of their island.

It took them several days to construct. Neither ever seemed quite satisfied with the other's work. A twig was too big, or too small, or perhaps just not in the right place. There were no arguments as such, as far as I could see. But my silver swan would rearrange things, tactfully, when her cob wasn't there. And he would do the same when she wasn't there.

Then, one bright cold morning with the ground beneath my feet hard with a late and unexpected frost, I arrived to see my silver swan enthroned at last on her nest, her cob proudly patrolling the loch close by.

I knew there were foxes about even then. I had heard their cries often enough echoing through the night. I had seen their footprints in the snow. But I had never seen one out and about, until now.

It was dusk. I was on my way back home from the loch, coming up through the woods, when I spotted a family of five cubs, their mother sitting on guard near by. Unseen and unsmelt, I crouched down where I was and watched.

I could see at once that they were starving, some of them already too weak even to pester their mother for food. But I could see too that she had none to give – she was thin and rangy herself. I remember thinking then: That's one family of foxes that's not likely to make it, not if the spring doesn't come soon, not if this winter goes on much longer.

But the winter did go on that year, on and on.

I thought little more of the foxes. My mind was on other things, more important things. My silver swan and her cob shared the sitting duties and the guarding duties, never leaving the precious nest long enough for me even to catch sight of the eggs, let alone count them. But I could count the days, and I did.

As the day approached I made up my mind I would go down to the loch, no matter what, and stay there until it happened – however long that might take. But the great day dawned foggy. Out of my bedroom window, I could barely see across the farmyard.

I ran all the way down to the loch. From the lochside I could see nothing of the island, nothing of the loch, only a few feet of limpid grey water lapping at the muddy shore. I could hear the muffled *aarking* of a heron out in the fog, and the distant piping of a moorhen. But I stayed to keep watch, all that day, all the next.

I was there in the morning two days later when the fog began at last to lift and the pale sun to come through. The island was there again. I turned my binoculars at once on the nest. It was deserted. They were gone. I scanned the loch, still mist-covered in places. Not a ripple. Nothing.

Then out of nothing they appeared, my silver swan, her cob and four cygnets, coming straight towards me. As they came towards the shore they turned and sailed right past me. I swear she was showing them to me, parading them. They both swam with such easy power, the cygnets bobbing along in their wake. But I had counted wrong. There was another one, hitching a ride in amongst his mother's folded wings. A snug little swan, I thought, littler than the others perhaps. A lucky little swan.

That night the wind came in from the north and the loch froze over. It stayed frozen. I wondered how they would manage. But I need not have worried. They swam about, keeping a pool of water near the island clear of ice. They had enough to eat, enough to drink. They would be fine. And every day the cygnets were growing. It was clear now that one of them was indeed much smaller, much weaker. But he was keeping up. He was coping. All was well.

Then, silently, as I slept one night, it snowed outside. It snowed on the farm, on the trees, on the frozen loch. I took bread crusts with me the next morning, just in case, and hurried down to the loch. As I came out of the woods I saw the fox's paw prints in the snow. They were leading down towards the loch.

I was running, stumbling through the drifts, dreading all along what I might find.

The fox was stalking around the nest. My silver swan was standing her ground over her young, neck lowered in attack, her wings beating the air frantically, furiously. I shouted. I screamed. But I was too late and too far away to help.

Quick as a flash the fox darted in, had her by the wing and was dragging her away. I ran out on to the ice. I felt it crack and give suddenly beneath me. I was knee-deep in the loch then, still screaming; but the fox would not be put off. I could see the blood, red, bright red, on the snow. The five cygnets were scattering in their terror. My silver swan was still fighting. But she was losing, and there was nothing I could do.

I heard the sudden singing of wings above me. The cob! The cob flying in, diving to attack. The fox took one look upwards, released her victim, and scampered off over the ice, chased all the way by the cob.

For some moments I thought my silver swan was dead. She lay so still on the snow. But then she was on her feet and limping back to her island, one wing flapping feebly, the other trailing, covered in blood and useless. She was gathering her cygnets about her. They were all there. She was enfolding them, loving them, when the cob came flying back to her, landing awkwardly on the ice.

He stood over her all that day and would not leave her side. He knew she was dying. So, by then, did I. I had nothing but revenge and murder in my heart. Time and again, as I sat there at the lochside, I thought of taking my father's gun and going into the woods to hunt down the killer fox. But then I would think of her cubs and would know that she was only doing what a mother fox had to do.

For days I kept my cold sad vigil by the loch. The cob was sheltering the cygnets now, my silver swan sleeping near by, her head tucked under her wing. She scarcely ever moved.

I wasn't there, but I knew the precise moment she died. I knew it because she sang it. It's quite true what they say about swans singing only when they die. I was at home. I had been sent out to fetch logs for the fire before I went up to bed. The world about me was crisp and bright under the moon. The song was clearer and sweeter than any human voice, than any birdsong, I had ever heard before. So sang my silver swan and died.

I expected to see her lying dead on the island the next morning. But she was not there. The cob was sitting still as a statue on his nest, his five cygnets around him.

I went looking for her. I picked up the trail of feathers and blood at the lochside, and followed where I knew it must lead, up through the woods. I approached silently.

The fox cubs were frolicking fat and furry in the sunshine, their mother close by intent on her grooming. There was a terrible wreath of white feathers near by, and telltale feathers too on her snout. She was trying to shake them off. How I hated her.

I ran at her. I picked up stones. I hurled them. I screamed at her. The foxes vanished into the undergrowth and left me alone in the woods. I picked up a silver feather, and cried tears of such raw grief, such fierce anger.

Spring came at long last the next day, and melted the ice. The cob and his five cygnets were safe. After that I came less and less to the loch. It wasn't quite the same without my silver swan. I went there only now and again, just to see how he was doing, how they were all doing.

At first, to my great relief, it seemed as if he was managing well enough on his own. Then one day I noticed there were only four cygnets swimming alongside him, the four bigger ones. I don't know what happened to the smaller one. He just wasn't there. Not so lucky, after all.

The cob would sometimes bring his cygnets to the lochside to see me. I would feed them when he came, but then after a while he just stopped coming.

The weeks passed and the months passed, and the cygnets grew and flew. The cob scarcely left his island now. He stayed on the very spot I had last seen my silver swan. He did not swim; he did not feed; he did not preen himself.

140

Day by day it became clearer that he was pining for her, dying for her.

Now my vigil at the lochside was almost constant again. I had to be with him; I had to see him through. It was what my silver swan would have wanted, I thought.

So I was there when it happened. A swan flew in from nowhere one day, down on to the glassy stillness of the loch. She landed right in front of him. He walked down into the loch, settled into the water and swam out to meet her. I watched them look each other over for just a few minutes. When they drank, they dipped their necks together, as one. When they flew, their wings beat together, as one.

Five years on and they're still together. Five years on and I still have the feather from my silver swan. I take it with me wherever I go. I always will.

It's a Dog's Life

Open one eye.
Same old basket, same old kitchen.
Another day.

Ear's itching.
Have a good scratch.
Lovely.

Have a good stretch.

Here comes Lula.

"Morning, Russ," she says.
"Do you know what day it is today?"
Silly question! Course I do!
It's the day after yesterday
and the day before tomorrow.

Out I go. Smarty's barking his 'good morning' at me from
    across the valley.
Good old Smarty. Best friend I've got, except Lula of course.

I bark mine back.

I can't hang about. Got to get the cows in.

There they are.
Lula's dad likes me to
have them ready for milking
by the time he gets there.

Better watch that one with the new calf.
She's a bit skippy.
Lie down, nose in the grass.
Give her the hard eye.

There she goes, in amongst the rest.

And here comes Lula's dad singing his way down to the
    dairy.
"Good dog," he says.
I wag my tail. He likes that.
He gives me another 'good dog'.
I get my milk. Lovely.

Off back up to the house.
Well, I don't want to miss my breakfast, do I?
Lula's already scoffing her bacon and eggs.

I sit down next to her
and give her my
very best begging look.
It always works.

Two bacon rinds in secret under the table,
and all her toast crusts too. Lovely.

There's good pickings
under the baby's chair this morning.
I hoover it all up. Lovely.

Lula always likes me to go with her
to the end of the lane.
She loves a bit of a cuddle, and
a lick or two before the school bus comes.

"Oh, Russ," she whispers. "A horse.
It's all I want for my birthday."
And I'm thinking, *'Scuse me, what's so great about a horse?*
Isn't a dog good enough?

Then along comes the bus and on she gets.
"See you," she says.

Lula's dad is whistling for me.

144

"Where are you, you old rascal you?"

I'm coming.
I'm coming.

Back up the lane,
through the hedge,
over the gate.

"Don't just sit there, Russ.
I want those sheep in for shearing."

And all the while he keeps on
with his whistling and whooping.

I mean, does he think
I haven't done this before?
Doesn't he know
this is what I'm made for?

Hare down the hill.
Leap the stream.
Get right around behind them.

Keep low. Don't rush them. That's good.

They're all going now. The whole flock of them are trotting
   along nicely.
And I'm slinking along behind, my eye on every one of
   them,
my bark and my bite deep inside their heads.

"Good dog," I get. Third one today. Not bad.

I watch the shearing
from the top of the haybarn.
Good place to sleep, this.

Tigger's somewhere here.
I can smell her.

There she is, up on the rafter,
waving her tail at me.
She's teasing me. I'll show her.

Later, I'll do it later.
Sleep now. Lovely.

"Russ! Where are you, Russ?
I want these sheep out.
Now! Move yourself."

All right, all right.
Down I go, and out they go,
all in a great muddle
bleating at each other,
bopping one another.

They don't recognise each other without their clothes on.
Not very bright, that's the trouble with sheep.

Will you look at that!
There's hundreds of crows out in my corn field.

Well, I'm not having that, am I?
After them! Show them who's boss!
Thirsty work, this.

What's this? Fox!
I can smell him.
I follow him down
through the bluebell wood to his den.
He's down there, deep down.
Can't get at him. Pity.

Need a drink.
Shake myself dry in the sun.
Time for another sleep.

Lovely.

Smarty wakes me.
I know what he's thinking.
How about
a Tigger hunt?

We find her soon enough.
We're after her.

We're catching her up.
Closer. Closer.
Right on her tail.

That's not fair.
She's found a tree.
Up she goes.
We can't climb trees, so we bark our heads off.
Ah well, you can't win them all.

"Russ, where were you, Russ?"
Lula's dad. Shouting for me again.
"Get those calves out in the field.
What's the point in keeping a dog
and barking myself?"

Nothing worse than trying to move young calves.
They're all tippy-toed and skippy.
Pretty things.
Pity they get so big and lumpy when they get older.

There, done it. Well done, me!

Back to the end of the lane to meet Lula.
I'm a bit late. She's there already,
swinging her bag and singing.

"*Happy birthday to me,*
happy birthday to me.
Happy birthday, dear Lula,
happy birthday to me!"

For tea there's a big cake with candles on it,
and they're singing that song again.

Will you look at them
tucking into that cake!
And never a thought for me.

Lula's so busy unwrapping her presents
that she doesn't even notice I'm there,
not even when I put my head on her knee.

Car! Car coming up my lane, and not one I know.
I'm out of the house in a flash.

I'm not just a farm dog, you know, I'm a guard dog too.
"Russ! Stop that barking, will you?"
That's all the thanks I get.
I'm telling you, it's a dog's life.

Looks like a horse to me.
Give him a sniff.
Yes, definitely a horse.

Lula goes mad.
She's hugging the horse
just like she hugs me, only for longer.
A lot longer.

"He's beautiful," she's saying.
"Just what I wanted."

Well, I'm not staying where I'm not wanted.
I haven't had any of that cake,
and they're not watching.

Nip back inside. Jump on a chair.
I'm a champion chomper.

Ooops.
The plate's fallen off the table.
I'm in trouble now.

They all come running in.
I look dead innocent.
Doesn't fool them though.
"You rascal, you. Out you go!"

I don't care. It was worth it.

I go and sit at the top of the hill
and tell Smarty all about it.
He barks back, "Good on you!
Who wants to be a good dog, anyway?"

Then Lula's sitting down beside me.
"I really love my horse," she says,
"but I love you more, Russ. Promise."

Give her a good lick. Make her giggle.
I like it when she giggles.
Lick her again.
Lovely.

DIDN'T WE HAVE A LOVELY TIME?

I have been teaching for over twenty years now, mostly around Hoxton, in north London. After all that time I am no longer at all sentimental about children. I don't think you could be. Twenty years at the chalk face of education gives you a big dose of reality.

I was sentimental to start with, I'm sure. I am still an idealist, though not as zealous perhaps as I used to be, but the fire's still there. You could say that I have given my life to it – I've never had children of my own. I'm headmistress at the school now and I believe more than ever we should be creating the best of all possible worlds for our children, giving every one of them the best possible chance to thrive. That's why every year for at least the past ten years I've been taking the children down to a farm in Devon, a place called Nethercott.

It takes six long hours by coach from London and there, in a large Victorian manor-house with views over to distant Dartmoor, we all live together, all forty of us, teachers and children. We eat three good hot meals a day, sing songs and tell stories around the fire at night, and we sleep like logs. By day we work. And that's the joy of it, to see the children working hard and purposefully out on the farm, feeding calves, moving sheep, grooming Hebe the Haflinger horse who everyone loves, mucking out stables and sheds, collecting eggs and logs, and apples too. The children do it all, and they love it – mostly, anyway. They work alongside real farmers, get to feel like real farmers, know that everything they are doing is useful and important to the farm, that they and their work are appreciated.

Every year we come back to school and the whole place is buzzing. In the playground and in the staff-room all the different stories of our week down on the farm are told again and again. The magic moments – a calf being born, the glimpse of a fox or a deer in Bluebell Wood; the little disasters – Mandy's welly sucked off in the mud, Jemal being chased by the goose. The children write a lot about it, paint pictures of it, and I know they dream about it too, as I do.

But something so extraordinary happened on one of these visits that I too felt compelled to write it down, just as it happened, so that I should never forget it – and because I know that in years to come, as memory fades, it is going to be difficult to believe. I've always found miracles hard to believe, and this really was a kind of miracle.

The boys and girls at our school, St Francis, come from every corner of the earth, so we are quite used to children who can speak little or no English. But until Ho arrived we never had a child who didn't speak at all – he'd have been about seven when he joined us. In the three years he'd been with us he had never uttered a word. As a result he had few friends, and spent much of his time on his own. We would see him sitting by himself reading. He read and he wrote in correct and fluent English, more fluent than many of his classmates who'd been born just down the street. He excelled in maths too, but never put his hand up in class, was never able to volunteer an answer or ask a question. He just put it all down on paper, and it was usually right. None of us ever saw him smile at school, not once. His expression seemed set in stone, fixed in a permanent frown.

We had all given up trying to get him to talk. Any effort to do so had only one effect – he'd simply run off, out into the playground, or all the way home if he could. The educational psychologist, who had not got a word out of him either, told us it was best simply to let him be, and do whatever we could to encourage him, to give him confidence, but without making demands on him to speak. He wasn't sure whether Ho was choosing not to speak or whether he simply couldn't.

All we knew about him was that ever since he'd arrived in England he'd been living with his adoptive parents. In all that time he hadn't spoken to them either, not a word. We knew from them that Ho was one of the Boat

People, that as the war in Vietnam was coming to an end he had managed to escape somehow. There were a lot of Boat People coming to England in those days, mostly via refugee camps in Hong Kong, which was still British then. Other than that, he was a mystery to us all.

When we arrived at the farm I asked Michael – he was the farm school manager at Nethercott, and, after all these years, an old friend – to be a little bit careful how he treated Ho, to go easy on him. Michael could be blunt with the children, pointing at them, firing direct questions in a way that demanded answers. Michael was fine about it. The truth was that everyone down there on the farm was fascinated by this silent little boy from Vietnam, mostly because they'd all heard about the suffering of the Vietnamese Boat People and this was the first time they'd ever met one of them.

Ho had an aura of stillness about him that set him apart. Even sweeping down the parlour after milking, he would be working alone, intent on the task in hand – methodically, seriously, never satisfied until the job was done perfectly.

He particularly loved to touch the animals, I remember that. Looking wasn't enough. He showed no fear as he eased his hand under a sitting hen to find a new-laid egg. When she pecked at him he didn't mind. He just stroked her, calmed her down. Moving the cows out after milking he showed no sign of fear, as many of the other children did. He stomped about in his wellies, clapping his hands at them, driving them on as if he'd been doing it all his life. He seemed to have an easiness around animals, an affinity with the cows in particular, I noticed. I could see that he was totally immersed in this new life in the country, loving every moment of every day. The shadow that seemed to hang over him back at school was lifting; the frown had gone.

On the Sunday afternoon walk along the river Okement I felt him tugging suddenly at my arm and pointing. I looked up just in time to see the flashing brilliance of a kingfisher flying straight as an arrow down the middle of the river. He and I were the only ones to see it. He so nearly smiled then. There was a new light in his eyes that I had not seen before. He was so observant and fascinated, so confident around the animals, I began to wonder about his past – maybe he'd been a country boy back in Vietnam when he was little. I longed to ask him, particularly when he came running up to walk alongside me again. I felt his cold hand creep into mine. That had certainly never happened before. I squeezed it gently and he squeezed back. It was every bit as good as talking, I thought.

At some point during our week-long visit, Michael comes up in the evening to read a story to the children. He's a bit of a writer, as well as a performer. He likes to test his stories out on the children, and we like listening to them too. He never seems to get offended if someone nods off – and they're so tired, they often do. We have all the children washed and ready in their dressing gowns (not easy, I can tell you, when there are nearly forty of them!), hands round mugs of steaming hot chocolate, and gather them in the sitting room round the fire for Michael's story.

On this particular evening, the children were noisy and all over the place, high with excitement. They were often like that when it was windy outside, and there'd been a gale blowing all day. It was a bit like rounding up cats. We thought we'd just about managed it, and were doing a final count of heads, when I noticed that Ho was missing. Had anyone seen him? No. The teachers and I searched for him all over the house. No one could find him anywhere. Long minutes passed and still no sign of Ho. I was becoming more than a little worried. It occurred to me that someone might have upset him, causing Ho to run off, just as he had a few times back at school. Out there in the dark he could have got himself lost and frightened all too easily. He had been in his dressing gown and slippers the last time anyone saw him, that much we had established. But it was a very cold night outside. I was trying to control my panic when Michael walked in, manuscript in hand.

"I need to speak to you," he said. "It's Ho." My heart

missed a beat. I followed him out of the room.

"Listen," he said, "before I read to the children, there's something I have to show you."

"What?" I asked. "What's happened? Is he all right?"

"He's fine," Michael replied. "In fact, I'd say he's happy as Larry. He's outside. Come and have a look." He put his fingers to his lips. "We need to be quiet. I don't want him to hear us."

And so it was that the two of us found ourselves, minutes later, tiptoeing through the darkness of the walled vegetable garden. It was so quiet, I remember hearing a fox barking down in the valley.

There was a light on over the stable door. Michael put his hand on my arm.

"Look," he whispered. "Listen. That's Ho, isn't it?"

Ho was standing there under the light stroking Hebe and talking to her softly. He was talking! Ho was talking, but not in English – in Vietnamese, I supposed. I wanted so much to be able to understand what he was saying. As though he were reading my thoughts, at that very moment he switched to English, speaking without hesitation, the words flowing out of him.

"It's no good if I speak to you in Vietnamese, Hebe, is it? Because you are English. Well, I know really you are from Austria, that's what Michael told us, but everyone speaks to you in English." Ho was almost nose to nose with Hebe now. "Michael says you're twenty-five years old. What's that in human years? Fifty? Sixty? I wish you could tell me what it's like to be a horse. But you can't talk out loud, can you? You're like me. You talk inside your head. I wish you could talk to me, because then you could tell me who your mother was, who your father was, how you learnt to be a riding horse. And you can pull carts too, Michael says. And you could tell me what you dream about. You could tell me everything about your life, couldn't you?

"I'm only ten, but I've got a story I could tell you. D'you want to hear it? Your ears are twitching. I think you understand every word I'm saying, don't you? Do you know we both begin with 'H', don't we? Ho. Hebe. No one else in my school is called Ho, only me. And I like that. I like to be like no one else. The other kids have a go at me sometimes, call me Ho Ho Ho – because that's how Father Christmas talks. Not very funny, is it?

"Anyway, where I come from in Vietnam, we never had Father Christmas. I lived in a village. My mum and dad worked in the rice fields, but then the war came and there were soldiers everywhere and aeroplanes. Lots of bombs falling. So then we moved to the city, to Saigon. I hated the city. I had two little sisters. They hated the city too. No cows and no hens. The city was so crowded. But not as crowded as the boat. I wish we had never got on that boat, but Mum said it would be much safer for us to leave. On the boat there were hundreds of us, and there wasn't enough food and water. And there were storms and I thought we were all going to die. And lots of us did die too, Mum and Dad, and my two sisters. I was the only one in the family left.

"A big ship came along and picked us up one day, me and a few others. I remember someone asked me my name, and I couldn't speak. I was too sad to speak. That's why I haven't spoken to anyone since then – only in my head like I said. I talk to myself in my head all the time, like you do. They put me in a camp in Hong Kong, which was horrible. I could not sleep. I kept thinking of my family, all dead in the boat. I kept seeing them again and again. I couldn't help myself. After a while I was adopted by Aunty Joy and Uncle Max and came to London – that's a long way from here. It's all right in London, but there are no cows or hens. I like it here. I want to stay here all my life. Sometimes at home, and at school, I'm so sad that I feel like running away. But with you and all the animals I don't feel sad any more."

All the time Ho was talking I had the strangest feeling that Hebe was not only listening to every single word he said, but that she understood his sadness, and was feeling for him, as much as we did, as we stood there listening in the darkness.

Ho hadn't finished yet. "I've got to go now, Hebe," he said. "Michael's reading us a story. But I'll come back tomorrow evening, shall I? When no one else is about. Night night. Sleep tight. Don't let the bedbugs bite." And he ran into the house then, almost tripping over the doorstep as he went.

Michael and I were so overwhelmed that for a minute we couldn't speak. We decided not to talk about it to anyone else. It would seem somehow like breaking a confidence.

For the rest of the week down on the farm Ho remained as silent and uncommunicative as before. But I noticed now that he would spend every moment he could in the stable yard with Hebe. The two had become quite inseparable. As the coach drove off on the Friday morning I sat down in the empty seat next to Ho. He was looking steadfastly, too steadfastly, out of the window. I could tell he was trying his best to hide his tears. I didn't really intend to say anything, and certainly not to ask him a question. It just popped out. I think I was trying to cheer him up.

"Well, Ho, didn't we have a lovely time?"

Ho didn't turn round.

"Yes, miss," he said, soft and clear. "I had a lovely time."

The Rainbow Bear

I am snow bear. I am sea bear. I am white bear. I wander far and wide, king in my wild white wilderness.

The snow has darkened around me again. I have dug my den deep into the mountainside. Here I am warm. Here I shall dream away the winter…

There will be plenty of hopping hares to pounce on. But hares are tricky. Plenty of frisking foxes. But foxes are fast. Plenty of wallowing walruses. But walruses are big.

Seals are slow. Seals are best. I stalk them silently. Silently. I am snow bear in a world of white and they cannot see me coming. But one sound, and a seal slips away into the sea.

A seal in the sea is slippery quick. Narwhals and beluga whales are strong, too strong. Fish flash by like silver light and are gone before they were ever there. Here all about me is whooping and whistling of whales. Here is groaning and grinding of ice. Here I am snow bear no more. I am green and blue and indigo and turquoise. Here I am sea bear.

I clamber out of the sea. I shake myself dry in the sun.

I am snow bear again. I look about me.

Rainbow! Rainbow over my wild white wilderness. Beautiful and bright he was, more wonderful than anything I had ever seen before. I knew at once I had to catch rainbow and make him mine. So I went after him. I went hunting rainbow.

I leapt from ice floe to ice floe. I galloped through snow. Ever closer, ever closer. I stalked him silently. Silently. And there at last was rainbow, just one leap away. I pounced.

But I pounced on snow, on white white snow. Rainbow was gone, vanished with the wind. I lay in wait for him, for days, for nights, but he never came back. So I went looking for him. I roamed my wild white wilderness. I would hunt nothing but rainbow.

How long I wandered I did not know. I was weary. I was hungry. I knew I must eat, or I would die.

I smelt man. Then I saw man. Man is clever. Man is danger. But this man was alone and I was hungry. This man was sitting on the ice. He was fishing.

I stalked him silently. Silently. When he saw me, he did not try to run. There was no fear in his eyes, only wisdom.

"So, my friend," he said, "so you have come to eat me. I'm old, very old, I'm not much of a meal for a king of a bear like you."

And it was true. He was old, little more than skin and bone. But a meal was a meal. I made ready to pounce.

"Only leave me to live out my days, my friend," he went on, "and I shall grant you your dearest wish. For I am wiser than man. I am shaman. I know all there is to know. I know you hunt rainbow. But rainbow cannot be hunted, cannot be caught. All you can do is let rainbow come to you. And when he does, you must not pounce on him, you must wish on him. Then all you wish will come true. This I promise you."

The wise old shaman turned back to his fishing again.

So I walked off and left him there on the ice. I did just as he had told me. I hunted no more for rainbow, only for seal and fox and hare. But I still looked everywhere for rainbow.

Every night I dreamt of him. Then one morning I woke and rainbow was there. It was him! It was rainbow leaping out over the sea and across the sky towards me. I remembered again the wise old shaman's words. So I sat on my mountainside and waited, and hoped. And waited and hoped. Nearer he came, nearer still, until he stopped right over me. I was soaked through in his colours. I was rainbow too! I knew at once what to wish for.

I closed my eyes and I wished. "Let me only stay like this, just as I am at this moment. Let me be rainbow bear."

When at last I opened my eyes, rainbow had gone from the sky above me. But I was rainbow, rainbow all over! I was rainbow bear!

I cavorted, I frolicked. I tumbled down the mountainside. I rolled in the snow. I plunged into the sea. When I came out I shook myself dry. I was still rainbow bear! No bear before me had ever been happier than I was then.

I went to find the old shaman, to tell him, to show him. It was far to go, so I hunted as I went. I smelt seal. I stalked him silently. Silently. But seal saw me coming and was quickly gone. I smelt fox. I stalked him silently. Silently. But fox saw me coming and was quickly gone. I smelt hare. I stalked him silently. Silently. But hare too saw me coming and was quickly gone.

By the time I found the wise old shaman again, I was weak with hunger.

"Ah, my friend," he said. "Wherever I go they speak of little else but you. Out at sea, the whales whistle and whoop of it. The waves murmur it. At night the snowy owl hoots to the moon of it. And all say the same: 'Have you seen the rainbow bear? Is he not the most beautiful bear the world has ever seen?' And you are. But there is much danger in beauty, my friend."

And even as he spoke, he pointed out to sea. A great ship was stealing towards us through the ice floes, silently. Silently.

"Look!" he cried. "They have come for you, my friend. Run! Hide yourself! Go, before it is too late!"

So I ran and ran, but the men from the great ship came

after me with their dogs and guns. I hid where I could, but wherever I hid they found me. I was no longer a white bear in a white world. I made for my mountainside, for my winter den. But the men soon dug me out. I was too weak to fight the net they threw over me.

"We have him!" they cried. "We have the rainbow bear! Let's take him back to the ship. He'll make us a fortune."

And so they took me away.

Oh, I had everything I had wished for. I was indeed rainbow bear, but my kingdom was now a cage. I could see the moon, I could see the stars – all through the bars of my cage.

In their thousands, they came to stare at me, to laugh at me. My only escape was in my dreams. But when I dreamt it was always of the wild white wilderness I had left behind and would never see again. I would be white bear again, white bear hunting, white bear stalking. But always I woke, and always the bars were still there.

And so my days passed, each day as long as a winter, each day the same – until early one morning when a voice roused me from my dreams.

"Mr Bear," came the voice. "Oh, Mr Rainbow Bear." A small boy was gazing up at me through the bars of my cage.

"I've been watching you, Mr Rainbow Bear," said the boy. "You just sit there and rock. You just walk up and down. You hate it in there. You hate being a rainbow bear, don't you? You're thinking, I want to be like other snow bears, I want to be back home where I belong, in all that ice and snow, with all those seals and walruses."

Suddenly he was up on the wall and pointing at the sky. "Look, Mr Rainbow Bear!" he cried. "Just like you! It's a rainbow, a rainbow! Don't you know, don't you know? Just find the end of a rainbow and you'll have all you could wish for. It's coming closer, closer. It's coming right over us now! We're at the very end of the rainbow. Quick! You wish. I'll wish. We'll both wish together."

He closed his eyes and lifted his hands into the rainbow above us. Now he was rainbow all over, just as I was.

"We wish this bear was white," cried the boy. "We wish this bear could go back home where he belongs, where he'll be happy. Now, this very minute."

And the boy wished, and I wished with him. I wished myself white. I wished myself away, and back home.

I am waking up, waking up. I have been dozing long enough down in my den. Time to get up. Time to hunt. There's the light of spring seeping through the snow above. I'll dig myself out.

Blue, blue sky. Eye-dazzling sun. Wonderful sun. New air. Icy air. I breathe in deep. The long winter sleep is done and forgotten now. How I wish I could remember my dreams. But I never can.

I clamber out. I cavort, I frolic, I tumble down the mountainside. I roll in the snow. I plunge into the sea. It is so good to be alive, so good to be wild.

I am snow bear. I am sea bear. I am white bear. I wander far and wide, king in my wild white wilderness.

CONKER

Most dogs have one name, but Pooch had three – one after the other. Pooch was what Grandma called him in the first place. But when Nick was a toddler he couldn't say Pooch very well and so Pooch soon became Pooh.

Then one day Pooh heard the rattle of the milk bottles outside and came bounding out of the house to say hello to the milkman – he liked the milkman. But today it was a different one. Pooh prowled around him sniffing at the bottom of his trousers. The new milkman went as white as his milk. Nick tried to drag Pooh back into the house, but he wouldn't come.

"'S'like a wolf," said the milkman, putting his hands on his head and backing down the path. "You ought to chain it up."

"Not a wolf," Nick said. "He's an old station."

"A what?" said the milkman.

"An old station," Nick said. "Pooh is an old station." At that moment Grandma came to the door.

"Nick gets his words muddled sometimes," she said. "He's only little. I think he means an Alsatian, don't you,

dear? Old Station! Old Station! You are a funny boy, Nick."
And she laughed so much that she nearly cried. So from
that day Pooh was called Old Station. There were always
just the three of them in the house. Nick had lived with
Grandma for as long as he could remember. She looked
after Nick, and Old Station looked after them both.

Everywhere they went Old Station went with them.
"Don't know what we'd do without him," Grandma would
say.

All his life Old Station had been like a big brother
to Nick. Nick was nine years old now. He had watched
Old Station grow old as he grew up. The old dog moved
slowly these days, and when he got up in the morning to go
outside you could see it was a real effort. He would spend
most of the day asleep in his basket, dreaming his dreams.

Nick watched him that morning as he ate his cornflakes
before he went off to school. It was the last day before
half-term. Old Station was growling in his sleep as he often
did and his whiskers were twitching.

"He's chasing cats in his dreams," said Grandma.
"Hurry up, Nick, else you'll be late." She gave him his
satchel and packed lunch, and Nick called out "Goodbye"
to Old Station and ran off down the road.

It was a windy autumn morning with the leaves falling
all around him. Before he got to school he caught twenty-
six of them in mid-air and that was more than he'd ever

caught before. By the end of the day the leaves were piled as high as his ankles in the gutters, and Nick scuffled through them on the way back home, thinking of all the bike rides he could go on now that half-term had begun.

Old Station wasn't there to meet him at the door as he sometimes was, and Grandma wasn't in the kitchen cooking tea as she usually was. Old Station wasn't in his basket either.

Nick found Grandma in the back garden, taking the washing off the line. "Nice windy day. Wanted to leave the washing out as long as possible," she said from behind the sheet. "I'll get your tea in a minute, dear."

"Where's Old Station?" Nick said. "He's not in his basket."

Grandma didn't reply, not at first anyway; and when she did Nick wished she never had done.

"He had to go," Grandma said simply, and she walked past him without even looking at him.

"Go where?" Nick asked. "What do you mean? Where's he gone to?"

Grandma put the washing down on the kitchen table and sat down heavily in the chair. Nick could see then that she'd been crying, and he knew that Old Station was dead.

"The vet said he was suffering," she said, looking up at him. "We couldn't have him suffering, could we? It had to be done. That's all there is to it. Just a pinprick it was, dear, and then he went off to sleep. Nice and peaceful."

"He's dead then," Nick said.

Grandma nodded. "I buried him outside in the garden by the wall. It's what was best for him, Nick," she said. "You know that, don't you?" Nick nodded and they cried quietly together.

After tea Grandma put Old Station's basket out in the shed and showed Nick where she had buried him. "We'll plant something over him, shall we, dear?" she said. "A rose perhaps, so we won't forget him."

"We'll never forget him," said Nick. "Never."

———

The day after Old Station died was Saturday. Saturdays and Sundays in the conker season meant conkers in Jubilee Park with his friends, but Nick didn't feel like seeing anyone, not that day. Every time he looked out of the kitchen window into the back garden he felt like crying.

It was Grandma's idea that he should go for a long ride, and so he did. The next best thing in the world after Old Station was the bike Grandma had given him on his birthday. It was shining royal blue with three-speed gears, a bell, a front light and everything. Just to sit on it made him feel happy. By the time he got back from his ride he felt a lot better.

The next morning Nick went off to Jubilee Park as he always did on a Sunday. All his friends were there, and so was Stevie Rooster. Stevie Rooster called himself the "Conker King of Jubilee Park". He was one of those bragging, brutish boys who could hit harder, run faster and shout louder than anyone else. There was only one thing Stevie had ever been frightened of, and that was Old Station. Perhaps it was because of Old Station that Nick was the one boy he had never bullied.

Of course they all knew about Old Station, but no one said anything about him, except for Stevie Rooster. "So that smelly old dog of yours kicked the bucket at last," he said. Perhaps he was expecting everyone to laugh, but no one did.

Nick tried to stop himself from crying.

Stevie went on, "'Bout time if you ask me."

In his fury Nick tore the conker out of Stevie Rooster's hand and hurled it into the pond.

"That's my twenty-fiver," Stevie bellowed, and he lashed out at Nick with his fist, catching him in the mouth.

Nick looked at the blood on the back of his hand and flew at Stevie's throat like an alley cat. In the end Nick was left with a split lip, a black eye and a torn shirt. He was lucky to get away with just that. If the Park Keeper had not come along when he did it might have been a lot worse.

Grandma shook her head as she bathed his face in the

kitchen. "What does it matter what Stevie Rooster says about Old Station?" she said. "Look what he's done to you. Look at your face."

"I had to get him," Nick said.

"But you didn't, did you? I mean he's bigger than you, isn't he? He's twice your size and nasty with it. If you want to beat him, you've got to use your head. It's the only way."

"What do you mean, Grandma?" Nick asked. "What else could I do?"

"Conkers," said Grandma. "Didn't you tell me once that he likes to call himself the 'Conker King of Jubilee Park'?"

"Yes."

"Well then," said Grandma. "You've got to knock him off his throne, haven't you?"

"But how?"

"You've got to beat him at conkers," she said. "And I'm going to teach you how. There's nothing I don't know about conkers, Nick, nothing. You'll see."

Somehow Nick had never thought of his Grandma as a conker expert.

"First we must find the right conkers," she said. "And there's only one place to find a champion conker and that's from the old conker tree out by Cotter's Yard. It's still standing. I saw it from the bus only the other day. I never had a conker off that tree that let me down. Always hard as nails they are. Mustn't be any bigger than my thumbnail. Small and hard is what we're after."

And so it was that Nick found himself that afternoon cycling along the road out of town, past the football ground and the gasworks, with a packet of jelly babies in his pocket. "Now don't eat them all at once, dear," Grandma had told him. "Go carefully and look for the tree on the left-hand side of the road just as you come to Cotter's Yard; you know, the scrapyard where they crunch up old cars. You can't miss it."

And Grandma's conker tree was just where she said it was, a great towering conker tree standing on its own by the scrapyard.

Nick must have spent half an hour searching through the leaves under the tree, but he couldn't find a single conker. He was about to give up and go home when he spotted a cluster of prickly green balls lying in the long grass on the other side of the fence. There was no sign of life in Cotter's Yard. No one would be there on a Sunday afternoon. No one would mind if he went in just to pick up conkers. There was nothing wrong with that, he thought.

He climbed quickly. At the top he swung his legs over and dropped down easily on the other side. He found the cluster of three small conkers and broke them open. Each one was shining brown and perfect, and just the right size. He stuffed them into his pocket and was just about to climb out again when he heard from somewhere behind him in Cotter's Yard, the distant howling of a dog. His first thought was to scramble up over the fence and escape, but then the howling stopped and the dog began to whine and whimper and yelp. It was a cry for help which Nick could not ignore.

Cotter's Yard was a maze of twisted rusting wrecks. The muddy tracks through it were littered with car tyres. Great piles of cars towered all about him now as he picked his way round the potholes. And all the while the pitiful howling echoed louder around him. He was getting closer.

He found the guard dog sitting by a hut in the centre of the yard. He was chained by the neck to a metal stake, and he was shivering so much that his teeth were rattling. The chain was twisted over his back and wrapped around his back legs so that he could not move.

Doesn't look ferocious, Nick thought, *but you never know*. And he walked slowly around the guard dog at a safe distance.

And then Nick noticed the dog's face. It was as if Old Station had come back from the grave and was looking up at him. He had the same gentle brown eyes, the same way of holding his head on one side when he was thinking. *Old*

Station liked jelly babies, Nick thought. *Perhaps this one will*. One by one the dog took them gently out of Nick's hand, chewed them, swallowed them and then waited for the next one.

When there were no more Nick gave him the paper bag to play with whilst he freed him from the chain. He ate the bag too, and when he stood up and shook himself, Nick could see that he was thin like a greyhound is thin. There were sores around his neck behind his ears where his collar had rubbed him raw.

Nick sat down beside him, took off his duffel coat and rubbed him and rubbed him until his teeth stopped chattering. He didn't like to leave him, but it was getting dark.

"Don't worry," Nick said, walking away. The dog followed him to the end of his chain. "I'll be back," he said. "I promise I will." Nick knew now exactly what he wanted to do, but he had no idea at all how he was going to do it.

It was dark by the time Nick got home and Grandma was not pleased with him. "Where have you been? I was worried sick about you," she said, taking off his coat and shaking it out.

"The conkers were difficult to find, Grandma," Nick said, but he said no more.

Grandma was pleased with the conkers though. "Just

177

like they always were," she said, turning them over in her hands. "Unbreakable little beauties." And then Grandma began what she called her "conker magic". First she put them in the oven for exactly twelve minutes. Then she took them out and dropped them still hot into a pudding basin full of her conker potion: a mixture of vinegar, salt, mustard and a teaspoon of Worcester Sauce. One hour later she took them out again and put them back into the oven for another twelve minutes. When they came out they were dull and crinkled. She polished them with furniture polish till they shone again. Then she drove a small brass nail through the conkers one after the other and examined each one carefully. She put two of them aside and held up the third in triumph.

"This is the one," she said. "This is your champion conker. All you have to do now, Nick, is sleep with that down the bottom of your bed tonight, and tomorrow you'll be 'Conker King of Jubilee Park'."

But Nick couldn't sleep that night. He lay there thinking of the dog he had left behind in Cotter's Yard, and about how he was going to rescue him.

By breakfast the next morning he was still not sure how to set about it.

"Remember, you must play on a short string," Grandma was saying. "And always play on grass so it won't break if he pulls it out of your hand. And try not to get tangled up – puts a strain on the knot. What's the matter with you, dear? You're not eating your breakfast."

"Grandma," Nick said, "what if you found a dog all chained up and lonely and miserable, would you try to rescue it?"

"What makes you ask a thing like that, dear?" Grandma said.

"Would you?" Nick asked.

"Of course, dear."

"Even if it meant stealing it, Grandma?"

"Ah well, that's different. Two wrongs don't make a right, Nick," she said. "What's all this about?"

"Oh nothing, nothing," Nick said quickly. "I was just thinking, that's all."

Nick could feel she was suspicious. He had said far too much already. He left quickly before she could ask any more questions.

"Good luck, Nick," Grandma called after him as he went off down the path.

He cycled right up to Stevie Rooster in the park and challenged him there and then. "I've got a conker that'll beat any conker you've got," he said. Stevie Rooster laughed at Nick and his little conker, but when his first conker broke in two the smile left his face.

He took conker after conker out of his sack, and each one was shattered into little pieces within seconds. A crowd gathered as Nick's conker became a twentier, a thirtier, a fiftier and then at last an eighty-fiver. Stevie Rooster's face was red with fury as he took his last conker out of his sack.

"Your turn," Nick said quietly and he held up his conker. There still wasn't a mark on it. Stevie swung again and was left holding a piece of empty string with a knot swinging at the end of it. Nick looked him in the face and saw the tears of humiliation start into his eyes. "You shouldn't have said that about Old Station," Nick said and he turned, got on his bike and cycled off, leaving a stunned crowd behind him.

———

It was a twenty-minute ride up to Cotter's Yard, but Nick did it in ten. All through the conker game he had been thinking about it and now at last he knew what to do. He had a plan. He was breathless by the time he got there. The gates were wide open. The yard was working today, the great crane swinging out over the crushing machine, a car hanging from its jaws.

"Hey, you, what're you after?" It was a voice from the door of the hut. It belonged to a weasel-faced man with mean little eyes.

"I've come to buy your dog," Nick said. "Haven't got any money, but I'll swap my bike for your dog. It's almost new, three speed and everything. Had it for my birthday, a month ago." Nick looked around for the dog, but there was no sign of him. The chain lay curled up in the mud by the hut.

"Haven't got no dog here," said the weasel-faced man. "Not any more. Wasn't any use anyway. Got rid of him, didn't I?"

"What do you mean?" Nick said.

"Just what I said. I got rid of him. Vet came and took him away this morning. No use to me he wasn't. Now push off out of here." And he went back inside the hut and slammed the door behind him.

As Nick cycled home, the rain came spitting down through the trees. He had never felt more miserable in his life. When Old Station died he had been sad enough, but this was different and much, much worse. This had been his fault. If only he had come back earlier, if only. By the time he reached home he was blinded with tears.

"Well, and how's the 'Conker King of Jubilee Park'?" Grandma called out from the kitchen as he closed the door behind him, and she came hurrying out to meet him. "Well, I told you, didn't I? I told you. It's all down the street. Everyone knows my Nick's the Conker King. Well, come on, let's see the famous conker. An eighty-fiver, isn't it?"

"Eighty-sixer," Nick said and burst into tears against her apron.

"What's all this?" Grandma said, putting her arm round him and leading him into the kitchen. "We can't have the 'Conker King of Jubilee Park' crying his eyes out."

And Nick blurted it all out, all about Cotter's Yard and the poor starving dog he had found there that looked just like Old Station, about how the vet had come and taken him away.

"I was going to buy him for you with my bike," Nick said, "to take Old Station's place, but I was too late."

"Who says you were?" said Grandma, and there was a certain tone in her voice.

"What do you mean?" Nick asked.

"What I mean, dear, is that if you'd wipe your eyes and look over in the corner there, you'd see a basket with a dog in it, and if you looked hard at that dog you might just recognise him."

Nick looked. The dog from Cotter's Yard lay curled up in Old Station's basket, his great brown eyes gazing up at him. The dog got up, stretched, yawned and came over to him.

"But how…?" Nick began.

Grandma held up her hand. "When you came home from Cotter's Yard with your duffel coat stinking of dog, I was a little suspicious. You see, old Cotter's known for the cruel way he looks after his guard dogs, always has been. And then when you asked me this morning if I would rescue a dog if I found him all chained up and hungry and miserable – well, I put two and two together."

"But he said the vet came and took him away – he told me," Nick said.

"So he did, dear, so he did. We went out there together, the vet and me, and we made old Cotter an offer he couldn't refuse. Either we took his dog with us or we reported him for cruelty to animals. Didn't take him long to make up his mind, I can tell you."

"So he's ours then, Grandma?" Nick said.

"Yours, Nick, he's yours. Old Station was mine. I had him even before I had you, remember? But this one's yours, your prize for winning the Conker Championship of Jubilee Park. Now can I see that famous conker or can't I?"

Nick fished the conker out of his pocket and held it up by the string. Before he knew it, the dog had jumped up and jerked it out of his hand. A few seconds later all that was left was a mass of wet crumbs and chewed string.

"It looks as if he likes conkers for his tea," Grandma said.

"Better call him 'Conker' then," Nick said.

And so they did.

THE BUTTERFLY LION

Bertie lives in the African veld, and one day he sees the rarest of creatures – a white lion cub. And so begins an incredible friendship of a lifetime…

One morning, a week or so later, Bertie was woken by a chorus of urgent neighing. He jumped out of his bed and ran to the window. A herd of zebras was scattering away from the waterhole, chased by a couple of hyenas. Then he saw more hyenas, three of them, standing stock still, noses pointing, eyes fixed on the waterhole. It was only now that Bertie saw the lion cub. But this one wasn't white at all. He was covered in mud, with his back to the waterhole, and he was waving a pathetic paw at the hyenas who were beginning to circle. The lion cub had nowhere to run to, and the hyenas were sidling ever closer.

Bertie was downstairs in a flash, leaping off the veranda and racing barefoot across the compound, shouting at the top of his voice. He threw open the gate and charged down the hill towards the waterhole, yelling and screaming and waving his arms like a wild thing. Startled at this sudden intrusion, the hyenas turned tail and ran, but not far. Once within range Bertie hurled a broadside of pebbles at them, and they ran off again, but again not far. Then he was at the waterhole and between the lion cub and the hyenas, shouting at them to go away. They didn't. They stood and watched, uncertain for a while. Then they began to circle again, closer, closer...

That was when the shot rang out. The hyenas bolted into the long grass, and were gone. When Bertie turned round he saw his mother in her nightgown, rifle in hand, running towards him down the hill. He had never seen her run before. Between them they gathered up the mud-matted cub and brought him home. He was too weak to struggle, though he tried. As soon as they had given him some warm milk, they dunked him in the bath to wash him. As the first of the mud came off, Bertie saw he was white underneath.

"You see!" he cried triumphantly. "He *is* white! He *is*. I told you, didn't I? He's my white lion!" His mother still could not bring herself to believe it. Five baths later, she had to.

They sat him down by the stove in a washing basket and fed him again, all the milk he could drink, and he drank the lot. They he lay down and slept. He was still asleep when Bertie's father got back at lunch time. They told him how it had all happened.

"Please, Father. I want to keep him," Bertie said.

"And so do I," said his mother. "We both do." And she spoke as Bertie had never heard her speak before, her voice strong, determined.

Bertie's father didn't seem to know quite how to reply. He just said: "We'll talk about it later," and then he walked out.

They did talk about it later when Bertie was supposed to be in bed. He wasn't, though. He heard them arguing. He was outside the sitting-room door, watching, listening. His father was pacing up and down.

"He'll grow up, you know," he was saying. "You can't keep a grown lion, you know that."

"And *you* know we can't just throw him to the hyenas," replied his mother. "He needs us, and maybe we need him. He'll be someone for Bertie to play with for a while." And then she added sadly: "After all, it's not as if he's going to have any brothers and sisters, is it?"

At this, Bertie's father went over to her and kissed her gently on the forehead. It was the only time Bertie had ever seen him kiss her.

"All right then," he said. "All right. You can keep your lion."

So the white lion cub came to live amongst them in the farmhouse. He slept at the end of Bertie's bed. Wherever Bertie went, the lion cub went too – even to the bathroom, where he would watch Bertie have his bath and lick his legs dry afterwards. They were never apart. It was Bertie who saw to the feeding – milk four times a day from one of his father's beer bottles – until later on when the lion cub lapped from a soup bowl. There was impala meat whenever he wanted it, and as he grew – and he grew fast – he wanted more and more of it.

For the first time in his life Bertie was totally happy. The lion cub was all the brothers and sisters he could ever want, all the friends he would ever need. The two of them would sit side by side on the sofa out on the veranda and watch the great red sun go down over Africa, and Bertie would read him *Peter and the Wolf*, and at the end he would always promise him that he would never let him go off to a zoo and live behind bars like the wolf in the story. And the lion cub would look up at Bertie with his trusting amber eyes.

"Why don't you give him a name?" his mother asked one day.

"Because he doesn't need one," replied Bertie. "He's a lion, not a person. Lions don't need names."

Bertie's mother was always wonderfully patient with the lion, no matter how much mess he made, how many cushions he pounced on and ripped apart, no matter how much crockery he smashed. None of it seemed to upset her. And strangely, she was hardly ever ill these days. There was a spring in her step, and her laughter pealed around the house. His father was less happy about it. "Lions," he'd mutter on, "should not live in houses. You should keep him outside in the compound." But they never did. For both mother and son, the lion had brought new life to their days, life and laughter.

RUNNING WILD

*Will and his mother have gone to Indonesia on holiday –
it's a chance to put their sadness behind them. But Oona,
the elephant Will is riding on the beach, begins acting
strangely. And when the tsunami comes crashing in, she
runs straight into the jungle…*

I should have been used by now to the sounds of the jungle at night, but the howling and screeching and hooting, all the endless racket of crickets and frogs would not let me sleep. Lying there, I often longed for the silence of the nights on the farm in Devon, when I'd been camping out with Dad. There I might have heard the occasional bark of a distant fox, or perhaps the hooting of a pair of owls calling to one another over the fields, but that was all I'd had to cope with. Here the full orchestra of the jungle, along with my fears, and my memories, as well as the insects, did their very best to prevent me from sleeping. Every night was a battle that had to be won before sleep would come, and every night it was Oona who helped me win it.

Time and time again I found that it was only when

my thoughts turned to Oona that I could begin to forget everything else. It was so dark at nights that I often could not see her even though she was always near. I could always hear her though, and that was all the reassurance I needed. I'd listen to her rumbling away, groaning and grunting softly. It was like a lullaby to me. Sometimes, when she came close enough, I could feel her ears wafting away the insects and fanning me gently, reminding me she was there when I was feeling at my very lowest. Somehow she seemed to know when that was, when she was needed most. I'd feel her breath warm my cheek and the soft tip of her trunk checking me out. Then I could relax, then I could sleep. Stuff everything, I thought, stuff all the sadness, stuff the leeches. I had Oona. In the morning everything would be fine again.

And it was.

How long it had been now since the day of the tidal wave I had no idea at all. All sense of time had long since vanished. When I thought about it, I did know it must have been a long while, several months at least – the waxing and waning of the moon told me that much. These were days and months that had changed me utterly, my whole being, my whole reason for living. Back at home, everything I'd done, I'd done for some specific reason and purpose. When I watched a DVD it was to see what would happen in the end. I used to get up at half past seven in the morning in order to go to school, in order to get there on time, because if I didn't I was in trouble. And when I got to school, I would maybe do a test in order to show I had learned what I was supposed to have learned. Back at home I would have to wash my hands before a meal, because I was told to, because they had to be clean, so that I wouldn't catch germs and get ill. When I went on a journey, it was always in order to arrive somewhere, at the library perhaps, at the doctor's, at the seaside, at the farm. Every hour of every day, everything I ever did seemed to have a different purpose. Life was full of endless purposes.

Here in the jungle there was only one simple purpose, and it was the same every day: to stay alive. Oona and I were travelling, not to get from one place to another, not to arrive, but only to find food and water, only to survive. It was a different way of being altogether, a new and uncomplicated kind of existence. And with it came a growing familiarity with the jungle around me, the world I now depended on. I was beginning to feel a kinship with this world, such as I had never known before. I was no longer a stranger in this place.

I was coming to believe more and more that the jungle was where I truly belonged, that I was becoming a part of it, that this new rhythm of life was the same for me as it was for every other creature in the jungle, from the leeches on the forest floor that I so loathed, to that distant shadowy orang-utan I loved to watch swinging majestically above us high in the trees, so unlike the sad little creature I'd seen in that magazine back home, lost and bewildered in the burnt-out wasteland of his home. I was sure this one was following us now. I'd see him up there so often. He looked to me like the same one. He was keeping an eye on us, I was sure of it. But orang-utan or leech, snake or gibbon, I was one of them now.

And even to look at I wasn't the same person any more. From time to time I'd catch sight of myself when I went down to fish in a river or to have a drink. The boy I saw staring back at me hardly resembled the same boy who had been carried off on Oona's back all that time ago. My shirt had long since been abandoned, ripped apart and shredded by the jungle, so all I had left were my tattered shorts. The buttons had mostly come off by now. So that they wouldn't fall off, I tied them up as best I could through the belt loops with jungle twine. I still had to keep hitching them up all the time, but it worked well enough, mostly. I was a mess. My hair hung down almost to my shoulders, and was no longer the colour of ripe corn, but was bleached almost white now – my eyebrows too. And my skin was nut brown, with sun or dirt or both. I looked as I felt, like someone else altogether.

It was this transformation, I think, that softened the pain of my grieving and stopped my tears altogether. I was able to believe now that everything before the tidal wave had happened to another boy, a different boy, the pink one, the one who went off to school every day with Tonk and Bart and Charlie, who went for holidays down to the farm in Devon, who drove Grandpa's tractor, and supported Chelsea and ate pies and crisps before the match, whose mum and dad were dead now. That was another boy, in another time, in another world. I was a wild boy now, with calloused hands, with the bottom of my feet as hard as leather, a boy of the jungle, and Oona was all the friends and family I had, all I needed. She was my teacher too, and she taught only by example. From her I was slowly learning to live with the heat and humidity of the jungle, and even with the insects too. Like her, I simply devised a better way of dealing with them. I didn't curse them or dread them so much, but instead tried to accept them as Oona did. It wasn't always easy, but I tried.

I learned from her that in the jungle everything and everyone has its place, that to survive you need to find ways of coexisting. You need knowledge of what is dangerous and what is not, what fruit is edible and what water is drinkable. But above all you have to live in rhythm with the jungle, as Oona did.

Patience is everything. If you see a snake – be still, let it pass. If a crocodile is basking on a river bank, mouth open, watching you, it means: this is my place, take care, keep out of my way. So much in the jungle depends on respecting the space of others. Some creatures eat one another – leeches ate me for a start – but most are fruit eaters, or insect eaters, or frog eaters, and just want to avoid trouble.

And one of the best ways of avoiding trouble, I was discovering, was being ready for it, being aware. See it coming, hear it coming, and most importantly of all, feel it coming. As Oona had shown me so often, she could do this supremely well. I really did have the very best of teachers.

THE DANCING BEAR

*A school teacher living high in the mountains recalls the
day that one of his pupils, a lonely orphan girl called
Roxanne, finds another orphaned creature in the woods...*

It was a Sunday morning in April. We were in the café before
lunch. The old man was going on about Roxanne again,
and how she ate him out of house and home. He'd had a bit
too much to drink, I think, but then he was often that way.

"Gone off again, she has," he grumbled. "God knows
what she gets up to. Nothing but trouble, that girl."

Just then we heard shouting in the village square and,
glad of any diversion, we all went out to look. Roxanne
was staggering towards us, clutching a bear cub in her
arms, with its arms wrapped around her neck. She'd been
scratched on her face and on her arms, but it didn't seem
to bother her. She was laughing and breathless with joy.

"Bruno!" she said. "He's called Bruno. I was down by
the stream. I was just throwing sticks and I felt something
stroking my neck. I turned round and there he was. He
patted my shoulder. He's my very own bear, Grandpa. He's
all alone. He's hungry. I can keep him, can't I? Please?"

If we hadn't been there – and half the village was there by now – I think the old man might have grabbed the bear cub by the scruff of the neck and taken him right back where he came from.

"Look at him," he said. "He's half starved. He's going to die anyway. And besides, bears are for killing, not keeping. You know how many sheep we lose every year to bears? Dozens, I'm telling you, dozens."

Some people were beginning to agree with him. I looked at Roxanne and saw she was looking up at me. Her eyes were filled with tears.

"Maybe –" I was still thinking hard as I spoke – "if you kept him, you know, just for a while. It wouldn't cost much: some waste milk and an old shed somewhere. And just suppose –" I was talking directly to the old man now – "just suppose you made 'bear' labels for your honey jars – you could call it 'Bruno's Honey'. Everyone would hear about it. They'd come from miles around, have a little look at the bear and then buy your honey. You'd make a fortune, I'm sure of it."

I'd said the right thing. Roxanne's grandfather had his beehives all over the mountainside, and everyone knew that he couldn't sell even half the honey he collected. He nodded slowly as the sense of it dawned on him. "All right," he said. "We'll try it. Just for a while, mind."

Roxanne looked at me and beamed her thanks. She

went off with Bruno, followed by an excited cavalcade of village children who took turns to carry him.

That afternoon, they made him a bed of bracken at the back of one of the old man's barns, and fed him a supper of warm ewe's milk from a bottle. They dipped his paw in honey and made him suck it. After that he helped himself. Later when I passed by the barn on my evening walk, I heard Roxanne singing him to sleep. She sang quite beautifully.

In no time at all, Bruno became one of the village children; nobody was afraid of him, as he was always gentle and biddable. He'd go splashing with them in the streams; he'd romp with them in the hay barns; he'd curl himself up in a ball and roll with them helter-skelter down the hillsides. He was more than a playmate, though. He was our mascot, the pride of the village.

To begin with, he never strayed far from Roxanne. He would follow her everywhere, almost as if he were guarding her. Then one day – and by this time, Roxanne was maybe ten or eleven – he broke out of his barn and followed her to school.

I was sitting at my desk sharpening pencils and the class was settled at its work, when Bruno's great panting face appeared at the window, tongue lolling out and drooling. Roxanne managed to shut him in the woodshed where he stayed till lunch, happily sharpening his claws on the logs.

Not much schoolwork was done *that* day.

BORN TO RUN

For Best Mate, being rescued is only the start of his adventures. He journeys from unwanted burden to favourite companion, and from pet dog to champion racing hound…

He hitched up his school bag and felt suddenly all bright and breezy, until he saw the swan some distance ahead of him, standing there on the towpath, looking at him, waiting for him. That worried him, because Patrick knew this swan, knew him all too well. They had met once before. It looked like the same one who had blocked his path on the way to school only a couple of weeks ago. He'd come running at Patrick wings outstretched, neck lowered to attack and hissing like a hundred snakes. Patrick had had to run into the undergrowth to escape him and had fallen into a patch of nettles. So Patrick did not like this swan, not one bit. Yet somehow he was going to have to get past him – it was the only way to get to school, and he had to get to school. The question was how to do it.

Patrick stood there eyeing the swan, just hoping that sooner rather than later the swan would decide it was time to go back into the water. But the swan stayed steadfastly where he was, glaring darkly at him, his great black feet planted firmly on the towpath. He was showing no signs of moving anywhere.

Patrick was still wondering what to do, when out of the corner of his eye he saw something floating out in the middle of the canal. It was bright green and looked plastic – a sack of some kind. He probably wouldn't have paid it any more attention – a sack's not that interesting, after all – if he hadn't heard the squeaking. It sounded as if it was coming from the sack itself, and that didn't make sense.

Patrick thought at first it might have been the piping of ducklings or moorhen chicks – he'd heard them often enough on the canal. But then he remembered that there weren't any chicks around, not any more, because it was autumn. The whole place was carpeted with yellow leaves, gold leaves, red leaves. They were all around his feet. Spring and summer were over. No, it really had to be the sack itself that was squeaking.

It was still early in the morning and Patrick's brain must have been working very slowly, because several moments passed before he realised that there was something alive inside the sack, and even then it wasn't only the squeaking that convinced him. The sack, he noticed, wasn't just drifting gently along like everything else, the leaves, the sticks, all the other flotsam in the canal. It was turning of its own accord, as if it was being propelled from the inside.

There was definitely something inside it, and whatever it was seemed to be struggling against the side of the plastic sack, kicking at it, trying to escape from it and squeaking and squealing in terror. He had no idea what it might be, only that it was alive and in danger of drowning. The canal wasn't that wide. It was dirty but it wasn't wide. He could do it.

Patrick didn't think about it any more. He shrugged off his school bag and leapt into the canal. He knew he was a good enough swimmer, so he wasn't worried about drowning, only about getting cold and wet. He didn't want the canal water in his mouth either, so he kept it tight shut. Just a few quick strokes out into the canal and he'd grabbed the sack, turned, and was swimming back again. Suddenly the bank seemed a long way away, but he got there.

Climbing out was the most difficult part because his clothes were heavy and clinging, and the sack was slippery in his hands, difficult to hold on to. He felt suddenly very weak, felt the cold of the water chilling him to the bone. But with one huge effort he heaved himself up, enough to hook one leg up, on to the bank, and then he was out. Standing there, dripping from everywhere, he untied the sack and opened it. There were five puppies inside, leggy, gangly looking creatures, skeletal almost, all of them trembling with cold and crawling over one another, squirming to get out, mouths open and squeaking frantically. They were like no puppies Patrick had even seen before.

He had two choices, and he knew neither of them were any good. He could go home at once and leave the puppies in his bedroom – he had a key, he could easily let himself into the flat. There'd be no one home, but at least they'd be warm there. This way he could change his wet clothes too. He could feed them when he got back after school. The trouble was that it would take for ever to get there and back, and by the time he got to school he'd be so late that Mrs Brightwell would probably have one of her eruptions and he'd be in detention for a week, and she'd be bound to send him home with another cross letter for his mum and dad.

She certainly wouldn't believe his excuse: "Please Mrs Brightwell, sorry I'm late, but I had to jump into the canal on the way to school to rescue some puppies." If he didn't have the puppies with him, and he'd already changed into dry clothes, she'd be bound to think he was making the whole thing up. She hated excuses anyway, especially incredible ones. She'd go ballistic.

Or he could go straight to school all wet and smelly from the canal, only a little bit late and carrying the puppies with him. At least she'd have to believe his story then, wouldn't she? But then he thought of what Jimmy Rington would say when he walked into school all dripping and sodden, how everyone would laugh at him.

They'd never let him forget it, that was for sure. And then there was that swan he had to get by, still there blocking his path, still glaring at him.

In the end it was Mr Boots, the lollipop man, who made up Patrick's mind for him. Patrick was standing there, numb with cold, still wondering what he should do, when he saw Mr Boots come hurrying along the towpath, lollipop stick in his hand, his white coat flying. Patrick had never much liked Mr Boots. He wasn't called "Bossy Boots" for nothing. He was a bit full of himself, a bit puffed up and pompous. And there was something about him Patrick had never quite trusted. He was a bit of a phoney, Patrick thought. But all the same he was glad to see him now.

Mr Boots arrived breathless. For a while he could only speak in gasps. "You jumped in!" he spluttered. "Whatever d'you want to go and do that for?"

By way of an answer Patrick showed him what he had in his sack. Mr Boots bent over to look. Then he was spluttering again. "Blow me down! Puppies, greyhound puppies they are. Little beauties!" He looked up at Patrick. "You could have drowned yourself, doing that. Look at you, you're soaked to the skin. You'll catch your death standing here. Best get you into school and fast. I'm telling you, when Mrs Brightwell hears about this... You come along with me. Here, you can take my lollipop stick if you like, and I'll carry your school bag and the puppies."

As the two of them hurried along the towpath a barge came chuntering past. "Been in for a bit of a dip, have you, son?" laughed the man at the wheel. But Patrick paid him no attention – he had his eye on that swan. He felt a little more confident though, because he had the lollipop stick to wave now. As it turned out he didn't need it. The swan moved aside as they came hurrying towards him and swam out into the canal, riding the wake of the barge. Then they were up the steps from the towpath and across the road into the school playground.

Patrick knew he was already late the moment he walked through the door. There was no one about. They'd all be in assembly by now. He'd be in really big trouble. He felt like running off home there and then. But he couldn't, because Mr Boots had him firmly by the hand and was walking him down the corridor towards the hall. He could hear Mrs Brightwell's voice now. She was making one of her important announcements, and by the sound of her she was in full flow and already cross about something. *Not a good moment to interrupt her*, Patrick thought. Mr Boots stopped at the door to straighten his tie and smooth down his hair – he didn't have much of it, but what he had he liked to keep immaculate. Then, clearing his throat, he threw open the double doors, and in they went.

Everyone turned and gawped. Up on the platform

Mrs Brightwell stopped in mid-sentence. A deep hush fell around them as they walked the entire length of the hall up towards Mrs Brightwell. Every step Patrick took seemed to squelch louder than the one before, and all the way the puppies in the sack were squealing and squeaking.

Mrs Brightwell did not look at all pleased. "Mr Boots," she said, "what is this? Why is Patrick standing there dripping all over my assembly hall? What on earth has happened?"

"Actually, it's a bit of a long story, Mrs Brightwell." Mr Boots sounded typically self-important. "You had to see it to believe it. There I am, just minding my own business on the crossing outside the school, when I hear this splash. So I look over the bridge, and what do I see? Only young Patrick here in the canal swimming like a fish. Well of course I think he's fallen in, and he's drowning. So I start running, don't I? I mean I've got to save him, haven't I? But then I see he's not drowning at all. He's got hold of this sack and he's swimming like billy-o for the bank. And I'm thinking to myself: *You're off your tiny rocker, my son, taking a dip in that filthy old canal just to fetch out a dirty old plastic sack*. Luckily for young Patrick here I was on hand to help him out, cos he wouldn't have made it on his own, that's for sure."

You fibber! Patrick thought. *You great big fibber!* But he didn't say anything.

Mr Boots hadn't finished yet. He was enjoying his moment in the limelight. "So Patrick's standing there now on the bank, all shivering and shaking, and that's when I have a little look inside the sack, don't I? And what do I find? It's full of puppies, that's what, five of the little beggars, and if I'm not mistaken, which I'm not, they're greyhounds, about seven weeks old by the look of them. We've got brindles in there, blacks and a fawn one too. I go down the greyhound track from time to time, so I know my greyhounds. I'm what you might call a greyhound connoisseur. They're lovely pups too, fine dogs. And young Patrick here jumped in the canal and saved them. I saw him with my own eyes. He's a bleeding hero, if you ask me – 'scuse my French, Mrs Brightwell – but that's what he is, a bleeding hero."

Patrick had never heard such a depth of silence as he heard in that hall when Bossy Boots had finished. Then one of the puppies squeaked, and suddenly they were all at it, a whole chorus of squealing, yelping puppies. "Aaah, sweet," said someone. Someone else started giggling, and soon there was laughter and clapping too, rippling round the hall. Within moments the assembly hall was loud with cheering and whooping – one or two were yelping like puppies. Patrick stood there soaking in the applause and feeling about ten foot tall. Even Mrs Brightwell was clapping now. Patrick saw there were tears in her eyes as she beamed at him. That was the first time, Patrick thought, that she'd ever beamed at him. He'd never seen her cry before either; he didn't know she could. Suddenly he found himself really quite liking her, and that hadn't happened before either.

As the applause died away at last, Mrs Brightwell came down off the platform, and peered into the sack. "One. Two. Three. Four, five, and they're all alive because of you, Patrick. What you did was very special. You risked your life to save them. I think that's about as special as it gets."

The Last Wolf

Miya's grandfather decides to trace his family tree, to find out who his ancestors were. Sometimes the most amazing stories are hidden in your own family history…

"You're an ostrich, Grandpa," Miya told me, sitting herself down on my bed and peeling an orange for me.

"And why's that then?" I asked her.

"Because whenever you see something you don't like, you just bury your head in the sand and pretend it's not there."

It was an old argument between us, not that you'd call it an argument as such, more of a tease. But whatever it was, I knew that sooner rather than later she was going to wear me down. Miya was determined to drag me into the twenty-first century whether I liked it or not. And now she'd found the perfect opportunity.

"You've got nothing else to do, Grandpa," she went on. "You're bored out of your mind. Why not try it, at least? I'll come in and teach you, if you like, every evening. Won't take long. It's easy-peasy – nothing to be frightened of."

"I'm not frightened," I replied. "I just don't see the point of all these new-fangled machines, that's all."

"Like I said, you're an ostrich. Here." She gave me my orange. "Eat. It's good for you," she said. "Listen, Grandpa, it's brilliant, honest it is. There's millions of different things you can do on it – email, word processing, games, shopping…"

"I hate shopping," I told her.

"You're a grumpy old ostrich too," she said, bending over to kiss me on the cheek. "We'll get started tomorrow. I'll bring over my laptop, all right? Byeee!"

And she was out of the door and gone, ignoring all my protests. She had won.

All this came about because I'd been ill – just flu at first, but then it became pneumonia. The doctor, who's a good friend of mine as well as my doctor, wagged his finger at me, and said, "Now you listen to me, Michael McLeod, this is serious. You're no spring chicken any more. You've got to stay in bed, and in the warm. No more gardening, no more golf, no more fishing. You've got to look after yourself." So, cooped up in my flat for weeks on end, I had become, as Miya had so rightly diagnosed, bored out of my mind.

Miya was fourteen, my eldest granddaughter and the apple of my eye. She was always popping in to cheer me up, bless her – she lives just round the corner. And she did cheer me up too, even if she did go on and on about the joys of her wretched computer. The truth was that so long as she came to see me, I didn't mind what we did, or what she talked about. It would pass the time, and talking about computers made a welcome change from losing to her at chess – again.

The computer lessons did not start well. I just could not get my head around it all. Then, bit by bit, day by day, with Miya's help, I began to make some sense of it; and once I'd made sense of it, I began to enjoy it – much to my surprise. A couple of weeks later Miya went off on her summer holidays, leaving me strict instructions as to how to plug in and keep in touch with her by email. She told me I must promise to practise every day on the computer. I promised, and I like to keep my promises.

So, except for occasional check-up visits from my doctor friend, and from my neighbour who very kindly did all my shopping for me, I was left alone in the house with Miya's computer. One morning, as I sat there in front of it, about to switch on, I began asking myself why I was doing this. I mean, what was this machine really for? What could it do for me? How, now I'd begun to master it, could I use it to help me through the long days of convalescence that still lay ahead of me? I needed a project, I thought. Something to occupy my mind, something I could really get my teeth into, and something this computer could help me to achieve.

I had a sudden idea. It was an old idea, one I'd had in the back of my mind for many years, but had never bothered to do anything much about. This was my opportunity. I had the time, and now I had the means – literally at my fingertips. I would set out on a quest, a quest I could achieve without ever leaving the flat. I could do it all, the whole thing, on the Internet, by email. I would search out my roots, piece together my family tree, discover where I came from, who I came from. I would trace my family line back as far as I could go.

On my mother's side, the Meredith side, this proved simple enough because they had lived in the country, in Suffolk mostly, for many generations, and I could track them down through parish records, through registers of births and marriages and deaths. I managed to trace that side of the family all the way back to a Hannah Meredith, who I discovered had been baptised in Southwold on 2 May 1730.

It was like detective work, genealogical detective work, and I was soon completely engrossed in it. I was emailing dozens of times a day. I had all the information I had gathered on a database. Miya and I exchanged emails often, particularly when I got stuck and needed her help. As Miya had said, her computer was "brilliant", utterly "brilliant".

But my father's family, the McLeod side, the Scottish side, proved much more difficult to trace even with the help of the computer, because they had moved about the world, one of the family to Argentina, one to Australia and another to the United States of America. Only a few generations back the trails kept going cold, and I was beginning to feel very frustrated. I simply had no more clues to follow up, not a single one.

Then, thank goodness, Miya came back home from her holiday and to my rescue. She told me I should upload my whole family tree on to a genealogical website, and appeal for help that way. So that's what I did. For several days I had no response at all. Then one evening Miya logged on for me and found an email from Marianne McLeod of Boston, Massachusetts, in the United States.

She had, she wrote, studied my father's side of my family tree with great interest and felt sure we must be distant cousins. She, like me, had been researching her family background – she called it her "lifelong obsession" – and had traced her family to Scotland, as far back as the 1700s, to her ancestor, and mine, she hoped – one Robbie McLeod of Inverness-shire. Quite by chance she had recently discovered hidden away amongst her family papers, Robbie McLeod's last will and testament. *It's the most wonderful story I have ever read. I've scanned it into my computer. Would you like to see it?* Would I! I emailed back to her at once. *Greetings, distant cousin, I can't wait.* Miya was as excited as I was now. There was no reply until nearly twenty-four hours later. Miya was there beside me when I first read it. One glance told me that it had been worth waiting for. As I read, my heart in my mouth with excitement, I knew that my quest had been achieved, that with the help of Miya's new-fangled machine, Miya and I had discovered something quite wonderful, as wonderful as any holy grail. I was reading the last words, in his own handwriting, of my great-great-great-great-great-grandfather. He was speaking to us from across the ages.

The Pity and the Shame

Illustration by Michael Foreman

HALF A MAN

When I was very little, more than half a century ago now, I used to have nightmares. You don't forget nightmares. The nightmare was always the same. It began with a face, a twisted, tortured face that screamed silently, a face without hair or eyebrows, a skull more than a face, a skull which was covered in puckered, scarred skin stretched over the cheekbones. It was Grandpa's face and he was staring at me out of his scream. And always the face was on fire, flames licking out of his ears and mouth.

I remember I always tried to force myself to wake up, so that I wouldn't have to endure the rest of it. But I knew every time that the rest would follow however hard I tried to escape – that my nightmare would not release me, would not allow me to wake until the whole horrible tale had played itself out.

I saw a great ship ablaze on the ocean. There were men on fire jumping overboard as she went down, then swimming in a sea where the water burned and boiled around them. I saw Grandpa swimming towards a lifeboat, but it was packed with sailors and there was no room for Grandpa. He begged them to let him on, but they wouldn't. Behind him, the ship's bow lifted out of the sea, and the whole ship groaned like a wounded beast in her death throes. Then she went down, slipping slowly under the waves, gasping great gouts of steam in the last of her agony. A silence came over the burning sea. Grandpa was clinging to the lifeboat now, his elbows hooked over the side. That was when I realised that I was in the lifeboat with the other sailors. He saw me looking down at him and reached out his hand for help. It was a hand with no fingers.

I would wake up then, shaking in my terror and knowing even now that my nightmare was not over. For my nightmare would always seem to happen just a day or two before Grandpa came to stay. It was a visit I always dreaded. He didn't come to see us in London very often, every couple of years at most, and usually at Christmas. Thinking about it now, I suppose this was part of the problem. There were perfectly good reasons why we didn't and couldn't see more of him. He lived far away, on the Isles of Scilly, so it was a long way for him to come, and expensive too. Besides which, he hated big cities like London. I'm sure if I'd seen him more often, I'd have got used to him – used to his face and his hands and his silent, uncommunicative ways.

I don't blame my mother and father. I can see now why they were so tense before each visit. Being as taciturn and unsmiling as he was, Grandpa can't have been an easy guest. But, even so, they did make it a lot worse for me than they needed to. Just before Grandpa came there were always endless warnings, from Mother in particular (he was my grandpa on my mother's side), about how I mustn't upset him, how I mustn't leave my toys lying about on the sitting-room floor because he didn't see very well and might trip over them, how I mustn't have the television on too much because Grandpa didn't like the noise. But most of all they drummed into me again and again that whatever I did I must not under any circumstances stare at him – that it was rude, that he hated people staring at him, particularly children.

I tried not to; I tried very hard. When he first arrived I would always try to force myself to look at something else. Once I remember it was a Christmas decoration, a red paper bell hanging just above his head in the front hall. Sometimes I would make myself look very deliberately at his waistcoat perhaps, or the gold watch chain he always wore. I'd fix my gaze on anything just as long as it was nowhere near the forbidden places, because I knew that once I started looking at his forbidden face or his forbidden hands I wouldn't be able to stop myself.

But every time, sooner or later, I'd do it; I'd sneak a crafty look. And very soon that look became a stare. I was never at all revolted by what I saw. If I had been, I could

OF LIONS AND UNICORNS

have looked away easily. I think I was more fascinated
than anything else, and horrified too, because I'd been told
something of what had happened to him in the war. I saw
the suffering he had gone through in his deep blue eyes –
eyes that hardly ever blinked, I noticed. Then I'd feel my
mother's eyes boring into me, willing me to stop staring,
or my father would kick me under the table. So I'd look
at Grandpa's waistcoat – but I could only manage it for
a while. I couldn't help myself. I had to look again at the
forbidden places. He had three half-fingers on one hand
and no fingers at all on the other. His top lip had almost
completely disappeared and one of his ears was little more
than a hole in his head.

As I grew up I'd often ask about how exactly it had
happened. My mother and father never seemed to want
to tell me much about it. They claimed they didn't know
any more than they'd told me already – that Grandpa had
been in the merchant navy in the Second World War, that
his ship had been torpedoed in the Atlantic, and he'd been
terribly burnt. He'd been adrift in a boat for days and days,
they told me, before he'd been picked up. He'd spent the
rest of the war in a special hospital.

Every time I looked at his face and hands the story
seemed to want to tell itself again in my head. I so much
wanted to know more. And I wanted to know more about
my grandmother too, but that was a story that made

220

everyone even more tight-lipped. I knew she was called Annie, but I had never met her and no one ever talked about her. All anyone would ever say was that she had "gone away" a very long time ago, before I was born. I longed to ask Grandpa himself about his ship being torpedoed, about my grandmother too, but I never dared, not even when I was older and got to know him a lot better.

I must have been about twelve when I first went to see him on my own in the Scilly Isles for my summer holiday, and by then the nightmares had gone. That was not to say I wasn't still apprehensive in those first few days after I arrived. But I was always happy to be there, happy just to get out of London. I'd go and stay with him in his cottage on Bryher – a tiny island, only about eighty people live there. He had no electricity, only a generator in a shed outside, which he'd switch off before he went to bed. The cottage wasn't much more than a shed, either. It was a different world for me and I loved it. He lived by himself and lived simply. The place smelt of warm damp and paraffin oil and fish – we had fish for almost every meal. He made some kind of living out of catching lobsters and crabs. How he managed to go fishing with his hands as they were I'll never know. But he did.

It was years before I discovered why he never smiled. It was because he couldn't. It was too painful. The skin simply wouldn't stretch. When he laughed, which wasn't often, it was always with a straight face. And when he smiled it was with his eyes only. I'd never understood that when I was little. His eyes were the same blue as the sea around Scilly on a fine day. He was silent, I discovered, because he liked to keep himself to himself. I'm a bit the same, so I didn't mind. He wasn't at all unkind or morose, just quiet. He'd read a lot in the evenings, for hours, anything about boats – Arthur Ransome, C. S. Forester and Patrick O'Brian. He didn't have a television, so I'd read them too. I think I must have read every book Arthur Ransome wrote during my holidays on Scilly.

During the day he'd let me do what I liked. I could run free. I'd wander the island all day; I'd go climbing on the rocks on Samson Hill or Droppy Nose Point. I'd go swimming in Rushy Bay, shrimping off Green Bay. But as I got older he'd ask me to go out fishing with him more and more. He liked the company, I think, or maybe it was because he needed the help, even if he never said so. I'd catch wrasse and pollack for baiting his lobster pots. I'd help him haul them in and extract the catch. We would work almost silently together, our eyes meeting from time to time. Sometimes he'd catch me staring at him as he had when I was little. All those years later and I still couldn't help myself. But now it was different. Now all the fear had gone. Now I knew him well enough to smile at him when our eyes met, and, as I was later to find out, he understood perfectly well why I was staring at him, at his forbidden face, his forbidden hands.

It wasn't until the summer I just left school that Grandpa first told me himself about what had happened to him when his ship went down. He talked more these days, but never as much as the day we saw the gannets. We were out in his fishing boat. We'd picked up the pots, caught a few mackerel for supper, and were coming back in a lumpy sea round the back of Bryher, when a pair of gannets flew over and dived together, spearing the sea just ahead of us. "See that, Grandpa?" I cried. "Aren't they brilliant?"

"Better than brilliant," he said. "They bring you good luck, you know."

We watched the gannets surface, swallow their catch and take off again. We caught each other's eye and smiled, enjoying the moment together.

"You know what I like about you, Michael?" he went on. "You look at me. Most people don't. Your mother doesn't, and she's my own daughter. She looks away. Most people look away. Not that I blame them. I did once. Not any more. But you don't look away." He smiled. "You've been having sneaky old looks at me ever since you were knee-high to a grasshopper. If you looked away it was only to be polite, I always knew that. You've always wanted to ask me, haven't you? You wanted to know, didn't you? How this happened, I mean."

He touched his face. "I never told anyone before, not your mother, not even Annie. I just told them what they needed to know and no more, that my ship went down and after a few days in a lifeboat I got picked up. That's all I said. The rest they could see for themselves." He was looking straight ahead of him, steering the boat as he was talking.

"I was a handsome enough devil before that – looked a bit like you do now. Annie and me got married a couple of years before the war broke out. A year later, I was in the merchant navy, in a convoy coming back from America. My third trip, it was." He looked out towards Scilly Rock and wiped his face with the back of his hand. "It was a day like this, the day we copped it – the day I became half a man. Early evening, it happened. I'd seen ships go down before, dozens of them, and every time I thanked God it wasn't me. Now it was my turn.

"I was on watch when the first torpedo struck. Never saw it coming. The first hit us amidships. The second blew off the stern – took it right off. All hell broke loose. A great ball of fire came roaring through the ship, set me on fire and cooked me like a sausage. Jim – Jim Channing, he came from Scilly too, him and me were mates, always were, even at school, joined up together – he smothered the flames, put them out. Then he helped me to the side. I'd never even have got that far without Jim. He made me jump. I didn't want to, because the sea was on fire. But he made me. He had hold of me and swam me away from the ship, so's we wouldn't get sucked down, he said. He got me to a lifeboat. There were too many in it already and they didn't want us."

I could see it! I could see it in my head. It was straight out of my nightmare.

"Jim said that he could hang on to the side but I'd been burnt and they had to help me into the boat. In the end they did, and Jim clung on beside me, still in the water, and we talked. We had to talk, and keep talking, Jim told me, so we didn't go to sleep, because if we went to sleep, like as not we'd never wake up again. So we told each other all the stories we knew: *Peter Rabbit*, the *Just So Stories* – anything we could remember. When we ran out of stories, we tried singing songs instead: 'Ten Green Bottles', 'Oranges and Lemons', anything. Time and again I dropped off to sleep, but Jim would always wake me up. Then one time I woke and Jim just wasn't there. He was gone. I've thought about Jim every day of my life since, but I've never spoken about him, until now.

"He's out there, Michael. Jim's out there, down in the deep somewhere. They all are, all the lads that went down

225

in that ship, good lads. And there's been plenty of times since, I can tell you, when I wished to God I'd gone down with them."

He said nothing more for a while. I'd never heard him talk like this before, never. But he hadn't finished yet.

"All we saw for days on end were gannets," he went on. "Except once we did see a whale, a ruddy great whale. But that was all. No ships. No aeroplanes. Nothing. Just sea and sky. Some of the lads were burnt even worse than I was. They didn't last long. We were out there on the open ocean for a week or more. No food, no water. I lost count of the days and the nights. By then I didn't know any more who was alive and who was dead, and what's more I didn't care. I only knew I was still alive. That was all that mattered to me. I lived on nothing but hope, and a dream. I had a dream and I clung on to it. I dreamt of getting back to Annie, of coming home. I thought if I dreamt it hard enough, hoped for it hard enough, it must come true.

"Then, one morning, I wake up and there's this huge destroyer right there alongside us and men looking down over the side and waving and shouting. I thought I was still in my dream, but I wasn't. Only three of us out of that whole lifeboat survived. They patched me up as best they could, and shipped me home. The next thing I knew I was in this hospital, down in Sussex it was, East Grinstead. That's where they put the pieces of me together again, like a sort of jigsaw puzzle, but the pieces were skin and bone and flesh. The trouble was, there were some pieces of my jigsaw missing, so they had a bit of a job, which is why I still look a bit of a mess. But I wasn't the worst in that hospital, not by a long shot.

"Dr McIndoe, he was called. Wonderful man he was, a genius. It was him that did it, put us back together, and I'm not just talking about the operations. He was a magician in the operating theatre, all right. But it's what he did afterwards for us. He made us feel right again inside, like we mattered, like we weren't monster men. It was a hospital full of men like me, but mostly air-force boys. We were all together, every one of us patched up in one way or another, so it didn't matter what we looked like even when we went out and about. Everyone treated us right: nurses and doctors, everyone. Annie came to see me when she could. Right away I saw she didn't look at me the same, didn't speak to me like I was normal, like the nurses did. She still loved me, I think, but all she saw was a monster man.

"After a while, when the war was over, I left the hospital and came home to Annie, home to Scilly. My dream had come true, I thought. But of course it hadn't. I soon found that out. Annie tried – tried her best. I tried too. We had a baby – your mother, Michael – but Annie still wasn't looking at me. I drank too much, said things I shouldn't have said. She did too, told me I should stop feeling sorry for myself, that I wasn't the man she'd married any more. Then we just stopped talking to one another. One day I came back home from a day's fishing and she'd left, just like that, taking my little girl, your mother, with her. She'd had enough. I don't blame her, not any more. No one wants a monster for a husband. No one wants half a man, and that's what I was, Michael, half a man. That's what I still am. But I blamed her then. I hated her. Every day it's all I could think of, how much I hated her.

"I lived with that hate inside me most of my life. Hate, anger, call it what you will. It's like a cancer. It eats away at you. She wouldn't let me see my little girl, even when she was older. I never forgave her for that. She said I drank too much, which was true – said I'd frighten her too much. Maybe she was right. Maybe she was right."

It wasn't the moment to say anything, so I didn't. We fell into our silence again.

We unloaded the catch, moored the boat and walked together back home up the hill. We cooked the mackerel and sat eating it, still in silence. I was silent because I was reliving his story in my head. But I had one thing I needed to say.

"She wasn't right," I told him. "Annie should have let you see your own daughter. Everyone has a right to see their own child."

"Maybe," he replied. "But the truth is, I think I do frighten your mother a little, even now. So Annie was right, in her way. Your mother came to see me for the first time after she'd left school, when she wasn't a little girl any more; practically grown up, she was. She came without ever asking her mother, to find out who her father was, she said; because she hadn't even known me, not properly. She was kind to me. She's always been kind to me ever since. But even now she can't look me in the eye like you do. She writes letters, keeps in touch, calls me Dad, lets me visit, does her best by me, always has. And I'm grateful, don't get me wrong. But every time I came to you for Christmas when you were little, I longed for her just to look at me. She wants to, but she can't. And she's angry too, like I was. She can't forgive her mother for what she did either, for taking her away from her dad. She hasn't spoken to her mother now in over twenty years. Time's come to forgive and forget; that's what I think."

So now I knew the whole story for the first time. We relapsed after that into our usual, quiet ways for the rest of the holidays. But by the time I left I think I was closer to him than I have ever been to anyone else in my life.

I went back a year later, this time with my mother to visit him in hospital. He was already too ill to get out of bed.

He said he was a lucky man because he could see the sea from his bed. He died the second night we were there. He'd left a letter for me on the mantelpiece in his cottage.

Dear Michael,

See they bury me at sea. I want to be with Jim and the others. I want Annie there, and I want your mother there too. I want you all there together. I want things put right. Thanks for looking at me like you did.

Love, Grandpa

A few days later Annie came over to Scilly for the funeral. She held hands with my mother as Grandpa's ashes were scattered out beyond Scilly Rock. We were lucky. We had a fine day for it. The gannets were flying, and everyone was together, just as Grandpa had wanted. So he was right about gannets. Grandpa was right about a lot of things. But he wasn't half a man.

WHAT DOES IT FEEL LIKE?

Rwanda, Bosnia, Kosovo, East Timor. Ethnic cleansing seems as rife today as it has been throughout history. Yet in our oh-so-comfy England, it can seem a world away – "just on the telly". I once visited, by chance, a village in France called Oradour, the scene of a dreadful massacre in the Second World War. The French have preserved the place as the German occupiers left it: burnt out and stark. As a memorial. I wrote this to remind me, and others, that it is not "just on the telly". It is happening, now, as you read this.

Seven o'clock, and it was just an ordinary kind of autumn morning, much like any other. The mist covered the valley floor and the cows grazed along the river meadows. Sofia was still half asleep. The wild roses smelt of apples. Sofia pulled a fat rosehip from the hedgerow and idly split it open with her thumbnail. It was packed with seeds. A perfect spider's web laced with mist linked the hedge to the gatepost. It trembled threateningly as she opened the gate into the meadow. She loved spiders' webs, but hated spiders.

Sofia sent the dog out to fetch in the cows and stayed

leaning on the gate, her chin resting on her knuckles. Chewing nonchalantly, they meandered past her, ignoring her, all except Myrtle who glanced at her with baleful eyes and licked deep into her nose. "Bad-tempered old cow," Sofia muttered. And she followed Myrtle back along the lane towards the milking parlour. She could hear Mother singing inside, 'Raining in My Heart'. Buddy Holly again, always Buddy Holly.

Sofia wandered home, picking the last of the seeds out of the rosehip. She was deep in her thoughts. Mother did all the milking these days. She had done since Father went off with the other men to the war. He had been gone nearly three months now, and still there had been no news. No news was good news. Mother said that often. Sofia believed her, but she knew that was only because she needed to believe her. It was hope rather than belief. There was a photo of Father on top of the piano at home. A team photo, after the village won the local football league last year. He was the one with the droopy moustache and balding head, crouching down in the front and holding his arms out in triumph.

There had been little warning of his going. He'd just come out with it at breakfast one morning. Nan had tried to talk him out of it, but he was adamant. Mother and Nan held hands together and tried not to cry. "There's five of us going from the village," Father had said. "We've got to, don't you see? Else the war will come here, and we none of us want that, do we?"

The fighting was somewhere down south a long way away, Sofia knew that much. People had talked of little else now for a year or more. She'd seen pictures of it on the television. There was the little girl without any legs, lying on a hospital bed. She'd never forgotten that. She never wanted to be without her legs, never. And at school, Mr Kovacs drew maps on the board, banged the desk, flashed his eyes and said that we had to fight for what was ours if we wanted to keep it. All of us had to fight if need be, he said. But until the day Father left, none of it seemed at all real to Sofia. Even now, she had seen no tanks or planes. She had heard no guns. She had asked Nan about the war – Mother didn't like to talk about it – about why Father was fighting.

"Because they want our land. They always have," she'd said. "And because we hate them. We always have. We've hated them for hundreds of years."

"And do they hate us?" Sofia had asked.

"I suppose they must," Nan had said.

Sofia remembered the last day Father had been with them. She had come home from school and he'd been there all smiling and smelling of the wood he'd been sawing. That evening was the last time they'd been milking together. She smiled as she recalled how Myrtle had whipped her mucky tail across Father's face. "Bad-tempered old cow," he'd said, wiping his face with the back of his hand. Sofia had laughed at the brown smudge on his face, and Father had chased her out of the parlour. She thought then of his strong, calloused hands and loved them.

Nan was calling her from her thoughts. She hurried her through her breakfast, grumbling all the time that the telephone was not working, that the electricity was cut off too.

"I can't understand it," she said. "Maybe there's thunder about, but it doesn't feel like thunder." She sent her on her way to school with a whiskery kiss.

It was ten to eight on Sofia's watch. Plenty of time. The farm was just on the edge of the village, not far. Sofia scuffled through the leaves, all the way down the road. By the time she reached the village square, there were no leaves left to scuffle. So she limped, one foot on the pavement, one in the road. She liked doing that. Sometimes, when no one was looking, she'd do the dance from *Singin' in the Rain*. This morning though, she couldn't. There were too many people around, but very little traffic on the move, she noticed, just a few bicycles. She crossed the road into the square. The café chairs were already out, and as usual Mighty Martha was scrubbing the pavement on her hands and knees. She looked up and blew the hair out of her face. Mighty Martha was the only famous person ever to be born in the village. She had won an Olympic silver medal for throwing the discus over twenty years before. Discus and medal hung proudly side by side on the café wall under a photo of Mighty Martha standing on a podium, smiling and waving. She was always smiling. That was why everyone wasn't just proud of her, they loved her too. It helped that she also happened to make the best apple cake in the entire world. That was why her café was always full, even at this early hour. She was smiling at Sofia now.

"Better hurry," she called out. "Kovacs will have your guts for garters if you're late."

Sofia turned into School Lane. She could hear the bell going now. She'd just make it. But then she stopped. It wasn't only the bell she was hearing. There was a distant rumble that sounded like thunder. So Nan had been right. There was thunder about. Sofia looked up at the mountains. It couldn't be thunder. There were no dark clouds. In fact there were no clouds at all, just jagged white peaks sharp against a clear blue sky.

That was the moment Sofia remembered last night's geography homework: 'Mountain ranges of the world'. She'd left it behind. She fought back the panic rising inside her and tried to think. Both the choices open to her were bad ones. She could run home to fetch it and be late for school, very late; or she could tell Mr Kovacs that she'd left it at home by mistake, but then he wouldn't believe her.

Either way Mr Kovacs would "have her guts for garters". Sofia chose what seemed to be the least painful option. She would fetch her homework, and on the way there and back, concoct some credible excuse for being late. She ran back across the square with Mighty Martha shouting after her, "Where are you off to?" Sofia waved, but did not reply.

The quickest way home was through the graveyard, but Sofia rarely took it. This morning she had to. She usually avoided the graveyard because Grandad had been buried there only two years before in the family grave and Nan went up there twice a week with fresh flowers. To pass the grave and see the flowers only made Sofia sad about Grandad all over again. There was a photograph of him on the grave that looked at her as she passed. She hated looking at it. She still half expected him to talk to her, which was silly and she knew it. Nonetheless she always hared past him before he had a chance to speak.

As she ran, her foot turned on a loose stone. She heard her ankle crack. It gave under her, and she fell heavily, grazing her knees and hands. She sat up to nurse her ankle, which was throbbing now with such a pain that she thought she might faint. When she finally looked up, Grandad was gazing at her sternly from his photograph. She tried to hold back her tears. He'd always hated her to cry. She rocked back and forth groaning, watching the blood from her knee trickle down her leg.

Her books were scattered all over the path, her English book face-down in a puddle. She was reaching for it when she heard the thunder again, much closer this time. For just a moment she thought it might be guns, but then she dismissed that at once. The war was down south, miles away, everyone said so. Mr Kovacs' maps said so. By now she was hearing an incongruous rattling and squeaking, more like the noise of a dozen tractors trailing their ploughs on the road. She stood up on her one good foot and looked down into the village.

Two tanks rumbled into the square from different ends of the village, engines roaring and smoking. Behind them came six open lorries. When they reached the square they all stopped. Soldiers jumped out. The engines died. The smoke lifted through the trees and a silence fell over the village. Doors opened, heads appeared at windows.

Mighty Martha stood alone in the square, her scrubbing brush in her hand. The soldiers were gazing around like tourists as the last of them climbed down out of the lorries. Mighty Martha's dog barked at them from the door of the café, his hackles raised. All the soldiers wore headbands, red headbands, except one who was wearing a beret, and there was a gunbelt round his waist like a cowboy. The soldiers – Sofia thought there must be perhaps thirty in all gathered around him – then wandered off in small groups into the narrow streets as if they were going to explore. They had their rifles slung over their shoulders. Sofia wondered if Father wore a red band round his head like they did. The man in the black beret leant back against a tank, crossed his legs and lit up a cigarette. Mighty Martha stood watching him for a few moments. Then she dropped her scrubbing brush into the bucket, slapped her hands dry and strode into the café.

Sofia gathered up her books and hobbled down the path back towards the square. Mighty Martha would see to her ankle for her, like she had done once before when she'd come off her bike. She'd been a nurse once. She knew about these things; and besides, Sofia wanted to know what was going on. She wanted to get a closer look at the tanks. The homework and Mr Kovacs had been forgotten.

She had got as far as the toilets on the corner of the square when she saw Martha coming out of the café. She was holding a rifle. Suddenly she stopped, brought it up to her shoulder and pointed it at the cowboy soldier.

"This is our village," she cried, "and you will never take it from us, never." A shot rang out and the rifle fell from Martha's hands. Her head twisted unnaturally on her neck and nodded loose for a moment like a puppet's head. Then she just collapsed, fell face forward on the cobbles and was still. The cowboy soldier was walking towards her, his pistol in his hand. He turned Martha over with the toe of his boot.

Sofia darted into the toilets, ran to the Ladies, closed the door behind her and bolted it. She sat down, squeezed her eyes tight shut and tried not to believe what she had just witnessed. She heard herself moaning and stopped breathing so that the moaning too would stop. But it did not. She knew then that it came from outside.

She climbed up on the toilet seat. The frosted window was a centimetre or two open. They were coming into the square from every corner. Mr Kovacs and all the schoolchildren came in twos down School Lane, the soldiers hustling them along. The children seemed more bewildered than frightened, except little Ilic, who clutched Mr Kovacs' hand and cried openly. None of them had seen Martha yet. The cowboy soldier was climbing up on to a tank. He stood legs apart, thumbs hooked into his belt and watched as everyone was marshalled into the square.

The doctor was there, pushing old Mrs Marxova in her wheelchair. Swathed in a shawl, her face ashen, she was pointing down at Martha. Some people were still in their dressing gowns and slippers. Stefan and Peter from the garage had their hands high in the air, a soldier behind them, jabbing them in their backs with his rifle barrel. Up the road from the bridge Sofia could see all the old folk from the retirement home, a couple of soldiers herding them along like cattle. They would pass by right underneath the toilet window. It was they who were moaning and wailing.

Sofia drew back so she wouldn't be seen. She waited until they had gone and then peered out again.

The square was filling. The schoolchildren were gathered around Mr Kovacs who was talking to them, trying to reassure them, but the children had seen Martha. Everyone had seen Martha. Mrs Marxova held her hands over her eyes and was shaking her head. The doctor was leaning over Martha and feeling her neck, then he was listening to her chest. After a while he took his jacket off and covered her face.

Little Ilic saw his mother and ran screaming across the square. One by one now the children ignored all Mr Kovacs' attempts to keep them together and went off to search for their mothers. Once found, they clung to them passionately as if they would never let go.

That was when Sofia saw Mother and Nan, arms linked, being marched into the square. All Sofia's neighbours were with them too. They'd even found Mr Dodovic who lived alone in his hut and kept his bees high up the mountainside. Like all the men, he too had his hands in the air. Mother went straight over to Mr Kovacs and took him by the arm. Mr Kovacs shook his head at her. Sofia longed to cry out, to run to her. But something inside her held her back. Everyone in the village was corralled in the square by now and surrounded by the soldiers.

A machine-gun was being set up on the steps of the

post office and another by the garage on the corner. Mother was talking to the doctor and looking about her frantically. Nan had sat down in a chair outside the café and was staring blankly at Martha.

The cowboy soldier on the tank held up his hands. The hush was almost instantaneous. Even the children stopped crying, except for Mrs Dungonic's new baby. Mrs Dungonic picked her up and shushed her over her shoulder. The whole square was silent now, expectant.

"You have seen now what happens if you resist," the cowboy soldier began. "No one will come to help you. All the telephone lines are cut. All the roads are blocked. You will do what we say. We do not want to harm any more of you, but if you make us, we will. Have no doubt about it. We are simply moving you. This land does not belong to you. You have been squatting here on our land for over three hundred years. You took it from my people. You stole it from us. Now we are taking back what is rightfully ours." No one said a word. "But we do not want to live in your stinking hovels so we are going to burn the whole place down. By this evening it will be as if it never existed. That way you'll have nothing to come back to, will you?" Still no one said anything.

Sofia was screaming inside herself, "Don't just stand there. Tell him he can't do it. Stop him. What's the matter with you all?"

"Now," the cowboy soldier went on as he swaggered along the side of his tank. "Here's what you do. The men, if you can call yourselves men, you get in those lorries outside the shop. Be good boys now. Off you go." No one moved. He took out his pistol and pointed it at the doctor. "Go," he said quietly.

"Where are we going?" the doctor asked.

"You'll see," replied the cowboy soldier.

Sofia ducked down. A soldier was walking towards the toilets. Sofia prayed, her eyes tight shut, fists and jaws clenched. "Don't let him come in. Don't let him come in. Be good, God. Don't let him come in."

He came in. She heard the tap running into the basin. He was drinking. Then he spoke. "Forgive me," he whispered. "Dear God, forgive me. I begged the captain. I begged him, but he wouldn't listen. Rats, he said, they breed like rats. You burn rats out. You destroy them. But they're not rats, they're flesh and blood. Oh God, oh God." He was sobbing and then he was kicking the wall. That was the moment Sofia shifted her weight on to her bad ankle and slipped. The sobbing stopped at once. Sofia shrank back as the footsteps came towards her. She could hear his breathing through the door.

"Whoever you are," his voice was urgent but gentle, "whoever's in there, just listen to me. Whatever happens, stay where you are. Believe me, where they're going, you don't want to go. Stay put. Don't move. I'll do what I can." And then he was gone.

It was some time after he'd left before Sofia screwed up enough courage to look out of her window again. When she did, she saw the last of the men from the village climbing up into the lorry. There were two lorry loads of them. A fierce anger welled up inside her. They were going like lambs, all of them. What of the rousing, triumphal songs they had sung so often in the café? What of Mr Kovacs' defiant exhortations that everyone must defend the homeland? How could they leave the women and the children without even a word of protest? How could they? The men were just sitting there with bowed heads, Mr Kovacs weeping openly. She hated him then even more than the cowboy soldier. She hated them all.

"Good," said the cowboy soldier, smiling. "Good boys. Now, women and children to the other lorries, and don't worry yourselves, you'll all meet up again soon enough. Hurry now." He waved his pistol, and the women and children drifted slowly, reluctantly, across to the other side of the square. The soldiers stood by and looked on as they struggled to clamber in. Only one of them stepped forward to pick up the smaller children and hand them up. Sofia wondered if it was her soldier. She hoped it was. He had long hair to his shoulders and a moustache like Father's. He seemed very young to be a soldier.

It took three of them to lift Mrs Marxova out of her wheelchair and up into the lorry. They were not gentle with her. One of them kicked away her chair so that it rolled down the road, hitting a kerb and turning over in the gutter. They laughed at that. Mother helped Nan up into the lorry beside her and they sat down together, Nan's head resting on her shoulder. The lorries started up. Mother was calling for her now, crying.

Sofia made up her mind in that instant. She had to be with them. Why should she trust the soldier? She didn't even know him. She had hardly seen him. She unlocked the door and ran past the basins, forgetting her ankle. She slipped and fell by the doorway. By the time she was up on her feet again, she could hear the lorries already moving off. It was too late. Maybe, she thought, maybe the soldier was right after all. Maybe she was safer here, undiscovered. She hobbled back into the toilet and shut the door. She climbed up just in time to see the last lorry leaving the square and her mother's scarved head still turning, still looking. She was still crying.

The cowboy soldier leapt down off his tank. "You know what to do. I don't want a building left standing. Understand? Nothing. You'll find all the petrol you need in the garage. Use hay, faggots, anything that'll burn. If it won't burn, then blow it up." The soldiers cheered at that. Whooping and yelling, they scattered in all directions, some diving directly into the houses on the square and others running off down the village streets. Soon the square was left to the cowboy soldier, who sat down on a bench and lit up another cigarette. He blew smoke rings into the air and poked his finger through them. Martha's dog was snuffling around her body, his tail between his legs.

Sofia could not look any more. She sat down. The blood had congealed on her leg. She took off her sock. Her ankle was puffed up and grey.

A window shattered somewhere in the village, then another, then another. Some way away, a gun began to chatter and did not stop.

"Are you still in there?" It was the soldier's voice from below her window.

"Yes," she replied at once, without thinking.

"For God's sake, don't try to run. You'll be seen. They'll kill you if they see you. They mustn't leave any witnesses."

"My mother, my nan. They were in the lorry. Where have you taken them? Where have they gone?"

"You don't want to know," said the soldier. "Just worry about yourself. And don't look out of the window. They'll see you. I could see the shape of your head from across the square. Keep down. I can't stay." Sofia heard him walk away. She wanted to ask him so much more but could not risk calling out. She sat down on the toilet and tried to gather her thoughts, but nothing would come but tears. Racked with sobbing, Sofia put her head between her knees and hugged herself into a tight ball and closed her eyes. So she sat for hour after hour as they burnt the village around her. Trying not to listen, not to smell.

The first explosion was from far away, but all the same, it rocked the building, blasted her ears and left a ringing inside her head that would not stop. The next was closer, in the square itself, maybe the post office she thought, and the next shortly afterwards was even closer still. Perhaps the café. She bit her lip till it bled, determined not to scream, not to give herself away. When plaster crashed down from the ceiling on to her shoulders, she could stand it no longer. She lifted her head and screamed and screamed. Through her own screaming, through the whistle in her ears, she heard the whoosh and crackle of the flames outside, the roar of the roofs collapsing, and always the soldiers whooping.

Then she saw smoke drifting in under the door, thick smoke that would stifle the life out of her. She had to get away. She climbed up on to the seat and put her nose to the window to breathe in the last of the cleaner air. That was when the tanks began to fire from under the trees, pounding, pounding, pounding. She fell backwards on to the floor, back down into the smoke. She rolled into a corner, covering her face, her mouth, her ears, clenching herself into herself as tight as she would fit. Then she prayed. The picture she had seen on television of the child without any legs flashed into her head. "Please, God, I want my legs. I need my legs. Let me die if you want, but I want my legs. I want my legs."

The smoke was thinning. Suddenly she could breathe without coughing, then there were voices outside.

"The toilets. Don't forget the toilets." It was the cowboy soldier. "A grenade will do it."

"Hardly worth the trouble, Captain," said another. Her soldier, her soldier's voice. "It's not as if there's anyone left to piss in it, is there? And anyway, why don't we leave it there as a monument? All that's left of them, their toilet."

The cowboy soldier laughed. "Good. Very good. I like it. Some bonfire, eh?" They were walking away now. The cowboy soldier went on, "D'you see the mosque come down? Obstinate beggar, he was. Took twenty rounds to topple him. This heat gives a man a thirst, eh? Let's get at the beer."

"Why not?" said Sofia's soldier.

There were no more shootings after that, no more explosions, but Sofia stayed where she was, curled up on the floor of the toilet. She could hear the soldiers carousing in the square and the sound of smashing beer bottles. One crashed against the window above her head, shattering the glass. Shortly after, their laughter was drowned out by the noise of the tank engines starting up. They were calling to each other. They were going. She waited a few minutes more until she was quite sure the tanks were on the move, their engines revving. Then she climbed up and looked out. The two tanks were rumbling away out of sight, belching black smoke out behind them. They were gone.

Everywhere she looked was utter destruction. The village was a flaming, smoking ruin. Like all the other buildings, the café had no roof. Flames licked out of the windows, leaping across the road into the trees. The parked cars were blackened shells now, the tyres still burning furiously. The front of the shop had entirely caved in. Sofia got down, opened the door and hobbled out into the square. The minaret had fallen right across School Lane, obliterating the houses beneath. Martha still lay outside her café, but now her dog was beside her. He was not moving. Sofia sat down on the bench in the middle of the square where she was farthest from the heat of the fires. She had no tears left to cry.

She was still sitting there late that evening when the reporters came in their Land Rover. She was rocking back and forth and there was a cow beside her, grazing the grass. She was humming 'Raining in My Heart'. She looked up at them as they approached.

"Hello," she said. "That's Myrtle. She's come to find me. She wants milking."

"Is this your village?" asked a reporter, pushing a microphone at her. Sofia looked at him blankly. "What does it feel like to see it like this?" he went on. "And what do you think of the people who've done it? Where the hell is everyone, anyway?"

"I've got my legs," said Sofia, and she smiled. "I've got my legs. God is great."

THE MOZART QUESTION

The question I am most often asked is always easy enough to answer. Question: how did you get started as a writer? Answer: funnily enough, by asking someone almost exactly that very same question, which I was only able to ask in the first place by a dose of extraordinarily good fortune.

I had better explain.

My good fortune was, of course, someone else's rotten luck – it is often that way, I find. The phone call sounded distraught. It came on a Sunday evening. I had only been working on the paper for three weeks. I was a cub reporter, this my first paid job.

"Lesley?" It was my boss, chief arts correspondent Meryl Monkton, a lady not to be messed with. She did not waste time with niceties; she never did. "Listen, Lesley, I have a problem. I was due to go to Venice tomorrow to interview Paolo Levi."

"Paolo Levi?" I said. "The violinist?"

"Is there any other Paolo Levi?" She did not trouble to hide her irritation. "Now look, Lesley. I've had an accident, a skiing accident, and I'm stuck in hospital in

Switzerland. You'll have to go to Venice instead of me."

"Oh, that's terrible," I said, smothering as best I could the excitement surging inside me. Three weeks into the job and I'd be interviewing the great Paolo Levi, and in Venice!

Talk about her accident, I told myself. Sound concerned. Sound very concerned.

"How did it happen?" I asked. "The skiing accident, I mean."

"Skiing," she snapped. "If there's one thing I can't abide, Lesley, it's people feeling sorry for me."

"Sorry," I said.

"I would postpone it if I could, Lesley," she went on, "but I just don't dare. It's taken me more than a year to persuade him to do it. It'll be his first interview in years. And even then I had to agree not to ask him the Mozart question. So don't ask him the Mozart question, is that clear? If you do he'll like as not cancel the whole interview – he's done it before. We're really lucky to get him, Lesley. I only wish I could be there to do it myself. But you'll have to do."

"The Mozart question?" I asked, rather tentatively.

The silence at the end of the phone was long.

"You mean to say you don't know about Paolo Levi and the Mozart question? Where have you been, girl? Don't you know anything at all about Paolo Levi?"

I suddenly felt I might lose the opportunity altogether

if I did not immediately sound informed, and well informed too.

"Well, he would have been born sometime in the mid-1950s," I began. "He must be about fifty by now."

"Exactly fifty in two weeks' time," Meryl Monkton interrupted wearily. "His London concert is his fiftieth birthday concert. That's the whole point of the interview. Go on."

I rattled off all I knew. "Child prodigy and genius, like Yehudi Menuhin. Played his first major concert when he was thirteen. Probably best known for his playing of Bach and Vivaldi. Like Menuhin he played often with Grappelli, equally at home with jazz or Scottish fiddle music or Beethoven. Has played in practically every major concert hall in the world, in front of presidents and kings and queens. I heard him at the Royal Festival Hall in London, five years ago, I think. He was playing Beethoven's Violin Concerto; he was wonderful. Doesn't like applause. Never waits for applause. Doesn't believe in it, apparently. The night I saw him he just walked off the stage and didn't come back. He thinks it's the music that should be applauded if anything, or perhaps the composer, but certainly not the musician. Says that the silence after the performance is part of the music and should not be interrupted. Doesn't record either. Believes music should be live, not canned. Protects his privacy fiercely. Solitary. Reticent. Lives alone in Venice, where he was born. Just about the most famous musician on the planet, and—"

"*The* most famous, Lesley, but he hates obsequiousness. He likes to be talked to straight. So no bowing or scraping, no wide-eyed wonder, and above all no nerves. Can you do that?"

"Yes, Meryl," I replied, knowing only too well that I would have the greatest difficulty even finding my voice in front of the great man.

"And whatever you do, stick to the music. He'll talk till the cows come home about music and composers. But no personal stuff. And above all, keep off the Mozart question. Oh yes, and don't take a tape recorder with you. He hates gadgets. Only shorthand. You can do shorthand, I suppose? Three thousand words. It's your big chance, so don't mess it up, Lesley."

No pressure, then, I thought.

So there I was the next evening outside Paolo Levi's apartment in the Dorsoduro in Venice, on the dot of six o'clock, my throat dry, my heart pounding, trying all I could to compose myself. It occurred to me again, as it had often on the plane, that I still had no idea what this Mozart question was, only that I mustn't ask it. It was cold, the kind of cruel chill that seeps instantly into your bones, deep into your kidneys, and makes your ears ache.

This didn't seem to bother the street performers in the square behind me: several grotesquely masked figures on stilts strutting across the square, an entirely silver statue-man posing immobile outside the café with a gaggle of tourists gazing wonderingly at him.

The door opened, and there he was in front of me, Paolo Levi, neat, trim, his famous hair long to his shoulders and jet black.

"I'm Lesley McInley," I said. "I've come from London."

"From the newspaper, I suppose." There was no welcoming smile. "You'd better come in. Shut the door behind you; I hate the cold." His English was perfect, not a trace of an accent. He seemed to be able to follow my thoughts. "I speak English quite well," he said as we went up the stairs. "Language is like music. You learn it best through listening."

He led me down a hallway and into a large room, empty except for a couch by the window piled high with cushions at one end, a grand piano in the centre and a music stand near by. There were just two armchairs and a table. Nothing else. "I like to keep it empty," he said.

It was uncanny. He *was* reading my thoughts. Now I felt even more unnerved.

"Sound needs space to breathe, just the same as we need air," he said.

He waved me to a chair and sat down. "You'll have

some mint tea?" he said, pouring me a cup. His dark blue cardigan and grey corduroy trousers were somehow both shabby and elegant at the same time. The bedroom slippers he wore looked incongruous but comfortable. "My feet, they hate the cold more than the rest of me." He was scrutinising me now, his eyes sharp and shining. "You're younger than I expected," he said. "Twenty-three?" He didn't wait to have his estimate confirmed – he knew he was right and he was. "You have heard me play?"

"Beethoven's Violin Concerto. The Royal Festival Hall in London, a few years ago. I was a student." I noticed his violin then, and his bow, on the window ledge by the couch.

"I like to practise by the window," he said, "so I can watch the world go by on the canal. It passes the time. Even as a child I never liked practising much. And I love to be near water, to look out on it. When I go to London I have to have a room by the Thames. In Paris I must be by the Seine. I love the light that water makes." He sipped his mint tea, his eyes never leaving me. "Shouldn't you be asking me questions?" He went on. "I'm talking too much. Journalists always make me nervous. I talk too much when I'm nervous. When I go to the dentist's I talk. Before a concert I talk. So let's get this over with, shall we? And not too many questions, please. Why don't we keep it simple? You ask me one question and then let me ramble on. Shall we try that?" I didn't feel at all that he was being dismissive or patronising, just straight. That didn't make it any easier, though.

I had done my research, made pages of notes, prepared dozens of questions; but now, under his expectant gaze, I simply could not gather my thoughts.

"Well, I know I can't ask you the Mozart question, Signor Levi," I began, "because I've been told not to. I don't even know what the Mozart question is, so I couldn't ask it even if I wanted to; and anyway, I know you don't like it, so I won't."

With every blundering word I was digging myself into a deeper hole. In my desperation I blurted out the first question that came into my head.

"Signor Levi," I said, "I wonder if you'd mind telling me how you got started. I mean, what made you pick up a violin and play that first time?" It was such an obvious question, and personal too, just the kind of question I shouldn't have asked.

His reaction only confirmed that. He sat back in his chair and closed his eyes. For fully a couple of minutes he said nothing. I was quite sure he was trying to control his impatience, his rage even, that he was going to open his eyes and ask me to leave at once. When he did open his eyes he simply stared up at the ceiling for a while. I could see from the seriousness of his whole demeanour that he was making a decision, and I feared the worst. But instead of throwing me out he stood up and walked slowly to the couch by the window. He picked up his violin and sat back on the cushions with his violin resting on his drawn-up knees. He plucked a string or two and tuned it.

"I will tell you a story," he began. "After it is over you will need to ask me no more questions. Someone once told me that all secrets are lies. The time has come, I think, not to lie any more."

He paused. I felt he was stiffening his resolve, gathering his strength.

"I will start with my father. Papa was a barber. He kept a little barber's shop just behind the Accademia, near the bridge, two minutes from here. We lived above the shop, Mama, Papa and I, but I spent most of my time downstairs in the barber's shop, sitting on the chairs and swinging my legs, smiling at him and his customers in the mirror, and just watching him. I loved those days. I loved him. At the time of these memories I must have been about nine years old. Small for my age. I always was. I still am."

He spoke slowly, very deliberately, as if he was living it again, seeing again everything he was telling me. My shorthand was quick and automatic, so I had time to look up at him occasionally as he spoke. I sensed right away that I was the first person ever to hear this story, so I knew even as he told it just how momentous the telling of it was for him, as in a totally different way it was for me too.

"Papa was infinitely deft with his fingers, his scissors playing a constantly changing tune. It seemed to me like a new improvisation for every customer, the snipping unhesitatingly skilful, so fast it was mesmerising. He would work always in complete silence, conducting the music of his scissors with his comb. His customers knew better than to interrupt the performance, and so did I. I think perhaps I must have known his customers almost as well as he did. I grew up with them. They were all regulars. Some would close their eyes as Papa worked his magic; others would look back in the mirror at me and wink.

"Shaving was just as fascinating to me, just as rhythmical too: the swift sweep and dab of the brush, the swish and slap of the razor as Papa sharpened it on the strap, then each time the miraculous unmasking as he stroked the foam away to reveal a recognisable face once more.

"After it was all over, he and his customers did talk, and all the banter amongst them was about football, Inter Milan in particular, or sometimes the machinations of politicians and women. What they said I cannot exactly remember, probably because I couldn't understand most of it, but I do know they laughed a lot. I do remember that. Then the next customer would take his seat and a new silence would descend before the performance started and the music of the scissors began. I am sure I first learnt about rhythm in that barber's shop, and about concentration. I learnt to listen too.

"Papa wasn't just the best barber in all of Venice – everyone said that – he was a musician too, a violinist. But strangely he was a violinist who never played the violin. I never heard him play, not once. I only knew he was a violinist because Mama had told me so. She had tears in her eyes whenever she told me about it. That surprised me because she was not a crying woman. He had been so brilliant as a violinist, the best in the whole orchestra, she said. When I asked why he didn't play any more, she turned away from me, went very quiet and told me I'd have to ask Papa myself. So I did. I asked him time and again, and each time he would simply shrug, and say something meaningless like: 'People change, Paolo. Times change.' And that would be that.

"Papa was never a great talker at the best of times, even at home, but I could tell that in this case he was hiding something, that he found my questions both irksome and intrusive. That didn't stop me. I kept on at him. Every time he refused to talk about it I became more suspicious, more sure he had something to hide. It was a child's intuition, I suppose. I sensed a deep secret, but I also sensed after a while that Papa was quite unmovable, that if I was ever going to unlock the secret it would be Mama who would tell me.

"As it turned out, my instinct was right. In the end

my almost perpetual pestering proved fruitful, and Mama capitulated – but not in a way I had expected. 'All right, Paolo,' she said after I'd been nagging her about it unmercifully one morning. 'If I show you the violin will you promise me you'll stop asking your wretched questions? And you're never ever to tell Papa I showed you. He'd be very angry. Promise me now.'

"So I promised, promised faithfully, and then stood in their bedroom and watched as she climbed up on a chair to get it down from where it had been hidden on top of the cupboard. It was wrapped up in an old grey blanket. I knelt on the bed beside her as she pulled away the blanket and opened the violin case. I remember it smelt musty. The maroon lining inside was faded and worn to tatters. Mama picked up the violin with infinite care, reverently almost. Then she handed it to me.

"I stroked the polished grain of the wood, which was the colour of honey, dark honey on the front, and golden honey underneath. I ran my fingers along the black pegs, the mottled bridge, the exquisitely carved scroll. It was so light to hold, I remember. I wondered at its fragile beauty. I knew at once that all the music in the world was hidden away inside this violin, yearning to come out. I longed to be the one to let it out, to rest it under my chin, to play the strings, to try the bow. I wanted there and then to bring it to life, to have it sing for me, to hear all the music we could make together. But when I asked if I could play it, Mama took sudden fright and said Papa might hear down below in the barber's shop, and he'd be furious with her for showing it to me; that he never wanted it to be played again. He hadn't so much as looked at it in years. When I asked why, she reminded me of my promise not to ask any more questions. She almost snatched the violin off me, laid it back in its case, wrapped it again in the blanket and put it back up on top of the cupboard.

" 'You don't know it exists, Paolo. You never saw it, understand? And from now on I don't want to hear another word about it, all right? You promised me, Paolo.'

"I suppose seeing Papa's old violin, holding it as I had, marvelling at it, must have satisfied my curiosity for a while, because I kept my promise. Then late one summer's evening I was lying half awake in my bed when I heard the sound of a violin. I thought Papa must have changed his mind and was playing again at last. But then I heard him and Mama talking in the kitchen below, and realised anyway that the music was coming from much further away.

"I listened at the window. I could hear it only intermittently over the sound of people talking and walking, over the throbbing engines of passing water buses, but I was quite sure now that it was coming from somewhere beyond the bridge. I had to find out. In my pyjamas I stole past the kitchen door, down the stair and out into the street. It was a warm night, and quite dark. I ran up over the bridge and there, all on his own, standing by the wall in the square, was an old man playing the violin, his violin case open at his feet.

"No one else was there. No one had stopped to listen. I squatted down as close as I dared. He was so wrapped up in his playing that he did not notice me at first. I could see now that he was much older even than Papa. Then he saw me crouching there watching him. He stopped playing. 'Hello,' he said. 'You're out late. What's your name?' He had kind eyes; I noticed that at once.

" 'Paolo,' I told him. 'Paolo Levi. My papa plays the violin. He played in an orchestra once.'

" 'So did I,' said the old man, 'all my life. But now I am what I always wanted to be, a soloist. I shall play you some Mozart. Do you like Mozart?'

" 'I don't know,' I replied. I knew Mozart's name, of course, but I don't think I had ever listened to any of his music.

" 'He wrote this piece when he was even younger than you. I should guess that you're about seven.'

" 'Nine,' I said.

" 'Well, Mozart wrote this when he was just six years old. He wrote it for the piano, but I can play it on the violin.'

"So he played Mozart, and I listened. As he played, others came and gathered round for a while before dropping a coin or two in his violin case and moving on. I didn't move on. I stayed. The music he played to me that night touched my soul. It was the night that changed my life for ever.

"Whenever I crossed the Accademia Bridge after that I always looked out for him. Whenever I heard him playing I went to listen. I never told Mama or Papa. I think it was the first secret I kept from them. But I did not feel guilty about it, not one bit. After all, hadn't they kept a secret from me? Then one evening the old man – I had found out by now that his name was Benjamin Horowitz and he was sixty-two years old – one evening he let me hold his violin, showed me how to hold it properly, how to draw the bow across the strings, how to make it sing. The moment I did that, I knew I had to be a violinist. I have never wanted to do or be anything else since.

"So Benjamin – Signor Horowitz I always called him then – became my first teacher. Now every time I ran over the bridge to see him he would show me a little more, how to tighten the bow just right, how to use the resin, how to hold the violin under my chin using no hands at all and what each string was called. That was when I told him about Papa's violin at home, and about how he didn't play it any more. 'He couldn't anyway,' I said, 'because it's a bit broken. I think it needs mending a bit. Two of the strings are missing, the A and the E, and there's hardly a hair left on the bow at all. But I could practise on it if it was mended, couldn't I?'

" 'Bring it to my house sometime,' Benjamin said, 'and leave it with me. I'll see what I can do.'

"It wasn't difficult to escape unnoticed. I just waited till after school. Mama was still at the laundry round the corner in Rio de la Romite where she worked. Papa was downstairs with his customers. To reach the violin on top of the cupboard I had to put a suitcase on the chair and then climb up. It wasn't easy but I managed. I ran through the streets hugging it to me. From the Dorsoduro to the Arsenale where Benjamin lived is not that far if you know the way – nowhere is that far in Venice – and I knew the way quite well because my Aunt Sophia lived there and we visited her often. All I had to do was find Benjamin's street. I had to ask about a bit, but I found it.

"Benjamin lived up a narrow flight of stairs in one small room with a bed in one corner and a basin in the other. On the wall were lots of concert posters. 'Some of the concerts I played,' he said. 'Milan, London, New York. Wonderful places, wonderful people, wonderful music. It's a wonderful world out there. There are times when it can be hard to go on believing that. But always believe it, Paolo, because it is true. And music helps to make it so. Now, show me that violin of yours.'

"He studied it closely, holding it up to the light, tapping

it. 'A very fine instrument,' he said. 'You say this belongs to your father?'

" 'And now I want to play it myself,' I told him.

" 'It's a bit on the large side for a young lad like you,' he said, tucking the violin under my chin and stretching my arm to see how far I could reach. 'But a big violin is better than no violin at all. You'll manage. You'll grow into it.'

" 'And when it's mended, will you teach me?' I asked him. 'I've got lots of money saved up from my sweeping; so many notes they cover all my bed when I spread them out, from the end of the bed right up to my pillow.'

"He laughed at that and told me he would teach me for nothing because I was his best listener, his lucky mascot. 'When you're not there,' he said, 'everyone walks by and my violin case stays empty. Then you come along and sit there. That's when they always stop to listen and that's when they leave their money. So a lesson or two will just be paying you back, Paolo. I'll have the violin ready as soon as I can and then we can start your lessons.'

"It was a week or two before the violin was mended. I dreaded that Mama or Papa might discover it was missing. But my luck held, and they didn't, and my lessons began. Whenever I wasn't having my lessons with Benjamin, Papa's violin, now restrung and restored, lay in its case wrapped in the grey blanket and hidden away on top of their bedroom cupboard. My secret was safe, I thought.

But secrets are never safe, however well hidden. Sooner or later truth will out, and in this case it was to be sooner rather than later.

"I took to the violin as if it had been a limb I had been missing all my life. I seemed to be able to pick up everything Benjamin taught me, effortlessly and instinctively. Under his kind tutelage my confidence simply burgeoned, my playing blossomed. I found I could make my violin – Papa's violin, rather – sing with the voice of an angel. Benjamin and I felt the excitement and pleasure of my progress as keenly as each other. 'I think this instrument was invented just for you, Paolo,' he told me one day. 'Or maybe you were made for it. Either way it is a perfect match.' I loved every precious moment of my lessons and always dreaded their ending. We would finish every lesson with a cup of mint tea made with fresh mint. I loved it. Ever since, I have always treated myself to a cup of mint tea after practice. It's something I always look forward to.

"I remember one day with the lesson over, we were drinking tea at his table when he looked across at me, suddenly very serious. 'It is strange, Paolo,' he said, 'but as I was watching you playing a moment ago, I felt I had known you before, a long, long time ago. And then just now I thought about your name, Levi. It is a common enough name, I know, but his name was Levi too. It is him you remind me of. I am sure of it. He was the youngest player in our orchestra, not more than a boy really. Gino, he was called.'

" 'But my father is called Gino,' I told him. 'Maybe it was him. Maybe you played with my father. Maybe you know him.'

" 'It can't be possible,' Benjamin breathed. He was staring at me now as if I were a ghost. 'No, it can't be. The Gino Levi I knew must be dead, I am sure of it. I have not heard of him in a long while, a very long while. But you never know, I suppose. Maybe I should meet your papa, and your mama too. It's about time anyway. You've been coming for lessons for over six months now. They need to know they have a wonderful violinist for a son.'

" 'No, you can't!' I cried. 'He'd find out! You can't tell him. You mustn't!' Then I told him, through my tears, all my secret, about how Mama had shown me Papa's violin and made me promise never to say anything, never to tell Papa, and how I'd kept it a secret all this while, mending the violin, the lessons, everything.

" 'Secrets, Paolo,' said Benjamin, 'are lies by another name. You do not lie to those you love. A son should not hide things from his papa and mama. You must tell them your secret, Paolo. If you want to go on playing the violin, you will have to tell them. If you want me to go on teaching you, you will have to tell them. And now is usually a good time to do what must be done, particularly when you don't want to do it.'

" 'Will you come with me?' I begged him. 'I can only do it if you come with me.'

" 'If you like,' he said, smiling.

"Benjamin carried Papa's violin for me that day, and held my hand all the way back to the Dorsoduro. I dreaded having to make my confession. I knew how hurt they would be. All the way I rehearsed what I was going to say over and over again. Mama and Papa were upstairs in the kitchen when we came in. I introduced Benjamin and then, before anyone had a chance to say anything, before I lost my courage entirely, I launched at once into my prepared confession, how I hadn't really stolen Papa's violin, just borrowed it to get it mended, and to practise on. But that's as far as I got. To my surprise they were not looking angry. In fact, they weren't looking at me at all. They were just staring up at Benjamin as if quite unable to speak. Benjamin spoke before they did. 'Your mama and papa and me, I think perhaps we do know one another,' he said. 'We played together once, did we not? Don't you remember me, Gino?'

" 'Benjamin?' As Papa started to his feet, the chair went over behind him.

" 'And if I am not much mistaken, Signora,' Benjamin went on, looking now at Mama, 'you must be little Laura Adler – all of us violins, all of us there, and all of us still here. It is like a miracle. It *is* a miracle.'

"What happened next I can see as if it were yesterday.
It was suddenly as if I was not in the room at all. The three
of them seemed to fill the kitchen, arms around each other,
and crying openly, crying through their laughter. I stood
there mystified, trying to piece together all I had heard, all
that was going on before my eyes. Mama played the violin
too! She had never told me that!

" 'You see, Paolo,' said Benjamin, smiling down at me,
'didn't I tell you it was a wonderful world? Twenty years.
It's been twenty years or more since I last saw your mama
and papa. I had no idea they were still alive. I always hoped
they survived, hoped they were together, these two young
lovebirds, but I never believed it, not really.'

"Mama was drying her eyes on her apron. Papa was so
overcome, he couldn't speak. They sat down then, hands
joined around the table as if unwilling to let each other go
for fear this reunion might turn out to be no more than a
dream.

"Benjamin was the first to recover. 'Paolo was about to
tell you something, I think,' he said. 'Weren't you, Paolo?'
I told them everything then: how I'd gone for my lessons,
how Benjamin had been the best teacher in the world. I
dared to look up only when I'd finished. Instead of the
disapproval and disappointment I had expected, both
Mama and Papa were simply glowing with joy and pride.

"Didn't I say Paolo would tell us, Papa?' she said. 'Didn't I tell you we should trust him? You see, Paolo, I often take down my violin, just to touch it, to look at it. Papa doesn't like me to, but I do it all the same, because this violin is my oldest friend. Papa forgives me, because he knows I love this violin, that it is a part of me. You remember I showed it to you that day, Paolo? It wasn't long after that it went missing, was it? I knew it had to be you. Then it came back, mended miraculously. And after school you were never home, and when you weren't home the violin was always gone too. I told Papa, didn't I, Papa? I told him you'd tell us when you were ready. We put two and two together; we thought you might be practising somewhere, but it never occurred to us that you were having lessons, nor that you had a teacher – and certainly not that your teacher was Benjamin Horowitz, who taught us and looked after us like a father all those years ago.' She cried again then, her head on Papa's shoulder.

" 'But you told me it was Papa's violin, that he'd put it away and never wanted to play it again, ever,' I said.

"At this the three of them looked at one another. I knew then they all shared the same secret, and that without a word passing between them they were deciding whether they should reveal it, if this was the right moment to tell me. I often wondered later whether, if Benjamin had not come that day, they would ever have told me. As it was they looked to Papa for the final decision, and it was he who invited me to the table to join them. I think I knew then, even before Papa began, that I was in some way part of their secret.

" 'Mama and me,' Papa began, 'we try never to speak of this, because the memories we have are like nightmares, and we want to forget. But you told us your secret. There is a time for truth, it seems, and it has come. Truth for truth, maybe.'

"So began the saddest, yet the happiest story I ever heard. When the story became too painful, as it often did, they passed it from one to the other, so that all three shared it. I listened, horrified, at the same time honoured that they trusted me enough with their story, the story of their lives. Each told their part with great care, explaining as they went along so that I would understand, because I was a boy of nine who knew very little then of the wickedness of the world. I wish I could remember their exact words, but I can't, so I won't even try. I'll just tell you their story my own way, about how they lived together, how they nearly died together and how they were saved by music.

"The three of them were brought by train to the concentration camp from all over Europe: Benjamin from Paris, Mama from Warsaw, Papa from here, from Venice; all musicians, all Jewish, and all bound for the gas chamber and extermination like so many millions. They survived only because they were all able to say yes to one question put to them by an SS officer on arrival at the camp. 'Is there anyone amongst you who can play an orchestral instrument, who is a professional musician?' They did not know when they stepped forward that they would at once be separated from their families, would have to watch them being herded off towards those hellish chimneys, never to be seen again.

"There were auditions, of course, and by now they knew they were playing for their lives. There were rehearsals then, and it was during these rehearsals that the three of them first met. Benjamin was a good thirty years older than Mama and Papa, who were very much the babies of the orchestra, both of them just twenty. Why the orchestra was rehearsing, who they would be playing for, they did not know and they did not ask. To ask was to draw attention to oneself. This they knew was not the way to survive, and in the camp to survive was everything. They played Mozart, a lot of Mozart. The repertoire was for the most part light and happy – *Eine kleine Nachtmusick*, the first Clarinet Concerto in A major, minuets, dances, marches. And Strauss was popular too, waltzes, always waltzes. Playing was very hard because their fingers were so cold that sometimes they could hardly feel them, because they were weak with hunger and frequently sick. Sickness had to be hidden, because sickness once discovered would mean death. The SS were always there watching, and everyone knew what awaited them if they did not play well enough.

"At first they gave concerts only for the SS officers. Papa said you just had to pretend they were not there. You simply lost yourself in the music – it was the only way. Even when they applauded you did not look up. You never looked them in the eye. You played with total commitment. Every performance was your best performance, not to please them, but to show them what you could do, to prove to them how good you were despite all they were doing to humiliate you, to destroy you in body and soul. 'We fought back with our music,' Papa said. 'It was our only weapon.'

"Papa could speak no Polish, Mama no Italian, but their eyes met as they were playing – as often as possible, Mama said. To begin with, it might have been their shared joy in music-making, but very soon they knew they loved one another. The whole orchestra knew it, even before they did, Benjamin told me. 'Our little lovebirds' they were called. For everyone else in the orchestra, he said, they represented a symbol of hope for the future; and so they were much loved, much protected. For Mama and Papa their love numbed the pain and was a blessed refuge from the constant fear they were living through, from the horror of all that was going on around them.

"But there was amongst them a shared shame. They were being fed when others were not. They were being kept alive while others went to the gas chamber. Many were consumed by guilt, and this guilt was multiplied a thousand times when they discovered the real reason the orchestra had been assembled, why they had been rehearsing all this time. The concerts for the SS officers turned out to be sinister dress rehearsals for something a great deal worse.

"One cold morning with snow on the ground, they were made to assemble out in the compound with their instruments and ordered to sit down and play close to the camp gates. Then the train arrived, the wagons packed with new prisoners. Once they were all out they were lined up and then divided. The old and young and the frail were herded past the orchestra on their way, they were told, to the shower block; the able-bodied, those fit for work, were taken off towards the huts. And all the while Mama and Papa and Benjamin and the others played Mozart. They all understood soon enough what it was for – to calm the terror, to beguile each new trainload into a false sense of security. They were part of a deadly sham. They knew well enough that the shower block was a gas chamber.

"Week after week they played, month after month, train after train. And twenty-four hours a day the chimneys of the crematorium spewed out their fire and their smoke and their stench. Until there were no more trains; until the day the camps were liberated. This was the last day Benjamin ever remembered seeing Mama and Papa. They were all terribly emaciated by now, he said, and looked unlikely to survive. But they had. Mama and Papa had walked together out of the camp. They had played duets for bread and shelter, all across Europe. They were still playing to survive.

"When at last they got home to Venice, Papa smashed his violin and burned it, vowing never to play music again. But Mama kept hers. She thought of it as her talisman, her saviour and her friend, and she would neither sell it nor abandon it. She said it had brought her through all the horrors of the camp, brought them safely across Europe, back to Papa's home in Venice. It had saved their lives.

"Papa kept his vow. He never played a note of music again. After all that had happened he could hardly bear to hear it, which is why Mama had not played her violin either in all these years. But she would not be parted from it and had kept it safe at the top of their bedroom cupboard, hoping against hope, she said, that one day Papa might change his mind and be able to love music again and even play it. He never had. But they had survived and they were in time blessed with a child, a boy they called Paolo – a happy ending, Benjamin said. And I was the one who had brought the three of them together again, he said. So two happy endings.

"As for Benjamin, he had found his way back to Paris after a while, and played again in his old orchestra. He had married a French girl, Françoise, a cellist who had died only recently. He had come to Venice because he had always loved visiting the city and always longed to live looking out over water, and because Vivaldi was born here – he had always loved Vivaldi above all other composers. He played in the streets not just for the money, though that was a help, but because he could not bear not to play his violin. And he loved playing solo violin at last. He was more like Mama, he said. It was music that had kept him alive in the camp, and music had been his constant companion ever since. He could not imagine living a single day of his life without it, which was why, he said, he would dearly like to go on teaching me, if Mama and Papa would allow it.

" 'Does he play well, Benjamin?' Mama asked. 'Can we hear him, Papa? Please.'

"Papa, I could see, was struggling with himself. 'So long as it's not Mozart,' he said finally. So I played the Winter movement from Vivaldi's *Four Seasons*, Benjamin's favourite piece. Papa sat listening with closed eyes throughout.

"When I had finished, Benjamin said, 'Well, Gino, what do you think? He has a great and wonderful talent, your son, a rare gift you have both given him.'

" 'Then it must not be wasted,' said Papa quietly.

"So every day without fail after that I went for my violin lessons with Benjamin in his little apartment in the Arsenale. Papa could not bring himself to listen to me playing, but sometimes Mama came along with me and sat and listened, and afterwards she always hugged me so tight it hurt; but I did not mind, not one bit. I began to play in the streets alongside Benjamin, and whenever I did the crowds became bigger and bigger each time. One day Papa was there amongst them watching, listening. He walked me home afterwards, saying not a word until we were walking over the Accademia Bridge. 'So, Paolo,' he said, 'you prefer playing the violin to sweeping up in my barber's shop, do you?'

" 'Yes, Papa,' I replied. 'I'm afraid I do.'

" 'Well then, I can see I shall just have to do my sweeping up myself.' He stopped then and put his hands on my shoulders. 'I shall tell you something, Paolo, and I want you never to forget it. When you play I can listen to music again. You have made music joyful for me once more, and that is a wonderful gift you have given me. You go and be the great violinist you should be. I shall help you all I can. You will play heavenly music and people will love you. Mama and I shall come to all your concerts, or as many as we can. But you have to promise me one thing: that until the day I die you will never play Mozart in public, not in my hearing. It was Mozart we played so often in the camp. Never Mozart. Promise me.'

"So I promised. I have kept my promise to Papa all these years. He died two weeks ago, the last of the three of them to go. At my fiftieth birthday concert in London

277

I shall be playing Mozart, and I shall be playing it on Mama's violin, and I shall play it so well that he will love it, they will all love it, wherever they are."

I was still finishing my shorthand when I looked up and saw him coming towards me. He was offering me his violin.

"Here you are," he said. "Mama's violin. My violin. You can hold it if you like while we have some more mint tea. You'll have another cup, won't you? I make the best mint tea in Venice."

So I held Paolo Levi's violin for several precious minutes as we sat talking quietly over a last cup of tea. I asked him no more questions. There were none to ask. He talked of his love of Venice, and how wherever he was in the world he longed to be back home. It was the sounds he always missed: the church bells, the walking and talking, the chuntering of boats, and the music in the streets. "Music belongs in the streets, where Benjamin played it," he said, "not in concert halls."

As I left, he looked me in the eye and said, still grasping my hand, "I am glad it was you I told."

"Why did you?" I asked him. "Why did you tell me?"

"Because it was time to tell the truth. Because secrets are lies, and because you have eyes that are kind, like Benjamin's. But mostly because you didn't ask the Mozart question."

THE BEST CHRISTMAS PRESENT
IN THE WORLD

I spotted it in a junk shop in Bridport, a roll-top desk. The man said it was early nineteenth century, and oak. I had been looking for a desk like this for years, but never found one I could afford. This one was in bad condition, the roll top in several pieces, one leg clumsily mended, scorch marks all down one side.

It was going for very little money, and I reckoned I was just about capable enough to have a go at restoring it. It would be a risk, a challenge, but here was my chance to have a roll-top desk at last. I paid the man and brought it back to my workroom at the back of the garage. I began work on it on Christmas Eve, mostly because the house was resonating with overexcited relatives and I wanted some peace and quiet.

I removed the roll top completely and pulled out the drawers. Each one of them confirmed that this would be a bigger job than I had first thought. The veneer had lifted almost everywhere – it looked like flood damage. Both fire and water had clearly taken their toll on this desk. The last drawer was stuck fast. I tried all I could to ease it out gently. In the end I used brute force. I struck it sharply with the side of my fist and the drawer flew open to reveal a shallow space underneath, a secret drawer. There was something in there. I reached in and took out a small black tin box. Taped to the top of it was a piece of lined note paper, and written on it in shaky handwriting: "Jim's last letter, received 25th January 1915. To be buried with me when the time comes."

I knew as I did it that it was wrong of me to open the box, but curiosity got the better of my scruples. It usually does.

Inside the box there was an envelope. The address read: "Mrs Jim Macpherson, 12 Copper Beeches, Bridport, Dorset". I took out the letter and unfolded it. It was written in pencil and dated at the top 26th December 1914.

Dearest Connie

I write to you in a much happier frame of mind because something wonderful has just happened that I must tell you about at once. We were all standing to in our trenches yesterday morning, Christmas morning. It was crisp and quiet all about, as beautiful a morning as I've ever seen, as cold and frosty as a Christmas morning should be.

I should like to be able to tell you that we began it. But the truth, I'm ashamed to say, is that Fritz began it. First someone saw a white flag waving from the trenches opposite. Then they were calling out to us from across no-man's-land, "Happy Christmas, Tommy! Happy Christmas!"

When we had got over the surprise some of us shouted back, "Same to you, Fritz! Same to you!"

I thought that would be that. We all did. But then suddenly one of them was up there in his grey greatcoat and waving a white flag.

"Don't shoot, lads!" someone shouted. And no one did. Then there was another Fritz up on the parapet, and another.

"Keep your heads down," I told the men. "It's a trick." But it wasn't.

One of the Germans was waving a bottle above his head. "It is Christmas Day, Tommy. We have schnapps. We have sausage. We meet you? Yes?"

By this time there were dozens of them walking towards us across no-man's-land and not a rifle between them.

Little Private Morris was the first up. "Come on, boys. What are we waiting for?"

And then there was no stopping them. I was the officer.

I should have called a halt to it there and then, I suppose, but the truth is that it never even occurred to me. All along their line and ours I could see men walking slowly towards one another, grey coats, khaki coats meeting in the middle. And I was one of them. I was part of this. In the middle of the war we were making peace.

You cannot imagine, dearest Connie, my feelings as I looked into the eyes of the Fritz officer who approached me, hand outstretched.

"Hans Wolf," he said, gripping my hand warmly and holding it. "I am from Dusseldorf. I play the cello in the orchestra. Happy Christmas."

"Captain Jim Macpherson," I replied. "And a happy Christmas to you too. I'm a school teacher from Dorset, in the west of England."

"Ah, Dorset," he smiled. "I know this place. I know it very well."

We shared my rum ration and his excellent sausage. And we talked, Connie, how we talked. He spoke almost perfect English. But it turned out that he had never set foot in Dorset. He had learnt all he knew of England from school, and from reading books in English. His favourite writer was Thomas Hardy, his favourite book Far from the Madding Crowd. *So out there in no-man's-land we talked of Bathsheba and Gabriel Oak and Sergeant Troy and Dorset. He had a wife and one son, born just six months ago. As I looked about me there were huddles of khaki and grey everywhere, all over no-man's-land, smoking, laughing, talking, drinking, eating. Hans Wolf and I shared what was left of your wonderful Christmas cake, Connie. He thought the marzipan was the best he had ever tasted. I agreed. We agreed about everything, Connie, and he was my enemy. There never was a Christmas party like it, Connie.*

Then someone, I don't know who, brought out a football. Greatcoats were dumped in piles to make goal posts, and the next thing we knew it was Tommy against Fritz out in the middle of no-man's-land. Hans Wolf and I looked on and cheered, clapping our hands and stamping our feet, to keep out the cold as much as anything. There was a moment when I noticed our breaths mingling in the air between us. He saw it too and smiled.

"Jim Macpherson," he said after a while, "I think this is how we should resolve this war. A football match. No one dies in a football match. No children are orphaned. No wives become widows."

"I'd prefer cricket," I told him. "Then we Tommies could be sure of winning, probably." We laughed at that, and together we watched the game. Sad to say, Connie, Fritz won, two goals to one. But as Hans Wolf generously said, our goal was wider than theirs, so it wasn't quite fair.

The time came, and all too soon, when the game was

finished, the schnapps and the cake and the rum and the sausage had long since run out, and we knew it was all over. I wished Hans well and told him I hoped he would see his family again soon, that the fighting would end and we could all go home.

"I think that is what every soldier wants, on both sides," Hans Wolf said. "Take care, Jim Macpherson. I shall never forget this moment, nor you."

He saluted and walked away from me slowly – unwillingly, I felt. He turned to wave just once and then became one of the hundreds of grey-coated men drifting back towards their trenches.

That night, back in our dugouts, we heard them singing a carol, and singing it quite beautifully. It was 'Stille Nacht' – 'Silent Night'. Our boys gave them a rousing chorus of 'While shepherds watched'. We exchanged carols for a while and then we all fell silent. We had had our time of peace and goodwill, a time I will treasure as long as I live.

Dearest Connie, by Christmas time next year, this war will be nothing but a distant and terrible memory. I know from all that happened today how much both armies long for peace. We shall be together again soon, I'm sure of it.

Your loving Jim

I folded the letter again and slipped it carefully back into its envelope. I told no one about my find, but kept my shameful intrusion to myself. It was this guilt, I think, that kept me awake all night. By morning, I knew what I had to do. I made an excuse and did not go to church with the others. Instead I drove to Bridport, just a few miles away. I asked a boy walking his dog where Copper Beeches was.

Number twelve turned out to be nothing but a burnt-out shell, the roof gaping, the windows boarded up. I knocked at the house next door and asked if anyone knew the whereabouts of a Mrs Macpherson. Oh yes, said the old man in his slippers, he knew her well. A lovely old lady, he told me, a bit muddle-headed, but at her age she was entitled to be, wasn't she? 101 years old. She had been in the house when it caught fire. No one really knew how the fire had started, but it could well have been candles. She used candles rather than electricity, because she always thought electricity was too expensive. The fireman had got her out just in time. She was in a nursing home now, he told me, Burlington House, on the Dorchester road, on the other side of town.

I found Burlington House Nursing Home easily enough. There were paper chains up in the hallway and a lighted Christmas tree stood in the corner with a lop-sided angel on top. I said I was a friend come to visit Mrs Macpherson to bring her a Christmas present. I could see through into the dining room where everyone was wearing a paper hat and singing along to 'Good King Wenceslas'. The matron had a hat on too and seemed happy enough to see me. She even offered me a mince pie. She walked me along the corridor.

"Mrs Macpherson is not in with the others," she told me. "She's rather confused today so we thought it best if she had a good rest. She's no family you know – no one visits. So I'm sure she'll be only too pleased to see you." She took me into a conservatory with wicker chairs and potted plants all around and left me.

The old lady was sitting in a wheelchair, her hands folded in her lap. She had silver white hair pinned into a wispy bun. She was gazing out at the garden.

"Hello," I said.

She turned and looked up at me vacantly.

"Happy Christmas, Connie," I went on. "I found this. I think it's yours."

As I was speaking her eyes never left my face. I opened the tin box and gave it to her. That was the moment her eyes lit up with recognition and her face became suffused with a sudden glow of happiness. I explained about the desk, about how I had found it, but I don't think she was listening. For a while she said nothing, but stroked the letter tenderly with her fingertips.

Suddenly she reached out and took my hand. Her eyes

were filled with tears. "You told me you'd come home by Christmas, dearest," she said. "And here you are, the best Christmas present in the world. Come closer, Jim dear, sit down."

I sat down beside her, and she kissed my cheek. "I read your letter so often, Jim, every day. I wanted to hear your voice in my head. It always made me feel you were with me. And now you are. Now you're back you can read it to me yourself. Would you do that for me? I just want to hear your voice again, Jim. I'd love that so much. And then perhaps we'll have some tea. I've made you a nice Christmas cake, marzipan all around. I know how much you love marzipan."

For Carlos, a Letter from Your Father

I *have never forgotten my tenth birthday. All my other* *childhood birthdays are lost somewhere in the mists of memory, blurred by sameness perhaps: the excitement of anticipation, the brief rapture of opening presents, and then the inevitable disappointment because birthdays, like Christmases, were always so quickly over. Not so my tenth.*

It is not only because of the gleaming silver bike my mother gave me that I remember it so well. I tried it out at once, in my pyjamas. In an ecstasy of joy and pride I rode it round and round the block, hoping all my friends would be up early and watching out of their windows, admiring, and seething with envy too. But even my memory of that has diminished over the years. It was when I came home, puffed out and glowing, and sat down for breakfast, that my mother gave me something else too. It is this second gift that I have never forgotten. I can't honestly remember what happened to my beautiful bike. Either it rusted at the back of the garage when I grew out of it, or it was thrown away. I don't know. I do know that I still have this second gift, that I have never grown out of it and I will never throw it away.

She put down beside me on the kitchen table what looked

at first like an ordinary birthday card. She didn't say who it was from but I could see that there was something about this card that troubled her deeply.

"Who's it from?" I asked her. I wasn't that interested at first – after all, birthday cards were never as intriguing as presents. She didn't answer me. I picked up the envelope. There, written in handwriting I did not know, was my answer:
For Carlos, a letter from your father.

The envelope had clearly been folded. It was soiled and there was a tear in one corner. The word father *was smeared and only just legible. I looked up and saw my mother's eyes filled with tears. I knew instantly she wanted me to ask no more questions. She simply said, "He wanted me to keep it for you, until your tenth birthday."*

So I opened the card and read.

Dearest Carlos,

I want to wish you first of all a very happy tenth birthday. How I should love to be with you on this special day. Maybe we could have gone riding together as I once did with my father on my birthday. Was it my tenth? I can't remember. I do remember we rode all day and picnicked on a high hill where the wind breathed through the long grass. I thought I could see for ever from that hill. Or maybe we could have gone to a football match and howled together at the referee and leapt up and down when we scored.

But then maybe you don't like horses or football. Why should you have grown up like me? You are a different person, but with a little of me inside you, that's all. I do know that your mother and I would have sung "Happy Birthday" to you and watched your eyes light up when you opened your presents, as you blew out the candles on your cake.

But all I have to give, all I can offer, is this letter, a letter I hope you will never have to read, for if you are reading it now it means that I am not with you, and have never been with you, that I died ten years ago in some stupid, stupid war that killed me and many, many others, and like all wars did no one any good.

Dying, Carlos, as you know, comes to each of us. Strangely, I am not afraid, not as much as I have been. I think maybe that love has conquered my fear. I am filled with so much love for you, and such a sadness too, a sadness I pray you will never have to know. It is the thought of losing you before I even get to know you that saddens me so. If I die in this terrible place then we shall never meet, not properly, father to son. We shall never talk. For a father to be parted from his son is always a terrible thing, yet if it has to be, then in a way I would rather it was now, this way, this soon. To have known you, to have watched you grow and then to have lost you, must surely be even worse. Or am I just telling myself that?

You will know me a little, I suppose, perhaps from photographs. And your mother may well have told you something about me, of my childhood, how I grew up on the farm in Patagonia and was riding horses almost before I could walk. Maybe she told you of our first meeting when her car had a puncture and I was riding by and stopped to change her tyre for her. I am quite good at tinkering with motors – you have to be on a farm. But I took a lot longer to change that tyre than I needed to – if you know what I mean. By the time I had finished I knew I loved her and wanted to spend my whole life with her. Later I learnt that she went home afterwards and told her sister that she'd met this young man on the road who had nice eyes, and a nice horse, but who talked too much and was hopeless at changing tyres. Anyway, much against the wishes of our families, who all said we were far too young, we got married six months later.

For a short while life seemed so sweet, so perfect. Then came my conscription papers and separation and the long weeks of military training. But I didn't mind that much because it was something we all had to do, and because I knew it would soon be over. I had so much to look forward to, most of all the birth of you. All the talk in the barracks was of war. I think we talked ourselves into this war – perhaps it is always like that.

I came home to see you just once, and now, only a few

weeks later, I find myself sitting here in the Malvinas, high in the rocky hills above Stanley Town. Night is coming on and I am waiting for battle.

As I write this I am so cold I cannot feel my feet. I can hardly hold the pencil I am writing with. The British are coming. They know where we are. They have been bombarding us all day. We cannot see them, but we know they are out there somewhere. We expect them to attack tonight. All of us know in our hearts, though we do not say it, that this will be the last battle. In battle men die. I do not want to think of that, but it is difficult not to. The officers say we can win, that if we can only hang on, reinforcements will soon be here. But we all know better. They have to say that, don't they?

I can see you now in my head as you were, three long months ago, on the morning I left home. When I looked down upon you that last time, cradled in your mother's arms, I remember I tried to picture you as a grown boy. I couldn't then, and I still can't. For me you are that sleeping child, yawning toothlessly, fists clenched, frowning through your milk-soaked dreams. But grow up you will, grow up you have, and now that you are old enough I want to tell you myself how I came to be here, fighting in a war in this dreadful place, how I died so far from home. I want to speak to you directly. At least you will know me a little because you can hear my voice in my writing. It is true that

I am writing to you also because it helps me – if I think of you I do not think of the battle ahead. I have already written to your mother. She will have read her letter ten years ago now. This is your letter, Carlos, our hello you might call it, and our goodbye.

I had not thought it would end like this. Like all my comrades I believed what we were told, what we saw on the television, what we read in the papers. The Malvinas belonged to Argentina, and that much is true. They had been stolen from us, they said. We would restore the honour of Argentina and take them back. Our flag would fly again over Stanley. It would be easy, they told us. We would attack in force, overwhelm the British garrison in a few hours. There would be very little shooting. The Malvinas would be ours again, Argentinian, and then we could all go home. I was excited – we all were excited and proud too, proud that we were the ones chosen to do this for our country. It was all going to be so simple.

And it began well. We came ashore in our landing craft. No one fired a shot at us. As we marched into Stanley we saw our flag already flying high over the town. The British marines in their green berets sat huddled by the roadside dejected, defeated. The war was over almost before it had begun. Or so we thought. We had won. The Malvinas were ours again. How the people back home would be cheering, I thought. What heroes we would be when we returned.

How we laughed and sang and drank that first night. We did not feel the cold in the wind, not then.

In those early days on the Malvinas, in that first flush of victory, the islands seemed to us like a paradise, a paradise regained. Our paradise. Argentinian.

Yet here I sit only a month or two later and we know that we are about to lose the last battle. The ships did not come. The supplies did not come. Instead the British came, their planes first, then their ships, then their soldiers. We did what we could, Carlos, but we were raw conscripts, poorly fed, poorly equipped, badly led, and we were up against determined fighters. From the moment they sank the great battleship *Belgrano*, the pride of our navy, we knew it could only end one way. I lost my cousin in that ship. I saw them die, good men, my friends, men with wives and mothers and children.

I grew up fast in the terrible weeks that followed. I learnt what I should already have understood, that in wars people really do kill one another. I did not hate those I have killed and those who try to kill me do not hate me either. We are like puppets doing a dance of death, our masters pulling the strings, watched by the world on television. What they don't know is that the puppets are made of flesh, not wood. War, Carlos, has only one result: suffering.

When I heard the British had landed at San Carlos Bay

I thought of you, and I prayed in the church in Stanley that I would be spared to see you again. They had no candles there. So I went out and bought a box of candles from the store and then I came back and lit them and prayed for me, for you, for your mother. An old lady in a scarf was kneeling at prayer. I saw her watching me as I came away. Her eyes met mine and she tried to smile. My English is not that good, but I remember her words. They echo still in my head.

"This is not the way," she said. "It is wrong, wrong."

"Yes," I replied, and left her there.

That was a few days ago now. Since then we have been stuck up here on these freezing hills above Stanley Town, digging in and waiting for the British, who come closer every day. And the bitter wind, from which we cannot hide, chills us to the bone, sapping the last of our strength and most of our courage too. What courage we have left we shall fight with, but courage will not be enough.

I must finish now. I must fold you away in an envelope and face whatever I must face. As you have grown up, you may not have had a father, but I promise you, you have always had a father's love.

Goodbye, dear Carlos.

And God bless.

Papa

SHADOW

*Aman and his mother live in war-torn Afghanistan. When
a Western dog appears at the mouth of their cave, it soon
becomes Aman's constant companion, his shadow as he
calls her. But life is becoming increasingly dangerous for
Aman and his family…*

After the phone call Mother stopped to buy some
flour in the market, and I walked on. When I turned
round after a while, to see if she was coming, I saw one
of the stallholders was shouting at her, waving his hands
angrily. I thought it was an argument about money, that
maybe she'd been short-changed. They were always doing
that in the market.

But it wasn't that.

She caught me up and hurried me away. I could see the
fear in her eyes. "Don't look round, Aman," she said. "I
know this man. He is Taliban. He is very dangerous."

"Taliban?" I said. "Are they still here?" I thought the
Taliban had been defeated long ago by the Americans, and
driven into the mountains. I couldn't understand what she
was saying.

"The Taliban, they are still here, Aman," she said, and she could not stop herself from crying now. "They are everywhere, in the police, in the army, like wolves in sheep's clothing. Everyone knows who they are, and everyone is frightened to speak. That man in the market, he was one of those who came to the cave and took your father away, and killed him."

I turned around to look. I wanted to run back and tell him face to face he was a killer. I wanted to look him in the eye and accuse him. I wanted to show him I was not afraid. "Don't look," Mother said, dragging me on. "Don't do anything, Aman, please. You'll only make it worse."

She waited till we were safely out of town before telling me more. "He was cheating me in the market," she said, "and when I argued, he told me that if I do not leave the valley, he will tell his brother, and he will have me taken to prison again. And I know his brother only too well. He was the policeman who put me in prison before. He was the one who beat me, and tortured me. It wasn't because of the apple you stole, Aman. It was so that I would not tell anyone about what his brother had done to your father, so that I would not say he was Taliban. What can I do? I cannot leave Grandmother. She cannot look after herself. What can I do?" I held her hand to try to comfort her, but she cried all the way home. I kept telling her it would be all right, that I would look after her.

That night I heard Mother and Grandmother whispering to each other in the cave, and crying together too. When they finally went to sleep, the dog crept into the cave and lay down beside me. I buried my face in her fur and held her tight. "It will be all right, won't it?" I said to her.

But I knew it wasn't going to be. I knew something terrible was going to happen. I could feel it.

Early the next day the police came to the cave. Mother had gone down to the stream for water, so I was there alone with Grandmother when they came, three of them. The stallholder from the market was with them. They said they had come to search the place.

When Grandmother struggled to her feet and tried to stop them, they pushed her to the ground. Then they turned on me and started to beat me and kick me. That was when I saw the dog come bounding into the cave. She didn't hesitate. She leapt up at them, barking and snarling. But they lashed out at her with their feet and their sticks and drove her out.

After that they seemed to forget about me, and just broke everything they could in the cave, kicked our things all over the place, stamped on our cooking pot, and one of them peed on the mattress before they left.

I didn't realise at first how badly Grandmother had been hurt, not till I rolled her over on to her back. Her eyes were closed. She was unconscious. She must have hit her head when she fell. There was a great cut across her forehead. I tried to wash the blood away, kept trying to wake her. But the blood kept coming, and she wouldn't open her eyes.

When Mother came back some time later, she did all she could to revive her, but it was no good. Grandmother died that evening. Sometimes I think she died because she just didn't want to wake up, because she knew it was the only way to make Mother and me leave, the only way to save us. So maybe Grandmother won her argument with Mother, in her own way, the only way she could.

We left Bamiyan the next day, the day Grandmother was buried. We did as Grandmother had told us. We took Father's donkey with us, to carry the few belongings we had, the cooking things, the blankets and the mattress, with Grandmother's jewels and Uncle Mir's money hidden inside it. We took some bread and apples with us, gifts from our friends for the journey, and walked out of the valley. I tried not to look back, but I did. I could not help myself.

War Horse

In the deadly chaos of the First World War, one horse witnesses the reality of battle from both sides of the trenches. Bombarded by artillery, Joey tells a powerful story of the truest friendships surviving in terrible times…

From both sides of me I heard a gradual crescendo of excitement and laughter rippling along the trenches, interspersed with barked orders that everyone was to keep their heads down and no one was to shoot. From my vantage point on the mound I could see only an occasional glimpse of a steel helmet, my only evidence that the voices I was hearing did indeed belong to real people. There was the sweet smell of cooking food wafting towards me and I lifted my nose to savour it. It was sweeter than the sweetest bran-mash I had ever tasted and it had a tinge of salt about it. I was drawn first one way and then the other by this promise of warm food, but each time I neared the trenches on either side I met an impenetrable barrier of loosely coiled barbed wire. The soldiers cheered me on as I came closer, showing their heads fully now over the trenches and beckoning me towards them; and when I had to turn back at the wire and crossed no-man's-land on to the other side, I was welcomed again there by a chorus of whistling and clapping, but again I could find no way through the wire. I must have crisscrossed no-man's-land for much of that morning, and found at long last in the middle of this blasted wilderness a small patch of coarse, dank grass growing on the lip of an old crater.

I was busying myself at tearing the last of this away when I saw, out of the corner of my eye, a man in a grey uniform clamber up out of the trenches, waving a white flag above his head. I looked up as he began to clip his way methodically through the wire and then pull it aside. All this time there was much argument and noisy consternation from the other side; and soon a small, helmeted figure in a flapping khaki greatcoat climbed up into no-man's-land. He too held up a white handkerchief in one hand and began also to work his way through the wire towards me.

The German was through the wire first, leaving a narrow gap behind him. He approached me slowly across no-man's-land, calling out to me all the while to come towards him. He reminded me at once of dear old Friedrich for he was, like Friedrich, a grey-haired man in an untidy, unbuttoned uniform and he spoke gently to me. In one hand he held a rope; the other hand he stretched out towards me. He was still far too far away for me to see clearly, but an offered hand in my experience was often cupped and there was enough promise in that for me to limp cautiously towards him. On both sides the trenches were lined now with cheering men, standing on the parapets waving their helmets above their heads.

"Oi, boyo!" The shout came from behind me and was urgent enough to stop me. I turned to see the small man in khaki weaving and jinking his way across no-man's-land, one hand held high above his head carrying the white handkerchief. "Oi, boyo! Where you going? Hang on a bit. You're going the wrong way, see."

The two men who were coming towards me could not have been more different. The one in grey was the taller of the two and as he came nearer I could see his face was lined and creased with years. Everything about him was slow and gentle under his ill-fitting uniform. He wore no helmet, but instead the peakless cap with the red band I knew so well sitting carelessly on the back of his head. The little man in khaki reached us, out of breath, his face red and still smooth with youth, his round helmet with the broad rim fallen askew over one ear. For a few strained, silent moments the two stood yards apart from each other, eyeing one another warily and saying not a word. It was the young man in khaki who broke the silence and spoke first.

"Now what do we do?" he said, walking towards us and looking at the German who stood head and shoulders above him. "There's two of us here and one horse to split between us. 'Course, King Soloman had the answer, didn't he now? But it's not very practical in this case, is it? And what's worse, I can't speak a word of German, and I can see you can't understand what the hell I'm talking about, can you? Oh hell, I should never have come out here, I knew I shouldn't. Can't think what came over me, and all for a muddy old horse too."

"But I can, I can speak a little bad English," said the older man, still holding out his cupped hand under my nose. It was full of black bread broken into pieces, a titbit I was familiar enough with but usually found too bitter for my taste. However I was now too hungry to be choosy and as he was speaking I soon emptied his hand. "I speak only a little English – like a schoolboy – but it's enough I think for us." And even as he spoke I felt a rope slip slowly around my neck and tighten. "As for our other problem, since I have been here the first, then the horse is mine. Fair, no? Like your cricket?"

"Cricket! Cricket!" said the young man. "Who's ever heard of that barbarous game in Wales? That's a game for the rotten English. Rugby, that's my game, and that's not a game. That's a religion that is – where I come from. I played scrum-half for Maesteg before the war stopped me, and at Maesteg we say that a loose ball is our ball."

"Sorry?" said the German, his eyebrows furrowed with

concern. "I cannot understand what you mean by this."

"Doesn't matter, Jerry. Not important, not any more. We could have settled all this peaceful like, Jerry – the war, I mean – and I'd be back in my valley and you'd be back in yours. Still, not your fault I don't suppose. Nor mine, neither, come to that."

By now the cheering from both sides had subsided and both armies looked on in total silence as the two men talked together beside me. The Welshman was stroking my nose and feeling my ears. "You know horses then?" said the tall German. "How bad is his wounded leg? Is it broken do you think? He seems not to walk on it."

The Welshman bent over and lifted my leg gently and expertly, wiping away the mud from around the wound. "He's in a mess right enough, but I don't think it's broken, Jerry. It's a bad wound though, a deep gash – wire by the look of it. Got to get him seen to quick else the poison will set in and then there won't be a lot anyone could do for him. Cut like that, he must have lost a lot of blood already. Question is though, who takes him? We've got a veterinary hospital somewhere back behind our lines that could take care of him, but I expect you've got one too."

"Yes, I think so. Somewhere it must be, but I do not know exactly where," the German said slowly. And then he dug deep in his pocket and produced a coin. "You choose the side you want, 'head or tail', I think you say. I will show the coin to everyone on both sides and everyone will know that whichever side wins the horse it is only by chance. Then no one loses any pride, yes? And everyone will be happy."

The Welshman looked up admiringly and smiled. "All right then, you go ahead, Jerry, you show them the coin and then you toss and I'll call."

The German held the coin up in the sun and then turned a full slow circle before spinning it high and glinting into the air. As it fell to the ground the Welshman called out in a loud, resonant voice so that all the world could hear, "Heads!"

"Well," said the German, stooping to pick it up. "That's the face of my Kaiser looking up at me out of the mud, and he does not look pleased with me. So I am afraid you have won. The horse is yours. Take good care of him, my friend," and he picked up the rope again and handed it to the Welshman. As he did so he held out his other hand in a gesture of friendship and reconciliation, a smile lighting his worn face. "In an hour, maybe, or two," he said, "we will be trying our best again each other to kill. God only knows why we do it, and I think he has maybe forgotten why. Goodbye, Welshman. We have shown them, haven't we? We have shown them that any problem can be solved between people if only they can trust each other. That is all it needs, no?"

The little Welshman shook his head in disbelief as he took the rope. "Jerry, boyo, I think if they would let you and me have an hour or two out here together, we could sort out this whole wretched mess. There would be no more weeping widows and crying children in my valley and no more in yours. If the worse came to the worst we could decide it all on the flip of a coin, couldn't we now?"

"If we did," said the German with a chuckle. "If we did it that way, then it would be our turn to win. And maybe your Lloyd George would not like that." And he put his hands on the Welshman's shoulders for a moment. "Take care, my friend, and good luck. *Auf Wiedersehen.*" And he turned away and walked slowly back across no-man's-land to the wire.

"Same to you, boyo," the Welshman shouted after him, and then he too turned and led me away back towards the line of khaki soldiers who began now to laugh and cheer with delight as I limped towards them through the gap in the wire.

Private Peaceful

Thomas Peaceful and his brother Charlie are on the battlefields of the First World War, trying to stay alive in the horror of the trenches…

The first snow of winter sees us back in the trenches. It freezes as it falls, hardening the mud – and that certainly is a blessing. Providing there is no wind we are no colder than we were before and can at least keep our feet dry. The guns have stayed relatively silent in our sector and we have had few casualties so far: one wounded by a sniper, two in hospital with pneumonia, and one with chronic trench foot – which affects us all. From what we hear and read we are in just about the luckiest sector we could be.

Word has come down from Headquarters, Wilkie says, that we must send our patrols to find out what regiments have come into the line opposite us and in what strength – though why we have to do that we do not know. There are spotter planes doing that almost every day. So most nights now, four or five of us are picked, and a patrol goes out into no-man's-land to find out what they can. More often than not they find out nothing. No one likes going, of course, but nobody's been hurt so far, and you get a double rum ration before you go and everyone wants that.

My turn soon comes up as it was bound to. I'm not particularly worried. Charlie's going with me, and Nipper Martin, Little Les and Pete – "the whole skittle team", Charlie calls us. Wilkie's heading the patrol and we're glad of that. He tells us we have to achieve what the other patrols have not. We have to bring back one prisoner for questioning. They give us each a double rum ration, and I'm warmed instantly to the roots of my hair, to the toes of my feet.

"Stay close, Tommo," Charlie whispers, and then we are climbing out over the top, crawling on our bellies through the wire. We snake our way forward. We slither into a shell hole and lie doggo there for a while in case we've been heard. We can hear Fritz talking now, and laughing. There's the sound of a gramophone playing – I've heard all this before on lookout, but distantly. We're close now, very close, and I should be scared witless. Strangely, I find I'm not so much frightened as excited. Maybe it's the rum. I'm out poaching again, that's what it feels like. I'm tensed for danger. I'm ready for it, but not frightened.

It takes an eternity to cross no-man's-land. I begin to wonder if we'll ever find their trenches at all. Then we see their wire up ahead. We wriggle through a gap, and still undetected we drop down into their trench. It looks deserted, but we know it can't be. We can still hear the voices and the music. I notice the trench is much deeper than ours, wider too and altogether more solidly constructed. I grip my rifle tighter and follow Charlie along the trench, bent double like everyone else. We're trying not to, but we're making too much noise. I can't understand why no one has heard us. Where are their sentries, for God's sake? Up ahead I can see Wilkie waving us on with his revolver. There is a flickering of light now coming from a dugout ahead, where the voices are, where the music is. From the sound of it there could be half a dozen men in there at least. We only need one prisoner. How are we going to manage half a dozen of them?

At that moment the light floods into the trench as the dugout curtain opens. A soldier comes out shrugging on his coat, the curtain closing behind him. He is alone, just what we are after. He doesn't seem to see us right away. Then he does. For a split second the Hun does nothing and neither do we. We just stand and look at one another. He could so easily have done what he should have done, just put up his hands and come with us. Instead he lets out a shriek and turns, blundering through the curtain back into the dugout. I don't know who threw the grenade in after him, but there is a blast that throws me back against the trench wall. I sit there stunned. There is screaming and firing from inside the dugout, then silence. The music has stopped.

By the time I get in there Little Les is lying on his side shot through the head, his eyes staring at me. He looks so surprised. Several Germans are sprawled across their dugout, all still, all dead – except one. He stands there naked, blood spattered and shaking. I too am shaking. He has his hands in the air and is whimpering. Wilkie throws a coat over him and Pete bundles him out of the dugout. Frantic now to get back we scrabble our way up out of the trench, the Hun still whimpering. He is beside himself with terror. Pete is shouting at him to stop, but he's only making it worse. We follow the captain through the German wire and run.

For a while I think we have got away with it, but then a flare goes up and we are caught suddenly in broad daylight. I hurl myself to the ground and bury my face in the snow. Their flares last so much longer than ours, shine so much brighter. I know we're for it. I press myself into the ground, eyes closed. I'm praying and thinking of Molly. If I'm going to die I want her to be my last thought. But she's not. Instead I'm saying sorry to Father for what I did, that I didn't mean to do it. A machine gun opens up behind us and then rifles fire. There is nowhere to hide, so we pretend to be dead. We wait till the light dies and the night is suddenly black again. Wilkie gets us to our feet and we go on, running, stumbling, until more lights go up, and the machine gunners start up again. We dive into a crater and roll down crashing through the ice into the watery bottom. Then the shelling starts. It seems as if we have woken up the entire German army. I cower in the stinking water with the German and Charlie, the three of us clinging together, heads buried in one another as the shells fall all about us. Our own guns are answering now, but it is little comfort to us. Charlie and I drag the Hun prisoner out of the water. Either he is talking to himself or he's saying a prayer, it's difficult to tell.

Then we see Wilkie lying higher up the slope, too close to the lip of the crater. When Charlie calls out to him he doesn't reply. Charlie goes to him and turns him over. "It's my legs," I hear the captain whisper. "I can't seem to move my legs." He's too exposed up there, so Charlie drags him back down as gently as he can. We try to make him comfortable. The Hun keeps praying out loud. I'm quite sure he's praying now. "*Du lieber Gott,*" I hear. They call God by the same name. Pete and Nipper are crawling over towards us from the far side of the crater. We are together at least. The ground shudders, and with every impact we are bombarded by showers of mud and stone and snow. But the sound I hate and fear most is not the sound of the explosion – by then it's done and over with, and you're either dead or not. No, it's the whistle and whine and shriek of the shells as they come over. It's the not knowing where they will land, whether this one is for you.

Then, as suddenly as the barrage begins, it stops. There is silence. Darkness hides us again. Smoke drifts over us and down into our hole, filling our nostrils with the stench of cordite. We stifle our coughing. The Hun has stopped his praying, and is lying curled up in his overcoat, his hands over his ears. He's rocking like a child, like Big Joe.

"I won't make it," Wilkie says to Charlie. "I'm leaving it to you to get them all back, Peaceful, and the prisoner. Go on now."

"No, sir," Charlie replies. "If one goes we all go. Isn't that right, lads?"

That's how it happened. Under cover of an early morning mist we made it back to our trenches, Charlie carrying Wilkie on his back the whole way, until the stretcher bearers came for him in the trench. As they lifted him, Wilkie caught Charlie by the hand and held it. "Come and see me in hospital, Peaceful," he said. "That's an order." And Charlie promised he would.

We had a brew up with our prisoner in the dugout before they came for him. He smoked a cigarette Pete had given him. He'd stopped shaking now, but his eyes still held their fear. We had nothing to say to one another until the moment he got up to leave. "*Danke*," he said "*Danke sehr.*"

"Funny that," Nipper said when he'd gone. "Seeing him standing there with not a stitch on. Take off our uniforms and you can hardly tell the difference, can you? Not a bad bloke, for a Fritz, that is."

That night I didn't think, as I should have done, of Little Les lying out there in the German dugout, with a hole in his head. I thought of the Hun prisoner we'd brought back. I didn't even know his name, yet, after that night cowering in the shell hole with him, I felt somehow I knew him better than I'd ever known Little Les.

An Elephant in the Garden

It is Dresden in 1945 and Karli and Elizabeth's mother works at the zoo. When the bombs begin to fall, they cannot bear to leave behind beloved elephant, Marlene...

I took Karli by the hand and we both followed Mutti, running through the snow after Marlene. But the snow was deep and we soon tired, and were reduced to a walk. Ahead of us the chase went on. However hard the dog tried to bound away over the snow and escape, Marlene kept after him. All the while her trumpeting was echoing through the park, and louder now in my ears than seemed possible – until I began to realise that it was not Marlene's trumpeting I was hearing at all, but the sound of the air-raid sirens wailing over the city. I stopped to listen, to be quite sure my ears were not playing tricks on me.

Karli gripped my arm. "An air raid!" he cried. "An air raid!" All I knew then was that we had to get to the shelter fast, as we had been taught. Ahead of us, Mutti too had stopped in her tracks. She was yelling out to Marlene to come back. Again and again she called, but Marlene just kept going. She was almost out of sight now in amongst the trees, as Mutti came stumbling back towards us.

"There is nothing more we can do for now, children," she said. "We shall find her later. We must get home, to the shelter. Come quickly!" She grabbed Karli's hand.

"No!" Karli cried, pulling away from her and turning to run. "No! We can't! We can't leave her. We have to catch her! I'm going after her. You go home if you like. I'm not coming."

"Karli! Karli, don't be silly! You come back here this minute, do you hear me?" Mutti was shouting after him, shrieking almost; but I could see it was pointless, that Karli had made up his mind. I started running after him then, so did Mutti. But he was already way ahead of us, and Marlene was by now no more than a shadowy shape moving through the trees, and then I lost sight of her altogether. We were catching Karli up fast, when, and not for the first time, he staggered, and fell to his knees, exhausted. Mutti and I were trying to help him up, doing all we could to persuade him that we had to get back to the shelter. He was still protesting, still struggling against us, fighting us, when we heard the sound we had been dreading for so long.

The bombers.

The bombers were coming. It sounded like a distant humming at first, then it became a droning, like a swarm of bees, a swarm that was coming closer, ever closer. We looked up. We could still see no planes. We could not tell from which direction they were coming because they seemed to be all around us, but invisible. Then, in no time at all, the sky above us was filled with a thunderous throbbing roar, so loud that I thought my ears might burst. Karli had his hands over his ears and was screaming. And then the bombs began to fall, behind us, on the city, on the far side of the park, on where we had come from, our street, our house. The whole world shuddered and shook with every blast. To me it felt like the end of the world had come.

Now we had no choice. We all of us knew at that moment that there could be no going back. Mutti picked Karli up in her arms. He clung on and buried his head in her shoulder, crying out for Marlene. And we ran, we ran and we ran. We did not know tiredness any more. Fear alone kept our legs running. I looked up once more, and saw the planes flying across the moon. There were hundreds of them up there. By now the bombs were falling all over Dresden. We heard the whine of them falling, the crump and crunch of them, saw the flash of explosions, saw fires raging everywhere.

There was no more argument, not about Marlene, who had disappeared into the night by now, and not about returning home to the shelter. Marlene we could do nothing more about, and it was obvious that if there was any way of escaping the bombs, it would be in the open country ahead of us beyond the suburbs, not in a shelter back in the burning city.

It was the city they were bombing, not the countryside. We only had to keep going, I told myself. We would soon be out of the park, into the outskirts of the city, closer all the time to the safety of the fields and the woods beyond.

We tried not to, but we had to stop from time to time, to catch our breath. And whenever we did, we would stand there, gazing back at the city. Our city it was, and it was being destroyed before our eyes. Searchlights crisscrossed the sky. Anti-aircraft guns were firing, firing, pounding away. But the planes just kept on coming, the blast of their bombs ever nearer, ever louder, roaring in our ears. The flames from burning houses and factories were licking high into the sky, leaping from one building to the next, from one street to the next, from one fire to another, each fire, it seemed to me, seeking out another fire to be with, so it could become an inferno, so it could burn more furiously.

Time and again we turned away from it and ran on, partly because the heat was so intense, and partly because we could bear to watch no longer. We were out of the park by now, out on to the road through the suburbs. A sudden wind was getting up, a strong fierce wind that gusted in our faces as we walked. We leaned into the wind and staggered on through the snow.

We followed the road to the top of a steep hill, and by then Mutti could carry Karli no further. She had to stop. We found ourselves on our knees in the snow, looking back down at the city, at the ring of fire that now encircled it entirely. Kneeling there, we heard quite distinctly through the drones of the bombers, the sound of shooting. And we could hear screaming. One look at Mutti's horrified face, and I knew this screaming for what it was, the shrieking of animals, of dying animals, and that it came from the direction of the zoo. They were shooting the animals. Mutti put her hands over Karli's ears, and hugged him to her. She wept then, uncontrollably, as much in anger as in grief, I thought. Karli and I put our arms around her to do our best to comfort her. There we knelt, the wind searing hot on our faces now, while the shooting went on, and the bombs fell, and the city burned.

In the end it was neither Karli nor me who brought her comfort. Instead it was the sound of breathing close behind us, and then, miraculously, Marlene's trunk winding itself around us, enfolding us. That was a moment I remember so well, because all three of us burst out laughing, laughing through our tears. We had gone looking for Marlene, lost her, and now she had found us. We were on our feet at once, overjoyed, Karli kissing her trunk again and again, and Mutti stroking her ear, but telling her how naughty she had been to run away like she had. I looked up into

Marlene's face, and saw the fires of the city burning in her troubled eye. She knew what was happening, understood everything. I was sure of it.

I think it was Marlene's sudden unexpected reappearance that gave us all fresh hope, new strength, Mutti most of all. "Well, children," she said, brushing the snow off her coat, "we have no house to go back to, and certainly there will be very little left of the city. So I have been thinking. There is only one place we can go to. We shall go to the farm, to Uncle Manfred and Aunt Lotti. It is a long, long way to go on foot, but there is nowhere else."

"But you and Papi," I said. "You told us we could never go back to the farm, not after…"

"I know," Mutti told him. "But we have no choice, have we? We shall be needing food, shelter. They will look after us, I know they will. It was a family row we had, that is all. I am sure everything is forgiven by now, and that we can all put it behind us. When we get there, they will welcome us in with open arms. It will be fine, I promise you. You will see."

The Kites are Flying

*A cameraman filming life in the West Bank befriends Said,
a silent young shepherd. He learns the terrible past of
Said's family but also sees hope for future generations…*

On the way back home to the village that evening with the sheep we came across Uncle Yasser harvesting his broad beans. I stopped and asked if he'd mind if I filmed him at his work. He shrugged. "There is not much to film," he told me. "It's a poor crop, but it's always a poor crop. There's never enough water, that's the trouble. They have taken most of it. And they have taken all our best land for themselves. They leave us only the dust to farm in. So what can you do?" He was watching Said as he walked on up into the village with his sheep. "I see he has sent his kite away. He let it go. The wind must have been just right. He never keeps his kites, not one of them. He just makes another one, waits for the next east wind, then sends it off again. Did you see what he writes on his kites? 'Salaam.' This means Peace. And on every one of them he writes both their names, 'Mahmoud and Said'." I had not expected him to want to talk so willingly.

"How many has he sent?" I asked him.

"We are not sure. And he cannot tell us of course. Maybe about one a week since Mahmoud… and that was nearly two years ago now."

I felt I could ask, because I felt he wanted to tell me. "Who is this Mahmoud? What happened?" He gave me a long and hard look. I thought I had gone too far then, intruded too much. I stopped filming, because I thought that was what he wanted.

"No," he said gravely. "You must film this. I want the world to hear about Mahmoud and how he lived and how he died. You are Said's friend. I think he trusts you. I think he would want you to know. Only Said knows what happened. He was there. He saw it with his own eyes." I was filming him again by the time he went on.

"Mahmoud was Said's older brother. He loved to make kites. He loved to fly kites, and always with Said. It happened two years ago next week, next Monday – before the occupiers built the wall. I knew there would be trouble that day, we all did. A settler's car was ambushed that morning, further down the valley. We heard that a woman was killed, and her daughter was in hospital with bad injuries to her legs, that maybe she would die too. So we said to all the children in the village: this is a dangerous time, you must stay inside, everyone is safer inside if the soldiers come. But Mahmoud, like his father, was a strong-willed boy, and he became angry with me when I said he could not go out with the sheep and fly his kite. He told me the sheep had to go out, that he would fly his kite whenever and wherever he wanted, that they had put his father in prison, that he would not let them make a prisoner of him in his own home, that he would not hide away like a coward. These were the last words Mahmoud spoke to me.

"And so they went off, the two of them together, with the sheep. Whenever Mahmoud went out, Said would always want to go with him. His mother tried to stop them too. They wouldn't listen.

"Maybe an hour later, we heard a helicopter come flying low over the village. There was some shooting. When it was over we all ran outside. We saw Mahmoud lying at the bottom of the hill, beside the road. Said was with him, Mahmoud's head on his lap. When we got there, his eyes were open, but he was dead. We asked Said how it happened. But he cannot tell us. Since that moment, he has not spoken. God willing, one day he will. God willing." His voice was breaking. He looked away from me, trying to compose himself. I was doing much the same thing. I couldn't bring myself to ask him any more questions. But when he turned to me again, I could see he was ready to tell me more.

"Said sent off his first kite the next day, the day we buried Mahmoud. Do you know why he sends his kites over there? He cannot tell us himself of course, but we think that for Said every kite that lands over there in the settlement is like a seed of friendship. This is why he writes 'Salaam' on each one. We think that he hopes and he believes that one day they'll send the kites back, and everything will be right, that his father will come home from prison, that somehow friendships will grow, all the killing will stop, and peace will come. For Said, his kites are kites of peace. You know what I think? I think, let Said have his dreams. It's all he has. He'll find out soon enough what they're like over there. Many people tell him this. Uncle Gasbag I may be, but I know when a thing must not be spoken. Let him dream, I say, let him dream."

"But what about the girl?" I asked him. "The one with the blue headscarf, the one in the wheelchair. She picked up Said's kite. She waved at him. I saw her. She was trying to be friendly. It's a beginning, surely."

He wasn't having any of it. "I have seen this girl. We all have," he said. "She's alive, isn't she? It is Mahmoud who is dead, is it not? Tell me, what does it cost to wave? They cannot wave away what they did. She is an occupier, isn't she? They are all occupiers. All occupiers are the same."

I spent the evening here in the family house, on my knees on the floor with Said, helping him make his new kite, everyone looking on. He caught my eye from time to time. I think there is so much he wants to tell me that he cannot tell me. I see in his eyes someone who believes completely in his dream, and I know he wants me to believe in it too. I want to, but I'm finding that very hard. I think he can sense my doubt. I hope he can't.

I should have phoned home today, and now it's too late. Anyway, I'm too sad to talk, and it would all be too difficult to explain how things are here over the phone. Tomorrow, I'll talk to them tomorrow. One thing I've decided I have to do. When I film the wall from the other side, that has to be the settlement I go to. I have to go to where Said's sending his kites. I'm going to try to meet up with that girl in the wheelchair, to talk to those kids playing football. I have to see and hear the whole story, to know it as it's lived on both sides. Everything's as silent as the stars up here, and as beautiful as peace. Time to sleep. G'night Jamie. G'night Penny.

———

Hey, Mahmoud? Are you there, Mahmoud? Are you listening? I waved to the girl, Mahmoud, and she waved back too. That's 94 of our kites she's got now. Mahmoud? Mahmoud? You will stay with me, won't you? I don't want to go to sleep. I don't want the nightmare again. I want to stay awake and talk to you. Don't leave me. You know how I hate the dark. I've got so much to tell you.

I flew the kite with Mister Max today. He was hopeless. He was making a real mess of it, and I didn't want him to crash it. So I took it off him in the end, and showed him how to do it. You should've seen me. It went so high. I mean, out of sight... well, almost. You won't want to hear this, but I'm as good at flying kites as you... well, almost. Anyway I'm a whole lot better at it than Mister Max, that's for sure. He's all right on the spool. I just have to nod and he lets out a little bit more. He's a bit slow. The last time I flew a kite with anyone else, it was with you, Mahmoud. It was that day, Mahmoud. Remember? Oh, Mahmoud, I don't want to remember, I don't want to, but I can't stop myself. It's my nightmare again, like a black hole waiting for me and I'm falling. I'm falling into it, Mahmoud! Mahmoud! Help me!

I'm flying the kite, and I'm loving it. You're on the spool, and you're going on and on about how Uncle Gasbag tried to keep us indoors, about how this was our hillside, and how no one could stop us flying our kites, not Uncle Yasser, not the soldiers, not the tanks, not anyone. I'm only half listening to you, because I'm trying to concentrate on the kite. I'm doing well too, diving it as fast as you, so fast I can hear the rush and the roar of it in the wind as it whizzes by over our heads. And I'm laughing, laughing to see it up there, looping and swooping. I'm still laughing when the roaring of the kite becomes a thunder and a throbbing in my ears. I'm so frightened because the ground underneath me is shaking, and I can't understand why, until I see the helicopter coming up over the hilltop behind us, and close, so close, almost touching the top of the kite tree. The sheep are going crazy, Mahmoud.

You're angry, Mahmoud. You're yelling at the helicopter, picking up a stone and throwing it, then another stone and another. The helicopter's right over us, and we're being blown away by it, and I'm losing all control of the kite. It's spiralling crazily away down towards the road and it's crashing into the rocks. You're yelling at me to stay where I am, and then I see you racing down the hill after it. I've got my hands over my ears and I'm crying because I know already that something terrible is going to happen. I see the tank coming round the bend in the road before you do, and I'm screaming at you, Mahmoud, trying to warn you, but you can't hear me.

You're crouching over the kite now, and then you look up and see the tank. I know what you're going to do, and I know that there's nothing I can do to stop you. You're too angry. "Mahmoud! Mahmoud! Don't do it!" But you do it. You run at the tank, shouting and screaming at it, hurling stones at it. When they open fire you still don't stop. You only stop when you fall, and when you fall you're lying still, so still.

The soldiers tell me it's a mistake. They were firing warning shots, they say. They are sorry, they say. One of the soldiers is crying, but I'm not going to cry any more, not in front of them. There's blood. There's so much blood. You are trying to tell me something. Mend the kite, Said. Can you hear me? Mend the kite.

Yes, I can hear you. I'll mend the kite. Then I'll make another and another. I promise. I promise.

I'm still promising when the light goes out of your eyes, Mahmoud. You're looking at me and you're not seeing me.

Friend or Foe

London is under siege during the bombing raids of the
Blitz. The morning that David has dreaded arrives, as he
and his friend Tucky become wartime evacuees, leaving
their homes and everything they know behind…

His mother woke him as usual that morning, shaking his shoulder and then kissing him gently as he rolled over. It was pitch black around him, but then he was used to that by now. For months they had slept down in the cellar on the bunks his father had made the last time he was home on leave.

"Here's your apple, dear," his mother said. "Sit up and have your apple now." And she patted the pillow behind him as he pushed himself up on to his elbows. He felt the saucer come into his hand. His early morning apple was the only thing that had not changed since the war started. Every morning as far back as he could remember his mother had woken him this way – with an apple peeled, cored and quartered lying opened up on a white saucer.

He felt his mother shifting off the bed and watched for the flare of yellow light as she struck the match for the oil lamp. The cellar walls flickered and then settled in the new light, and the boy saw his mother was dressed to go out. She had her coat on and her hat with the brown feather at the back. It was only then that he remembered. His stomach turned over inside him and tears choked at his throat. The morning he had thought would never come, had come. Every night since he'd first heard about it, he prayed it might not happen to him; and the night before, he had prayed he would die in his sleep rather than wake up and have to go.

"You were restless again last night, dear. Did you sleep?" He nodded, not trusting himself to speak. "Come on now. Eat your apple and get dressed. Quick as you can, dear. It's six o'clock by the station, they said. It's a quarter-to now. I left you as long as I could."

Fifteen minutes left. Fifteen minutes and he'd be gone. Thirty minutes and she would be back in this house without him. She was bending over him, shaking his shoulder. "Please, dear. We must hurry. Eat it down, quickly now. Miss Roberts said you'd be having a roll and jam on the train, but you must have something before you go."

"Don't want it, Mum." He handed the saucer back to her. Only moments before he had been savouring that first bite of his apple. They were always crisp, always juicy, like nothing else. But now he felt sick at the sight of it.

"You must, David. You always have your apple. You

know you do."

He had upset her and ate it to make her happy, swallowing it like medicine, trying not to taste it. Each bite reminded him that this was the last apple.

Once out of bed he dressed to keep the cold out. His mother was packing his suitcase and he watched everything going in and wondered where he'd be when he took it all out again.

"They said only one case, so there's only room for one change of clothes. All the things you wanted, they're at the bottom. I'll send on the rest as soon as I know where you'll be." She smoothed down his coat collar and brushed through his hair with her fingers. "You'll do," she said, smiling softly.

"Do I have to, Mum? Do I have to go?" Even as he asked he knew it was useless. Everyone was going from school – no one was staying behind. He was ashamed of himself now. He'd promised himself he'd be brave when he said goodbye. He clung to his mother, pressing his face into her coat, fighting his tears.

She crouched down in front of him, holding him by the shoulders. "You remember what I said, David, when I told you your father had been killed? Do you?" David nodded. "I said you'd have to be the man in the house, remember?" He took the handkerchief she was offering. "You never saw your father crying, did you?"

"No, Mum."

"Men don't cry, see? Try to be a man, David, like your father was, eh?" She chucked him under the chin, and straightened his cap on to the front of his head. "Come on now. We'll be late."

It was still dark up in the street, and a fine drizzle sprayed their faces as they walked away from the house. David looked back over his shoulder as they came to the postbox at the corner and caught a last glimpse of the front steps. He felt his mother's hand on his elbow, and then they were round the corner.

Ahead of them there was a glow of fire in the sky. "South of the river," his mother said. "Battersea, I should say. Poor devils. At least you'll be away from all that, David, away from the bombs, away from the war. At least they won't get you as well." He was surprised by the grim tone in her voice.

"Where will you go, Mum?"

"Wherever they send me. Probably to the coast – Kent or somewhere like that. Somewhere where there's anti-aircraft guns, that's all I know. Don't worry, I'll write."

Their footsteps sounded hollow in the empty street. They had to step off the pavement to pick their way round the edge of a pile of rubble that was still scattered halfway across the street. That was where the Perkins family had lived. They had been bombed out only a week before; they were all killed. Special prayers were said at school assembly for Brian and Garry Perkins, but no one ever mentioned them after that. They were dead, after all.

In the gloom outside Highbury and Islington Underground Station there was already a crowd of people. Miss Evers's voice rang out above the hubbub and the crying. She was calling out names. His mother pulled at his hand and they ran the last few yards.

"Tony Tucker. Tony Tucker." Miss Evers's voice rose to a shriek. "Where's Tucky? Has anyone seen Tucky?"

"He's coming, miss. I saw him."

"And what about David Carey? Is he here yet?"

"Yes, miss. I'm here, miss." David spoke out, pleased at the strength in his voice.

"Here's Tucky, miss. He's just coming."

"Right then." Miss Evers folded her piece of paper. "We're all here, and it's time to go. Say goodbye as quick as ever you can. The train leaves Paddington at half past eight, and we have to be there at least an hour before. So hurry it up now – and don't forget your gas masks."

David felt the case being handed to him. "Goodbye, David. And don't worry. It'll be all right. I'll send a letter as soon as I can. God bless." She kissed him quickly on the cheek and turned away. He watched her until she disappeared at the end of the street. All around him there was crying:

boys he'd never dreamt could cry, weeping openly, and mothers holding on to each other as they walked away. He was glad his mother hadn't cried, and it helped him to see so many of his friends as miserable as he felt himself. He blinked back the tears that had gathered in his eyes and wiped his face before turning towards the station.

The warmth of the Underground came up to meet them as the school trooped down the silent, unmoving escalator. They followed Miss Evers along the tunnels, down the stairways and out on to the platform. Tucky came up alongside David and dropped his suitcase.

"H'lo, Davey."

"H'lo, Tucky." They were old friends and there was nothing more to be said.

They did not have long to wait. There was a distant rumble and then a rush of warm, oily wind that blew their eyes closed as it rushed into the platform. Miss Evers counted them as they pushed and jostled into the carriage, herding them in like sheep, so that every corner of the carriage was filled. The doors clicked and hissed shut, and the train jerked forward, throwing everyone against each other.

David watched the last Highbury and Islington sign as long as he could, craning his neck until the carriage plunged into the darkness of the tunnel and it was gone.

"That's that, then," said Tucky next to him. David

nodded and looked up at the parallel rows of handles that swung from the roof of the carriage, always out of reach. And he remembered his father lifting him up high above everyone, and how he'd hung on to the strap next to his father's looking down on a sea of upturned faces.

Miss Evers was shouting at them again. "Boys, boys. Can you all hear me, boys? Sam, you're not listening. I can see you're not listening. You can't listen and talk at the same time – it's not possible. Now, we've been through all this many times before, but I'll do it just once more to make sure. We're going to… where are we going, Tucky?"

"Devon, miss."

"What station do we have to go to, to get to Devon, Tucky?"

"Don't know, miss."

"Paddington, Tucky. We're going to Paddington Station." Whenever Miss Evers wanted to tell them all something, she always asked Tucky first; and when Tucky didn't know, and he never did know, that was her excuse to tell them herself. She picked on Tucky mercilessly, and David hated her for it.

"And what am I going to give you at Paddington Station, Tucky? Can you remember that, Tucky?"

"No, miss."

"Your placards, Tucky. With your name and address on. Remember? In case you get lost."

"And the string, miss," someone else said. Tucky was already sniffing, his hands screwed into his eyes. Another question from Miss Evers and he would dissolve into floods of tears.

"Well, I'm glad someone was paying attention. Placards and string. You'll be wearing the placards round your neck. Remember now, Tucky?" Tucky nodded into his raincoat sleeve, and Miss Evers left him alone after that.

They had to change trains once and Sam left his case behind on the train. Miss Evers screamed at the guard and the doors hissed open again and she went back in for it. When she came out she screamed at Sam, but Sam braved it out and then grinned sheepishly as soon as her back was turned.

Placards strung round their necks, and two by two, the boys climbed the long stairs up into Paddington Station. David and Tucky were almost last in the crocodile and as far away from Miss Evers as possible.

Up to that moment it had been just his school that was being evacuated, but now David discovered that every other child in London seemed to be at the station. Miss Evers shouted back at them to hold on to the belt of the boy in front and they wound their way like a long snake through the crowds of milling children and screaming teachers, who paused only to blow their whistles. And above it all came the thunder and rhythmic pounding of steam engines, and the rich, exciting smell of the smoke.

David had been on a train once before. Just before the war started he'd been on a school journey to Birchington, but then his mother and father had been on the platform waving him off. He felt the belt in his hand jerk and the crocodile stuttered forward again towards the platform.

Miss Roberts, the headmistress, was waiting for them by the ticket barrier; and so was Miss Hardy. Miss Roberts was in her usual bird's nest hat, and Miss Hardy, as usual, was clucking around her like a worried hen. Miss Evers seemed relieved to see them, and smiled for the first time that morning. Miss Roberts took charge and beckoned everyone closer.

"The train's at least two hours late, boys, so we'll have to wait. Put your cases down and sit on them." It was good to have Miss Roberts there in her hat and bright clothes. There wasn't a boy in the school who didn't like her, and now her smiles and laughter were familiar and comforting in the strangeness and noise of the station.

David spent the two hours chatting to Tucky and looking at everyone else – that was all there was to do. The marches blared out of the loudspeakers, but they were so loud he could hardly make out the tune – and when there was a tune he recognised, a great explosion of steam would ruin it for him. Miss Hardy gave everyone a roll and jam with a mug of warm milk, and Miss Roberts sat heavily on her suitcase and smoked her way through a packet of cigarettes.

It seemed as if the train would never leave, but it did – three hours late. The boys piled into the train, fourteen to a carriage, and the train stood there, hissing gently.

David and Tucky found themselves sitting in Miss Roberts's carriage. They knew it would mean cigarette smoke all the way to Devon, but that was better than Miss Hardy's fussing, and a lot better than Miss Evers's waspish tongue. Miss Roberts collected all their placards and put them in the luggage rack above their heads.

"You won't need those for a bit. I think I know who you all are." Miss Roberts sat down next to Tucky, and the seat sank. "You'll need them again when we get to Devon – if we ever do." She took off her bird's nest hat with a flourish and shook out her red hair, and then settled down to a packet of Senior Service cigarettes and a pile of orange paperbacks.

She was a huge lady, and Tucky wondered if he would ever be able to stop himself from sliding down towards her into the crater she had made in the cushioned seat.

Doors were banging all the way down the train and a group of sailors ran past waving and shouting. More banging, the shrill whistle, the pressure building up in short blasts of steam; and then the train heaved forward, the engine settling into a slow pulling rhythm as they watched the platform slip away.

"We're off," said Tucky.

"On our way, boys," said Miss Roberts. "Say goodbye to London, and good luck. Not for ever, you know. We'll be back."

David stared out of the window and wondered what his mother was doing at that moment and how long it would be before he'd see her again.

The Lonely Sea and the Sky

Illustration by Quentin Blake

The Giant's Necklace

The necklace stretched from one end of the kitchen table to the other, around the sugar bowl at the far end and back again, stopping only a few inches short of the toaster. The discovery on the beach of a length of abandoned fishing line draped with seaweed had first suggested the idea to Cherry; and every day of the holiday since then had been spent in one single-minded pursuit, the creation of a necklace of glistening pink cowrie shells. She had sworn to herself and to everyone else that the necklace would not be complete until it reached the toaster; and when Cherry vowed she would do something, she invariably did it.

Cherry was the youngest in a family of older brothers, four of them, who had teased her relentlessly since the day she was born, eleven years before. She referred to them as "the four mistakes", for it was a family joke that each son had been an attempt to produce a daughter. To their huge delight Cherry reacted passionately to any slight or insult whether intended or not. Their particular targets were her size, which was diminutive compared to theirs, and her dark flashing eyes that could wither with one scornful look, her "zapping" look, they called it. Although the teasing was interminable it was rarely hurtful, nor was it intended to be, for her brothers adored her; and she knew it.

Cherry was poring over her necklace, still in her dressing gown. Breakfast had just been cleared away and she was alone with her mother. She fingered the shells lightly, turning them gently until the entire necklace lay flat with the rounded pink of the shells all uppermost. Then she bent down and breathed on each of them in turn, polishing them carefully with a napkin.

"There's still the sea in them," she said to no one in particular. "You can still smell it, and I washed them and washed them, you know."

"You've only got today, Cherry," said her mother, coming over to the table and putting an arm round her. "Just today, that's all. We're off back home tomorrow morning first thing. Why don't you call it a day, dear? You've been at it every day – you *must* be tired of it by now. There's no need to go on, you know. We all think it's a fine necklace and quite long enough. It's long enough, surely?"

Cherry shook her head slowly. "No," she said. "Only that little bit left to do and then it'll be finished."

"But they'll take hours to collect, dear," her mother said weakly, recognising and at the same time respecting her daughter's persistence.

"Only a few hours," said Cherry, bending over, her brows furrowing critically as she inspected a flaw in one of her shells, "that's all it'll take. D'you know, there are five thousand, three hundred and twenty-five shells in my necklace already? I counted them, so I know."

"Isn't that enough, Cherry?" her mother said desperately.

"No," said Cherry. "I said I'd reach the toaster, and I'm going to reach the toaster."

Her mother turned away to continue the drying-up.

"Well, I can't spend all day on the beach today, Cherry," she said. "If you haven't finished by the time we come away, I'll have to leave you there. We've got to pack up and tidy the house – there'll be no time in the morning."

"I'll be all right," said Cherry, cocking her head on one side to view the necklace from a different angle. "There's never been a necklace like this before, not in all the world. I'm sure there hasn't." And then, "You can leave me there, Mum, and I'll walk back. It's only a mile or so along the cliff path and half a mile back across the fields. I've done it before on my own. It's not far."

There was a thundering on the stairs and a sudden rude invasion of the kitchen. Cherry was surrounded by her four brothers who leant over the table in mock appreciation of her necklace.

"Ooh, pretty."

"Do they come in other colours? I mean, pink's not my colour."

"Who's it for? An elephant?"

"It's for a giant," said Cherry. "It's a giant's necklace, and it's still not big enough."

It was the perfect answer, an answer she knew would send her brothers into fits of laughter. She loved to make them laugh at her and could do it at the drop of a hat. Of course she no more believed in giants than they did, but if it tickled them pink to believe she did, then why not pretend?

She turned on them, fists flailing and chased them back up the stairs, her eyes burning with simulated fury. "Just cos you don't believe in anything 'cept motorbikes and football and all that rubbish, just cos you're great big, fat, ignorant pigs..." She hurled insults up the stairs, and the worse the insult the more they loved it.

Boat Cove just below Zennor Head was the beach they had found and occupied. Every year for as long as Cherry could remember they had rented the same granite cottage, set back in the fields below the Eagle's Nest, and every year they came to the same beach because no one else did. In two weeks not another soul had ventured down the winding track through the bracken from the coastal path. It was a long climb down and a very much longer one up.

The beach itself was almost hidden from the path that ran along the cliff top a hundred feet above. It was private and perfect and theirs. The boys swam in amongst the rocks, diving and snorkelling for hours on end. Her mother and father would sit side by side on stripey deck chairs. She would read endlessly and he would close his eyes against the sun and dream for hours on end.

Cherry moved away from them and clambered over the rocks to a narrow strip of sand in the cove beyond the rocks, and here it was that she mined for the cowrie shells. In the gritty sand under the cliff face she had found a particularly rich deposit. She was looking for pink cowrie shells of a uniform length, colour and shape – that was what took the time. Occasionally the boys would swim around the rocks and in to her little beach, emerging from the sea all goggled and flippered to mock her. But as she paid them little attention they soon tired and went away again. She knew time was running short. This was her very last chance to find enough shells to complete the giant's necklace, and it had to be done.

The sea was calmer that day than she had ever seen it. The heat beat down from a windless, cloudless sky; even the gulls and kittiwakes seemed to be silenced by the sun. Cherry searched on, stopping only for a picnic lunch of pasties and tomatoes with the family before returning at once to her shells.

In the end the heat proved too much for her mother and father, who left the beach earlier than usual in mid-afternoon to begin to tidy up the cottage. The boys soon followed because they had tired of finding miniature crabs and seaweed instead of the sunken wrecks and treasure they had been seeking. So, by teatime Cherry was left on her own on the beach with strict instructions to keep her hat on, not to bathe alone and to be back well before dark. She had calculated she needed one hundred and fifty more cowrie shells and so far she had only found eighty. She would be back, she insisted, when she had finished collecting enough shells and not before.

Had she not been so immersed in her search, sifting the shells through her fingers, she would have noticed the dark grey bank of cloud rolling in from the Atlantic. She would have noticed the white horses gathering out at sea and the tide moving remorselessly in to cover the rocks between her and Boat Cove. When the clouds cut off the warmth from the sun as evening came on and the sea turned grey, she shivered with cold and put on her sweater and jeans. She did look up then and saw the angry sea, but she saw no threat in that and did not look back over her shoulder to Boat Cove. She was aware that time was running out so she went down on her knees again and dug feverishly in the sand. She had to collect thirty more shells.

It was the baleful sound of the foghorn somewhere out

at sea beyond Gurnard's Head that at last forced Cherry to take some account of the incoming tide. She looked for the rocks she would have to clamber over to reach Boat Cove again and the winding track that would take her up to the cliff path and safety, but they were gone. Where they should have been, the sea was already driving in against the cliff face. She was cut off. In a confusion of wonder and fear she looked out to sea at the heaving ocean that moved in towards her, seeing it now as a writhing grey monster breathing its fury on the rocks with every pounding wave.

Still Cherry did not forget her shells, but wrapping them inside her towel she tucked them into her sweater and waded out through the surf towards the rocks. If she timed it right, she reasoned, she could scramble back over them and into the Cove as the surf retreated. She reached the first of the rocks without too much difficulty; the sea here seemed to be protected from the force of the ocean by the rocks further out. Holding fast to the first rock she came to and with the sea up around her waist, she waited for the next incoming wave to break and retreat. The wave was unexpectedly impotent and fell limply on the rocks around her. She knew her moment had come and took it. She was not to know that piling up far out at sea was the first of the giant storm waves that had gathered several hundred miles out in the Atlantic, bringing with it all the momentum and violence of the deep ocean.

The rocks were slippery underfoot and more than once Cherry slipped down into seething white rock pools where she had played so often when the tide was out. But she struggled on until, finally, she had climbed high enough to be able to see the thin strip of sand that was all that was left of Boat Cove. It was only a few yards away, so close. Until now she had been crying involuntarily; but now, as she recognised the little path up through the bracken, her heart was lifted with hope and anticipation. She knew that the worst was over, that if the sea would only hold back she would reach the sanctuary of the Cove.

She turned and looked behind her to see how far away the next wave was, just to reassure herself that she had enough time. But the great surge of green water was on her before she could register either disappointment or fear. She was hurled back against the rock below her and covered at once by the sea.

She was conscious as she went down that she was drowning, but she still clutched her shells against her chest and hoped she had enough of them at last to finish the giant's necklace. Those were her last thoughts before the sea took her away.

Cherry lay on her side where the tide had lifted her and coughed until her lungs were clear. She woke as the sea came in once again and frothed around her legs. She rolled on her back, feeling the salt spray on her face and saw that it was night. The sky above her was dashed with stars and the moon rode through the clouds.

She scrambled to her feet, one hand still holding her precious shells close to her. Instinctively she backed away from the sea and looked around her. With growing dismay she saw that she had been thrown back on the wrong side of the rocks, that she was not in Boat Cove. The tide had left only a few feet of sand and rock between her and the cliff face. There was no way back through the sea to safety.

She turned round to face the cliff that she realised now would be her last hope, for she remembered that this little beach vanished completely at high tide. If she stayed where she was she would surely be swept away again and this time she might not be so fortunate. But the cold seemed to have calmed her and she reasoned more deliberately now, wondering why she had not tried climbing the cliff before. She had hurried into her first attempt at escape and it had very nearly cost her her life. She would wait this time until the sea forced her up the cliff. Perhaps the tide would not come in that far. Perhaps they would be looking for her by now. It was dark. Surely they would be searching. Surely they must find her soon. After all, they knew where she was. *Yes*, she thought, *best just to wait and hope*.

She settled down on a ledge of rock that was the first step up on to the cliff face, drew her knees up to her chin to keep out the chill, and waited. She watched as the sea crept ever closer, each wave lashing her with spray and eating away gradually at the beach. She closed her eyes and prayed, hoping against hope that when she opened them the sea would be retreating. But her prayers went unanswered and the sea came in to cover the beach. Once or twice she thought she heard voices above her on the cliff path, but when she called out no one came. She continued to shout for help every few minutes, forgetting it was futile against the continuous roar and hiss of the waves. A pair of raucous white gulls flew down from the cliffs to investigate her and she called to them for help, but they did not seem to understand and wheeled away into the night.

Cherry stayed sitting on her rock until the waves threatened to dislodge her and then reluctantly she began her climb. She would go as far as she needed to and no further. She had scanned the first few feet above for footholds and it did look quite a simple climb to begin with, and so it proved. But her hands were numbed with cold and her legs began to tremble with the strain almost at once. She could see that the ledge she had now reached was the last deep one visible on the cliff face. The shells in her sweater were restricting her freedom of movement so she decided she would leave them there. Wrapped tight in the towel they would be quite safe. She took the soaking bundle out of her sweater and placed it carefully against the rock face on the ledge beside her, pushing it in as far as it would go. "I'll be back for you," she said, and reached up for the next lip of rock. Just below her the sea crashed against the cliff as if it wanted to suck her from the rock face and claim her once again. Cherry determined not to look down but to concentrate on the climb.

At first, she imagined that the glow above her was from a torch. She shouted and screamed until she was weak from the effort of it. But although no answering call came from the night, the light remained pale and beckoning, wider than that of a torch. With renewed hope Cherry found enough strength to inch her way up the cliff, until she reached the entrance to a narrow cave. It was filled with a flickering yellow light like that of a candle shaken by the wind. She hauled herself up into the mouth of the cave and sat down exhausted, looking back down at the furious sea frothing beneath her. She laughed aloud in triumph. She was safe! She had defied the sea and won! Her one regret was that she had had to leave her cowrie shells behind. She would fetch them tomorrow after the tide had gone down again.

For the first time now she began to think of her family and how worried they would be, but the thought of walking in through the front door all dripping and dramatic made her almost choke with excitement.

As she reached forward to brush a sharp stone from the

sole of her foot, Cherry noticed that the narrow entrance to the cave was half sealed in. She ran her fingers over the stones and cement to make sure, for the light was poor. It was at that moment that she recognised exactly where she was. She recalled now the giant fledgling cuckoo one of her brothers had spotted being fed by a tiny rock pipit earlier in the holidays, how they had quarrelled over the binoculars and how, when she had finally usurped them and made her escape across the rocks, she had found the cuckoo perched at the entrance to a narrow cave some way up the cliff face from the beach.

She had asked about the man-made walling, and her father had told her of the old tin mine whose lodes and adits crosscrossed the entire coastal area around Zennor. This one, he said, might have been the mine they called Wheal North Grylls, and he thought the adit must have been walled up to prevent the seas from entering the mine in a storm. It was said there had been an accident in the mine only a few years after it was opened over a hundred years before, and that the mine had had to close soon after when the mine owners ran out of money to make the necessary repairs. The entire story came back to her now, and she wondered where the cuckoo was and whether the rock pipit had died with the effort of keeping the fledgling alive. *Tin mines*, she thought, *lead to the surface, and the way home*. That thought and her natural inquisitiveness about the source of light persuaded her to her feet and into the tunnel.

The adit became narrower and lower as she crept forward, so that she had to go down on her hands and knees, sometimes flat on her stomach. Although she was out of the wind now, it seemed colder. She felt she was moving downwards for a minute or two, for the blood was coming to her head and her weight was heavy on her hands. Then, quite suddenly, she found the ground levelling out and saw a large tunnel ahead of her. There was no doubt as to which way she should turn, for one way the tunnel was black, and the other way was lighted with candles that lined the lode wall as far as she could see. She called out, "Anyone there? Anyone there?" She paused to listen for the reply, but all she could hear now was the muffled roar of the sea and the continuous echoing of dripping water.

The tunnel widened now and she found she could walk upright again; but her feet hurt against the stone and so she moved slowly, feeling her way gently with each foot. She had gone only a short distance when she heard the tapping for the first time, distinct and rhythmic, a sound that was instantly recognisable as hammering. It became sharper and noticeably more metallic as she moved up the tunnel. She could hear the distant murmur of voices and the sound of falling stone. Even before she came out of the tunnel and into the vast cave she knew she had happened upon a working mine.

The cave was dark in all but one corner and here she could see two men bending to their work, their backs towards her. One of them was inspecting the rock face closely whilst the other swung his hammer with controlled power, pausing only to spit on his hands from time to time. They wore round hats with turned-up brims that served also as candlesticks, for a lighted candle was fixed to each, the light dancing with the shadows along the cave walls as they worked.

Cherry watched for some moments until she made up her mind what to do. She longed to rush up to them and tell of her escape and to ask them to take her to the surface, but a certain shyness overcame her and she held back. Her chance to interrupt came when they sat down against the rock face and opened their canteens. She was in the shadows and they still could not see her.

"Tea looks cold again," one of them said gruffly. "'Tis always cold. I'm sure she makes it wi' cold water."

"Oh, stop your moaning, Father," said the other, a younger voice, Cherry felt. "She does her best. She's five little ones to look after and precious little to do it on. She does her best. You mustn't keep on at her so. It upsets her. She does her best."

"So she does, lad, so she does. And so for that matter

do I, but that don't stop her moaning at me and it'll not stop me moaning at her. If we didn't moan at each other, lad, we'd have precious little else to talk about, and that's a fact. She expects it of me, lad, and I expects it of her."

"Excuse me," Cherry said tentatively. She felt she had eavesdropped for long enough. She approached them slowly. "Excuse me, but I've got a bit lost. I climbed the cliff, you see, cos I was cut off from the Cove. I was trying to get back, but I couldn't and I saw this light and so I climbed up. I want to get home and I wondered if you could help me get to the top?"

"Top?" said the older one, peering into the dark. "Come closer, lad, where we can see you."

"She's not a lad, Father. Are you blind? Can you not see 'tis a filly? 'Tis a young filly, all wet through from the sea. Come," the young man said, standing up and beckoning Cherry in. "Don't be afeared, little girl, we shan't harm you. Come on, you can have some of my tea if you like."

They spoke their words in a manner Cherry had never heard before. It was not the usual Cornish burr, but heavier and rougher in tone, more old-fashioned somehow. There were so many questions in her mind.

"But I thought the mine was closed a hundred years ago," she said nervously. "That's what I was told, anyway."

"Well, you was told wrong," said the old man, whom Cherry could see more clearly now under his candle. His eyes were white and set far back in his head, unnaturally so, she thought, and his lips and mouth seemed a vivid red in the candlelight.

"Closed, closed indeed, does it look closed to you? D'you think we're digging for worms? Over four thousand tons of tin last year and nine thousand of copper ore, and you ask is the mine closed? Over twenty fathoms below the sea this mine goes. We'll dig right out under the ocean, halfway to 'Merica afore we close down this mine."

He spoke passionately now, almost angrily, so that Cherry felt she had offended him.

"Hush, Father," said the young man, taking off his jacket and wrapping it round Cherry's shoulders. "She doesn't want to hear all about that. She's cold and wet. Can't you see? Now let's make a little fire to warm her through. She's shivered right through to her bones. You can see she is."

"They all are," said the old tinner, pulling himself to his feet. "They all are." And he shuffled past her into the dark. "I'll fetch the wood," he muttered, and then added, "for all the good it'll do."

"What does he mean?" Cherry asked the young man, for whom she felt an instant liking. "What does he mean by that?"

"Oh, pay him no heed, little girl," he said. "He's an old man now and tired of the mine. We're both tired of it, but we're proud of it see, and we've nowhere else to go, nothing else to do."

He had a kind voice that was reassuring to Cherry. He seemed somehow to know the questions she wanted to ask, for he answered them now without her ever asking.

"Sit down by me while you listen, girl," he said. "Father will make a fire to warm you and I shall tell you how we come to be here. You won't be afeared now, will you?"

Cherry looked up into his face which was younger than she had expected from his voice; but like his father's, the eyes seemed sad and deep set, yet they smiled at her gently and she smiled back.

"That's my girl. It was a new mine this, promising, everyone said. The best tin in Cornwall and that means the best tin in the world. 1865 it started up and they were looking for tinners, and so Father found a cottage down by Treveal and came to work here. I was already fourteen, so I joined him down the mine. We prospered and the mine prospered, to start with. Mother and the little children had full bellies and there was talk of sinking a fresh shaft. Times were good and promised to be better."

Cherry sat transfixed as the story of the disaster unfolded. She heard how they had been trapped by a fall of rock, about how they had worked to pull them away, but behind every rock was another rock and another rock. She heard how they had never even heard any sound of rescue. They had died, he said, in two days or so because the air was bad and because there was so little of it.

"Father has never accepted it; he still thinks he's alive, that he goes home to Mother and the little children each evening. But he's dead, just like me. I can't tell him though, for he'd not understand and it would break his heart if he ever knew."

"So you aren't real. I'm just imagining all this. You're just a dream."

"No dream, my girl," said the young man, laughing out loud. "No more'n we're imagining you. We're real right enough, but we're dead and have been for a hundred years and more. Ghosts, spirits, that's what living folk call us. Come to think of it, that's what I called us when I was alive."

Cherry was on her feet suddenly and backing away.

"No need to be afeared, little girl," said the young man, holding out his hand towards her. "We won't harm you. No one can harm you, not now. Look, he's started the fire already. Come over and warm yourself. Come, it'll be all right, girl. We'll look after you. We'll help you."

"But I want to go home," Cherry said, feeling the panic rising to her voice and trying to control it. "I know you're kind, but I want to go home. My mother will be worried about me. They'll be out looking for me. Your light saved my life and I want to thank you. But I must go else they'll worry themselves sick, I know they will."

"You going back home?" the young man asked, and then he nodded. "I s'pose you'll want to see your family again."

"Course I am," said Cherry, perplexed by the question. "Course I do."

"'Tis a pity," he said sadly. "Everyone passes through and no one stays. They all want to go home, but then so do I. You'll want me to guide you to the surface, I s'pose."

"I'm not the first then?" Cherry said. "There's been others climb up into the mine to escape from the sea? You've saved lots of people."

"A few," said the tinner, nodding. "A few."

"You're a kind person," Cherry said, warming to the sadness in the young man's voice. "I never thought ghosts would be kind."

"We're just people, people who've passed on," replied the young man, taking her elbow and leading her towards the fire. "There's nice people and there's nasty people. It's the same if you're alive or if you're dead. You're a nice person, I can tell that, even though I haven't known you for long. I'm sad because I should like to be alive again with my friends and go rabbiting or blackberrying up by the chapel near Treveal like I used to. The sun always seemed to be shining then. After it happened I used to go up to the surface and move amongst the people in the village.

I went often to see my family, but if I spoke to them they never seemed to hear me, and of course they can't see you. You can see them, but they can't see you. That's the worst of it. So I don't go up much now, just to collect wood for the fire and a bit of food now and then. I stay down here with Father in the mine and we work away day after day. From time to time someone like you comes up the tunnel from the sea and lightens our darkness. I shall be sad when you go."

The old man was hunched over the fire rubbing his hands and holding them out over the heat.

"Not often we have a fire," he said, his voice more spritely now. "Only on special occasions. Birthdays, of course, we always have a fire on birthdays back at the cottage. Martha's next. You don't know her; she's my only daughter – she'll be eight on September 10th. She's been poorly, you know – her lungs, that's what the doctor said." He sighed deeply. "'Tis dreadful damp in the cottage. 'Tis well nigh impossible to keep it out." There was a tremor in the old man's voice that betrayed his emotion. He looked up at Cherry and she could see the tears in his eyes. "She looks a bit like you, my dear, raven-haired and as pretty as a picture; but not so tall, not so tall. Come closer, my dear, you'll be warmer that way."

Cherry sat with them by the fire till it died away to nothing. She longed to go, to get home amongst the living, but the old man talked on of his family and their little one-roomed cottage with a ladder to the bedroom where they all huddled together for warmth, of his friends that used to meet in the Tinners' Arms every evening. There were tales of wrecking and smuggling, and all the while the young man sat silent, until there was a lull in the story.

"Father," he said. "I think our little friend would like to go home now. Shall I take her up as I usually do?" The old man nodded and waved his hand in dismissal.

"Come back and see us sometime, if you've a mind to," he said, and then put his face in his hands.

"Goodbye," said Cherry. "Thank you for the fire and for helping me. I won't forget you." But the old man never replied.

The journey through the mine was long and difficult. She held fast to the young tinner's waist as they walked silently through the dark tunnels, stopping every now and then to climb a ladder to the lode above until finally they could look up the shaft above them and see the daylight.

"It's dawn," said the young man, looking up.

"I'll be back in time for breakfast," said Cherry, setting her foot on the ladder.

"You'll remember me?" the young tinner asked, and Cherry nodded, unable to speak through her tears. She felt a strange affinity with him and his father. "And if you should ever need me, come back again. You may need me and I shall be here. I go nowhere else."

"Thank you," said Cherry. "I won't forget. I doubt anyone is going to believe me when I tell them about you. No one believes in ghosts, not up there."

"I doubt it too. Be happy, little friend," he said. And he was gone, back into the tunnel. Cherry waited until the light from the candle in his hat had vanished and then turned eagerly to the ladder and began to climb up towards the light.

She found herself in a place she knew well, high on the moor by Zennor Quoit. She stood by the ruined mine workings and looked down at the sleeping village shrouded in mist, and the calm blue sea beyond. The storm had passed and there was scarcely a breath of wind even on the moor. It was only ten minutes' walk down through the bracken, across the road by the Eagle's Nest and down the farm track to the cottage where her family would be waiting. She began to run, but the clothes were still heavy and wet and she was soon reduced to a fast walk. All the while she was determining where she would begin her story, wondering how much they would believe. At the top of the lane she stopped to consider how best to make her entrance. Should she ring the bell and be found standing there, or should she just walk in and surprise them there at breakfast? She longed to see the joy on their faces, to feel the warmth of their arms round her and to bask once again in their affection.

She saw as she came round the corner by the cottage that there was a long blue Land Rover parked in the lane, bristling with aerials. "*Coastguard,*" she read on the side. As she came down the steps she noticed that the back door of the cottage was open and she could hear voices inside. She stole in on tiptoe. The kitchen was full of uniformed men drinking tea, and around the table sat her family, dejection and despair etched on every face. They hadn't seen her yet. One of the uniformed men had put down his cup and was speaking. His voice was low and hushed.

"You're sure the towel is hers, no doubts about it?"

Cherry's mother shook her head.

"It's her towel," she said quietly, "and they are her shells. She must have put them up there, must have been the last thing she did."

Cherry saw her shells spread out on the open towel and stifled a shout of joy.

"We have to say," he went on. "We have to say then, most regrettably, that the chances of finding your daughter alive now are very slim. It seems she must have tried to climb the cliff to escape the heavy seas and fallen in. We've scoured the cliff top for miles in both directions and covered the entire beach, and there's no sign of her. She must have been washed out to sea. We must conclude that she is missing. We have to presume that she is drowned."

Cherry could listen no longer, but burst into the room shouting.

"I'm home, I'm home. Look at me, I'm not drowned at all. I'm here! I'm home!"

The tears were running down her face.

But no one in the room even turned to look in her direction. Her brothers cried openly, one of them clutching the giant's necklace.

"But it's me," she shouted again. "Me, can't you see? It's me and I've come back. I'm all right. Look at me."

But no one did, and no one heard.

The giant's necklace lay spread out on the table.

"So she'll never finish it after all," said her mother softly. "Poor Cherry. Poor dear Cherry."

And in that one moment Cherry knew and understood that she was right, that she would never finish her necklace, that she belonged no longer with the living, but had passed on beyond.

This Morning I Met a Whale

This morning I met a whale. It was just after five o'clock and I was down by the river. Sometimes, when my alarm clock works, and when I feel like it, I get up early, because I like to go bird-watching, because bird-watching is my favourite hobby. I usually go just before first light. Mum doesn't mind, just so long as I don't wake her up, just so long as I'm back for breakfast.

It's the best time. You get to hear the dawn chorus. You get to see the sunrise and the whole world waking up around you. That's when the birds come flying down to the river to feed, and I can watch them landing in the water. I love that.

If you're already there when they come, they hardly notice you, and then you don't bother them. Hardly anyone else is down by the river at five o'clock, sometimes no one at all, just the birds and me. The rest of London is asleep. Well, mostly, anyway.

From our flat in Battersea it takes about five minutes to walk down to the river. The first bird I saw this morning was a heron. I love herons because they stand so still in the shallows. They're looking for fish, waiting to strike. When they strike they do it so fast, it's like lightning, and when they catch something they look so surprised and so pleased with themselves, as if they've never done it before. When they walk they will walk in slow motion. When they take off and fly they look prehistoric, like pterodactyls almost. Herons are my best. But soon enough they all came, all the other birds, the moorhens and coots, the crested grebes and the swans, the cormorants and the ducks. This morning I saw an egret too, perched on a buoy out in the river, and you don't see many of those. They're quite like herons, only much smaller, and white, snow-white. He was so beautiful. I couldn't take my eyes off him.

I was watching him through my binoculars, and he was looking right back at me. It was like he was asking me, "Hey you, what are you doing here? This is my river, don't you know?" Suddenly, without any warning, he lifted off. Then they all lifted off, all the birds on the shore, all the birds in the river. It was really strange. It was just as if I'd fired a gun or something, but I hadn't. I looked around. There wasn't a single bird anywhere. They'd all disappeared. For a while the river was completely still and empty and silent, like it was holding its breath almost, waiting for something that was about to happen. I was doing the same.

Then I spotted something slicing slowly through the water towards me. It was a fin. *Shark!* I thought. *Shark!* And a warm shiver of fear crept up my back. Then I saw the head and knew at once it couldn't be a shark. It was more like a dolphin, but it wasn't. It wasn't quite the right shape. It was too big and too long to be a dolphin. It was big enough to be a whale, a real whale. Now I knew what it was. With a face like that I knew at once that it had to be a bottle-nosed whale. It's the only whale that's got a face like a dolphin. (I know quite a lot about whales because my uncle sent me a whale poster he'd got out of a newspaper, and I've had it pinned up in my bedroom over my bed ever since. So that's why I can recognise just about all the whales in the world, narwhals, belugas, sperm whales, pilot whales, minkies, bottle-nose whales, the lot.)

To begin with I just stood there and stared. I thought I was still dreaming. I couldn't take it in. I couldn't believe my eyes. I mean, a whale in the Thames, a whale in Battersea! He was close to the shore now, in shallower water, and still coming towards me. I could see almost all of him, from his head to his tail. But after a bit, I could see he wasn't really swimming any more, he was just lying there in the shallows, puffing and blowing a bit from time to time. *He must be resting*, I thought, *tired out after a long journey perhaps*. And then I noticed he was watching me as hard as I was watching him, almost like he was trying to stare me out, except I could tell from the gentleness in his eye that he wasn't being unfriendly towards me. He was interested in me, that's all, as interested as I was in him.

That's when I knew – don't ask me how, I just knew – that he wanted me to come closer to him. I climbed the wall and ran along the shore. The tide was already going out fast. I could see at once that he was in great danger. If he stayed where he was, he'd soon be stranded. I was walking slowly, so as not to alarm him. Then I crouched down as close as I could get to him, the water lapping all around me. His great domed head was only just out of my reach. We were practically face to face, eye to eye. He had eyes that seemed to be able to look right into me. He was seeing everything I was thinking.

I was sure he was expecting me to say something. So I did.

"What are you doing here?" I asked him. "You're a bottle-nose whale, aren't you? You shouldn't be here at all. You don't belong in the Thames. On my whale poster it says you live in the North Atlantic somewhere. So you should be up there, near Iceland, near Scotland maybe, but not down here. I've seen bottle-nose whales on the telly too, on *Planet Earth*, I think it was. There were lots of you all together. Or maybe it was pilot whales, I can't remember. But anyway, you always go around in schools, don't you, in huge family groups. I know you do. So how come you're all alone? Where's the rest of you? But maybe you're not all alone. Maybe some of your family came with you, and you got yourself a bit lost. Is that it?"

He kept staring back at me out of his big wide eye. I thought the best thing I could do was to just keep talking. I couldn't think what else to do. For a moment or two I didn't know what else to say, and anyway I suddenly felt a bit stupid talking to him. I mean, what if someone was watching me? Luckily, though, there was no one about. So instead, I looked upriver, back towards Battersea Bridge, to see if any of his family might have come with him, but everywhere the river was empty and glassy and still. There was nothing there, nothing that broke the surface anyway. He was alone. He'd come alone.

And that was when it happened. The whale spoke! I'm telling you the truth, honest. The whale spoke to me. His voice was like an echoing whisper inside my head, like a talking thought. But it was him talking. It really was, I promise you. "No," he said. "My family's not with me. I'm all on my own. They came some of the way with me, and they're waiting for me back out at sea. And you're right. We usually stay close to our families – it's safer that way. But I had to do this bit alone. Grandfather said it would be best. Grandfather would have come himself, but he couldn't. So I've come instead of him. Everyone said it was far too dangerous, that there was no point, that it's too late anyway, that people won't listen, that they just won't learn, no matter what. But Grandfather knew differently. He always said I should go, that time was running out, but there was still hope. I was young enough and strong enough to make the journey, he said. One of us had to come and tell you. So I came. There are some things that are so important that you just have to do them, whatever anyone says, however dangerous it might be. I believe that. And besides, I promised Grandfather before he died. I promised him I'd come and find you. And I always keep my promises. Do you keep your promises?"

I could just about manage a nod, but that was all. I tried, but I couldn't speak a word. I thought maybe I was going mad, seeing things that weren't there, hearing voices that weren't real, and suddenly that really terrified me. That was why I backed away from him. I was just about ready to run off when he spoke again.

"It's all right," he said. "Don't be frightened. I want you to stay. I want you to listen to me. I've come a very long way to talk to you, and I haven't got long."

His tail thrashed suddenly, showering me with water, and that made me laugh. But then I could see it was serious. He was rolling from one side to the other, rocking himself violently. Now I saw what it was that he was struggling to do. He was trying to back himself out into deeper water, struggling to keep himself afloat. I wanted to help him, but I didn't know how. All I could do was stand there and watch from the shore. It took him a while before he was out into deeper water and able to swim free again. He was blowing hard. I could tell he'd given himself a terrible fright. He swam off into the middle of the river, and then just disappeared completely under the water.

I stood there for ages and ages, looking for him up and down the river – he could have gone anywhere. I was longing for him to surface, longing to see him again, worried that he'd never dare risk it again. But he did, though when he came back towards me this time he kept his distance. Only his head was showing now, and just occasionally his fin. "I've got to watch it," he said. "The tide is going out all the time. Grandfather warned me about it, they all warned me. 'Stay clear of the shore,' they told me. 'Once you're beached, you're as good as dead.' We can breathe all right out of the water, that's not the problem. But we need water to float in. We can't survive long if we get stranded. We're big, you see, too heavy for our own good. We need water around us to survive. If we're not afloat we soon crush ourselves to death. And I don't want that to happen, do I?"

Maybe I got used him speaking to me like this, I don't know. Or maybe I just wanted to hear more. Either way, I just didn't feel at all scared any more. I found myself walking back along the shore to be closer to him, and crouching down again to talk to him. I had things I needed to ask him.

"But I still don't really understand," I said. "You said you'd come to talk to me, didn't you? That means you didn't get lost at all, did you?"

"No, I didn't get lost," he told me. "Whales don't get lost, well not that often anyway. We tell each other where we are all the time, what's going on all around the world. What we see we share. So each and every one of us has a kind of map of the oceans, all the mountains and valleys under the sea, all the rivers and creeks, the coast of every continent, and every island, every rock – it's inside our heads. We grow up learning it. That's why we don't get lost." He paused for a while, puffing hard through his blowhole. Talking was exhausting for him, I could see that.

"But we do get tired," he went on, "and we get old too, and we get sick, just like people do. We've a lot more in common with people than you know. We've got this earth in common for a start – and that's why I've come all this way to see you. We don't just share it with whales, but with every living thing. With people too. I've come to help you to save yourselves before it's too late, because if you save yourselves, then you'll be saving us too. It's like Grandfather said: we can't survive without you and you can't survive without us."

I didn't have a clue what he was on about, but I didn't dare say so. But I felt his eye searching out my thoughts. "You don't really know what I'm talking about, do you?" I shook my head. "Then I think the best thing I can do is to tell you about Grandfather, because it all began with

Grandfather. When I was little, Grandfather was always going off on his travels, voyages of discovery, he called them. All over the world he went. We hardly ever saw him. Sometimes he was away for so long we all thought he was never coming back, and he wasn't all that good about keeping in touch either. He was a sort of adventurer, my grandfather, an explorer. He liked to go to places where no whale had ever been before.

"Then one day – it was some time ago now, when I was quite little – he came back from his travels and told us an amazing story. Ever since I first heard that story, I dreamed of going where Grandfather had gone, of seeing what he had seen. Grandfather had gone off to explore an unknown river, to follow it inland as far as he could go. No other whale had ever before dared to go there, as far as anyone knew anyway. All he knew of this river was that a couple of narwhals had been beached there in the mouth of the river a long time ago. They never made it back out to sea. The warning had gone out all over the oceans, and that was why whales had avoided the river ever since.

"It took a while for Grandfather to find it, but when he did he just kept on swimming. On and on he swam right into the middle of the biggest city he'd ever seen. It was teeming with life. Everywhere he looked there were great cranes leaning out over the river, and towering wharfs and busy docks. Everywhere there were boats and barges. He saw cars and trains and great red buses. And at night the lights were so bright that the whole sky was bright with them. It was a magical city, a place of bridges and towers and spires. And everywhere there were people, crowds of them, more than he'd ever seen before, more than he'd ever imagined there could be. He wanted to stay longer, to explore further upstream, to discover more. It was a wonderful place, but Grandfather knew it was dangerous too. The further upriver he swam, the shallower the waters around him were becoming. There were boats and barges everywhere, and he knew that if he wasn't very careful any one of them could run him down, and be the death of him. When a propeller took a nick out of his fin, he decided it was time to leave. And besides, he was weak with hunger by this time. He knew he couldn't go any further.

"So he turned around and tried to swim back the way he'd come, back out to sea. But that was when he found that the tide was going down fast. He was having to keep to the deep channels, but so were all the boats and barges of course. There was danger all around him. He was so busy looking out for boats, that he didn't notice how shallow the water was getting all around him. Grandfather knew, as all whales do, just how easy it is to get yourself stranded. He always said it was his own fault that he got stranded. He lost concentration. But Grandfather got lucky. Some children saw him floundering there in the shallows, and came running down to the river to help him. They helped him back into the water, and then stayed with him till they were sure he was going to be all right. They saved his life, those children, and he never forgot it. 'When you get there, find a child,' he told me, 'because children are kind. They'll help you, they'll listen, they'll believe you.' So you see, it was only because of those children that Grandfather managed to find his way back out to the open sea again, and come back to us and tell us his story."

That was when I noticed that all the birds were back again, the egret too on his buoy out in the river. They had gathered nearby. There were pigeons and blackbirds perching on the trees behind me. On the shore not far away from me a beady-eyed heron stood stock still, and there was a family of ducks bobbing about on the river, a couple of cormorants amongst them, all looking at the whale but none of them too close. And like me, they were listening. Even the trees seemed to be listening.

The whale spoke again. "Grandfather told me exactly how to get here, just how many days south I had to swim. He said I had to look out for the fishing boats and their nets, not to hug the coastline, because that was where there were always more boats about. He warned me about the currents and the tides, told me where the deep channels were in the river, and not to show myself till I had to. I mustn't stay too long. I mustn't swim too far upriver. I mustn't go any further than I had to. 'You'll want to,' he told me, 'just like I did. When you find a child that'll be far enough. And when you find him, tell him all I've told you, what we whales all know and people refuse to understand. Tell him it's our last chance and their last chance. And you must make sure it's a child you tell. The old ones are greedy. They have hard hearts and closed minds, or they would not have done what they have done. They're too old to listen, too old to change. The young ones will listen and understand. Just like they saved me, they can save the world. If they know, they will want to put it right – I know they will. They just need telling. All you have to do is tell them.' That's what Grandfather told me. So that's why I have found you, and that's why I have come."

That was when I saw he was drifting closer and closer to the shore again. I was just about to warn him when he must have realised the danger himself, because suddenly his tail began to thrash wildly in the shallows. The birds took off in a great flurry of panic. The whale didn't stop flailing around till he'd found his way back out into deeper waters, where he dived down and vanished altogether. This time I wasn't really worried. I knew in my heart that he would come back, that he had much more to tell me. All the same, he was gone a long while before he appeared again, and I was so pleased to see him when at last he did.

It was the strangest thing, but when he began speaking

to me again this time, I found I wasn't just hearing his words and understanding them. It was as if I could see in my mind everything he was telling me. I was seeing it all happen right there in front of my eyes. He wasn't just telling me. He was taking me round the world, round his world and showing me.

He showed me the bottom of the sea, where a coral reef lay dying and littered with rubbish. I saw a sperm whale being winched bleeding out of the sea, a leatherback turtle caught up in vast fishing nets, along with sharks and dolphins. There was an albatross too, hanging there limp and lifeless.

I saw the ice-cliffs in the Arctic falling away into the sea, and a polar bear roaming the ice, thin and hungry.

He showed me skies so full of smoke that day had become night, and below them the forests burning. An orang-utan was running for her life along a beach, clutching her infant, the hunters coming after her. I watched as they shot her down, and wrenched the screaming baby out of her arms. And then he showed me people, thousands upon thousands of them in a tented city by the sea, and a skeletal child lying alone and abandoned on the sand. She wasn't crying, because she was dead.

"Grandfather said all this killing has to stop. You are killing the sea we live in! You are killing the air we breathe. You are killing the world. Tell a child, Grandfather said.

Only the children will put it right. That's why I came. That's why I found you. Will you put it right?"

"But how can I?" I cried.

"Tell them why I came. Tell them what I said. Tell them they have to change the way they live. And don't just tell them. Show them. Will you do that?"

"Yes," I cried. "I promise!"

"But do you keep your promises?" he asked.

"I'll keep this one," I told him.

"That's all I needed to hear," he said. "Time for me to go now. I don't want to get myself beached, do I? I like your town. I like your river. But I'm more at home back in my sea."

"But what if you are beached?" I asked. "What if you die?"

"I'd rather not, of course," he said. "But like I told you, I had to come. It was important, the most important thing I ever did. I promised I'd do it, didn't I? Now I've done it. The rest is up to you."

And away he swam then, blowing loudly as he passed upriver under Battersea Bridge, so that the whole river echoed with the sound of it. There was a final flourish of his tail before he dived. It was like he was waving goodbye, so I waved back. I stayed there watching for a while just in case he came up again. All around me the birds were watching too. But that was the last we saw of him.

And that's the end of my story.

Mrs Fergusson was so delighted to see Michael writing away that she let him go on long after the others had finished. That's why she let him stay in all through breaktime too. She stayed in the classroom with him because she had some marking to do anyway. Every time she looked up Michael was still beavering away at his story. She'd never seen him so intent on anything, and certainly not on his writing. Until now, he'd always seemed to find writing rather difficult. She was intrigued. She was longing to ask him what he was writing about, but she didn't want to interrupt him.

Michael finished just as the bell went and everyone came rushing back into the classroom again, filling the place with noise. When they'd settled down Mrs Fergusson thought she'd try something she hadn't tried before with this class. She asked if any of them would like to read their story out loud to the rest of the class. It was the last thing Michael wanted. They wouldn't believe him. They'd laugh at him, he knew they would. So he was very relieved when Elena, who always sat next to him, put up her hand. He was quite happy to sit there and listen to another of Elena's horsey stories. Elena was mad about horses. It was all she ever wrote about or talked about, all she ever painted too. Mrs Fergusson said it was good, but a bit short, and that perhaps it might be nice if she wrote about something else besides horses once in a while. Michael was looking out of the window, thinking of his whale deep down in the sea with his family all around him. So it caught him completely by surprise when she suddenly turned to him, and said, "Well, Michael, why don't you read us yours? What's it about?"

"A whale, miss," Michael replied.

She was coming over to his table. She was picking up his book. "A whale? That sounds really interesting," she said. "Goodness gracious. You've written pages and pages, Michael. You've never written this much before, have you? Would you like to read it for us?" Michael shook his head, which didn't surprise Mrs Fergusson at all. Michael was never one to volunteer himself for anything. "Your handwriting's a bit squiggly, but I think I can read it." She leafed through the pages. "Yes, I'm sure I can. Shall I read it out for you? You don't mind, do you, Michael?" Then she spoke to the whole class. "Would you like to hear Michael's whale story, children?" And they all did, so there was nothing Michael could do to stop her.

He had to sit there and listen like everyone else. He wanted to put his hands over his ears. He didn't dare to look up. He didn't want to have to see all those mocking smiles. To begin with, Mrs Fergusson read it like she always did, in her teachery voice, as if it was just a story.

Then gradually, her whole tone seemed to change, and she was reading it as if she was inside the story and down by the river, as if she was seeing it all, hearing it all, feeling it all, as if she was longing to know what was going to happen. Michael dared to look around him now. No one was laughing. No one was even smiling. The longer the story went on, the more Mrs Fergusson's voice trembled, and the more silent the class became. When she'd finished she stood there for a long while, so moved she was unable to speak. But Michael was still waiting for the first sound of laughter, dreading it. Then, all of a sudden, Elena started clapping beside him, and moments later they were all clapping, including Mrs Fergusson who was smiling at him through her tears.

"An amazing story, Michael, the best I've read in a long, long time – and certainly the best you've ever written. Quite wonderful," she said. "Only one thing I would say, Michael," she went on. "It doesn't really matter of course, but if you remember, Michael, I did tell you it had to be a true story, about something that really happened."

"It is true, miss," Michael told her. "It all happened, just like I said. Honest."

That's when Jamie Bolshaw started sniggering and snorting. It spread all around the classroom until everyone was laughing out loud at him. It didn't stop until Mrs Fergusson shouted at everyone to be quiet.

"You do understand what 'true' means, Michael, don't you?" she said. "It means not made up. If it is true, as you say it is, then that means that right now, just down the road, there's a bottle-nose whale swimming about in the river. And it means you actually met him, that he actually talked to you."

"Yes, miss. He did, miss," Michael said. "And I did meet him, this morning, early. Promise. About half past five, or six. And he did talk to me. I heard his voice and it was real. I wasn't making it up. But he's not there any more, miss, because he's gone back out to sea, like I said. It's true, all of it. I promise you, miss. It was just like I wrote it." And when Jamie Bolshaw started tittering again, Michael felt tears coming into his eyes. Try as he did, he couldn't hold them back, nor could he hold back the flood of words. He so wanted to make them believe him.

"It's true, miss, really true. When it was all over I ran all the way back home. Mum was already having her breakfast. She told me I was late, that I'd better hurry or I'd be late for school. I told her why I was late. I told her all about the whale, the whole thing. She just said it was a good story, but that she didn't have time for stories just now, and would I please sit down and eat my breakfast. I said it was all true, every word of it. I crossed my heart and hoped to die. But she didn't believe me. So I gave up in the end and just ate my breakfast like she said.

"And when I got to school I didn't dare tell anyone, because I thought that if Mum didn't believe me, then no one else would. They'd just laugh at me, or call me a liar. I thought it would be best to keep quiet about it. And that's what I would have done. But you said we all had to write about something that had really happened to us. It could be funny or sad, exciting or frightening, whatever we wanted, you said, but it had to be true, really true. 'No fantasy, no science fiction, and none of your shock-horror stories, Jamie Bolshaw, none of that dripping blood stuff. I want you to write it down just as it happened, children, just as you remember it.' That's what you told us.

"And I couldn't think of anything else to write about except my whale. So that's what I wrote about. It was very long, the longest story and the most important story I've ever written. That's because I didn't want to leave anything out. I don't usually like writing stories, I'm no good at them. Can't get started, can't find a good ending. But this time it was like it was writing itself almost. All I had to do was to let it flow on to the page, down from my head, along my arm, through my fingers. Sometimes, though, it was really hard to concentrate, because I kept thinking about my whale, hoping and hoping he was out in the open sea by now, with his family again, safe again. The more I hoped it, the more I believed it, and the more I believed it the more I wanted to tell his story. That's why

I stayed in all through breaktime to get it finished. It was raining anyway, so I didn't really mind."

When he'd finished there was a long silence.

"Yeah, yeah," Jamie sneered.

"That'll be quite enough of that, Jamie," Mrs Fergusson snapped, clapping her hands for silence. She could see now how upset Michael was becoming. "All right, Michael, all right. We'll say no more about it for the moment. Now children, what I want is for you to illustrate the story you've just written. Like that poem poster on the wall above the bookshelf – the tiger one, over there. I read it to you last week, remember? 'Tiger, tiger, burning bright'. I told you, didn't I? The poet illustrated it himself. And that's what I want you to do."

Through blinding tears Michael drew his bottle-nose whale, with the birds all around, the heron and the ducks and the cormorants, and the snowy white egret watching from the buoy. Then he drew himself, crouching down by the river's edge, with the sun coming up over London, all just as he'd seen it that morning. He had almost finished when, very surreptitiously, and making sure Mrs Fergusson wasn't looking, Elena slipped him a folded piece of paper. Michael opened it and read it. "Liar, liar, pants on fire." Elena was shaking her head and pointing at Jamie Bolshaw, who was making a face at him. That was the moment Michael lost it. He scrunched up the paper, got up, walked across the classroom and hurled it at Jamie's grinning face. "I'm not a liar," he screamed at him. "I'm not, I'm not!"

Mrs Fergusson put Jamie in one corner and Michael in another. They hadn't been there five minutes before Mr Jenner, the Headteacher, came in. Much to Michael's surprise and relief he didn't seem even to notice him standing there in the corner. He was pulling on his hat and coat. He was clearly going somewhere, and in an almighty hurry too. "Mrs Fergusson," he was saying. "I want your class to stop whatever it is that they're doing right now. I want them to get their coats on and assemble at once in the playground. And hurry please."

"Why? What's going on?" Mrs Fergusson asked. "Is it a fire drill?"

"No, no, nothing like that. You're not going to believe this," Mr Jenner said, "but apparently there's a huge great whale in the river, right here, right now, just down the road from us. It's true. Not every day a whale comes to town, is it? It's on the telly. But we can see it for real. So I thought we'd all go and take a look. Quick as you can, please, else he could be gone before we get there, and we don't want that, do we?" And then he was gone.

Everyone was gaping at Michael. For some time after Mr Jenner had left, no one said a word, not even Mrs Fergusson. But in spite of the look of utter amazement on

387

Jamie Bolshaw's face, Michael could not for one moment enjoy his triumph. All he could think of was that his whale hadn't made it to the sea, that he must still be floundering in the river, still there, and trapped. He knew only too well what that might mean. He had to be there, now. He was out of the classroom, across the playground already full of excited children being herded into lines, and on his way down to the river before anyone could stop him.

By the time Michael arrived, there were crowds everywhere, hundreds of them lining the river on both sides, and all along Battersea Bridge too. He pushed through the crowds and hoisted himself up on to the wall so he could see over. There were police down on the shoreline keeping everyone back behind the wall. From the moment he saw the whale Michael could see he was in serious trouble. He was wallowing helpless in the shallows, at the mercy of the tide, unwilling or unable to move.

Standing next to Michael was a building worker in a yellow hard-hat and muddy boots. He was screaming down his mobile hone. "It's huge! Humungous, I'm telling you. Looks more like a bleeding shark to me. And he's going to get himself well and truly stuck in the mud if he's not careful, and that'll be his lot. Yeah, just below Battersea Bridge. I've got my yellow hat on, you can't miss me. I'll look out for you. No, he'll still be here. He's not going anywhere, poor blighter. And don't forget to bring the camcorder, right? This won't happen again. Once in a lifetime this."

There were half a dozen people around the whale, a couple of divers amongst them, trying to encourage him back into the water, but Michael could see it was no use. Without him the whale seemed to have lost all will to live. He was trying to decide what he could do, how he could get to the whale without being stopped by the police, when he found Mr Jenner beside him and Mrs Fergusson too, both breathless.

"You shouldn't have gone running off like that, Michael," said Mrs Fergusson. "You had us worried sick."

"He needs me," Michael told her. "I've got to go to him."

"You leave it to the experts," said Mr Jenner. "Come on over with the other children now. We've got a great view where we are."

"I don't want a great view," Michael shouted. "Don't you understand? I have to save him."

Michael didn't think twice after that. He climbed over the wall and raced along the shore towards the whale, dodging the police as he went. When Mr Jenner tried to call him back, Mrs Fergusson put her hand on his arm. "Best leave him be," she told him. "It's his whale. I'll go after him."

By the time the police managed to catch up with

Michael, Mrs Fergusson was there to explain everything. They took some persuading, but in the end they said they could make an exception just this once, provided she stayed with him all the time, and provided both of them wore lifejackets, and didn't interfere.

So, along with several others, Michael and Mrs Fergusson were there when the tide began to rise, and at last the whale began to float free of the mud. Michael stayed as close to his head as he could get, and talked to him all the while to reassure him. "You'll be all right now," he said. "There's lots of us here, and we all want to help you. You'll swim out of here just like your grandfather did. All you have to do is swim. You must swim. You've got your whole family waiting for you out there. Do it for them. Do it for me."

They walked knee high with the whale out into the river, one of the divers swimming alongside him the whole time. Michael could see how hard the whale was trying. He was trying all he could, but he was so weak. Then, to the rapturous cheers of everyone around the whale seemed suddenly to find strength enough to move his tail, and he managed to swim away from the shore, blowing hard as he went. They watched him turning slowly out in the middle of the river. And when everyone saw he was swimming the right way, another huge cheer went up. But Michael just wished they'd keep quiet. He sensed that all this noise must be bewildering and disorientating for him. But when the whale swam away under the bridge back towards the sea, even Michael joined in the cheering.

Like everyone else, when the whale dived down and disappeared, Michael thought he would be all right now, that he was well and truly on his way, that he'd make it this time for sure. But for some reason, by the time the whale surfaced again, he had turned and was coming back towards them. Within no time at all he had drifted back into the shallows, and despite all they tried to do to stop him, he had beached himself again.

Mrs Fergusson tried to stop him, so did the others, but Michael broke free of them and waded as far out into the river as he could, until he was as near to him as he could get. "You've got to swim!" he cried. "You've got to. Go under the bridge and just keep going. You can do it. Don't turn around. Don't come back. Please don't come back!"

There were people and boats everywhere, bustle and ballyhoo all around, so much of it that Michael could barely hear the whale when he spoke. "I'm trying," he said. "I'm trying so hard. But I'm very tired now, and I don't seem to know where I'm going any more. I'm feeling muddled in my head, and I'm so tired. I just want to sleep. I'm afraid that maybe I stayed too long. Grandfather warned me, they all warned me." His eyes closed. He seemed almost too exhausted to say anything more. Then his eyes opened again. "You do remember everything I said?" he whispered.

"Of course I do. I'll never forget. Never."

"Then it was worth it. No matter what happens, it was worth it. Stay with me if you can. I need you with me."

So Michael did stay. He stayed all that day, and Mrs Fergusson stayed with him, long after all the other children had gone back home. By late afternoon his mother was there with them – they'd got a message to her at work. And the white egret stayed too, watching everything from his buoy.

As evening came on they tried to make Michael go home to sleep for a while.

"There's nothing more you can do here," his mother told him. "And anyway, you can watch it on the television. You can't stay here all night. You'll catch your death. We'll get a pizza on the way. What do you say?" Michael stayed crouching down where he was. He wasn't moving.

"I tell you what, Michael," Mrs Fergusson said, "I'll stay. You go home and get some rest, and then you can come back in the morning. I won't leave him, honestly I won't. And I'll phone if anything happens. How's that?"

Between them they managed to persuade him. Michael knew everything they said was true. He was tired, and he was cold, and he was hungry. So in the end he agreed, just so long as he could come back in the morning, at first light, he said.

"I won't be long," he whispered to the whale. "I'll be back soon, I promise."

Back at home in a hot bath he shivered the cold out of him, but all the while he was thinking only of his whale.

He ate his pizza watching his whale on the television. He knew he couldn't go to bed. He didn't want to sleep. He wanted only one thing, to be back down by the riverside with his whale. He begged his mother again and again to let him go, but she wouldn't let him. He had to get some sleep, she said.

There was only one thing for it. He would wait till his mother had gone to bed, then he'd get dressed and slip out of the flat. That's what he did. He ran all the way back down to the river.

All the rescue team and the divers were still there, and so was Mrs Fergusson, sitting by the wall wrapped in a blanket. And everywhere there were still dozens of onlookers. The egret was there on his buoy. And the whale was floundering near the shore, not far from where Michael had left him. But there was something else out on the river. It looked like a barge of some kind, and it hadn't been there before – Michael was sure of it. He ran over to Mrs Fergusson.

"Miss, what's that barge there for?" he asked her. "What's going on?"

"They're going to lift him, Michael," she said. "They had a meeting, and they decided it's the only way they can save him. They don't think he can do it on his own, he's too weak and disorientated. So they're going to lift him on to that barge and carry him out to sea."

"They can't!" Michael cried. "They'll kill him if they do. He can't live out of the water, he told me so. He's my whale. I found him. They can't, they mustn't! I won't let them!"

Michael didn't hesitate. He dashed down to the shore and waded out into the river. When he found he couldn't wade any more, he began to swim. A few short strokes and he was alongside the whale. He could hear Mrs Fergusson and the others shouting at him to come back. He paid them no attention. The whale looked at him out of his deep dark eye.

"I need you with me," he whispered.

"I know. I'm back," Michael said. "Are you listening? Can you hear me?"

"I hear you," replied the whale.

"I'm going to swim with you," Michael told him. "I'm a really good swimmer. We're going together. You just have to follow me. Can you do that?"

"I'll try," said the whale.

From the bank they all saw it, Michael and the whale swimming away side by side towards Battersea Bridge.

They could hardly believe their eyes. They could see the whale was finding it hard, puffing and blowing as he went, that Michael was battling against the tide. But incredibly, they were both making some headway. By now the rescue team had sent out an inflatable to fetch Michael in. Everyone could see what was bound to happen in the end, that the tide was against them, that it was too cold, that it was impossible. Both the boy and the whale tired together. They hauled Michael out of the water, and brought him back to the shore. From there he had to watch his whale swim bravely on for a few more minutes, before he had to give up the unequal struggle. Even Michael knew now that there was nothing more he could do, that the barge was the whale's only chance of survival.

Michael was there on the shore with his mother and Mrs Fergusson later that morning when they hoisted the whale slowly out of the water, and swung him out in a great sling on to the barge that would take him out to sea. With the world watching on television, followed by a procession of small boats, the barge carried him along the river, under the bridges, past Westminster and the London Eye and St Paul's, out towards Greenwich and the Thames Barrier and to the sea beyond. There was a vet on hand to monitor his progress all the way. And Michael too never left the whale's side, not for one moment. He stayed by him, pouring water over him from time to time, to keep his skin moist, soothing him and talking to him to reassure him, to keep his spirits up, all the while hoping against hope that the whale would have the strength to survive long enough to reach the open sea.

Michael didn't have to ask, he could see the vet was not optimistic. He could see his whale was failing fast. His eyes were closed now, and he had settled into a deep sleep. He was breathing, but only barely. Michael thought he did hear him breathe just one more word.

"Promise?" he said.

"I promise," Michael replied. He knew exactly what he was promising, that he would spend his whole life keeping it. And then the whale simply stopped breathing. Michael felt suddenly very alone.

The vet was examining him. After a while he looked up, wiping the tears from his face. "Why?" he asked. "I don't understand. Why did he come? That's what I'd like to know."

Ahead of them, as they came back into the heart of London, flew a single white bird. It was the snowy egret that had never left the whole way out and the whole way back. The whole of London seemed still with sadness as they passed by under Tower Bridge.

On 20 January 2006, an eighteen-foot (five metre) northern bottle-nosed whale was spotted swimming up the Thames past the Houses of Parliament. She swam up as far as Battersea Bridge where she became stranded. For two days rescuers battled to save the whale, as the world looked on, hoping for the best. But in spite of everyone's efforts that whale died before the rescue pontoon on which she was being transported could reach the safety of the open sea.

The Saga of Ragnar Erikson

14 July 1965

As I sailed into Arnefjord this morning, I was looking all around me, marvelling at the towering mountains, at the still dark waters, at the welcoming escort of porpoises, at the chattering oyster-catchers, and I could not understand for the life of me why the Vikings ever left this land.

It was beautiful beyond belief. Why would you ever leave this paradise of a place, to face the heaving grey of the Norwegian Sea, and a voyage into the unknown, when you had all this outside your door?

The little village at the end of the fjord looked at first too good to be true – a cluster of clapboard houses gathered around the quay, most painted ox-blood red. On top of the hill beyond them stood a simple wooden church with an elegant pencil-sharp spire, and a well-tended graveyard, surrounded by a white picket fence. There seemed to be flowers on almost every grave. A stocky little Viking pony grazed the meadow below.

The fishing boat tied up at the quay had clearly seen better days. Now that I was closer, I noticed that the village too wasn't as well kept as I had first thought. In places the paint was peeling off the houses. There were tiles missing from the rooftops, and a few of the windows were boarded up. It wasn't abandoned, but the whole place looked tired, and sad somehow.

As I came in on the motor there was something about the village that began to make me feel uncomfortable. There was no one to be seen, not a soul. Only the horse. No smoke rose from the chimneys. There was no washing hanging out. No one was fishing from the shoreline, no children played in the street or around the houses.

I hailed the boat, hoping someone might be on board to tell me where I could tie up. There was no reply. So I tied up on the quay anyway and jumped out. I was looking for a café, somewhere I could get a drink, or even a hot meal. And I needed a shop too. I was low on water, and I had no beer left on board, and no coffee.

I found a place almost immediately that looked as if it might be the village stores. I peered through the window. Tables and chairs were set out. There was a bar to one side, and across the room I could see a small shop, the shelves stacked with tins. Things were looking up, I thought. But I couldn't see anyone inside. I tried the door, and to my surprise it opened.

I'd never seen anything like it. This was shop, café,

nightclub, post office, all in one. There was a Wurlitzer juke box in the corner, and then to one side, opposite the bar, the post office and shop. And there was a piano right next to the post office counter, with sheet music open on the top – Beethoven Sonatas.

I called out, but still no one emerged. So I went outside again and walked down the village street, up the hill towards the church, stopping on the way to stroke the horse. I asked him if he was alone here, but he clearly thought that this was a stupid question and wandered off, whisking his tail as he went.

The church door was open, so I went in and sat down, breathing in the peace of the place, and trying at the same time to suppress the thought that this might be some kind of ghost village. It was absurd, I knew it was, but I could feel the fear rising inside me.

That was when the bell rang loud, right above my head, from the spire. Twelve times. My heart pounded in my ears. As the last echoes died away I could hear the sound of a man coughing and muttering to himself. It seemed to come from high up in the gallery behind me. I turned.

We stood looking at one another, not speaking for some time. I had the impression he was as surprised to see me as I was to see him. He made his way down the stairs, and came slowly up the aisle towards me.

He had strange eyes this man, unusually light, like his hair. He might have been fifty or sixty, but weathered, like the village was.

"Looking at you," he began, "I would say you might be English."

"You'd be right," I told him.

"Thought so," he said, nodding. Then he went on, "I ring the bell every day at noon. I always have. It's to call them back. They will come one day. You will see, they will come."

I didn't like to ask who he was talking about. My first thought was that perhaps he was a little mad.

"You need some place to stay, young man? I have twelve houses you can choose from. You need to pray? I have a church. You need something to eat, something to drink? I have that too. Yes, you're looking a little pale. I can tell you need a drink. Come."

Outside the church he stopped to shake my hand and to introduce himself as Ragnar Erikson. As we walked down the hill he told me who lived in each of the houses we passed – a cousin here, an aunt there – and who grew the best vegetables in the village, and who was the best pianist. He spoke as if they were still there, and this was all very strange because it was quite obvious to me by now that no one at all was living in any of these houses. Then I saw he

401

was leading me back to where I'd been before, into the bar-cum-post office-cum-village stores.

"You want some music on the Wurlitzer?" he asked me. "Help yourself, whatever you like, 'A Whiter Shade of Pale', 'Sloop John B', 'Rock Around the Clock'. You choose. It's free, no coins needed."

I chose 'A Whiter Shade of Pale', while he went behind the bar and poured me a beer.

"I don't get many people coming here these days," he said, "and there's only me living here now, so I don't keep much in the bar or the shop. But I caught a small salmon today. We shall have that for supper, and a little schnapps. You will stay for supper, won't you? You must forgive me – I talk a lot, to myself mostly, so when I have someone else to talk to, I make up for lost talking time. You're the first person I've had in here for a month at least."

I didn't know what to say. Too much was contradictory and strange. I longed to ask him why the place looked so empty and if there were people really living in those houses. And who was he ringing the church bell for? Nothing made any sense. But I couldn't bring myself to ask. Instead, I made polite conversation.

"You speak good English," I told him.

"That is because Father and I, we went a lot to Shetland in the old days. So we had to speak English. We were always going over there."

"In that fishing boat down by the quay?" I asked him.

"It is not a fishing boat," he said. "It is a supply boat. I carry supplies to the villages up and down the fjords. There is no road, you see; everything has to come by boat, the post as well. So I am the postman too."

After a couple of beers he took me outside and back down to the quayside to show me his boat. Once on board, I could see it was the kind of boat that no storm could sink. It was made not for speed but for endurance, built to bob up and down like a cork and just keep going. The boat suited the man, I thought. We stood together in the wheelhouse, and I knew he wanted to talk.

"My family," he said, "we had two boats, this one and one other just the same. Father made one, I made the other. This is the old boat, my father's boat. He made it with his own hands before I was born, and we took it over to Shetland, like the Vikings did before us. But we were not on a raid like they were. It was during the wartime, when the Germans were occupying Norway.

"We were taking refugees across the Norwegian Sea to Shetland, often twenty of them at a time, hidden down below. Sometimes they were Jews escaping from the Nazis. Sometimes it was airmen who had been shot down, commandos we had been hiding, secret agents too. Fifteen times we went there and back and they didn't catch us. Lucky, we were very lucky. This is a lucky boat. The other one, the one I built, was not so lucky."

Ragnar Erikson wasn't the kind of man you could question or interrupt, but I was wondering all through our supper of herring and salmon, in the warmth of his kitchen that evening, what he had meant about the other boat. And still I hadn't dared to broach the subject that puzzled me most: why there seemed to be no one else living in the village. When he fell silent I felt he wanted to be lost in his thoughts, and so the right moment never came.

But after supper by the fire, he began to question me closely about why I had come sailing to Norway, about what I was doing with my life. He was easy to talk to because he seemed genuinely interested. So I found myself telling him everything: how at thirty-one I had found myself alone in the world, that my mother had died when I was a child, and just a couple of months ago my father had too. I was a schoolteacher, but not at all sure I wanted to go on being one.

"But why did you come here?" he asked me. "Why Norway?"

So I told him how, when I was a boy, I had been obsessed by the Vikings; I'd loved the epic stories of Beowulf and Grendel; I'd even learnt to read the runes. It had become a lifelong ambition of mine to come to Norway one day. But arriving here in this particular fjord had been an accident – I was just looking for a good sheltered place to tie up for the night.

"I'm glad you came," he said after a while. "As I said, no one comes here much these days. But they will, they will."

"Who will?" I asked him, without thinking, and at once regretted it for I could see he was frowning at me, looking at me quite hard suddenly, and I feared I might have offended him.

"Whoever it is, they will be my family and my friends, that's all I know," he said. "They will live in the houses, where they all once lived, where their souls still live."

I could hear from the tone of his voice that there was more to tell and that he might tell it, if I was patient and did not press him. So I kept quiet, and waited. I'm so pleased I did. When at last he began again, he told me the whole story, about the empty village, about the other boat, the boat he talked about as if it had been cursed.

"I think perhaps you would like to know why I'm all alone in this place?" he said, looking directly at me. It felt as if he was having to screw up all his courage before he could go on.

"I should have gone to the wedding myself," he said, "with everyone else in the village, but I did not want to. It was only in Flam, down the fjord just north of here, not that far. The thing was, that ever since I was a little boy, the bride had been my sweetheart, the love of my life, but I was always too timid to tell her. I looked for her every time I went to Flam to collect supplies, met her whenever I could, went swimming with her, picking berries, mountain climbing, but I never told her how I felt. Now she was marrying someone else. I didn't want to be there, that's all. So my father skippered my boat that day instead of me. There were fourteen people in the boat – everyone from the village except for me and two very old spinster sisters. They did everything together, those two. One of them was too sick to go, so the other insisted on staying behind to look after her. I watched the boat going off into the morning mists. I never saw it again, nor anyone on board.

"To this day, no one really knows what happened. But we do know that early in the evening, after the wedding was over, there was a rock-slide, a huge avalanche which swept down the mountainside into the fjord, and set up a great tidal wave. People from miles around heard it and saw it. No one saw the boat go down, but that's what must have happened.

"For a few years the two old sisters and I kept the village going. When they died, within days of one another, I buried them in the churchyard. Then I was alone. To start with, very often, I thought of leaving, but someone had to tend the graves, had to ring the church bell, so I stayed. I fished, I kept a few sheep in those days. I had my horse. I learnt how to be alone.

"I discovered there is one thing you have to do when

you are alone, and that is to keep busy. So every day I work on the houses, opening windows in the summers to air rooms, lighting fires in the winters to warm them through, painting windows and doors, fixing where I can, just keeping them ready for the day they return. There's always something. I know it's looking more and more untidy as the years go by, but I do my best. I have to. They're all living here still, all my family and friends. I can feel them all about me. They're waiting, and I'm waiting, for the others to come and join them."

"I don't understand," I told him.

"No, young man," he said, laughing a little. "I'm not off my head, not quite. I know the dead cannot come back. But I do know their spirits live on, and I do know that one day, if I do not leave, if I keep ringing the bell, if I keep the houses dry, then people will find this place, will come and live here. In the villages nearby, they are still frightened of the place. They think it is cursed somehow. But they are wrong about that. It was the boat that was cursed, I tell them, not the village. Anyway, they do not come. Most of them are so frightened, they won't even come to visit me. They say it is a dying village and will soon be a dead village. But it is not, and it will not be, not so long as I stay. One day people will come and then the village will be alive once more. I know this for sure."

*

Ragnar Erikson offered me a bed in his house that night, but I said I was fine in the boat. I am ashamed to admit it, but after hearing his story I just didn't want to stay there any longer. It was too easy to believe that the place – paradise that it looked – might be cursed. He did not try to persuade me. I am sure he knew instinctively what I was feeling. I told him that I had to be up early in the morning, thinking I might not see him again. But he said he would be sure to see me off. And he was as good as his word. He was down on the quay at first light. We shook hands warmly, friends for less than a day, but I felt, because he had told me his story, that in a way we were friends for life. He told me to come back one day and see him again if ever I was passing. Although I said I would, I knew how unlikely it would be. But, through all the things that have happened to me since, I never forgot the saga of Ragnar Erikson. It was a story that I liked to tell often to my family, to my friends.

                                     1 August 2010. Midnight

Today I came back to Arnefjord. It has been over forty years and I've often dreamed about it, wondering what happened to Ragnar Erikson and his dying village. This time I have brought my family, my grandchildren too, because however often I tell them the story, they never quite seem to believe it.

    I had my binoculars out at the mouth of the little fjord

and saw the village at once. It was just as it had been. Even the boat was there at the quay, with no one on it, so far as I could see. There was no smoke rising from the chimneys; when we tied up, no one came to see us. I walked up towards the village shop, the grandchildren running off into the village, happy to be ashore, skipping about like goats, finding their land legs again.

Then, as I walked up towards the church, I saw a mother coming towards me with a pushchair.

"Do you live here?" I asked her.

"Yes," she said, and pointed out her house, "over there."

My granddaughter came running up to me.

"I knew it, Grandpa," she cried, "I always knew it was just a story. Of course there are people living here. I've seen lots and lots of them."

And she was right. There was a toy tractor outside the back door of a newly painted house, and I could hear the sound of shrieking children coming from further away down by the seashore.

"What story does she mean?" the mother asked me.

So I told her how I'd come here over forty years before and had met Ragnar Erikson, and how he was the only one living here then.

"Old Ragnar," she said, smiling. "He's up in the churchyard now."

She must have seen the look on my face. "No, no," she said, "I don't mean that. He's not dead. He's doing the flowers. We wouldn't be here if it wasn't for him. Ragnar saved this village, Ragnar and the road."

"The road?" I asked.

"Fifteen years ago they built a road to the village, and suddenly it was a place people could come to and live in. But there would have been no village if Ragnar hadn't stayed, we all know that. There are sixteen of us living here – six families. He's old now and does not hear so well, but he is strong enough to walk up the hill to ring the bell. It was the bell that brought us back, he says. And he still likes to go on ringing it every day. Habit, he says."

I went up the hill with my granddaughter, who ran on ahead of me up the steps and into the church. When she came out there was an old man with her, and he was holding her hand.

"She has told me who you are," he said. "But I would have recognised you anyway. I knew you would come back, you know. You must have heard me ringing. If I remember rightly, you liked 'A Whiter Shade of Pale' on the Wurlitzer. And you liked a beer. Do you remember?"

"I remember," I said. "I remember everything."

'GONE TO SEA'

William Tregerthen had the look of a child who carried all the pain of the world on his hunched shoulders. But he had not always been like this. He is remembered by his mother as the happy, chortling child of his infancy, content to bask in his mother's warmth and secure in the knowledge that the world was made just for him. But with the ability to walk came the slow understanding that he walked differently from others and that this was to set him apart from everyone he loved. He found he could not run with his brothers through the high hay fields, chasing after rabbits; that he could not clamber with them down the rocks to the sea, but had to wait at the top of the cliffs and watch them hop-scotching over the boulders and leaping in and out of the rock pools below.

He was the youngest of four brothers born on to a farm that hung precariously along the rugged cliffs below the Eagle's Nest. The few small square fields that made up the farm were spread, like a green patchwork between the granite farmhouse and the grey-grim sea, merging into gorse and bracken as they neared the cliff top. For a whole child it was a paradise of adventure and mystery, for the land was riddled with deserted tin miners' cottages and empty, ivy-clad chapels that had once been filled with boisterous hymns and sonorous prayer. There were deserted wheel houses that loomed out of the mist, and dark, dank caves that must surely have been used by wreckers and smugglers. Perhaps they still were.

But William was not a whole child; his left foot was turned inwards and twisted. He shuffled along behind his older brothers in a desperate attempt to stay with them and to be part of their world. His brothers were not hard-souled children, but were merely wrapped in their own fantasies. They were pirates and smugglers and revenue men, and the shadowing presence of William was beginning already to encroach on their freedom of movement. As he grew older he was left further and further behind and they began to ignore him, and then to treat him as if he were not there. Finally, when William was just about school age, they rejected him outright for the first time. "Go home to Mother," they said. "She'll look after you."

William did not cry, for by now it came as no shock to him. He had already been accustomed to the snide remarks, the accusing fingers in the village and the assiduously averted eyes. Even his own father, with whom he had romped and gambolled as an infant, was becoming estranged and would leave him behind more and more when he went out on the farm. There were fewer rides on

the tractor these days, fewer invitations to ride up in front
of him on his great shining horse. William knew that he had
become a nuisance. What he could not know was that an
inevitable guilt had soured his father who found he could
no longer even look on his son's stumbling gait without a
shudder of shame. He was not a cruel man by nature, but
he did not want to have to be reminded continually of his
own inadequacy as a father and as a man.

Only his mother stood by him and William loved her
for it. With her he could forget his hideous foot that would
never straighten and that caused him to lurch whenever
he moved. They talked of the countries over the sea's end,
beyond where the sky fell like a curtain on the horizon.
From her he learnt about the wild birds and the flowers.
Together they would lie hidden in the bracken watching
the foxes at play and counting the seals as they bobbed
up and down at sea. It was rare enough for his mother
to leave her kitchen, but whenever she could she would
take William out through the fields and clamber up on to
a granite rock that rose from the soil below like an iceberg.
From here they could look up to Zennor Quoit above
them and across the fields towards the sea. Here she would
tell him all the stories of Zennor. Sitting beside her, his
knees drawn up under his chin, he would bury himself in
the mysteries of this wild place. He heard of mermaids,
of witches, of legends as old as the rock itself and just as

enduring. The bond between mother and son grew strong during these years; she would be there by his side wherever he went. She became the sole prop of William's life, his last link with happiness; and for his mother her last little son kept her soul singing in the midst of an endless drudgery.

For William Tregerthen, school was a nightmare of misery. Within his first week he was dubbed "Limping Billy". His brothers, who might have afforded some protection, avoided him and left him to the mercy of the mob. William did not hate his tormentors any more than he hated wasps in September; he just wished they would go away. But they did not. "Limping Billy" was a source of infinite amusement that few could resist. Even the children William felt might have been friends to him were seduced into collaboration. Whenever they were tired of football or of tag or skipping, there was always "Limping Billy" sitting by himself on the playground wall under the fuchsia hedge. William could see them coming and screw up his courage, turning on his thin smile of resignation that he hoped might soften their hearts. He continued to smile through the taunting and the teasing, through the limping competitions that they forced him to judge. He would nod appreciatively at their attempts to mimic the Hunchback of Notre Dame, and conceal his dread and his humiliation when they invited him to do better. He trained himself to laugh with them back at himself; it was his way of riding the punches.

His teachers were worse, cloaking their revulsion under a veneer of pity. To begin with they overburdened him with a false sweetness and paid him far too much loving attention; and then because he found the words difficult to spell and his handwriting was uneven and awkward, they began to assume, as many do, that one unnatural limb somehow infects the whole and turns a cripple into an idiot. Very soon he was dismissed by his teachers as unteachable and ignored thereafter.

It did not help either that William was singularly unchildlike in his appearance. He had none of the cherubic innocence of a child; there was no charm about him, no redeeming feature. He was small for his age; but his face carried already the mark of years. His eyes were dark and deep-set, his features pinched and sallow. He walked with a stoop, dragging his foot behind him like a leaden weight. The world had taken him and shrivelled him up already. He looked permanently gaunt and hungry as he sat staring out of the classroom window at the heaving sea beyond the fields. A recluse was being born.

On his way back from school that last summer, William tried to avoid the road as much as possible. Meetings always became confrontations, and there was never anyone who wanted to walk home with him. He himself wanted less and less to be with people. Once into the fields and out of sight of the road he would break into a staggering, ugly run, swinging out his twisted foot, straining to throw it forward as far as it would go. He would time himself across the field that ran down from the road to the hay barn, and then throw himself at last face down and exhausted into the sweet warmth of new hay. He had done this for a few days already and, according to his counting, his time was improving with each run. But as he lay there now panting in the hay he heard someone clapping high up in the haystack behind him. He sat up quickly and looked around. It was a face he knew, as familiar to him as the rocks in the fields around the farm, an old face full of deeply etched crevasses and raised veins, unshaven and red with drink. Everyone around the village knew Sam, or "Sam the Soak" as he was called, but no one knew much about him. He lived alone in a cottage in the churchtown up behind the Tinners' Arms, cycling every day into St Ives where he kept a small fishing boat and a few lobster pots. He was a fair-weather fisherman, with a ramshackle boat that only went to sea when the weather was set fair. Whenever there were no fish and no lobsters to be found, or when the weather was blowing up, he would stay on shore and drink. It was rumoured there had been some great tragedy in his life before he came to live at Zennor, but he never spoke of it so no one knew for certain.

"A fine run, Billy," said Sam; his drooping eyes smiled gently. There was no sarcasm in his voice but rather a kind sincerity that William warmed to instantly.

"Better'n yesterday anyway," William said.

"You should swim, dear lad." Sam sat up and shook the hay out of his hair. He clambered down the haystack towards William, talking as he came. "If I had a foot like that, dear lad, I'd swim. You'd be fine in the water, swim like the seals I shouldn't wonder." He smiled awkwardly and ruffled William's hair. "Got a lot to do. Hope you didn't mind my sleeping awhile in your hay. Your father makes good hay, I've always said that. Well, I can't stand here chatting with you, got a lot to do. And, by the by, dear lad, I shouldn't like you to think I was drunk." He looked hard down at William and tweaked his ear. "You're too young to know but there's worse things can happen to a man than a twisted foot, Billy, dear lad. I drink enough, but it's just enough and no more. Now you do as I say, go swimming. Once in the water you'll be the equal of anyone."

"But I can't swim," said William. "My brothers can but I never learnt to. It's difficult for me to get down on the rocks."

"Dear lad," said Sam, brushing off his coat. "If you can run with a foot like that, then you can most certainly swim. Mark my words, dear lad; I may look like an old soak – I know what they call me – but drink in moderation

417

inspires great wisdom. Do as I say, get down to the sea and swim."

William went down to the sea in secret that afternoon because he knew his mother would worry. Worse than that, she might try to stop him from going if she thought it was dangerous. She was busy in the kitchen so he said simply that he would make his own way across the fields to their rock and watch the kestrel they had seen the day before floating on the warm air high above the bracken. He had been to the seashore before of course, but always accompanied by his mother who had helped him down the cliff path to the beach below.

Swimming in the sea was forbidden. It was a family edict, and one observed by all the farming families around, whose respect and fear of the sea had been inculcated into them for generations. "The sea is for fish," his father had warned them often enough. "Swim in the rock pools all you want, but don't go swimming in the sea."

With his brothers and his father making hay in the high field by the chapel William knew there was little enough chance of his being discovered. He did indeed pause for a rest on the rock to look skywards for the kestrel, and this somehow eased his conscience. Certainly there was a great deal he had not told his mother, but he had never deliberately deceived her before this. He felt however such a strong compulsion to follow Sam's advice that he soon left the rock behind him and made for the cliff path. He was now further from home than he had ever been on his own before.

The cliff path was tortuous, difficult enough for anyone to negotiate with two good feet, but William managed well enough using a stick as a crutch to help him over the streams that tumbled down fern-green gorges to the sea below. At times he had to go down on all fours to be sure he would not slip. As he clambered up along the path to the first headland, he turned and looked back along the coast towards Zennor Head, breathing in the wind from the sea. A sudden wild feeling of exuberance and elation came over him so that he felt somehow liberated and at one with the world. He cupped his hands to his mouth and shouted to a tanker that was cruising motionless far out to sea:

"I'm Limping Billy Tregerthen," he bellowed, "and I'm going to swim. I'm going to swim in the sea. I can see you but you can't see me. Look out, fish, here I come. Look out, seals, here I come. I'm Limping Billy Tregerthen and I'm going to swim."

So William came at last to Trevail Cliffs where the rocks step out into the sea, but even at low tide never so far as to join the island. The island where the seals come lies some way off the shore, a black bastion against the sea,

419

warning it that it must not come any further. Cormorants and shags perched on the island like sinister sentries and below them William saw the seals basking in the sun on the rocks. The path down to the beach was treacherous and William knew it. For the first time he had to manage on his own, so he sat down and bumped his way down the track to the beach.

He went first to the place his brothers had learnt to swim, a great green bowl of sea water left behind in the rocks by the tide. As he clambered laboriously over the limpet-covered rocks towards the pool, he remembered how he had sat alone high on the cliff top above and watched his brothers and his father diving and splashing in the pool below, and how his heart had filled with envy and longing. "You sit there, with your mother," his father had said. "It's too dangerous for you out there on those rocks. Too dangerous."

"And here I am," said William aloud as he stepped gingerly forward on to the next rock, reaching for a handhold to support himself. "Here I am, leaping from rock to rock like a goat. If only they could see me now."

He hauled himself up over the last lip of rock and there at last was the pool down below him, with the sea lapping in gently at one end. Here for the first time William began to be frightened. Until this moment he had not fully understood the step he was about to take. It was as if he had woken suddenly from a dream: the meeting with Sam in the hay barn, his triumphant walk along the cliff path, and the long rock climb to the pool. But now as he looked around him he saw he was surrounded entirely by sea and stranded on the rocks a great distance out from the beach. He began to doubt if he could ever get back; and had it not been for the seal William would most certainly have turned and gone back home.

The seal surfaced silently into the pool from nowhere. William crouched down slowly so as not to alarm him and watched. He had never been this close to a seal. He had seen them often enough lying out on the rocks on the island like great grey cucumbers and had spotted their shining heads floating out at sea. But now he was so close he could see that the seal was looking directly at him out of sad, soulful eyes. He had never noticed before that seals had whiskers. William watched for a while and then spoke. It seemed rude not to.

"You're in my pool," he said. "I don't mind really, though I was going to have a swim. Tell you the truth, I was having second thoughts anyway, about the swimming, I mean. It's all right for you, you're born to it. I mean you don't find getting around on land that easy, do you? Well nor do I. And that's why Sam told me to go and learn to swim, said I'd swim like a seal one day. But I'm a bit frightened, see. I don't know if I can, not with my foot."

The seal had vanished as he was speaking, so William lowered himself carefully step by step down towards the edge of the pool. The water was clear to the bottom, but there was no sign of the seal. William found it reassuring to be able to see the bottom, a great slab of rock that fell away towards the opening to the sea. He could see now why his brothers had come here to learn, for one end of the pool was shallow enough to paddle whilst the other was so deep that the bottom was scarcely visible.

William undressed quickly and stepped into the pool, feeling for the rocks below with his toes. He drew back at the first touch because the water stung him with cold, but soon he had both feet in the water. He looked down to be sure of his footing, watching his feet move forward slowly out into the pool until he was waist-high. The cold had taken the breath from his body and he was tempted to turn around at once and get out. But he steeled himself, raised his hands above his head, sucked in his breath and inched his way forward. His feet seemed suddenly strange to him, apart from him almost and he wriggled his toes to be sure that they were still attached to him. It was then that he noticed that they had changed. They had turned white, dead white; and as William gazed down he saw that his left foot was no longer twisted. For the first time in his life his feet stood parallel. He was about to bend down to try to touch his feet, for he knew his eyes must surely be deceiving him, when the seal reappeared only a few feet away in the middle of the pool. This time the seal gazed at him only for a few brief moments and then began a series of water acrobatics that soon had William laughing and clapping with joy. He would dive, roll and twist, disappear for a few seconds and then materialise somewhere else. He circled William, turning over on his back and rolling, powering his way to the end of the pool before flopping over on his front and aiming straight for William like a torpedo, just under the surface. It was a display of comic elegance, of easy power. But to William it was more than this, it became an invitation he found he could not refuse.

The seal had settled again in the centre of the pool, his great wide eyes beckoning. William never even waited for the water to stop churning but launched himself out into the water. He sank of course, but he had not expected not to. He kicked out with his legs and flailed his arms wildly in a supreme effort to regain the surface. He had sense enough to keep his mouth closed, but his eyes were wide open and he saw through the green that the seal was swimming alongside him, close enough to touch. William knew that he was not drowning, that the seal would not let him drown; and with that confidence his arms and legs began to move more easily through the water. A few rhythmic strokes up towards the light and he found the air his lungs had been craving for. But the seal was nowhere to be seen. William struck out across to the rocks on the far side of the pool quite confident that the seal was still close by. Swimming came to William that day as it does to a dog. He found in that one afternoon the confidence to master the water. The seal however never reappeared, but William swam on now by himself until the water chilled his bones, seeking everywhere for the seal and calling for him. He thought of venturing out into the open ocean but thought better of it when he saw the swell outside the pool. He vowed he would come again, every day, until he found his seal.

William lay on the rocks above the pool, his eyes closed against the glare of the evening sun off the water, his heart still beating fast from the exertion of his swim. He lay like this, turning from time to time until he was dry all over. Occasionally he would laugh out loud in joyous celebration of the first triumph in his life. Out on the seal island the cormorants and shags were startled and lifted off the rocks to make for the fishing grounds out to sea, and the colony of seals was gathering as it always did each evening.

As William made his way back along the cliff path and up across the fields towards home he could hear behind him the soft hooting sound of the seals as they welcomed each new arrival on the rocks. His foot was indeed still twisted, but he walked erect now, the stoop gone from his shoulders and there was a new lightness in his step.

He broke the news to his family at supper that evening, dropped it like a bomb and it had just the effect he had expected and hoped for. They stopped eating and there was a long heavy silence whilst they looked at each other in stunned amazement.

"What did you say, Billy?" said his father sternly, putting down his knife and fork.

"I've been swimming with a seal," William said, "and I learnt to swim just like Sam said. I climbed down to the rocks and I swam in the pool with the seal. I know we mustn't swim in the sea, but the pool's all right, isn't it?"

"By yourself, Billy?" said his mother, who had turned quite pale. "You shouldn't have, you know, not by yourself. I could have gone with you."

"It was all right, Mother," William smiled up at her. "The seal looked after me. I couldn't have drowned, not with him there."

Up to that point it had all been predictable, but then his brothers began to laugh, spluttering about what a good tale it was and how they had actually believed him for a moment; and when William insisted that he could swim now, and that the seal had helped him, his father lost his patience. "It's bad enough your going off on your own without telling your mother, but then you come back with a fantastic story like that and expect me to believe it. I'm not stupid, lad. I know you can't climb over those rocks with a foot like that; and as for swimming with seals, well it's a nice story, but a story's a story, so let's hear no more of it."

"But he was only exaggerating, dear," said William's mother. "He didn't mean—"

"I know what he meant," said his father. "And it's your fault, like as not, telling him all these wild stories and putting strange ideas in his head."

William looked at his mother in total disbelief, numbed by the realisation that she too doubted him. She smiled sympathetically at him and came over to stroke his head.

"He's just exaggerating a bit, aren't you, Billy?" she said gently.

But William pulled away from her embrace, hurt by her lack of faith.

"I don't care if you don't believe me," he said, his eyes filling with tears. "I know what happened. I can swim I tell you, and one day I'll swim away from here and never come back. I hate you, I hate you all."

His defiance was punished immediately. He was sent up to his room and as he passed his father's chair he was cuffed roundly on the ear for good measure. That evening, as he lay on his bed in his pyjamas listening to the remorseless ker-thump, ker-thump of the haybaler outside in the fields, William made up his mind to leave home.

His mother came up with some cocoa later on as she always did, but he pretended to be asleep, even when she leant over and kissed him gently on the forehead.

"Don't be unhappy, Billy," she said. "I believe you, I really do."

He was tempted at that moment to wake and to call the whole plan off, but resentment was still burning too strongly inside him. When it mattered she had not believed him, and even now he knew she was merely trying to console him. There could be no going back. He lay still and tried to contain the tears inside his eyes.

Every afternoon after school that week William went back down to the beach to swim. One of his brothers must have said something for word had gone round at school that "Limping Billy" claimed that he had been swimming with the seals. He endured the barbed ridicule more patiently than ever because he knew that it would soon be over and he would never again have to face their quips and jibes, their crooked smiles.

The sea was the haven he longed for each day. The family were far too busy making hay to notice where he was and he was never to speak of it again to any of them. To start with he kept to the green pool in the rocks. Every afternoon his seal would be there waiting for him and the lesson would begin. He learnt to roll in the water like a seal and to dive deep exploring the bottom of the pool for over a minute before surfacing for air. The seal teased him in the water, enticing him to chase, allowing William to come just so close before whisking away out of reach again. He learnt to lie on the water to rest as if he were on a bed, confident that his body would always float, that the water would always hold it up. Each day brought him new technique and new power in his legs and arms. Gradually the sea would let him come closer until one afternoon just before he left the pool William reached out slowly and stroked the seal on his side. It was a gesture of love and thanks. The seal made no immediate attempt to move away, but turned slowly in the water and let out a curious groan of acceptance before diving away out of the pool and into the open sea. As he watched him swim away, William was sure at last of his place in the world.

With the sea still calm next day William left the sanctuary of the pool and swam out into the swell of the ocean with the seal alongside him. There to welcome them as they neared the island were the bobbing heads of the entire seal colony. When they swam too fast for him it seemed the easiest, most natural thing in the world to throw his arms around the seal and hold on, riding him over the waves out towards the island. Once there he lay out on the rocks with them and was minutely inspected by each member of the colony. They came one by one and lay beside him, eyeing him wistfully before lumbering off to make room for the next. Each of them was different and he found he could tell at once the old from the young and the female from the male. Later, sitting cross-legged on the rocks and surrounded entirely by the inquisitive seals, William tasted raw fish for the first time, pulling away the flesh with his teeth as if he had been doing it all his life. He began to murmur seal noises in an attempt to thank them for their gift and they responded with great hoots of excitement and affection. By the time he was escorted back to the safety of the shore he could no longer doubt that he was one of them.

The notepad he left behind on his bed the next afternoon read simply: "Gone to sea, where I belong." His mother found it that evening when she came in from the fields at dusk. The Coastguard and the villagers were alerted and the search began. They searched the cliffs and the sea shore from Zennor Head to Wicca Pool and beyond, but in vain. An air-sea rescue helicopter flew low over the coast until the darkness drove it away. But the family returned to the search at first light and it was William's father who found the bundle of clothes hidden in the rocks below Trevail Cliffs. The pain was deep enough already, so he decided to tell no one of his discovery, but buried them himself in a corner of the cornfield below the chapel. He wept as he did so, as much out of remorse as for his son's lost life.

Some weeks later they held a memorial service in the church, attended by everyone in the village except Sam, whom no one had seen since William's disappearance. The Parochial Church Council was inspired to offer a space on the church wall for a memorial tablet for William, and they offered to finance it themselves. It should be left to the family, they said, to word it as they wished.

Months later Sam was hauling in his nets off Wicca Pool. The fishing had been poor and he expected his nets to be empty once again. But as he began hauling it was clear he had struck it rich and his heart rose in anticipation of a full catch at last. It took all his strength to pull the net up through the water. His arms ached as he strained to find the reserves he would need to haul it in. He had stopped hauling for a moment to regain his strength, his feet braced on the deck against the pitch and toss of the boat, when he heard a voice behind him.

"Sam," it said quietly.

He turned instantly, a chill of fear creeping up his spine. It was William Tregerthen, his head and shoulders showing above the gunwale of the boat.

"Billy?" said Sam. "Billy Tregerthen? Is it you, dear lad? Are you real, Billy? Is it really you?" William smiled at him to reassure him. "I've not had a drink since the day you died, Billy, honest I haven't. Told myself I never would again, not after what I did to you." He screwed up his eyes. "No," he said, "I must be dreaming. You're dead and drowned. I know you are."

"I'm not dead and I'm not drowned, Sam," William said. "I'm living with the seals where I belong. You were right, Sam, right all along. I can swim like a seal, and I live like a seal. You can't limp in the water, Sam."

"Are you really alive, dear lad?" said Sam. "After all this time? You weren't drowned like they said?"

"I'm alive, Sam, and I want you to let your nets down," William said. "There's one of my seals caught up in it and there's no fish there, I promise you. Let them down, Sam, please, before you hurt him."

Sam let the nets go gently, hand over hand until the weight was gone.

"Thank you, Sam," said William. "You're a kind man, the only kind man I've ever known. Will you do something more for me?" Sam nodded, quite unable to speak any more. "Will you tell my mother that I'm happy and well, that all her stories were true, and that she must never be sad. Tell her all is well with me. Promise?"

"Course," Sam whispered. "Course I will, dear lad."

And then as suddenly as he had appeared, William was gone. Sam called out to him again and again. He wanted confirmation, he wanted to be sure his eyes had not been deceiving him. But the sea around him was empty and he never saw him again.

William's mother was feeding the hens as she did every morning after the men had left the house. She saw Sam coming down the lane towards the house and turned away. It would be more sympathy and she had had enough of that since William died. But Sam called after her and so she had to turn to face him. They spoke together for only a few minutes, Sam with his hands on her shoulders, before they parted, leaving her alone again with her hens clucking impatiently around her feet. If Sam had turned as he walked away he would have seen that she was smiling through her tears.

The inscription on the tablet in the church reads:

WILLIAM TREGERTHEN
AGED 10
Gone to sea, where he belongs

Dolphin Boy

Once upon a time, the little fishing village was a happy place. Not any more.

Once upon a time, the fishermen of the village used to go out fishing every day. Not any more.

Once upon a time, there were lots of fish to catch. Not any more.

Now the boats lay high and dry on the beach, their paint peeling in the sun, their sails rotting in the rain.

Jim's father was the only fisherman who still took his boat out. That was because he loved the *Sally May* like an old friend and just couldn't bear to be parted from her.

Whenever Jim wasn't at school, his father would take him along. Jim loved the *Sally May* as much as his father did in spite of her raggedy old sails. There was nothing he liked better than taking the helm, or hauling in the nets with his father.

One day, on his way home from school, Jim saw his father sitting alone on the quay, staring out at an empty bay. Jim couldn't see the *Sally May* anywhere. "Where's the *Sally May*?" he asked.

"She's up on the beach," said his father, "with all the

other boats. I've caught no fish at all for a week, Jim. She needs new sails and I haven't got the money to pay for them. No fish, no money. We can't live without money. I'm sorry, Jim."

That night Jim cried himself to sleep.

After that, Jim always took the beach road to school because he liked to have a look at the *Sally May* before school began.

He was walking along the beach one morning when he saw something lying in the sand amongst the seaweed. It looked like a big log at first, but it wasn't. It was moving. It had a tail and a head. It was a dolphin!

Jim knelt in the sand beside him. The boy and the dolphin looked into each other's eyes. Jim knew then exactly what he had to do.

"Don't worry," he said. "I'll fetch help. I'll be back soon, I promise."

He ran all the way up the hill to school as fast as he could go. Everyone was in the playground.

"You've got to come!" he cried. "There's a dolphin on the beach! We've got to get him back in the water or he'll die."

Down the hill to the beach the children ran, the teachers as well. Soon everyone in the village was there – Jim's father and his mother too.

"Fetch the *Sally May*'s sail!" cried Jim's mother. "We'll

roll him on to it."

When they had fetched the sail, Jim crouched down beside the dolphin's head, stroking him and comforting him. "Don't worry," he whispered. "We'll soon have you back in the sea."

They spread out the sail and rolled him on to it very gently. Then, when everyone had taken a tight grip of the sail, Jim's father gave the word, "Lift!"

With a hundred hands lifting together, they soon carried the dolphin down to the sea where they laid him in the shallows and let the waves wash over him.

The dolphin squeaked and clicked and slapped the sea with his smiley mouth. He was swimming now, but he didn't seem to want to leave. He swam around and around.

"Off you go," Jim shouted, wading in and trying to push him out to sea. "Off you go." And off he went at last.

Everyone was clapping and cheering and waving goodbye. Jim just wanted him to come back again. But he didn't. Along with everyone else, Jim stayed and watched until he couldn't see him any more.

That day at school Jim could think of nothing but the dolphin. He even thought up a name for him. "Smiler" seemed to suit him perfectly.

The moment school was over, Jim ran back to the beach hoping and praying Smiler might have come back. But Smiler wasn't there. He was nowhere to be seen.

435

Filled with sudden sadness he rushed down to the pier. "Come back, Smiler!" he cried. "Please come back. Please!"

At that very moment, Smiler rose up out of the sea right in front of him! He turned over and over in the air before he crashed down into the water, splashing Jim from head to toe.

Jim didn't think twice. He dropped his bag, pulled off his shoes and dived off the pier.

At once Smiler was there beside him – swimming all around him, leaping over him, diving under him. Suddenly Jim found himself being lifted up from below. He was sitting on Smiler! He was riding him!

Off they sped out to sea, Jim clinging on as best he could. Whenever he fell off – and he often did – Smiler was always there, so that Jim could always get on again. The further they went, the faster they went. And the faster they went, the more Jim liked it.

Around and around the bay Smiler took him, and then back at last to the quay. By this time everyone in the village had seen them and the children were diving off the quay and swimming out to meet them.

All of them wanted to swim with Smiler, to touch him, to stroke him, to play with him. And Smiler was happy to let them. They were having the best time of their lives.

Every day after that, Smiler would be swimming near

the quay waiting for Jim, to give him his ride. And every day the children swam with him and played with him too. They loved his kind eyes and smiling face.

Smiler was everyone's best friend.

Then one day, Smiler wasn't there. They waited for him. They looked for him. But he never came. The next day he wasn't there either, nor the next, nor the next.

Jim was broken-hearted, and so were all the children. Everyone in the village missed Smiler, young and old alike, and longed for him to come back. Each day they looked and each day he wasn't there.

When Jim's birthday came, his mother gave him something she hoped might cheer him up, a wonderful carving of a dolphin – she'd made it herself out of driftwood. But not even that seemed to make Jim happy.

Then his father had a bright idea. "Jim," he said, "why don't we all go out in the *Sally May*? Would you like that?"

"Yes!" Jim cried. "Then we could look for Smiler too."

So they hauled the *Sally May* down to the water and set the sails. Out of the bay they went, out on to the open sea where, despite her raggedy old sails, the *Sally May* flew along over the waves.

Jim loved the wind in his face, and the salt spray on his lips. There were lots of gulls and gannets, but no sight of Smiler anywhere. He called for him again and again, but he didn't come.

The sun was setting by now, the sea glowing gold around them.

"I think we'd better be getting back," Jim's father told him.

"Not yet," Jim cried. "He's out here somewhere. I know he is."

As the *Sally May* turned for home, Jim called out one last time, "Come back, Smiler! Please come back. Please!"

Suddenly the sea began to boil and bubble around the boat, almost as if it was coming alive. And it WAS alive too, alive with dolphins! There seemed to be hundreds of them, leaping out of the sea alongside them, behind them, in front of them.

Then, one of them leapt clear over the *Sally May*, right above Jim's head. It was Smiler! Smiler had come back, and by the look of it he'd brought his whole family with him.

As the *Sally May* sailed into the bay everyone saw her coming, the dolphins dancing all about her in the golden sea. What a sight it was!

Within days the village was full of visitors, all of them there to see the famous dolphins and to see Smiler playing with Jim and the children.

And every morning, the *Sally May* and all the little fishing boats put to sea crammed with visitors, all of them only too happy to pay for their trip of a lifetime. They loved every minute of it, holding on to their hats and laughing with delight as the dolphins frisked and frolicked around them.

Jim had never been so happy in all his life. He had Smiler back, and now his father had all the money he needed to buy new sails for the *Sally May*. And all the other fishermen too could mend their sails and paint their boats. Once again, the village was a happy place.

As for the children…

… they could go swimming with the dolphins whenever they wanted to. They could stroke them, and swim with them and play with them, and even talk to them. But they all knew that only one dolphin would ever let anyone sit on him.

That was Smiler.

And they all knew that there was only one person in the whole world who Smiler would take for a ride.

And that was Jim.

ALONE ON A WIDE WIDE SEA

Arthur Hobhouse was shipped to Australia after WWII, losing his sister, his country and his home. Now at the end of his life, Arthur's daughter Allie has set sail in a very special boat across the roughest seas in the world to try to reunite their long-lost family...

Dad used to love old black and white Spencer Tracy movies, any Spencer Tracy movie. If it was on we watched it. And one film in particular he loved. It was called *Captain Courageous*. Tracy plays this old fisherman on a whaling ship. He looks after a young boy who's very spoilt and teaches him what's what, right from wrong, fair from unfair. He sings him an old fishing song, and I loved this song. It was one of those songs that just stayed in my head. I used to sing it all the time, out on the boat with Dad, in the bath at home, wherever I was happy. And now here I was in the Southern Ocean on my way to the Horn on *Kitty Four* catching and killing my first fish (I've never liked that part of it), tears pouring down my cheeks and singing out Spencer Tracy's fishing song:

"Hey ho little Fish, don't cry, don't cry. Hey ho little

Fish don't cry."

That first one I couldn't bring myself to eat, so I tossed it overboard for my albatross who had been watching me, probably hoping I'd do just that. He didn't have to be asked twice. He was in the sea in a flash and swallowed it down. He didn't actually lick his lips, but he looked pretty pleased as he sat there in the sea waiting for more. When I caught my next fish, I ate it myself, despite lots of hurt looks from my albatross. But I did chuck him the head, which he gobbled down more than happily.

Whenever I caught a fish after that my albatross seemed to be waiting, so I always threw him the head. I got less squeamish about boning and gutting them too, and I learnt how to cook them better each time. The truth is that I began to enjoy the whole process, from the excitement of seeing the line go taut to the eating itself. So now unless it was really stormy I'd have a line out astern of me most of the time.

Routine was all important to living on *Kitty Four*. It kept my spirits up. Routine checks of everything up on deck – regular adjustments to the halyards and the steering lines. Regular meals and hot meals too, if the weather allowed. The weather rules everything at sea, so sailing the boat came first. But I tried to live as normal a life as possible, tried not to allow the sea to dictate how I spent every moment of my day. So I learnt my *Ancient Mariner*. I wrote my emails. I tidied the cabin. I played my

CDs. I mended what had to be mended – there was always something. I fitted the spare membrane to my troublesome desalinator, superglued what had to be superglued. I washed clothes, not as often as I should, and hung them out to dry. I liked to keep myself clean too – to begin with I hadn't cared about it, but the longer I was at sea the more important it became. So I washed whenever I could – I always felt so much better for having made the effort. And on fine nights, however hard it was blowing, I'd always do the same thing. I'd go up into the cockpit if possible with my cup of hot chocolate and I'd watch the stars. I'd do a lot of singing up there too – everything from *London Bridge* to *Hey ho Little Fish* to *Yellow Submarine*.

It was on just such a night that I first saw it. I was sitting there gazing up at the zillions of stars, wondering if Grandpa back home was also sitting there with his telescope doing the very same thing at the very same moment, remembering how he loved to tell me what each of them was called, how he'd help me to hold his telescope myself. I was remembering all this when I saw a shooting star pass overhead, much lower and brighter and slower than shooting stars usually were. I watched in amazement as this light arced across the sky, knowing already it couldn't be a shooting star. It had to be a satellite of some kind. I went down below at once and emailed home to see if Grandpa knew what it could be. Until now I'd never had an email direct from Grandpa – they had always come through Mum. But the next day he emailed me back himself. "I checked. Got to be the ISS. International Space Station."

I saw it up there again a few nights later even brighter this time, even closer, and I got to thinking: those astronauts up there are closer to me at this moment than any other human being on earth. I'm sailing the seas down here. They're sailing through space up there. I wondered then if with all their high-tech gizmos they could see me. I felt like waving. So I stood there in the cockpit and waved and shouted till my arms ached, till my throat was sore. I was just so excited, so so happy to see them up there. That was when the idea first came to me to try to make contact with them, proper contact. *Wouldn't it be wonderful*, I thought, *to meet up by email or even by phone, so we could actually talk to one another as they passed over?* I sent an email to Grandpa. It was just a crazy idea to start with, just a lovely dream. Grandpa emailed back. "No worries. I'll fix it." I thought he was joking. Meanwhile I had a boat to sail.

I was still about 1000 miles from the Horn. I was down to 57°S. There was ice about in the south, lots of it. It was cold you couldn't forget, the kind that got into your bones, deep into your kidneys. Feet and hands went numb, so when I cut myself, and I often did, I couldn't feel it. My ears and my nose ached with it. I used to warm my socks and gloves on the kettle, but the trouble was that my toes and fingers were always colder than my socks and gloves were warm. So the bliss never lasted long. I'd never known cold like it. I'd do all I could to stay down below in the warm fug I'd created for myself. But sooner or later I'd always have to go back up there again, and the snugger I'd make myself, the colder the blast that hit me when I got up into the cockpit.

It was too rough for fishing now, and far too cold anyway, but my albatross was usually still there. He'd go off for a day or two, but I knew he'd always come back, and he did. I had such faith in him, that he'd stay with me and see me safely round the Horn. And I knew why too, knew it for sure, though I'd stopped writing about it in my emails because I thought it might upset Mum, and because I know it sounded at best a bit crazy. But I knew I wasn't hallucinating, that I wasn't mad. I now knew for sure that it was Dad's spirit soaring up above *Kitty Four*. He was an albatross, of course he was, but he was Dad too.

It was a different world I was sailing in down there, the wildest place I'd ever been. I could see and feel the swell building all the time. South of 60° between Cape Horn and the Antarctic peninsula there's no land to break up the ocean swells, so the waves travel uninterrupted for hundreds of miles and they're just massive – I kept using the word "awesome" in my emails, and that was about right. I knew *Kitty Four* could handle them, but I also knew I couldn't leave it all to her. I had to be out there avoiding the breaking waves, especially the hollow ones, the ones that look as if they're going to swallow you up. Sleep was almost impossible in seas like this, in weather like this. The wind screamed all the time. It was a constant pounding. I was on edge, listening to the boat, trying to work out if she was just complaining, or whether she was telling me something was really wrong. Like me, she was finding this very hard. We were both being tested as never before.

Below in the cabin was my whole world for hours on end. It was cramped, but down there I felt warm and safe. My bunk was a tight fit – it had to be because falling out was very painful and dangerous too. But it wasn't comfortable. I'd lie there surrounded by all the stuff that was keeping me alive – the medical box, generator, stove, charts, almanacs, sextant, PC, spares for everything, harnesses, life vests and sails – and kept telling myself that *Kitty Four* and all this equipment would get me through. And when I went up on deck there was my albatross telling me exactly the same thing. It was scary, it was heart-thumpingly scary at times, but I never for one moment thought we wouldn't make it. And whenever I felt like human company, I'd sing to myself or listen to a CD, or email home. In my emails I tried to hide just how scary it really was sometimes. There was no point in upsetting Mum and Grandpa unnecessarily. *Tell them some of it*, I thought, *but there's no need to tell them everything*.

I was finding the keyboard slow to use now because my fingers were becoming very swollen. I couldn't feel them, and they looked like a bunch of white bananas. I was doing all I could to look after them, smothering them with lanolin, but still the cracks came, still my cuticles split around my nails – what nails I had left. My hands were not a pretty sight, but I didn't mind. I just wanted them to work, to be able to do what I told them to do – cook, tie knots, pull ropes, email.

I've never forgotten the morning I saw Cape Horn up there on the laptop screen at last. Sometime before I left home I'd seen the movie *Master and Commander*, seen the frigate battling its way through ferocious seas off the Horn. It was terrifying enough sitting in a comfy seat next to Dad in the cinema in Hobart. Soon now I'd be going round the Horn myself, doing it for real, but Dad was still beside me. He was there in the boat he'd made for us, in the albatross that guarded us, and in my heart too. I took out *The Ancient Mariner* which by now had become like a Bible to me. It gave me new determination, a new courage every time I read it out loud.

The ice was here, the ice was there,
The ice was all around:
It cracked and growled, and roared and howled,
Like noise in a swound!

At length did come an Albatross,
Thorough the fog it came;
As if it had been a Christian soul,
We hailed it in God's name.

Every time I spoke those words now, I felt that somehow I was living inside the poem, that it had been written just for Dad and me, just for this moment as we approached the Horn on the 9th March.

Why the Whales Came

*Gracie and Daniel have been warned to stay away from the
mad Birdman. But when they find a message written in
the sand, Gracie can't help asking her parents about him,
or the legend of the curse on Sansom Island…*

Tea when I was a child was always fish, fish and
potatoes; and that evening it was mullet, a great pink
fish that stared up at me with glazed eyes from the platter.
I had no appetite for it. All I could think of were those two
letters in the sand on Rushy Bay. I had to know one way or
the other – I had to be sure it was the Birdman.

I forced myself to eat the fish for I knew Mother and
Father would suspect something if I did not, for mullet was
known to be my favourite fish. We ate in silence, busying
ourselves over the fish, so I had the whole meal to work
out how best to ask them about the initials in the sand,
without incriminating myself.

"Saw the Birdman today," I said at last, as casually as
I could.

"Hope you kept your distance," said Father, pushing
his plate away. "With young Daniel Pender again were you?

Always with him aren't you?" And it was true I suppose. Daniel Pender and Gracie Jenkins were a pair, inseparable. We always had been. He lived just across the way from our front gate at Veronica Farm. Whatever we did, we did together. Father went on. "Proper young scallywag his father says he is and I can believe it. You be sure he doesn't lead you into any trouble, my girl. Always looks like a big puppy that one with his arms and legs too long for the rest of him. Hair's always stood up on his head like he's just got out of bed. Proper scallywag he looks."

"Looks aren't everything," said Mother quietly; and then she smiled and added, "they can't be, can they, else how would I ever have come to pick you?"

"My beard, perhaps, Clemmie," Father laughed, and he stroked his beard and smoothed his moustache. He always called her "Clemmie" when he was happy. It was "Clem" when he was angry.

"You leave Daniel be," said Mother. "He's a clever boy, clever with his hands. You seen those boats he makes?"

"I help him," I insisted. "I paint them and I make the sails."

"Been sailing them all day, I suppose," said Father. "Out by the pool were you? That where you saw the Birdman?"

"Yes, Father," I said; and then, "About the Birdman, Father; everyone just calls him 'The Birdman', but he must have a real name like other people, mustn't he?"

"Woodcock," said Father, sitting back in his chair and undoing a notch in his belt as he always did after a meal. "Woodcock, that's what his mother was called anyway. You can see for yourself if you like – she's buried down in the churchyard somewhere. Last one to leave Samson they say she was, her and the boy. Starving they were by all accounts. Anyway, they came over to Bryher and built that cottage up there on Heathy Hill away from everyone else. The old woman died a few years after I was born. Must have been dead, oh, thirty years or more now. The Birdman's lived on his own up there ever since. But you hear all sorts of things about his old mother. There's some will tell you she was a witch, and some say she was just plain mad. P'raps she was both, I don't know. Same with the Birdman; I don't know whether he's just mad or evil with it. Either way it's best to keep away from him. There's things I could tell you…"

"Don't go frightening her now with your stories," said Mother. "Anyway it's only rumours and tittle-tattle. I don't believe half of it. If anything goes wrong on this island they blame it on the Birdman. Lobsters aren't there to be caught – it's his fault. Blight in the potatoes – it's his fault. Anyone catches the fever – it's his fault. Dog goes missing – they say he's eaten it. Lot of old nonsense. He's just a bit simple, bit mad perhaps, that's all."

"Simply, my aunt," Father said, getting up and going over to his chair by the stove. "And what's more, it's not all tittle-tattle, Clemmie, not all of it. You know it's not."

"There's no need to tell her any more," said Mother. "Long as she doesn't go anywhere near him, long as she keeps off Samson, that's all that matters. Don't you go filling her head with all those stories."

"But they're not all stories, are they, Clemmie? Remember what happened to Charlie Webber?"

"Charlie Webber? Who's he?" I asked.

"Never you mind about Charlie Webber," said Mother; and she spoke firmly to Father.

"That's enough – you'll only frighten her."

But Father ignored her. He leant forward towards me in his chair, stuffing his pipe with tobacco. "Charlie Webber was my best friend when I was a boy, Gracie. Got into all sorts of scrapes and capers together, Charlie and me. Nothing we wouldn't tell each other; and Charlie wouldn't ever have lied to me, not in a million years. He wasn't like that, was he, Clemmie?" But Mother wouldn't answer him. She walked away and busied herself at the sink. His voice dropped to a whisper now, almost as if he was afraid of being overheard. "There's always been strange stories about Samson, Gracie. Course, people only half believed them, but they've always steered clear of Samson all the same, just in case. But it was all on account of the Birdman

451

and his mother that Samson became a place no one dared go near. They were the ones who put it about that there was a curse on the place. They were always warning everyone to keep off, so we did. They told everyone it was an island of ghosts, that whoever set foot on the place would bring the terrible curse of Samson down on his family. No one quite believed all that about ghosts and curses; but just the same everyone kept well clear of the place, everyone except Charlie."

Father lit up his pipe and sat back in his chair which creaked underneath him as it always did whenever he moved. "I never went over there, but Charlie did. It was a day I'll never forget, never, never – low tide, no water to speak of between Bryher and Samson. You could walk across. It was my idea, and not one I'm proud of, Gracie, I can tell you. It was me that dared Charlie Webber. I dared him to walk over to Samson. We were always daring each other to do silly things, that's just how we were; and Charlie Webber never could resist a dare. I stood on top of Samson Hill, and watched him running over the sands towards Samson, leaping the pools. It took him about ten minutes I suppose and there he was jumping up and down on the beach waving and shouting to me, when suddenly this man in a black sou'wester appeared out of the dunes behind him, came from nowhere. He began screaming at Charlie like some kind of mad fiend and Charlie ran and ran and ran. He ran like a hare all the way back across the sand, stumbling and splashing through the shallows. By the time he reached me he was white with fear, Gracie, white with it I tell you. But that's not all of it. That very same night Charlie Webber's house was burnt to the ground. It's true, Gracie. Everyone managed to get out alive, but they never did find out what caused the fire; but Charlie knew all right, and I knew. Next day Charlie went down with the scarlet fever. I caught it after him and then near enough every child on the island got it. Aunty Mildred – you know Daniel's Aunty Mildred – she was just a baby at the time and she nearly died of it."

"Did Charlie Webber die of it?" I asked.

"Now that's enough," said Mother sharply. "You've said enough."

"Clem," said Father, "she's ten years old and she's not a baby any more. She's old enough to hear the rest of it." He lit his pipe again, drawing on it deeply several times before he shook out the match. "No, Gracie, Charlie didn't die, but he had to leave the island. His family was ruined, couldn't afford to rebuild the house. But before Charlie left for good he told me something I'll never forget. The day after the fire, Charlie was sitting on the quay when he felt someone behind him. He looked around and there was the Birdman. There was nowhere for Charlie to run to. He'd come, he said, to say sorry to Charlie, to explain to him that it wasn't his fault. There was nothing he could do once Charlie had set foot on Samson. He told Charlie that there was a curse on the island, that the ghosts of the dead haunted the place and could not rest, not until the guilt of Samson had been redeemed, whatever that meant. And when Charlie asked him why there was a curse on Samson, why the ghosts could not rest – this is what he told him. He was a little boy when it happened, younger than Charlie, he said. The people of Samson woke up one morning to find a ship run aground on a sandbank off Samson. Like a ghost ship it was on a flat calm sea. No fog, no wind, no reason for it to be there. They rowed out and hailed it, but no one answered; so they clambered on board. There was no one there. The ship was deserted. Well you don't look a gift horse in the mouth, do you? Every man on Samson, sixteen of them there were in all, he said – every one of them was on that ship when it refloated at high tide. They sailed it off to Penzance to claim the salvage money, but they never got there. The ship foundered on the Wolf Rock, off Land's End, went down in broad daylight, mind you; gentle breeze, no fog. Every man on board was lost. The Birdman's own father went down on that ship, Gracie."

"It's a horrible story," said Mother, "horrible. Every time I hear it it makes me shiver."

"True nonetheless, Clemmie," Father said. "And that wasn't the last of it. It seems things went from bad to worse on Samson after that. With no men left to go fishing or to work up the fields, the women and children soon began to go hungry. All they had to eat was limpets. The Birdman told Charlie that they even had to eat the dogs. It's true, Gracie, that's what Charlie told me. Then with the hunger came the fever, and the old folk and the babies began to die. So they left. One by one the families left the island until the Birdman and his mother were alone on Samson."

Father drew on his pipe again and found it had gone out – his pipe was always going out. "And I believe every word Charlie told me, Gracie. I don't pretend to understand the whys and wherefores; and I tell you straight, I don't know if it's him that's cursed or Samson. All I do know is that it's better to keep away from the both of them – that's for sure. So you keep well clear of him, you hear me now?"

I sat silent for some time lost in Father's story, my head full of questions. "So he can put spells and curses on people like they say he can?" I asked.

"Maybe," said Father, tapping his pipe out on the side of the stove. And I shivered as I thought of how close we had been to his cottage that day, and how he must have been watching us on Rushy Bay. Then there were those letters in the sand. Perhaps they were initials, but perhaps they were part of some spell. I wanted to be sure.

"What about his first name, Father?" I asked. "Do you know his first name?" But immediately I regretted it for I felt Mother looking at me. I was being over inquisitive, too interested; and she was suspicious.

"Why all these sudden questions about the Birdman, Gracie?" she asked. "You've never shown any interest in him before."

"Just saw him today, like I said. Just wondered, that's all. Daniel and me, we just wondered about him."

Mother came over and stood in front of me. She took my chin in her hand and pulled it up so that I had to look her in the eyes. She always did this when she thought I'd been up to some mischief and she wanted to get the truth out of me. "You haven't been speaking to him, have you, Gracie? You haven't been over on Heathy Hill, have you? You know you're not supposed to go there, don't you?"

"No, Mother, course I haven't, honest I haven't." It was just as well I did not have to lie, for Mother would have known. Father I could deceive any time I wanted, but Mother knew me far too well. She looked down at me out of tired, kind eyes, a knowing smile on her lips, so knowing that I had to look away.

"You leave him to his birds, Gracie," Father said. "You keep well away like I said. Promise me now. You be a good girl and stay away."

"I promise," I said. "I'll stay away."

And so I did, for a day or so at least. It took only that long for Daniel to persuade me to go with him back to

Rushy Bay, that we had been silly to run away in the first place just because we'd heard a donkey braying. I told him everything Father had told me about the Birdman and Samson and Charlie Webber. He listened, but I could see he didn't really believe any of it. He said he had heard something about the fire before, and that it didn't matter anyway because we weren't going to Samson like Charlie Webber did. We were only going to Rushy Bay. And the Birdman might be a bit loony, but what did that matter? He just wanted to make friends, that was all. Why else would he give us back our boat? Why else would he be leaving messages for us in the sand? We didn't have to go anywhere near him, did we? Perhaps I agreed to go with Daniel because I was half convinced by his arguments, or perhaps I was inquisitive.

When I crawled up over Samson Hill with Daniel that next day I kept flat on my stomach in the heather until I was sure the Birdman was not down there on Rushy Bay waiting for us.

The Birdman was not waiting for us, but something else was.

Kaspar, Prince of Cats

Johnny Trott, bellboy at the Savoy Hotel, has made the unlikeliest friends in young heiress Lizziebeth and Kaspar the Prince of Cats. And it is this friendship that takes them all on the maiden voyage of RMS Titanic...

I never saw the iceberg, nor did any of us stokers, but we soon met one of the crew who was there when the ship struck, and who had seen it all. He said the iceberg was at least a hundred feet high, looming above the ship, and not white like icebergs are supposed to be, but dark, almost black. But it had been a glancing blow, he said, no cause for alarm, no need for panic. And no one was panicking. No one was rushing anywhere. By now more and more passengers were beginning to appear on deck, to find out what was happening, just as we had. I saw a couple strolling arm in arm. They looked completely unconcerned, as if they were simply taking the air. Even after the collision, like everyone on board, they clearly still accepted, as I did, the absolute assumption – and one that had after all been confirmed to me in person of course by Captain Smith himself – that the *Titanic* was unsinkable, that everything would be all right.

It was when the ship began to list, and this happened quite soon, that the first doubts began to creep in. But only when I saw men and women gathering in numbers on deck, and putting on life-preservers, did I truly begin to understand the dreadful danger we were now in, and only then did I think of Lizziebeth and Kaspar in their stateroom on deck C. It took me a while to locate the right corridor, and when I did I had some difficulty in finding my way to number 52. There was no time to stand on ceremony. I hammered on the door, yelling for them. A moment or two later Mr Stanton was standing there, in front of me, his face grey with anxiety. He was fully dressed, with his life-preserver already on, as were the rest of the family.

They looked at me as if I'd come from another planet. I just blurted it out. "I stowed away." That was all I said by way of explanation. There wasn't time for any more, and now it didn't matter anyway.

"Are we sinking?" Mrs Stanton asked me. She was quite calm and controlled.

"I don't know," I said. "I don't think so. But I think we should get out on deck."

Mrs Stanton was picking up her bag.

"We must take nothing with us, my dear." Mr Stanton spoke to her very gently but firmly, as he took it from her.

"But all my precious things, my mother's necklace, my

photographs," she cried.

"You and Lizziebeth are all that's precious," he said quietly. He turned to me. "Johnny, you will take care of Lizziebeth." Lizziebeth's hand had crept into mine. It was cold. She looked up at me, her eyes full of bewilderment. She seemed still only half awake. It was only as we were leaving the cabin that she seemed to begin to comprehend what was going on. She grabbed her father's arm suddenly. "Papa, what about Kaspar? We can't leave Kaspar."

"We leave everything behind, Lizziebeth, and I mean everything." Mr Stanton spoke very firmly to her. "Now follow me and stay close." Staying close was not easy because the corridors and gangways were full of people, and many of them were carrying or dragging heavy bags. Lizziebeth kept saying it again and again, to me now, "What about Kaspar? We can't leave him, Johnny, we can't. Please. All those people, they've got bags, they're carrying things. Please." She was trying to tug me back all the time, but I knew there was nothing I could say to comfort her. I had to ignore her and keep going.

As we got up on to the Boat Deck and out into the cold air I realised that the ship was listing noticeably more severely than before. I saw dozens of post bags being piled up on deck, and abandoned luggage everywhere. Boats were being lowered away, and the band was playing. Everywhere people were gathered in small groups, huddling together against the cold, some with blankets round their shoulders. A few were praying aloud, but most stood in silence, waiting patiently.

I recognised Mr Lightoller, the officer we'd seen in the Captain's cabin, going about the deck, organising, spreading calm as he went, and explaining to everyone that it would be women and children first, that when all the women and children were safely away in the lifeboats, then the men could leave. When he turned to Mrs Stanton and told her it was her turn to get into one of the boats, she clung to her husband and refused.

"I won't leave my family," she said. "We belong together, and if it's God's will, then we will die together."

Mr Stanton took her gently by the shoulders and, looking deep into her eyes, he spoke to her very softly, almost in a whisper. "You will take Lizziebeth, my dear, and you will do as the officer says, and go to the boat. Johnny Trott and I will come after you, I promise you. Go, my dear. Go now."

At that moment Lizziebeth broke free of my hand and ran for it. I knew straight away that she was going back for Kaspar. I went after her at once, and caught her at the top of the gangway. She struggled against me, but I held her tight. "I can't leave him!" she cried. "I can't! I won't!"

"Lizziebeth," I said. "Listen to me. I must take you to the boat. It'll be gone soon. You have to go with your mother. You have to save yourself. Leave Kaspar to me. I'll find him. I'll save him."

She looked up at me, her eyes full of sudden hope. "You promise me?"

"I promise," I told her.

"And you, Johnny, what will happen to you?"

"I'll be all right, there's plenty of boats," I said.

When we got back to the railings, the lifeboat was nearly full and almost ready to launch, but I could see the crew were having the greatest difficulty in lowering it. With the help of Mr Stanton and a sailor we helped Lizziebeth and her mother into the boat. But still the boat could not be lowered. One of the crew was slicing away at the rope with his knife, cursing as he did so, and cursing even louder when he dropped his knife into the sea below. There were several lifeboats in the water already and rowing away from the *Titanic*. I glanced towards the stern and saw it was a great deal higher than it had been before. I could feel the great ship settling ever lower into the sea.

I caught Lizziebeth's eye then. She was willing me to do it, and to do it now. I knew that if I left it any longer it may well be too late. I would show her there and then that I meant to keep my promise if I could. I turned to Mr Stanton beside me. "I'm going for Kaspar," I said. "I shan't be long." He shouted after me to come back, but I ignored him.

By now the decks were crowded with men, all of them corralled by the crew who had made a human cordon to keep them back as the last of the women and children were being helped into the boats. But there was no pushing, no shoving. I saw among them dozens of my fellow stokers, most of them black with coal dust, and all unnaturally quiet. As I pushed my way through them to get back down below, one of them called out to me. "You should be in one of they boats, Johnny lad. You're only a slip of a boy. You're young enough. You've got the right."

The gangway was packed with passengers trying to make their way up on deck, some of the older and more infirm still in their nightgowns. One of the sailors who was trying to help them tried to stop me going down. "You can't go. There's water coming in everywhere down there, the whole ship's flooding fast." I dodged past him. "Idiot!" he yelled after me. "You blithering idiot! You go down there and you won't come back up again!" I ran on.

After losing my way in the warren of corridors, I reached the right corridor on deck C and I knew then that the sailor had been right. The sea water was ankle deep, and rising all the time. And once I opened the door to number 52, I saw the carpets were already under water. I looked around me frantically for Kaspar, but couldn't see him anywhere, not at first. It was Kaspar himself who told me where he was, yowling at me from the top of the wardrobe. I looked around for the picnic basket to carry him in, but couldn't find it. I reached up and took him off the wardrobe, and held him tight; but then, as I went out, I had the presence of mind to snatch a blanket off the nearest bed. All the way back along the corridor, I was wrapping Kaspar up in the blanket, not against the cold, but to stop him clawing at me, for I knew that even if he wasn't frightened now, he very soon would be.

But as I ran back down the corridor I was beginning to realise that the blanket had another use, and a much more essential one too. If no luggage was being allowed in the boats, I reasoned, then they would hardly accept a cat. This was why, by the time I got back up on deck again, Kaspar was well hidden deep inside the blanket. And now he was beginning to yowl.

"None of your fuss, please, Kaspar," I whispered to him. "Quiet now, and stay quiet. Your life could depend on it."

I pushed my way through the stokers, ducked under the cordon of crewmen, and saw to my great relief that the lifeboat was still hanging there. But then I found my way suddenly blocked by an officer in a peaked cap, who grabbed me by the shoulder. "No, you don't, lad. No men allowed in the boats until all the women and children are loaded," he said. "I can't let you on. I can't let you pass."

"He's not a man," someone shouted behind me. "He's

only a kid, can't you see?" All around me the stokers were suddenly clamouring at him to let me through, and they began pushing angrily against the ring of sailors desperately trying to hold them back. I could see the officer was taken by surprise at the sudden rage of the crowd, and that he was hesitating.

I saw my chance. "I'm not going on the boat," I told him. "I just went to fetch a blanket. It's for a child, a friend of mine. She'll freeze to death out there without it." I still don't think he'd have let me through if Mr Stanton hadn't come up at that moment and vouched for me.

"It's all right. He's my son," he said to the officer, "and the blanket's for his sister." I was through. With Mr Stanton holding me fast round the waist I leant across and handed the blanket, and the miraculously silent Kaspar, into Mrs Stanton's outstretched arms.

"Be careful," I told her as meaningfully as I could. She knew as she was taking it from me that Kaspar was inside the blanket. She hugged it to her and sat down again in the boat. I could see from the way Lizziebeth was smiling up at me that she knew it too.

Distress rockets were fired up into the sky, lighting the ocean all around us, lighting too the scattering of little white boats out on the open sea, each of them crammed with women and children.

I remember thinking how extraordinarily beautiful

465 🐈

it all was, and wondering how something as terrible as this could be so beautiful. On board behind us the band played on, as Lizziebeth's boat was finally lowered into the water. Mr Stanton and I stood side by side and watched from the railings as it was rowed slowly away. "That was a fine and noble thing you did, Johnny," he said, putting his hand on my shoulder. "God will guard them, I know it. And for us there'll be a boat along soon enough to take us off. Mr Lightoller says they've seen the lights of a ship not five miles away. The *Carpathia*. She'll be on her way. They'll see these rockets for sure. They'll be alongside soon enough. Meanwhile, I think we should help with the women and children, don't you?" That was how we busied ourselves for the next hour or so, passing the women and the children into the boats.

I marvel now when I think of it, at the courage I witnessed around me that night. I saw one American lady waiting to get into a boat with her elderly sister, but she was told there was no room. She didn't object or protest in any way, but merely stepped back and said: "Never mind. I will get on a later boat." I never saw her again. I saw no man ever try to push his way to the boats. To a man they accepted that it was perfectly right and proper for women and children to go first. I heard later that some men on the starboard side of the ship had tried to rush one of the lifeboats, and that shots had to be fired over their heads to drive them back. But I never saw it with my own eyes.

There were many heroes that night, but if there was one I remember best it was Mr Lightoller. He was everywhere, quietly ensuring the safe loading and launching of the boats, and picking out the seamen to row each one. I can hear his voice even now echoing in my head. "Lower away there. Lower away. Are there any more women? Are there any more women?" And one of the waiting men answered him back, I remember.

"No more women, officer. There's plenty of men though, but I don't see plenty of boats."

It was something every one of us now had come to realise, that there were hardly any boats left to take the rest off, and that many of the lifeboats that remained could not now be launched because of the severe list of the ship. When I saw the sea water come washing over the bow, and rushing down the deck towards us, I knew that our chances of survival were fading fast. Like so many others, I scanned the horizon desperately for the lights of the *Carpathia*. We were all aware by now that she was the only ship close enough to come to our rescue. But there were no lights to be seen.

The *Titanic* was sinking fast, and we knew now we were going down with her. With every minute that passed now the list to port was telling us the end was near. The deck was at such an angle that it was well-nigh impossible to keep our footing. We heard Mr Lightoller's voice ringing out. "All passengers to the starboard side."

So that's where Mr Stanton and I went, slipping and sliding, clutching at each other for support, until we reached the rail on the starboard side and clung on. Here we looked out at the sea, and waited silently for our end. There was nothing more to be done. "I should like to say," Mr Stanton said, his hand resting on my shoulder, "that if I am to die tonight and I cannot die with my family, then I'd rather die in your company than any other. You're a fine young man, Johnny Trott."

"Will the sea be cold?" I asked him.

"I fear so," he replied, "but don't worry, that's all to the good. It will all be over very quickly for us both."

KENSUKE'S KINGDOM

*Michael and his parents are on the voyage of a lifetime,
sailing their yacht around the world. But on one dreadful
night, Michael and his dog Stella are swept away
by the waves...*

The terrors came fast, one upon another. The lights of the *Peggy Sue* went away into the dark of the night, leaving me alone in the ocean, alone with the certainty that they were already too far away, that my cries for help could not possibly be heard. I thought then of the sharks cruising the black water beneath me – scenting me, already searching me out, homing in on me – and I knew there could be no hope. I would be eaten alive. Either that or I would drown slowly. Nothing could save me.

I trod water, frantically searching the impenetrable darkness about me for something, anything to swim towards. There was nothing.

Then a sudden glimpse of white in the sea. The breaking of a wave perhaps. But there were no waves. Stella! It had to be. I was so thankful, so relieved not to be all alone. I called out and swam towards her. She would keep bobbing away from me, vanishing, reappearing, then vanishing again. She had seemed so near, but it took several minutes of hard swimming before I came close enough to reach out and touch her. Only then did I realise my mistake. Stella's head was mostly black. This was white. It was my football. I grabbed it and clung on, feeling the unexpected and wonderful buoyancy of it. I held on, treading water and calling for Stella. There was no answer. I called and I called. But every time I opened my mouth now, the sea water rushed in. I had to give her up. I had to save myself if I could.

There was little point in wasting energy by trying to swim. After all, I had nowhere to swim to. Instead, I would simply float. I would cling to my football, tread water gently and wait for the *Peggy Sue* to come back. Sooner or later they had to discover I was overboard. Sooner or later they would come looking for me. I mustn't kick too much, just enough to keep my chin above the water, no more. Too much movement would attract the sharks. Morning must come soon. I had to hang on till then. I had to. The water wasn't that cold. I had my football. I had a chance.

I kept telling myself that over and over again. But the world stayed stubbornly black about me, and I could feel the water slowly chilling me to death. I tried singing to stop myself from shivering, to take my mind off the sharks. I sang every song I could remember, but after a while I'd forget the words. Always I came back to the only song I was sure I could finish: 'Ten Green Bottles'. I sang it out loud again and again. It reassured me to hear the sound of my own voice. It made me feel less alone in the sea. And always I looked for the grey glint of dawn, but it would not come and it would not come.

Eventually I fell silent and my legs just would not kick any more. I clung to my football, my head drifting into sleep. I knew I mustn't, but I couldn't help myself. My hands kept slipping off the ball. I was fast losing the last of my strength. I would go down, down to the bottom of the sea and lie in my grave amongst the seaweed and the sailors' bones and the shipwrecks.

The strange thing was that I didn't really mind. I didn't care, not any more. I floated away into sleep, into my dreams. And in my dream I saw a boat gliding towards me, silent over the sea. The *Peggy Sue*! Dear, dear *Peggy Sue*. They had come back for me. I knew they would. Strong arms grabbed me. I was hauled upwards and out of the water. I lay there on the deck, gasping for air like a landed fish.

Someone was bending over me, shaking me, talking to me. I could not understand a word that was being said. But it didn't matter. I felt Stella's hot breath on my face, her tongue licking my ear. She was safe. I was safe. All was well.

I was woken by a howling, like the howling of a gale through the masts. I looked about me. There were no masts above me, there were no sails. No movement under me either, no breath of wind. Stella Artois was barking, but some way off. I was not on a boat at all, but lying stretched out on sand. The howling became a screaming, a fearful crescendo of screeching that died away in its own echoes.

I sat up. I was on a beach, a broad white sweep of sand, with trees growing thick and lush behind me right down to the beach. Then I saw Stella prancing about in the shallows. I called her and she came bounding up out of the sea to greet me, her tail circling wildly. When all the leaping and licking and hugging were done, I struggled to my feet.

I was weak all over. I looked all about me. The wide blue sea was as empty as the cloudless sky above. No *Peggy Sue*. No boat. Nothing. No one. I called again and again for my mother and my father. I called until the tears came and I could call no more, until I knew there was no point. I stood there for some time trying to work out how I had got here, how it was that I'd survived. I had such confused memories, of being picked up, of being on board the *Peggy Sue*. But I knew now I couldn't have been. I must have dreamed it, dreamed the whole thing. I must have clung to my football and kept myself afloat until I was washed up. I thought of my football then, but it was nowhere to be seen.

Stella, of course, was unconcerned about all the whys and wherefores. She kept bringing me sticks to throw, and would go galloping after them into the sea without a care in the world.

Then came the howling again from the trees, and the hackles went up on Stella's neck. She charged up the beach barking and barking, until she was sure she had silenced the last of the echoes. It was a musical, plaintive howling this time, not at all menacing. I thought I recognised it. I had heard howling like it once before on a visit to London Zoo. Gibbons, "funky gibbons", my father had called them. I still don't know why to this day. But I loved the sound of the word 'funky'. Perhaps that was why I remembered what they were. "It's only gibbons," I told Stella, "just funky gibbons. They won't hurt us." But I couldn't be at all sure I was right.

From where I now stood I could see that the forest grew more sparsely up the side of a great hill some way inland, and it occurred to me then that if I could reach the bare rocky outcrop at the summit, I would be able to see further out to sea. Or perhaps there'd be some house or farm further inland, or maybe a road, and I could find someone to help. But if I left the beach and they came back looking for me, what then? I decided I would have to take that chance.

I set off at a run, Stella Artois at my heels, and soon found myself in the cooling shade of the forest. I discovered a narrow track going uphill, in the right direction, I thought. So I followed it, only slowing to a walk when the hill became too steep. The forest was alive with creatures. Birds cackled and screeched high above me, and always the howling wailed and wafted through the trees, but more distantly now.

It wasn't the sounds of the forest that bothered me, though, it was the eyes. I felt as if I was being watched by a thousand inquisitive eyes. I think Stella did too, for she had been strangely quiet ever since we entered the forest, constantly glancing up at me for reassurance and comfort. I did my best to give it, but she could sense that I, too, was frightened.

What had seemed at first to be a short hike now felt more like a great expedition into the interior. We emerged exhausted from the trees, clambered laboriously up a rocky scree and stood at long last on the peak.

The sun was blazing down. I had not really felt the burning heat of it until then. I scanned the horizon. If there was a sail somewhere out there in the haze, I could not see it. And then it came to me that even if I were to see a sail, what could I do? I couldn't light a fire. I had no matches. I knew about cavemen rubbing sticks together, but I had never tried it. I looked all round me now. Sea.

Sea. Sea. Nothing but sea on all sides. I was on an island. I was alone.

The island looked perhaps two or three miles in length, no more. It was shaped a bit like an elongated peanut, but longer at one end than the other. There was a long swathe of brilliant white beach on both sides of the island, and at the far end another hill, the slopes steeper and more thickly wooded, but not so high as mine. With the exception of these twin peaks the entire island seemed to be covered in forest. So far as I could see there was no sign of any human life. Even then, as I stood there, that first morning, filled with apprehension at the terrifying implications of my dreadful situation, I remember thinking how wonderful it was, a green jewel of an island framed in white, the sea all about it a silken shimmering blue. Strangely, perhaps comforted somehow by the extraordinary beauty of the place, I was not at all downhearted. On the contrary I felt strangely elated. I was alive. Stella Artois was alive. We had survived.

Dear Olly

Hero is a migrating swallow, about to undertake the long journey south to Africa. But as the flock sets out there are dangers in the skies…

Hero joined the others as they flocked to a nearby lake, and for several days he hunted there, skimming over the water after midges and mosquitoes. He was safe here with his family, in amongst the thousands upon thousands of milling swallows and martins; and all the while his strength grew within him. At dusk they gathered to roost in the trees and reed beds around the lake. Every night in the roost the air of expectancy grew. Every night the birds were slower to settle to their silence and their sleep.

Then one morning, early, the hobby falcon came gliding high over the lake. They heard his killer *kew-kew* call and scattered in terror. Down came the hobby, swifter than any bird Hero had ever seen. Hero felt the wind of him as he passed by, and swerved aside only just in time. But the hobby was not after him, he was after a young martin, slower and more stuttering in flight than Hero – and for the martin there was no escape.

The flock flew that same morning, a spontaneous lift-off, swirling out over the lake, a whispering cloud, darkening the sky as it went. They wheeled south, south towards the sea, hoping they had seen the last of the hobby falcon. But the hobby was not far behind, for he too was bound for Africa. He would fly all the way with them, picking off the youngest, the slowest, the weakest, whenever he felt like it. He had done it before.

Out over the coast of France he struck once again. Hero knew, as they all knew, that they must stay together, stay close and never fall behind. They flew high, where they could see the danger, where the flying was easier anyway, where they could float on the warm air. But they had to come down to drink, to feed, and that was when the hobby falcon pounced. He would appear in amongst them out of nowhere, wings cutting through the air like scythes, shadowing them, stalking them. He took his time, but once the hobby falcon had singled out his prey, there could be only one outcome. No amount of fancy aerobatics could deceive him. He would simply follow, close and kill. He was remorseless, tireless, merciless. There was always a strange sense of relief when he had killed – the survivors knew they were safe, then, for a while at least.

On they flew, on over the vineyards, on over the mountains.

It was evening over Spain, and the air was heavy with a gathering storm. The birds tried to rise above it, but the storm was suddenly upon them and could not be avoided. They bunched as they flew into it, desperately seeking each other's shelter, but were scattered at once by a whirling wind that whipped them about the blackening sky. Hero found himself alone. Lightning flashed and crackled all around him. Pounded by the rain and by hailstones too, Hero dived earthwards, faster now in his fear than he'd ever flown before. Still the storm was all around him, still he could not see the ground. Then, below, a glow of sudden light, some small hope of escape. But Hero found that his sodden wings would not beat as they should. He was falling like a stone – down, down towards the light. He could only spread his wings wide, willing them to take flight again. When at long last they did, he found himself floating down into the pool of light, a light dazzling bright and full of noise. But Hero was not afraid. He was out of the storm and that was all that mattered.

It was a football stadium. He sought out a convenient perch, the crossbar of the goalpost, settled and fluttered the wet from his wings. Here he would rest.

The goalkeeper looked up at him and laughed. "Hello, friend," he said. "Stay as long as you like. I'll be doing my best to see you're not disturbed, but I can't guarantee anything."

Hero knew that he could not rest for long, that all the while the flock would be moving further away, would be more difficult to find. He had to go, and go now. He fluffed up his feathers and shook himself ready. At that moment, the television cameras found him and focused on him. There he was – a giant swallow – up on the big screen. Twenty thousand voices cheered him as he took off and flew, up out of the light into the darkness beyond.

Even in the black of night, even without the others to guide him, Hero sensed in which direction he must go, where south must be. But he could not know where his friends were, how far away, nor how high they would be flying. Hero heard the storm still rumbling overhead. He would fly low, low and fast, and just hope to find them at first light. It was the dread of losing them, of being left behind altogether that gave new power to his wings.

All night long Hero flew, but as the sun came up and warmed his back he saw he was still quite alone. He fed constantly on the wing, and the feeding was good, the flies fat and plentiful. There was water whenever he needed it, which was often. It was as he was drinking, as he was skimming the blue stillness of a mountain lake, that he felt a sudden cold shadow pass over him. He saw the reflection in the water below. The hobby falcon! He shrieked in his terror and tried frantically to gain height and speed, twisting and turning to avoid the talons outstretched just above him, ready to snatch him from the air. One claw ripped a feather from his back, but did not touch the flesh. Then Hero was up and away, climbing towards the sun. But the hobby falcon came after him, his wing beats stiff and strong.

Now, Hero's only chance lay in his agility, and in his ability to deceive his enemy in flight. For sheer speed the hobby falcon would have the better of him. He feinted, he weaved, he dodged – but the hobby was always still there, right behind him, and waiting for just the right moment. For hour upon hour the chase went on over the parched high sierras, along lush river valleys, in amongst the roofs and chimneys and aerials of hilltop villages and towns.

Hero was tiring, and tiring fast now. There was a forest below filling the valley. He saw his one last chance. With the hobby still on his tail, he dived suddenly down in amongst the shadows of the cork trees. He flitted through the branches, flashed through the dappled light, seeking the darkest depths of the forest. A glance back, and then another. The hobby was nowhere to be seen. On he sped, just to be sure, to be very sure. His eyes scanned the forest about him. The hobby had not followed him. He had lost him. He was safe at last. He landed, his heart beating wildly, and perched there for some time, on the lookout all the while for the stubby-tailed silhouette he so much dreaded, listening for the killer *kew-kew* call he never again wanted to hear.

Hero had stayed long enough. He had to go, he had to risk it sometime. He lifted off his perch out of the dark depths of the forest and flew away south, straight as an arrow, high over the sunlit sierras.

The hobby came down on him like a bolt from the blue, missing him by only a whisker at the first pass, so close Hero could see the dark glint in his eye. The bare sierras stretched away to the horizon – they offered no hiding place. Hero dived, and the death shadow followed him. He cried out, steeling himself for cruel claws that would tear the life out of him.

A gunshot blasted the air around him. Hero saw the hobby stagger and stutter in flight, and hurtle to earth, where he bounced and bounced, and then was still. Hunters came running over the hills with their dogs.

Hero could feel the wind off the sea ahead, and the heat of the desert beyond, beckoning him on. The sea was quickly crossed. He drank from a swimming pool, beside a hotel of white marble, in Morocco. Children were playing there, laughing with delight every time he came swooping down to dip into the blue of the water beside them. But once the children had gone inside, once he had drunk and fed his fill, Hero set off across the desert. He flew by the moon, by the stars, keeping low over the sand.

The great red sun came up over the desert and chased

481

away the cold of the night. Still no water, still alone. Hero cried out for his friends again and again as he flew. *Tswit. Tswit. Tswit.* Never an answering call, never a sign of them. All day and another night and another day, Hero flew, gliding, resting on the thermals whenever he could, for he felt his strength ebbing away fast. Without water he could not go on much longer. And now there came a hot desert wind blowing against him, slowing him. He saw the billowing sandstorm in the distance, and heard its dreadful roaring. To be caught in it would be certain death. He would have to fly over it. With the very last of his strength he beat his way skywards. Try as he did, Hero could not entirely avoid the stinging lash of the fringes of the storm, but at least the murderous heart of it had passed safely beneath him.

Hero glided now because there was no power in his wings to do anything else. He was completely exhausted. That last stupendous effort had finished him utterly. He floated on the air as far as he could. He called out desperately for his companions. *Tswit. Tswit. Tswit.* Suddenly, the whole desert seemed to be answering him. He called again, and from the heat haze below came a clamouring chorus of welcome. The haze darkened and became trees – an oasis of palm trees amongst the sand dunes below him, where every tree was alive with birds, all of them singing out their greetings.

Hero floated down to join them. They were there in their thousands, swallows and martins, and swifts too. Hero landed where he needed to, right at the water's edge. It didn't matter a bit to him when a camel came down to drink beside him. Camel and swallow drank together, oblivious to anything but the sweet cooling relief of the water.

Tales Told and New

Illustration by Emma Chichester Clark

Cockadoodle-doo, Mr Sultana

In a far-off Eastern land, a long, long time ago, there once lived a great and mighty Sultan. He was, without doubt, the richest, laziest, greediest and fattest Sultan there had ever been. He was so rich his palace was built of nothing but shining marble and glowing gold, so rich that even the buttons on his silken clothes were made of diamonds.

He was so lazy he had to have a special servant to brush his teeth for him, and another one to dress him.

He did nothing for himself, except eat. He was so greedy that every meal – breakfast, lunch and dinner – he'd gobble down a nice plump peacock just to himself, and a great bowl of sweetmeats too. And then he'd wash it all down with a jug of honeyed camel's milk.

It was because he was so very lazy and so very greedy that he was so very, very fat.

He had to sleep in a bed wide enough for five grown men, and his pantaloons were the baggiest, most capacious pantaloons ever made for anyone anywhere.

But believe it or not there was something the Sultan cared about even more than his food – his treasure. He loved his treasure above anything else in the whole world.

Before he went to sleep every night, he would always open his treasure chest and count out his jewels – emeralds, rubies, diamonds, pearls, sapphires, hundreds and hundreds of them – just to be quite sure they were all still there. Only then could he go to bed happy and sleep soundly.

But outside the walls of his palace, the Sultan's people lived like slaves, poor, wretched and *hungry*. They had to work every hour God gave them. And why?

To keep the Sultan rich in jewels. Everything they harvested – their corn, their grapes, their figs, their dates, their pomegranates – all had to be given to the Sultan. He allowed them just enough food to keep body and soul together – no more.

One fine morning, the Sultan was out hunting. He loved to hunt, because all he had to do was sit astride his horse and send the hawks off to do the hunting. There was only one horse in the land strong enough to carry him, a great stout old warhorse. But strong though he was, to be sat on by the great fat Sultan for hour after hour under the hot, hot, sun, proved too much even for him.

Lathered up and exhausted, the old warhorse staggered suddenly and stumbled, throwing the Sultan to the ground.

It took ten servants to get him to his feet and brush him down. He wasn't badly hurt, just a bit bumped and bruised, but he was angry; very angry.

He ordered his servants to whip the old horse soundly, so that he wouldn't do it again. Then they all helped him back up on his horse, which took some time, of course; and off they went back to the palace.

———

The Sultan didn't know it, not yet, and no more did anyone else, but he'd left something behind lying in the dirt on the dusty farmyard track, something that had popped off his waistcoat when he'd fallen from his horse.

It was a button, a shining, glittering diamond button.

Just a little way off down the farmyard track, was a tumbledown farmhouse where there lived a poor old woman. She had little enough in this world – though she never complained of it – only a couple of nanny goats for her milk, a few hens for her eggs, *and* a little red rooster. She always kept the goats hidden away inside her house, and the hens too, for fear that the Sultan's servants might come by and steal them away for the Sultan. She had always tried to keep her little red rooster in the house too, because she loved him dearly, and because she wanted him to keep her hens happy. But this was a little red rooster with a mind of his own, and whenever he could, he would go running off to explore the big, wide world outside, to find friends – and to find food, for he was always very hungry.

***

That same day, when the poor old woman went out to fetch the water for her goats and hens, the little red rooster scooted out from under her skirts. Before she could stop him he was out through the open door and running off down the farm track.

"Come back, Little Red Rooster!" cried the poor old woman. "Come back! If the Sultan finds you, he'll catch you and eat you up. Come back!"

But the little red rooster had never in his life been frightened of anything or anyone. He just kept on running. "Catch me if you can, mistress mine," he called out.

On and on he ran, until he came to the farm track where the cornfield and the vineyard met. He knew this was just the perfect place to scratch around for a good meal. Here he'd find all the ripe corn and dried-up sultanas he could eat. As he pecked about busily in the earth, he came across dozens of wriggling worms and singing cicadas and burrowing beetles, but he never ate these. After all, these were his friends. He couldn't eat his friends – though he had thought about it once or twice.

Meanwhile, back in his gold and marble palace, the great Sultan was stamping up and down. He was in a horrible temper, his stomachs and his chins wobbling with fury.

"The diamond button off my waistcoat," he roared. "I have lost my diamond button. Search, you miserable beggars, search everywhere, every nook and cranny."

His servants were scurrying here and there and everywhere, all over the palace, but they could not find it anywhere.

"I'll lop off your heads if you don't find it," he bellowed. But no matter how loud he shouted, how terrible the threats, no one could find the missing diamond button.

"Am I surrounded by nothing but fools and imbeciles?" he thundered. "I see I shall have to find it myself. We shall go back and search every inch of the ground we hunted over this morning. And you will go in front of me, all of you on your knees in the dust where you belong, and search for my diamond button. Fetch me my horse."

He clapped his hands.

"At once. At once."

Out in the countryside, the little red rooster was scratching around in the dusty farm track at the edge of the cornfield. He scratched and he scratched. Suddenly there was something strange in the earth, something different, something very pretty that glistened and shone and twinkled in the sun. He tried eating it, but it didn't taste very good. So he dropped it. And then he had a sudden and brilliant idea.

"I know," he said to himself. "Poor old mistress mine loves pretty things. She's always saying so, and she's got nothing pretty of her own. I'll take it home for her. Then she won't be cross with me for running away, will she?"

But just as he picked it up again, along the farm track came the great fat Sultan on his horse, and in front of him, dozens of his servants, all of them crawling on their hands and knees in the dirt.

Closer and closer they came. All at once they spotted the little red rooster *and* the diamond button too, glinting in his beak.

"There, my lord Sultan!" they cried. "Look! That little red rooster. He's got your diamond button."

"So that's what it is," the little red rooster said to himself.

The great fat Sultan rode up, scattering his servants hither and thither as he came. "Little Red Rooster," he said from high up on his horse. "I see you have my diamond button. I am your great and mighty Sultan. Give it to me at once. It's valuable, very valuable. And it's mine."

"I don't think so, Mr Sultana," replied the little red

rooster, who had never in his life been frightened of anyone or anything. "Cockadoodle-doo, Mr Sultana. Finders keepers. If it's so valuable, then I'm going to give it to poor mistress mine. She needs it a lot more than you, I think. Sorry, Mr Sultana."

"What!" spluttered the Sultan. "Mr Sultana? How dare you speak to me like that! How dare you! Did you hear what that infernal bird called me? Fetch me that rooster. Fetch me my diamond button! Grab him! Grab that rooster!"

There was a frightful kerfuffle of dust and feathers… and squawking, as the Sultan's servants tried to grab the little red rooster. Whatever they did, they just could not catch him. In the end, the little red rooster ran off into the cornfield. But although he'd escaped their clutches, he was very cross with himself, for in all the kerfuffle he had dropped the diamond button.

———

One of the Sultan's servants found it lying in the dust and brought it back to the Sultan. The Sultan was delighted, of course, and all his servants were mightily relieved, too. Now, at least, none of them would have his head lopped off, not that day anyway.

But had the Sultan seen the last of the little red rooster? Not by any means. The little red rooster wasn't going to give up that easily – he wasn't like that. He followed the

Sultan and his servants back to the palace. Then, in the middle of the night, as everyone slept, he flew up to the Sultan's window, perched on the window ledge, took a deep breath and crowed, and crowed.

Cockadoodle-doo!

He let out the loudest, longest, cockadoodle-doo he'd ever doodled in all his life.

"Cockadoodle-doo, Mr Sultana," he crowed. "Cocka-doodle-doo!"

The Sultan tried to cover his ears. It didn't work.

"Cockadoodle-doo!"

The Sultan tried to bury his head in his pillow. It didn't work.

"Cockadoodle-doo, Mr Sultana! Give me back my diamond button."

By now the Sultan was in a terrible rage. He had had quite enough of this. He called in his servants. "Grab me that infernal bird," he cried. "I know what I'll do. I know. We'll throw him in the well and drown him. That should shut him up, and shut him up for good."

All night long, the Sultan and his servants chased around the palace after the little red rooster. The little red rooster had lots of fun. He played hide-and-seek behind the peacocks.

He flew,

he hopped,

he ran.

He perched on cornices,

on chandeliers,

on the Sultan's throne itself!

And that was where they finally caught him. One of the servants crept up behind and grabbed him by his tail feathers. The little red rooster didn't really mind – he'd had enough of the game anyway. He wasn't at all frightened of water. He knew what to do with water. He wasn't worried.

"Aha!" cried the exultant Sultan. "We've got you now. You've crowed your very last doodle-doo."

"I don't think so, Mr Sultana," said the little red rooster. But the Sultan took him by the neck and dropped him down the well. It was a long flutter down, and of course it was a bit wet when he landed. But the little red rooster didn't mind. He simply said to himself: "*Come, my empty stomach. Come, my empty stomach and drink up all the water.*"

It took a bit of time, but that's just what he did. He drank up all the water, every last drop of it. Up and out of the well he flew, up and away, until he reached the Sultan's window.

"Cockadoodle-doo, Mr Sultana!" he cried, "Give me back my diamond button!"

The Sultan could not believe his eyes. He could not believe his ears. "What!" he spluttered. You again!"

He called his servants. "Look!" he shrieked. "Can't you see? That infernal bird is back. I know what I'll do, I know. We'll grab him and throw him into the fire. Let him burn." So the Sultan's servants rushed at the little red rooster and caught him.

"Aha!" cried the exultant Sultan. "We've got you now. You've crowed your very last doodle-doo."

"I don't think so, Mr Sultana," said the little red rooster. But the Sultan took him by the neck and threw him on the fire. He wasn't at all frightened of fire. He knew what to do with fire. He wasn't worried. He simply said to himself: "*Come, my full-up stomach. Come, my full-up stomach, let out all the water and put out all the fire.*"

It took a bit of time, but that's just what he did. He gushed out all the water and put out all the fire, every last spark of it. And up he flew again to the Sultan's window.

"Cockadoodle-doo, Mr Sultana," he cried. "Give me back my diamond button."

"What!" spluttered the Sultan. "You again!"

Now the Sultan was really mad. He was beside himself with fury. He called his servants again. "Look! That infernal bird is back. I know what I'll do this time. I know. We'll grab him and throw him into the beehive. Let the bees sting him." And the Sultan's servants rushed at the little red rooster and caught him.

"Aha!" cried the exultant Sultan. "We've got you now. You've crowed your very last doodle-doo."

"I don't think so, Mr Sultana," said the little red rooster. But the Sultan took him by the neck and threw him into the beehive.

The little red rooster wasn't at all frightened by the bees. He knew what to do with bees. He wasn't worried. As the bees buzzed angrily all around him he simply said to himself: "*Come, my empty stomach. Come, my empty stomach and eat up all the bees.*"

And that's just what he did. He ate up all the bees, every last one of them.

Back in the palace, the Sultan was rubbing his hands with glee. He thought for sure he had seen the last of the little red rooster. But he hadn't, had he?

He was happily tucking into his lunch of roast peacock, when suddenly he heard this:

"Cockadoodle-doo, Mr Sultana! Give me back my

diamond button." The little red rooster was back on the window ledge.

"What!" spluttered the Sultan, his mouth full of peacock. "You again!"

Like a crazed camel, he was, like a vengeful vulture, like a jibbering jackal. He stamped and stormed about the palace, shouting and screaming at his servants.

"Who will rid me of this infernal bird?" he cried. "Tell me. Tell me how to do it, or I'll lop off your heads. I will! I will!"

And the servants knew he meant it too. So naturally they all thought about how they could get rid of the little red rooster. They thought very hard, very hard indeed.

"Hang him by the neck from the pomegranate tree, my lord Sultan," said one. But the Sultan shook his head.

"Lop off his head, my lord Sultan," said another.

"It's no good," wailed the Sultan. "He'd only run around without it." And he sat down in deep despair on his cushions.

But then, just as he was sitting down, he heard the cushions sighing and groaning underneath him. He was squashing them flat!

"That's it!" he cried, leaping to his feet. "I know what I'll do. I'll sit on him and flatten him. I'll squash him. I'll squish him. I'll obsquatulate him!"

From the window ledge the little red rooster heard it

all and smiled inside himself.

The Sultan's servants rushed at the little red rooster and caught him.

"Aha!" cried the exultant Sultan. "We've got you now. You've crowed your very last doodle-doo."

"I don't think so, Mr Sultana," said the little red rooster. But the Sultan took the little red rooster by the neck, stuffed him down the back of his pantaloons and then sat down on him, hard, very hard indeed.

The little red rooster wasn't at all frightened of being obsquatulated. He knew what to do about that. He wasn't worried. He simply said to himself: "*Come, my full-up stomach. Come, my full-up stomach, let out all the bees and sting the Sultan's bottom.*"

And were those bees angry? I should say so. And did they all sting the great and mighty Sultan's bottom? I should say so. There was plenty of room in those capacious pantaloons for every bee to sting wherever he wanted. And remember, that great and mighty Sultan had a very large, very round bottom, probably the biggest bottom the world had ever seen!

Did the great fat Sultan jump up and down? I should say so. Did he screech and yowl and whimper? I should say so. And did the little red rooster hop out of those great pantaloons and fly off safe and sound? Of course he did.

"Aiee! Ow! Youch! Oosh, ooh!" cried the Sultan, as he

sat with his stinging bottom dunked in a bath of ice-cold water.

"Cockadoodle-doo, Mr Sultana!" cried the little red rooster. "Now, will you let me have back my diamond button?"

"All right, all right," said the Sultan. "I give in. Anything, anything to get you out of my sight. Take him up to my room and give him his confounded diamond button. It's in my treasure chest."

So the Sultan's servants took the little red rooster up to the Sultan's bedchamber, and gave him the diamond button from out of the Sultan's treasure chest.

"Now go," they cried. "Fly away! *Shoo!* You've got what you came for. Go, before you get us into any more trouble."

"I'm going. I'm going," replied the little red rooster, the diamond button in his beak. But he was in no hurry to go, for something had caught his eye. He could not believe his luck. The Sultan's treasure chest! The servants had left it open! So he flew away only as far as the window ledge, and he waited there till all the servants had left. Then he flew down and hopped across the room and up on to the treasure chest. Emeralds, rubies, diamonds, pearls, sapphires – the finest jewels in the entire world.

"Ah well. In for a penny, in for a pound," said the little red rooster to himself. "*Come, my empty stomach and gobble down the Sultan's jewels."*

And that's just what he did. He gobbled down all the Sultan's jewels, every last one of them. Then out he flew, out of the window and out over the palace walls, which was not at all easy, because he was rather heavy now. He had to waddle all the rest of the way back home, rattling as he went.

As he neared the farm, he happened to meet up with his friends again, the wriggling worms and the singing cicadas and the burrowing beetles. So, of course, he just had to tell them all about his great adventures in the Sultan's palace. He was only halfway through his story when the poor old woman, who had been looking high and low for him, spied him at last. She came scuttling along the farm track.

"Where have you been, Little Red Rooster?" she cried. "I've been worried sick."

"Ah, mistress mine," replied the little red rooster. "Never in your life will you ever have to worry again. And never will we have to go hungry again, either. Look what I have for you."

And he said to himself: *"Come, my full-up stomach. Come, my full-up stomach and give up all your jewels."*

Out they poured on to the ground, all of them, all the Sultan's jewels, until there was a great sparkling pile of them at the poor old woman's feet.

Only, she wasn't poor any more, was she?

It took the breath right out of her. She sat down with a bump, still trying to believe her eyes.

"Goodness me!" she cried. "Goodness me!"

And she *was* good too, goodness itself. Do you know what she did? She gave those jewels to all her poor friends in the countryside round about, just enough for each of them so that no one had too much. She kept for herself all she needed, and no more. But, of course, the little red rooster got to keep his diamond button.

Just you try and take it from him!

AESOP'S FABLES
FOR MR AESOP FROM MR MORPURGO, A THANK YOU

*T*here *was once a lion who never hunted any more because
he was too old and too tired; who didn't roar any more
because he was too sad. So he spent all day and every day in
his cave feeling very bored and very hungry. All the animals
who passed by would stop and tease him. "Who's roaring
now?" they'd chant.*

*One morning he woke up and saw a young man sitting
reading a book at the mouth of his cave.*

"What are you reading?" asked Lion.

*"Some stories," replied the young man. "I've just written
a story about you; about an old lion who won't leave his cave
because he feels he's too old. He feels he's not what he was,
a bit slow, a bit stupid."*

"What happens to him?" asked Lion.

*"He meets a young man one day called Aesop, a
storyteller, who comes to his cave and reads him all the
fables he has written. And the lion loves the stories so much
he wants to read them again himself."*

"What happens next?" asked Lion.

"That's up to you," said Aesop. And leaving him the

book, he went on his way.

Sitting at the mouth of his cave the next morning Lion roared and roared so loud that all the animals heard and came running to the cave at once.

"My friends," said Lion, "come into my cave and I will read you the best stories ever written." And they did. All the animals marvelled at Lion and how clever he was.

"This lion may be old and slow," they thought, "but this lion is not stupid."

Story after story he read, and after each one explained the moral of the story. All afternoon, all evening, all night, he read, so that one by one the animals dropped off to sleep. By morning he'd finished all of Aesop's fables and he'd also eaten up all his sleeping listeners too.

A STORY IS AS GOOD AS A FEAST.
BUT WATCH OUT YOU DON'T GO TO SLEEP!

GENTLE GIANT

On a small island way out in the middle of a silver lake there once lived a sad young man. He had been unhappy ever since he was a child, when his mother had died and left him alone in the world, still quite unable to talk.

But he was sad for another reason too. He had grown up into a giant of a man, very big, very strong and very frightening. Because of this, no one liked to go near him, and so he had no friends at all.

Every day he rowed across the silver lake to work in the village of Ballyloch, where he thatched all the houses and barns and hayricks with barley straw. But, however hard he worked, the villagers were always unkind. If ever he opened his mouth to try to talk they simply laughed at him. "He caws like a crow," they jeered. "He croaks like a frog."

They called him the Beastman of Ballyloch.

"The Beastman's coming," the villagers would cry. "Look out, look out, Mister Ugly's about!" Time and again they warned their children to keep away from him. "He's mad. He's bad," they said. "He'll gobble you up for his supper. Don't go near him."

Every evening after work, the Beastman would row back to his island home where he lived on his own. But he was never quite alone, for around him lived all the wild creatures he loved – squirrels, otters, ducks, herons, kingfishers – and dearest of all, his beloved swans. To every one of them he was neither a Beastman nor ugly, but a true and trusted friend.

Early one spring morning the Beastman looked out over the lake and saw there was already someone out fishing. It was a young woman in a wide-brimmed straw hat. And then she began to sing. The Beastman had never heard anything so beautiful.

But suddenly, as he watched, the boat tipped, and with a cry the girl was over the side, vanishing at once under the water. The Beastman did not think twice. He ran down to the lake and plunged in. He swam out to where her straw hat still floated, and dived down into the murky depths beneath. It was icy cold in the water, but the Beastman searched and searched until at last he found her, lying in amongst the weeds at the bottom of the lake.

Gathering her in his arms he swam up to the surface and back to his island. He did all he could to bring her back to life, but still she did not move and she did not breathe. The Beastman held his face in his hands and wept.

"Why are you crying?" She was speaking! She was alive

after all! "You saved me," she said.

He wanted so much to talk, to tell her how happy he was, but all that came out was a hideous croaking.

She smiled at him. "Back home in the village, we call you the Beastman of Ballyloch. But you're not a Beastman, are you? All I see in your eyes is gentleness."

She took his hand. "My name is Miranda," she told him, "and I shall be your friend for ever."

All that day Miranda rested by the fire, while the Beastman made the best potato soup she had ever tasted. As she slept, he looked down at her and knew that he loved her more than life itself.

That evening, as they rowed back over the silver lake, she could see that he was sad. "I'll come back again tomorrow," she promised. "Don't worry."

But someone had seen them out together in the Beastman's boat. By the time she got home, her father knew about it, and he was furious. "You dare to disobey me! Haven't I told you never, ever, to go near that monster?"

Miranda tried to explain how the Beastman had saved her life, but her father was too angry to listen. He took her upstairs and locked her in her room.

That same evening, there came to the village a stranger, a smiling stranger with twinkling eyes. He was carrying a load of sacks on the back of his cart.

"What do you want most in all the world?" he asked

the villagers.

"To be rich, of course," they cried.

"And so you shall be, my friends, but only if you buy my magic stardust. All you have to do is sprinkle my magic stardust on your lake. Believe me, within one day you will be catching fish as big as whales."

And they believed every word he told them. With his twinkling eyes he charmed them, and in no time at all the villagers had bought all the stardust he had.

Next morning, early, they were out in their fishing boats sprinkling the stardust on the water. By evening the silver lake rang with shouts of joy. The stardust was doing its magic! They were catching the biggest, fattest fish they had ever seen.

But the Beastman was becoming more and more troubled. His swans and all his wild creatures seemed suddenly bewildered and frightened, as if they knew that something terrible was about to happen. And still Miranda had not come back to him as she had promised.

That night, thunder rumbled and rolled about the mountains. Lightning crackled, and the lake howled all around him in the wind. The Beastman stood on the shore of his island, waiting and watching for Miranda. But she did not come and she did not come.

By morning, the storm had passed. The Beastman was still standing there, still hoping to see Miranda's boat.

But there was no boat. Instead, in the first light of dawn, he saw to his horror that his beautiful lake was no longer silver, but a ghastly green all over.

Then, from across the lake he heard the sound of wailing. He soon saw why. Ballyloch was in ruins. Every roof of every house and barn had been blown off by the storm, and the straw was strewn about the streets. The Beastman crouched down and ran his hand through the water. Slime, green slime.

An otter ran along the shore, green from head to tail. Everywhere the fish lay dead or dying. Worst of all, his beloved swans were choking as they dipped their necks into the water to drink.

That was when the Beastman noticed a bright circle of clear silver water, and floating in the middle of it, was Miranda's straw hat. He waded out and plucked it from the water. Then he saw that underneath, it was covered in thick green slime.

At once, the Beastman knew what had to be done. But he needed help. Miranda. Miranda would help him.

He leapt into his boat and rowed over to Ballyloch. As he hurried through the village streets, no one noticed him. "Our lake is dying," wailed the villagers. "It's the smiling stranger's fault! Where is he?" But the smiling stranger had long since taken his money and vanished.

From her bedroom window, Miranda saw the Beastman

and called down to him. In no time, he had unlocked her door and set her free.

"Look at the lake!" she cried. "What are we to do?"

At first, Miranda could make no sense of the Beastman's frantic croaking. Only when he held out her straw hat, and showed her the green slime underneath, did she understand what he was trying to tell her.

At once, Miranda gathered the villagers together.

"Do you want to save our beautiful silver lake?" she asked them. "And all our wild creatures?"

"Yes!" they cried. So Miranda told them exactly what the Beastman wanted them to do. No one argued, for they knew this was their only hope.

Soon, everyone was busy picking up the fallen thatch from the streets. All day they worked, spreading it out, weaving it into great straw mats. Their backs ached, their hands were raw; but on they worked until at last the job was done. Then, at dusk, the fishing boats towed the mats out on to the lake and left them floating there. "Now all we can do is wait and hope," said Miranda.

That night, out on the island, Miranda and the Beastman gathered together his beloved swans and all the wild creatures they could find, and cleaned them until their feathers and their fur were bright and shining again.

When they had finished, Miranda taught the Beastman to say her name. Soon, he could say "Manda", which sounded, she told him, just as good as Miranda, if not better. She taught him many more words that night, but his favourite was "Manda". He kept saying it over and over, until they both fell asleep.

Next morning they woke to the sound of whooping and cheering and laughing. They could hardly believe their eyes…

Every fishing boat in Ballyloch was out on the lake, and heading towards the island. And the lake was silver again, dancing in the light of the early morning sun. The green had entirely vanished.

And the straw had done its work, just as they had hoped it would. Overhead flew the Beastman's beloved swans, white again, as white as snow, their wings singing in the air.

The people of Ballyloch were overjoyed. As for Miranda's father, he begged his daughter's forgiveness, and the Beastman's too, for the way he had been treated for so many years.

"We know now," he said, "how wise you are and kind, for you knew the secret of the barley straw and saved us from ourselves. For as long as men tell stories, they will tell of you – and of Miranda's marvellous hat!"

Everyone hung garlands of flowers around the Beastman's neck, and Miranda's too. All day long they danced and sang and feasted.

As the villagers' boats left the island that evening, the sun went down over the silver lake. Miranda's hand stole into his.

"You are no longer the Beastman of Ballyloch," she whispered. "You are my Gentle Giant."

"And you are my Manda," said the Gentle Giant. "My Manda."

And it's quite true about straw and water.
Lay a mat of straw on a murky green pond for a while,
and the water will soon be bright and clean again.
Try it! There's truth in every fairy tale.

On Angel Wings

*T*he truth is that once we weren't children any more
we never did believe Grandpa's story, not really,
much as we might have wanted to. It was just too
improbable, too fantastical. We still loved listening to it,
though. Christmas nights would never have been the same
without it.

*We'd be out there on the hillside, all of us together,
keeping watch over the sheep by night. That's where he'd
been on the first Christmas night all those years before,
the night it happened – or that's what he told us. We'd
be wrapped in our cloaks and huddled round the fire, the
sheep shifting around us in the darkness, and we'd be
ready and waiting for the story to begin. That's just how
it was last night. Grandpa poked his shepherd's crook into
the fire and sent a shower of sparks flying up into the
night sky.*

"When I was very little," he began, "I remember I used
to think all the stars were made out of sparks like those,
sparks that went on for ever, that never went out. Then
one night, I'd have been nine, or maybe ten years old,

something quite wonderful happened. Father and Uncle Zac were there, and my older brothers, Reuben and Jacob. We were all tired and irritable. It had been a long, hard day. We'd lost a couple of lambs the night before, to a wolf maybe, or a jackal. So no one was singing around the fire that night. No one was even talking. I remember I was stabbing at the fire with my crook, making stars of the sparks, as I loved to do. Then it happened.

Instead of flying up high to join the stars, they seemed to be playing with one another, then arranging themselves into a figure, a human figure, that was bathed in sudden glorious light, hovering over us, wings outstretched. It was an angel!

I threw myself into Father's arms and buried my face in his shoulder. When I dared look up again Uncle Zac and Reuben and Jacob were lying face down on the ground, Jacob sobbing like a baby. The sheep had scattered everywhere, bleating piteously.

"I'm sorry to drop in on you unexpectedly like this," said the angel. And at the sound of his voice the sheep fell silent around us. "It must be an awful shock. But believe me you've got nothing to worry about, nothing at all."

There was a comforting warmth to his voice, and a gentleness about him that was instantly reassuring. Uncle Zac and Reuben and Jacob were up on their knees by now, their faces filled not with fear, but with awe and wonder. The sheep were drifting back towards us, gazing up at the angel adoringly as if he were their shepherd. It was Uncle Zac who dared to speak first.

"Are you really an angel?" he breathed.

"I am," said the angel. "And my name is Gabriel."

"Are you really real?" Father asked, clutching me as tightly as I was clutching him. "Or are you a dream?"

"No dream," the Angel Gabriel replied. "What I am is real, and what I've come to tell you is true. I bring you news of great joy. For tonight, only a few miles away from here in Bethlehem a child has been born, a Saviour who is Christ the Lord. He will bring peace and goodwill to the whole world. Even as I speak, this child King, this son of God and son of man, is lying wrapped in swaddling clothes and cradled in a manger. I can see from your faces that you don't quite believe me, do you?"

"Kings are born in palaces," said Father.

"Not this King," replied the angel. "But seeing is believing, isn't it? How would you like to go there? Would you like to see him for yourselves?"

"We'll go, of course we will," said Uncle Zac, getting to his feet. "But you'll have to tell us where to find him. There are dozens of stables in Bethlehem. How are we to know which one he is in?"

"It's simple," the Angel Gabriel said. "When I've gone

you'll see a star in the eastern sky. Just follow it and it'll stop right over the stable. That's where you'll find the baby. What are you waiting for? Do you want to go, or don't you?"

"Why us?" asked Uncle Zac. "Why have you chosen us?"

"Because," replied the Angel Gabriel, "because one day he too will be a shepherd as you are, a shepherd not of sheep, but of all mankind."

"I don't like it," Reuben whispered to Uncle Zac. "How do we know it's true? It could be some sort of trick, to get us to leave our sheep."

"Oh dear," sighed the Angel Gabriel. "I can see you're going to need some convincing."

As he spoke the sky above was suddenly filled with angels, hundreds of them, and the whole earth rang with their singing. "Glory to God on high. And on earth, peace, goodwill towards men."

Even as they sang, they hovered above us, their wings beating the air so that there was a great rushing wind all about us that fanned the embers of the fire into sudden roaring flames.

Reuben and Jacob and Uncle Zac were flat on their faces again, but I watched. I watched all the time. I didn't want to miss a thing. I wasn't frightened at all, I was simply spellbound.

The angels were gone as unexpectedly as they had appeared, the Angel Gabriel too, leaving us alone with our sheep in the silence and the darkness of the hillside. It took a while for our eyes to become accustomed to the dark again. Father threw some more wood on to the fire, and when the sparks flew up I half expected them to become the Angel Gabriel again, but this time they just vanished into the blackness above.

"Look," Uncle Zac whispered. "Look up there in the east. That star! It's moving!"

And sure enough, there it was: a moving star low in the eastern sky, as bright a star as I'd ever seen.

"Come on. Let's follow it," Uncle Zac said. "We have to find out if this Saviour has really come. We have to know if the child King is there."

"What about the sheep?" Father asked. "Who'll look after the sheep? We can't just leave them."

"Well, I'm not staying," said Reuben and Jacob in unison.

And suddenly everyone was looking at me and I could see at once the way it was going.

"Why me?" I protested. "What about the wolves? What about the jackals?"

"He's frightened of the dark," Jacob scoffed. "He's a scaredy-cat."

"You've got the fire," Uncle Zac told me. "They won't

come near the fire."

"We won't be gone long, son." Father might have sounded more sympathetic than my brothers, but he was still going with them. They were still leaving me alone. "Bethlehem's just over the hill. We'll be back before dawn."

"But we could take the sheep with us," I pleaded. "Then we could all go."

"You can't move sheep in the dark, stupid," Reuben said.

"But why me?" I cried. "It's just because I'm the youngest. It's not fair." No one was listening to me.

"Don't worry," said Father, trying to console me as they made ready to go. "We'll tell you all about the baby when we get back. Promise. You just keep the fire going and look after the sheep. You'll be quite safe."

And off they went, shadows drifting away into the night, leaving me. I had never felt so alone, nor so miserable as I did then. Sitting by the fire, pulling my cloak around me, I cursed my luck for being the youngest, and my father for abandoning me, and began to sob my heart out. Lifting my head I let out a huge wail of anger and despair that echoed over the hills.

"It's not fair! It's not fair!"

As the echoes died I became suddenly aware that I was not alone any more. There, opposite me in the glowing light of the fire, sat the Angel Gabriel.

"You don't sound very happy," he said. "They left you behind, didn't they? Well, someone had to look after the sheep, I suppose."

"I suppose," I said, so relieved not to be alone any more.

"You're right, though," said the Angel Gabriel, "about life not being fair. So I've had this idea, to make it a little fairer. I could fly you there to the stable. We could be there and back, lickety-split, and no one would ever know you'd been gone."

"You could fly me there?" I cried, more excited than I had been in all my life. "You could really do that?"

"Easy as pie," he said.

At that moment a sheep and her lamb came and lay down beside me, as if to remind me of my duty. I knew I couldn't leave them.

"The sheep," I said, suddenly downcast. "There'd be no one to look after the sheep."

"Have you forgotten my heavenly chorus?" said the Angel Gabriel. "They don't just sing, you know."

And even as he spoke the sky above us burst into light and out of the light they came floating down – who knows how many? – landing softly on their feet in amongst the sheep who seemed not in the least alarmed.

"Enough to do the job, I think, don't you?" laughed the Angel Gabriel. "Now, hop on. We haven't a moment to lose."

I did as he told me. Still clutching my shepherd's crook, I vaulted on to his back and clung on. So I left the sheep with their guardian angels and lifted off, my arms around the Angel Gabriel's neck.

"Hang on," he said, laughing, "but don't throttle me, there's a good lad."

And so we rose into the sky, leaving the sheep below with the guardian angels now as their shepherds. On we flew along the black glassy rivers, up and down hills, his great wings beating strongly, slowly. And always we went eastwards, the star ahead of us, beckoning us on. I wanted it to go on for ever and ever, even though the cold numbed my fingers, numbed my face, and made my eyes water. I saw the lights of the little town flickering beneath us. We saw where the star had stopped, saw the lights of the stable below. We floated gently to earth in the courtyard of an inn.

The town lay asleep all around us, still and silent, except for a couple of dogs that barked at one another. Cats slunk everywhere into dark alleyways, their eyes glinting.

"You go in alone," said the Angel Gabriel. "His mother is called Mary, his father is Joseph. Off you go now."

The guttering glow of yellow lamplight seemed to be inviting me in. The door was half open. I stepped in.

It was much like any other stable I'd been in – warm

and dusty and smelly. A couple of donkeys were lying side by side, their great ears following me, their eyes watching me with dreamy indifference. In the dim light of the stable I could see several oxen chewing their cud, grunting contentedly. One of them licked deep into her nose as I passed by. I could still see no baby, no Christ child, no King. I was beginning to wonder if the angel had brought me to the wrong place. Then from a stall at the far end of the stable came a man's voice.

"We're over here," he said. "Where the sheep are. Careful you don't tread on them."

The sheep shifted as I walked slowly through them. A lamb came skittering out of the shadows and suckled his mother furiously, his tail waggling with wild delight.

It was then I saw them, at last, their faces bright in the lamplight.

"Come closer," said Mary. "You won't be disturbing him. He's wide awake."

She was sitting propped up in the hay, the baby cradled in her arms. All I could see of him was a pink face and one tiny hand, which he waved a little and then promptly shoved in his mouth. He was looking at me, straight at me, and when at last he took his fist out of his mouth, he smiled, and it was a smile I have never forgotten, a smile of such love that it moves my heart to this day whenever I think of it.

I crouched down in the straw beside them and when I offered him my finger, he clung on to it and didn't seem to want to let go.

"He's strong," I said.

"He'll need to be," said Joseph.

We talked in whispers, the three of us, and Joseph told me how ashamed he was not to have found a better place for Mary to give birth, but that everywhere in Bethlehem, all the inns, were full.

"It's fine," said Mary. "It's warm in here and his manger's full of soft hay for a cradle. He has all he needs, and now he has his first visitor. Would you like to hold him for a while?"

I had never in all my life held a baby before – plenty of lambs, but never a baby. Joseph showed me how to do it. Babies were easier, I discovered. They didn't wriggle so much.

"What's he called?" I asked, cradling him in my arms, hoping against hope he wouldn't cry.

"Jesus," Mary said. "We're calling him Jesus."

So for a few precious minutes I held him in my arms, the child that has been the light of my life ever since.

I stayed until they laid him in his manger of hay, until he fell asleep, and Mary too. Then Joseph took me back through the sheep to the stable door to say goodbye.

"There may be more visitors tonight," said Joseph.

"But you were the first. We shan't forget you."

"Nor I you," I replied. It was only then, as I was about to go, that it occurred to me I had forgotten something.

"Whenever a child is born in our village," I said, "everyone brings a present. This is all I've got with me." And I handed Joseph my shepherd's crook. "Father made it for me. He said it should last a lifetime."

"Thank you," Joseph said, running his hand along the crook. "This is wonderful work, the work of a craftsman. He will have no finer gift than this." And with that he turned and went back inside.

Moments later the Angel Gabriel was winging me away, out over the walls of the stable yard, over the sleeping town, away from the light of the star and back towards the darkness of the hills.

As we flew I was full of questions. I wanted to know so much about Jesus, this child King who was going to save the world.

"How will he do it?" I shouted into Gabriel's ear against the sound of the wind. "How will he bring us peace and goodwill?"

The Angel Gabriel flew on, never answering any of my questions. It was almost as if he hadn't heard me at all. Only when we landed in amongst the sheep and the shepherd angels did he at last give me an answer.

"Love," he said. "He will bring us love, and through

love we will at last have peace and goodwill on earth. Now, make sure you keep the fire going, there's a good lad."

Those were the last words he spoke to me. There were no goodbyes. There was no time. He rose at once into the night sky, and with him all the other angels too, each a beacon of sparkling light. And as they went I heard first the singing of their wings, then the singing of their voices until the sky above me and the whole earth rang with such a joyful sound that I thought my heart would burst.

"Glory to God on high. And on earth, peace, goodwill towards men."

Slowly the music faded and the light died. I felt suddenly alone in the night until the sheep gathered about me, all of us, I know, sharing the wonder of everything we had just witnessed.

Father and the others came back just after sunrise, full of everything, of course, and very pleased with themselves. They'd followed the star and found the stable and the child King wrapped in swaddling clothes. He'd been fast asleep in his manger, they said, all the time they were there.

"Such a pity you couldn't have been with us," Reuben sniggered.

"Then these three Kings from far-off Persian lands turned up, and there wasn't room for us and we had to go," said Uncle Zac, who sounded more than a little put out. "You should've seen the presents they brought: gold, frankincense, myrrh. We had nothing to give him except our crooks and we couldn't hardly give him those, could we?"

"Proper stupid we felt," Jacob added.

"Sheep all right?" Father asked me. "Anything happen while we were gone?"

"Not a thing," I replied. "Not a thing."

I nearly told them then, so nearly. I was bursting to tell them everything. But I didn't, because I knew they'd never have believed me anyway. Reuben and Jacob would only have scoffed and laughed at me even more than usual. Just keep quiet about it, I told myself. When the time comes you can tell your children and your grandchildren, because they'll know about Jesus by then – everyone will. And you do too, don't you, his whole life, everything he did and said. You may not believe my story, but you don't laugh at me, you don't scoff. You just think I'm a bit old, a bit doolally. And I suppose I am at that."

And Grandpa always ended his story the same way, his voice almost a whisper. "And that shepherd's crook I gave him – I told Father I'd lost it in the dark that night and he made me another – Jesus carried it with him all his life. It was there at the Sermon on the Mount; when he fed the five thousand; when he rode into Jerusalem. He had it with him almost to the end, till they took it off him, till that last day when he carried the cross instead."

And so Grandpa finished his story. But that wasn't the end of it, not last night. Last night the story had a very different ending altogether, something amazing, incredible – which is why I've written it down at once. This way I'll always be able to remember it as it was and I'll never be able to believe it didn't happen.

As we sat there around the fire, silent in our thoughts, I thought, as all of us did, that Grandpa's Christmas story was over for another year. It was such a lovely story, but just a story. We knew how Grandpa had followed Jesus all his life, how much he loved him. Wishful thinking, we thought, that's all it had been, just wishful thinking. But I remember sitting there last night and wondering whether any of it could possibly be true. That was when it happened.

Grandpa began prodding at the fire with his shepherd's crook. Showers of sparks rose into the night sky and as I watched them I saw that they did not fly up towards the stars, but gathered themselves into a great light. And within the light I saw beacons of brightness that took shape and became angels, hundreds of them, thousands of them, their wings singing in the air, then their voices too, until the skies above us rang with such joyful sounds that I thought my heart would burst.

"Glory to God on high!" they sang. "And on earth, peace, goodwill towards men!"

The Best of Times

There are times when all seems well with the world. It was just such a time when this story begins. Everyone in the whole country was happy. The harvest was looking good. The corn grew gold in the fields. The vines and the trees were heavy with fruit. The shining rivers teemed with silver fish.

But the happiest of all in this lucky land was Prince Frederico. He was more like a brother than a prince to his people, and much loved, which was why everyone was so happy for him when he found at last the Princess of his heart, Princess Serafina. She was a girl of such beauty and kindness that everyone who saw her took her to their heart at once. She only had to smile and there was joy all around her. She sang, she danced. She only had to laugh and the world laughed with her.

The two married on New Year's Day, and the people went mad with joy. They rang the bells all over the land. They danced in the streets, they rousted and revelled, they feasted and fêted, from morning till night. Never had anyone seen such a happy couple.

But a year or so later, all this had changed. The joy

and the gladness had gone. Everyone could see that a great sorrow was settling over the Princess, like a dark shadow.

She never smiled any more, nor laughed any more. She did not sing. She did not dance. She did not speak for days on end. Sometimes she would not even eat. Prince Frederico simply could not understand what had come over his beloved Princess, nor could anyone else. It was a complete mystery.

The light left her eyes. The glow left her cheeks. Every evening, the Princess would sit beside her Prince in the great hall of the palace, not touching her food, speaking to no one. She seemed lost in her own sadness, and could find no way out.

Prince Frederico was desperate to make her happy again. He did all he could to cheer her heart.

At Christmas time, as a token of his love for her, he lavished gifts upon her. Dresses of the finest silk. Rubies and emeralds and sapphires he gave her too, and a pair of white doves that cooed to her from her window when she woke in the mornings. He gave her parakeets and peacocks, meerkats and monkeys, and two whippets to stay always by her side and love her faithfully.

But nothing seemed to raise her spirits. No husband could have been more kind and loving than the Prince. He tried his very best to find out why it was, how it was, that she had become so wrapped up in her sorrows.

"We can be happy together again, dearest," he told her. "All will be well, I promise. If only you would just tell me what is troubling you so, then I could help to make things right for you, and make you happy again. Is it something I have done?"

But the Prince's kind words, like all his wonderful gifts, simply left her cold. She turned her head away and kept her silence. Even when he held her in his arms and kissed her fondly, she still seemed far away from him and lost in her sadness. The Prince was heartbroken. There seemed to be nothing whatever he could do to help her. The royal physician visited her every day, but he was as baffled and mystified as everyone else. No medicine he gave her made any difference.

For poor Princess Serafina there was no escape from her sorrows, even in her dreams. All night long she would lie awake. All day long she would sit in her room, ignoring all the food Prince Frederico brought to her, however sweet it smelt, however spicy. A little fruit was all she would eat, and a little water to drink. That was all. She was overwhelmed by sorrow. Maybe after the grey skies of Winter had passed, the Prince thought, maybe then she would be happier.

Spring came at long last, and there was birdsong again, and daffodils danced in the sunshine. But the

Princess remained as sad as ever. Prince Frederico was now becoming worried for her life, as was the royal physician.

"She is pining away, my Prince," the physician told him, his eyes full of tears. "She seems to have lost the will to live. If she does not want to live, then there is little I can do, little anyone can do. All I can suggest is that she should get out into the fresh Spring air. Maybe she should go for a ride each day. That might help."

So, the next morning, Prince Frederico took her for a long ride up in the hills, where the air was bright and bracing, where they could look out over the land and see how green and lovely it was under a cloudless blue sky. He put his arm around her.

"Isn't this the most beautiful place on earth, dearest?" he whispered. "It makes you feel good to be alive, doesn't it?"

But Princess Serafina spoke not a word in reply. She gazed out over the cornfields, seeing nothing but emptiness, feeling nothing but loneliness.

By the time Spring turned to Summer, the Princess had become too weak even to ride. The Prince loved her far too much to give up trying. Day after day, he took her out walking in the countryside. But nothing seemed to mean anything to her any more; not the warmth of the breeze on her face, not the buzzards wheeling and mewing over the hillsides, not the lark rising into the sky from the cornfield, not the leaping salmon, nor the whisper of the willows by the river. Nothing touched her heart.

Now it was Autumn. The Princess was too ill by this time to go out any more for her daily walks with the Prince. Instead he sat with her at her window, holding her hand, hoping and praying for the first sign of a miraculous recovery. None came. Gentle morning mists lay over the water-meadows. Trees glowed red and gold and yellow in the afternoon sun. But the Princess saw no beauty in it, took no joy from it at all.

Winter came in with its whining winds and savage storms. The Prince and Princess sat by the fire now in her room, and he would read her stories through the long dark evenings, even though he could tell she wasn't listening. Then, just a week or so before Christmas it was, the Princess became too weak even to rise from her bed. The royal physician shook his head and told the Prince that he knew of nothing that could save her now, that he must prepare himself for the worst.

"No!" cried the Prince. "She will not die. I will not let her die."

But he feared in his heart of hearts that there was nothing more that he could do.

Inside the palace, and outside too, the news quickly spread that the Princess was close to death, that it could only be a matter of time. The Master of the Prince's

Household ordered that all preparations for Christmas were to be stopped, that the holly was to be removed, the tree taken down from the great hall, that there would be no Christmas celebrations that year.

All about him, the Prince saw only sympathy and sadness. Friends and family wept openly. It was more than he could bear. He just wanted to get away from it all. He leapt on to his horse and galloped off into the countryside where he could be alone. He rode and he rode, crying out his grief, shouting it into the wind, into the blinding blizzard that was suddenly swirling all around him. On he rode through the snowstorm, not knowing any more how far he had gone, nor where he was, and not caring much either.

Soon his horse could go no further. The snow was too deep, the wind too harsh. So when the Prince saw the light of a cottage window nearby, he knew he had to stop and seek shelter.

But as he came closer and dismounted from his horse, the Prince realised that it wasn't a cottage at all, but a caravan, a travellers' caravan.

He climbed the steps and knocked on the door.

A smiling young lad opened the door and invited him in at once. He did not appear at all surprised to see him. In fact, it seemed to the Prince that this whole family of travellers must somehow have been expecting him, so generous and immediate, so unquestioning was the warmth of their welcome. They saw to the Prince's horse, stabled her with theirs, made sure she had a good rub-down and a feed. Then they sat the Prince down by the stove and gave him a bowl of piping-hot soup to warm him through. In the glow of the lanterns there were a dozen or more faces watching him as he drank down his soup, old and young, but all of them welcoming. There was no sadness here, only smiles and laughter wherever he looked.

None of them seemed to know who he was. He was simply a stranger they had taken in out of the storm.

All evening he stayed with them as they sang their songs and told their stories. Then the old grandfather, the head of the family, leant forward to speak to the Prince.

"You've heard our songs, stranger, and you've heard our stories. Haven't you got a song you'd like to sing for us? Haven't you got a story you'd like to tell?"

The Prince thought for a while. He had only one story on his mind. "It's about a Prince who lived in a palace, and a beautiful Princess whom he loved more than life itself, how they had once been so happy, until…" And so he told the story.

As he neared the end of his story, one of the children sitting at his feet looked up at him and cried, "And did the Princess die? I don't want her to die."

"Nor do I," said the Prince. "I want my story to have a happy ending. I so want her to live. But, you see, I don't know how to save her from her sadness, how to make her happy again. All of you here seem to be so happy. What's your secret?"

"Oh, that's quite simple," replied the old grandfather, knocking out his pipe on the stove. "We are who we want to be. We're travellers, and we keep travelling on. We just follow the bend in the road. Like everyone, we have our troubles, we have our sadnesses. But we try to keep smiling. That's the most important thing of all, to keep smiling. Now, if that Princess in your story could only smile, then she'd be right as rain, and your story would have a happy ending. I like a happy ending. But there's a strange thing about happy endings, they often make you cry, don't they? Funny that. Very close those two, crying and laughing. We need a bit of both, I reckon." The old grandfather lit up his pipe again before he went on. "This prince of yours, in the story, he loves his princess very much, doesn't he?"

"More than his whole kingdom," said the Prince. "He'd give his whole kingdom to have her happy again."

"Well then, maybe that's just what he'll have to do," said the old man.

The Prince lay awake all night beside the stove, the travelling family sleeping on the floor around him, and all the while he was thinking of everything the old grandfather had said. Outside the storm was blowing itself out.

By morning, the Prince had made up his mind what

must be done to save his beloved Serafina. He ate a hearty breakfast with the family, and thanked all of them for their kindliness from the bottom of his heart. Then, wishing them a happy Christmas, he set spurs to his horse and rode homeward through the snow, hoping and praying all the way that Princess Serafina would be no worse when he got there.

She was no worse, but she was no better either. Prince Frederico knew there was no time to lose. He called his Council together at once.

"Send out messengers into every corner of this land," he told them. "Tell the people that I will give away my whole kingdom, all my titles, lands and property to anyone who is able to make Princess Serafina smile again."

The Council protested loudly at this, but the Prince would hear no argument from them.

"I want it proclaimed that whoever can do this, whoever wishes to win my kingdom, must come here to the palace on Christmas Day – and that is only two days away now." He turned to the Master of the Household. "Meanwhile, we shall make merry throughout the palace, throughout the land, as we always do at Christmas time. I want there to be no more sadness. I want the Princess to feel the joy of Christmas all around her. I want this palace to be loud with laughter. I want to hear the carols ringing out. I want her to smell all the baking pies and puddings, all the roasting pork and geese. I want everything to be just as it should be. We may be sad, but we must make believe we are glad. Let her know that Christmas is the best of times. Let her see it, let her hear it."

And so messengers were sent out far and wide, into every valley, into every hamlet and town in the land.

Meanwhile, as the Prince had commanded, every room and hall in the palace was bedecked again for Christmas, and all the festive fun and games began.

By the first light of dawn on Christmas Day, the courtyard of the palace was filled with all manner of jesters and clowns, jugglers and acrobats and contortionists, all in bright and wonderful costumes, all busy rehearsing their acts. There were animals too – elephants from India, ponies from Spain and chimpanzees from Africa.

Inside the great hall, everyone waited for Prince Frederico to appear and, when at last they saw him coming down the staircase carrying Princess Serafina in his arms, they were on their feet and cheering them to the rafters, willing her to be better, longing for her to smile.

How pale she looked, how frail, so frail that many thought she might not live to see in the new year. But everyone there that Christmas Day knew that this would be her last chance, her only hope, and that they had their part to play. They would do all they could to lift her spirits, to let her know how much she was loved. When at last the great doors opened and in came the first of the performers, a clown with a bucket on his head, they all roared with laughter, all of them glancing from time to time at the Princess, hoping for a flicker of a smile.

One after the other, the clowns and jesters came in to do their turns. They cavorted and capered, they tripped and tumbled, but through it all the Princess sat stony-faced. Jugglers and acrobats, the best in the land, cartwheeled and somersaulted around the hall. They amazed and enthralled everyone there, but not the Princess. Everyone howled with laughter at the contortionists' tangled tricks, but not the Princess.

When the elephants came trumpeting in, the chuckling chimpanzees riding on their backs, when the ponies danced and pranced in time to the music, the Princess looked on bemused, unamused and empty-hearted. As the last of them left, and the great doors closed after them, a silence fell upon the hall, a silence filled with sorrow. Prince Frederico knew, as everyone did, that it was hopeless now, that nothing on earth could lighten the darkness for the Princess, that she was lost to them for ever.

But just then, slowly, very slowly, one of the great doors groaned open, and a face peered around. A masked face.

"Who are you?" Prince Frederico asked, as into the hall there came a whole troupe of players. They wore no costumes, only masks. Some were older, some were younger, they could see that. And some were women and some men. But all moved lightly on their feet, like dancers. Together, hands joined, they walked the length of the great hall to where the Prince and Princess sat.

"Who are you?" the Prince asked them once again.

"We are a donkey," said one.

"We are a camel," said another.

"We are a cow."

"We are a sheep."

"We are a goat."

"I am a goose."

"And I am a star," a small voice piped up, holding up high a golden star on a long pole. "And we have all made a puppet play for the Princess, a Christmas play, to please her heart." With that, everyone except the child with the star went out again.

Moments later, a goose appeared at the great door, looking imperiously this way and that, as if the palace belonged to him. And then, bold as brass, as if no one else had any right to be there, he waddled into the great hall, stopping to beckon in after him a sheep and a goat and a cow, life-size all of them, and all of them – the goose too – manipulated by masked puppeteers. They breathed such life into their puppets that, very soon, everyone had eyes only for the animals themselves, and the puppeteers became almost invisible. Organised by this bossy goose, who was fast becoming a favourite with the audience, the animals settled down to sleep under the golden star.

A donkey walked in then, a weary-looking donkey. On his back he was carrying a lady who wore a dark cloak about her – everyone knew it was Mary by now, of course. And leading the donkey was Joseph, who helped her down off the donkey, and led her in amongst the sleeping animals, where he sat her down to rest. They sang a carol together then: "Silent Night, holy night, all is calm, all is bright." As they finished singing, Mary opened up her cloak very slowly, and everyone saw there was a baby inside.

A gasp ran around the hall, as everyone saw that the child too was a puppet. His little fists waved in the air. He kicked his legs. He cried out. He gurgled. Suddenly, the Princess was sitting bolt upright, her hand to her mouth, the tears running down her cheeks. Seeing how upset she was, the Prince leapt to his feet at once to stop the play, but before he could do so, she put a hand on his arm.

"Let them go on, dearest," she whispered to him. "I want to see it all, the whole play."

At that moment, in through the great doors there came three camels, masked puppeteers inside them. Living, breathing creatures they were, their heads tossing against their bridles, their tails whisking, chewing and grunting as they came, and each of them ridden by a king bearing gifts.

The goose woke up suddenly, not at all pleased at this unwelcome intrusion. He prowled and hissed around the three kings, head lowered, wings outstretched, as they presented their gifts to Mary and the baby. Then, hissing like a dozen angry snakes, he turned on the camels and chased them off into the night, the three kings running helter-skelter after them. Laughter and clapping filled the hall. The goose took a bow, and then went to have a look at the baby, before settling down again to sleep beside the sheep and the goat and the cow.

Just then, who should come in but several shepherds, looking a bit lost and bewildered. The goose slept on, for the moment. The shepherds found the baby and knelt before him to worship him. Then they sang a carol to him, a lullaby:

"Hush my babe, lie still in slumber,
holy angels guard thy bed,
Sweetest blessings without number,
gently fall upon thy head."

As they sang, the Prince saw the Princess was crying still. Then, like a sudden miracle, she was smiling, smiling through her tears. And by the time the goose woke up, saw the shepherds, and proceeded to chase them, around and around the hall, she was on her feet and crying again, but with laughter this time.

"I love that goose!" she cried. "I love that goose!"

Everyone was on their feet now, clapping and cheering as the puppeteers came forward to take their bow. The applause went on and on, because everyone could see that the Princess too was clapping and laughing with them, her eyes bright again with life. It was many minutes before the hall had quietened and the Prince could speak.

"You have made my Princess smile," he told the players. "You have made her laugh. So, as I promised, my kingdom is yours."

One by one, players took off their masks, and then the Prince knew them for who they were, that same family of travellers who had sheltered him from the snowstorm, to whom he had told his story.

"We do not want your kingdom," said the old grandfather. "We wanted only to be sure your story had a happy ending, that the Princess could learn to smile again. And now she has. It will soon be the best of times again for her, and for all of you in this happy land."

"Then at least stay with us a while, stay for our feasting," said the Prince, "so that in some small way I can repay your kindliness and hospitality."

So the players stayed, and feasted, but they would not stay the night. "Travellers," said the old grandfather, as he climbed up into their caravan, "never stay for long. We like to keep travelling on. We just follow the bend in the road. But before we go, we should like to leave you a Christmas gift. Our little goose. We've talked to him about it. He says he's quite happy to live in a palace – just so long as you don't eat him!" And so, leaving the goose behind them, they went on their way into the night. No one knew where they had come from. No one knew where they went. No one ever saw them again.

By Christmas time the next year, Princess Serafina was not only restored to full health and happiness, but she had her own precious baby in her arms, which, of course, was just what the Princess had been longing for all this time. In the play they put on in the great hall that Christmas, the Princess played Mary, and her own child played the baby, kicking his little legs and waving his fists just as he should.

The goose, of course, still insisted on playing the goose. He wasn't the kind of goose you could argue with, everyone knew that. And in his honour – just in case he ever found out – no one in that land ate roast goose at Christmas ever again.

PINOCCHIO

"My name is Pinocchio. I reckon I must be just about the most famous puppet the world has ever known. But I'm more than just bits of wood and string. I'm me. So it's about time that I, Pinocchio, told you my story…"

So here's how I began. I was a tiny cherry-pip in a blackbird's beak. The blackbird dropped me in an orchard below a town called Naples, and I fell to earth.

After a while, I grew into a fine cherry tree, blossoming wonderfully every year, until one winter's day a raging storm blew me over, and the next thing I know, I am nothing but a piece of wood, a branch in a pile of other branches, waiting to be burnt. And that would have been that. There would have been no Pinocchio.

But… as luck would have it, along came an old woodcarver. He was whistling away as he searched through the pile, and talking to himself. He picked me up, turned me this way and that, peered at me, smelt me even.

"This will do very well," he said. "Cherry-wood, the best for carving. Just what I've been looking for."

He looked about him nervously. "No one's around.

No one will notice, will they?" He tapped me with his knuckle, knocked me against a tree. "Yes, you'll carve perfectly."

That was when I spoke my first words – I'd heard a lot of speaking in my life, so words came easily. I'd just never needed them before.

"Excuse me," I said, "but I do wish you wouldn't keep knocking me about like that. It hurts. And carving me up, I'm sure, will hurt a great deal more – I don't like the sound of that one bit."

He heard me. I know that because in his surprise he dropped me on his foot. When he'd stopped hopping about, he began to search around, wondering where on earth the voice had come from.

"Anyway, you can't just steal me," I went on.

"All right, all right," he said, clapping his hands to his ears. "I will pay. Here, look. I'm leaving a coin for you on the woodpile."

And with that he tucked me under his arm and legged it. All the way I kept shouting and shouting, begging him to take me back. By the time we reached his house I'd been shouting so loud and for so long that I'd lost my voice completely.

All around the walls of his house hung the tools of his trade: chisels, planes, hammers, drills. I was terrified. To me they were nothing but instruments of torture. But when I tried to protest, nothing would come out, not a squeak, not a whisper. Then I saw the lady sitting by the fire, staring sadly into the flames.

"*Carissima mia*," said the woodcarver. "See what I have for you, my darling."

She turned and looked.

"Not another log," she sighed. "How many times have you tried before? I want a real boy for a son, not a puppet."

"But this is the finest cherry-wood, *carissima mia*. And when I touch it, it has life. I feel it. I smell it. I can almost hear it. You'll see, my darling. With this piece of wood, I will make you at last the son you have always longed for."

Gepetto's wife shook her head, and I could see there were tears in her eyes. "You are the kindest of men, Gepetto. And I love you because you never stop trying, you never stop hoping. But it is hopeless, I tell you, hopeless. We'll never have a son of our own." And again she turned her face to the fire and wept.

Gepetto the woodcarver took down his tools from the wall, rolled up his sleeves, and wiped his nose with the back of his hand. Then, looking down on me, he said, "I will make a boy of you, block of wood. I will make a son for my darling wife and me. So lie still and be good. It won't hurt."

I was terrified. I tried to yell, I tried to screech, but no sound came out, so of course he heard nothing. But I need not have worried. Gepetto was right. It didn't hurt at all. It felt as if he was tickling me!

My hair, my ears, my forehead – as he worked on them, chiselling them into shape, they simply tickled. I wanted to giggle, to laugh out loud, but I couldn't. And when he made my eyes, I couldn't move them either, not at first. All I could do was stare at him.

"It's rude to stare, you know," he said. "I knew a little boy once who stared, and he picked his nose too. He was called Pinocchio. There we are! That shall be your name: Pinocchio! Now for your nose, which you should never pick – because that is ruder even than staring, and *carissima mia* would not like it."

Gepetto had trouble with my nose – it seemed to be too long for my face. But he didn't want to risk cutting it off altogether, so, in the end, he left it too long – something I often blamed him for later on. Children often blame their fathers and mothers later on, it's quite natural.

The real trouble came when he made my mouth. Now I could giggle and laugh, but not out loud yet – because I still had no voice, you remember – but *inside*, and I was killing myself laughing, if you know what I mean. It tickled *so* much. The face was the most complicated part. That's what took the time. After that the neck, the shoulders, the stomach, the legs, the arms, the hands, all came fairly easily.

I could see how excited Gepetto was, how delighted he was with his handiwork. At last, as I lay there on the table, arms and legs outstretched, staring up at him, he stood back, hands on hips, smiling down at me.

"You'll do, Pinocchio," he whispered. "You'll do." Then he picked me up gently in his arms and carried me over to where his wife still sat gazing into the fire, brushing her tears away. He set me on her knee, took her arms and put them round me so that I was cradled in her lap. One large tear fell on my cheek and suddenly I could move, suddenly my voice came back to me too.

"Mama," I cried. "Papa!"

"Pinocchio!" They were both so happy.

Mama held me up higher and then hugged me to her. They took a hand each to help me walk. But after going once or twice around the room I didn't need them any more. Within moments I was walking on my own, a little wobbly maybe, but not falling over, not once. Then I was running, running all around the room, skipping with joy, jumping over the stools. I could do the splits; I could do somersaults; I could stand on my head!

"Our brave little Pinocchio," Gepetto cried, catching me up and setting me on his shoulder. "We have a son at last, a boy of our own." And together my new mama and papa took me out into the streets to show me off to the world.

As word spread about the town, everyone in Naples came running to see me.

"He's not a boy," they shouted, pointing at me and mocking me. "He's just a puppet, a puppet without any strings maybe, but a puppet nonetheless. He can't talk," they cried.

"He can," Gepetto told them triumphantly. "Say something to them, Pinocchio."

"Of course I can talk," I said. "I can walk with no one holding me," I said. And I did. "I can dance," I said. And I did – tap-dancing was easy with wooden feet. "I can do somersaults and handstands too."

They were amazed, everyone was, but they didn't stop laughing at me, and, what was worse, they laughed at Mama and Papa too, who I could tell were so proud of me.

"Look how his wooden head wobbles when he walks! He isn't a proper boy," they said. "A proper boy has a mind of his own, goes on adventures. You can't make a mind out of wood, Signor Gepetto! He's not a real boy at all. Wobble head! Clumpy feet! Big nose!"

That was it. I'd had enough of all their insults. I took off, legged it, did a runner. And could I run! In leaps and bounds I ran, *tickety-tackety tickety-tackety* went my wooden feet on the cobbled streets. They tried to catch me, but I dodged and ducked.

"Grab him!" they shouted. "Catch Pinocchio!" The

whole town was after me.

I had almost escaped them when, ahead of me, barring my way, there was a huge, burly policeman, a *carabiniere*, legs apart, arms wide open to catch me.

Go through his legs, I thought. *It's the only way to get past him*. But he grabbed me by my nose. Can you imagine? The indignity of it!

And then he carried me under his arm, back to Papa and Mama, who took me home at once and put me to bed.

"Never run away again, Pinocchio," Mama said, hugging me tight and kissing me. Then she brought me a mug of hot milk.

"You gave us such a fright," Gepetto said. "We thought we'd lost you for good. No matter what anyone says, you are our dear son, our little boy, and this is your home. Tomorrow you will go to school, like all the other boys and girls."

"What happens at school?" I asked them.

"You will read books and learn to spell and to write and to add up and to take away. You will learn to have a mind of your own."

"But I have a mind of my own already," I said. "I don't like this school idea at all."

"You'll love it," they told me. "You'll soon make lots of friends."

But I didn't love it and I didn't make lots of friends – in fact, not one. All the others did was laugh at me and tease me because I was different. And the teachers were just as bad. The moment they found me staring out of the window dreaming, which was often – I wanted to be out there exploring the world, not stuck in a classroom – they'd put me in the corner with a dunce's cap on my head.

I was standing there in the corner one day when I made up my mind. I knew it would upset Mama and Papa, and I felt bad about that because after all they fed me and looked after me and loved me, but I couldn't stand it any longer. I would run away and see the world. I would make my fortune. I'd show the world I wasn't a puppet, that I was a boy with a mind of my own. I'd make Mama and Papa proud of me, but I'd do it my way.

All right, all right, I know now that it was stupid. But don't think too badly of me. I don't think I was that different from most of you who are reading this – except of course I was made of wood. But that wasn't my fault, was it? I was a wooden-head, a puppet with very little sense. I just wanted to have a good time, do my own thing. That's natural, right?

THE PIED PIPER OF HAMELIN

*The fable of the mysterious piper who comes to Hamelin
town and leaves with its children is one of the world's
greatest tales. And here it begins, retold in a
wonderfully modern way…*

I don't know who my mother was, nor my father. There were a lot of children like that, like me, in Hamelin town in those days. We lived in a shanty town of shacks, around the rubbish tips outside the walls of the town, scavenging for scraps, like the crows, like the dogs, like the rats. Some of us were orphans, some simply abandoned. The truth is that most of us didn't know which, and it didn't much matter anyway. Either way, we were "thief dogs" – that's what the townspeople called us when they spat on us, threw stones at us or set their dogs on us. And we were thieves too, there's no denying it.

But don't imagine there were just a few of us. The streets and alleyways of Hamelin town were full of beggars and children like us. In every square, on every street corner, under every bridge, you'd see us. We had nowhere else to go. We begged because we had to, stole because we had to.

When you're starving you have to, I promise you. There was no other way for us to survive.

Meanwhile, the rich and the greedy lived like kings and queens behind the walls and gates of their grand houses. And their children grew up – through no fault of their own, I've got to say – like spoilt little princes and princesses, with far too much of everything they wanted. Richest and greediest of all though, was the Mayor himself and his councillors in the Town Hall. They were proud of it too, for ever showing how rich and powerful they were, dressed in their ermine cloaks, with their shining gold chains and their sparkling jewels. And the Mayor and his councillors were the nastiest of all. The truth was that they were the real thieves. They'd got rich by taking money from the working people, by the extortionate taxes they made them pay, more than three quarters of everything they earned. But if ever they caught us stealing, they'd set their servants on us. They'd beat us with sticks, and sometimes let their dogs loose on us as well.

To see me now, you'd think I'd been lame all my life. It wasn't like that. It was just bad luck. I was in the wrong place at the wrong time. It was a cold frosty morning, I do remember that, so cold I could see my breath in the air. I'd been sitting on the corner of the Market Square, my usual pitch, playing my penny whistle and hoping that some passer-by would take pity on me and drop a coin or two in my hat. But my hat was still empty. I was tired, weak with hunger and chilled to the bone after a night out in the open. I think that must have been why I fell asleep, why I didn't hear the carriage coming, didn't hear the horses galloping over the cobbles. They were on me before I knew it. Somehow the horses didn't trample me. They told me afterwards that none of them even touched me. It was the wheels of the carriage that did the damage. They ran right over my leg and crushed it. It was Emma who found me – she was my best friend and a thief dog like me. She patched me up as best she could. Emma saved my life, but there was nothing she could do about my leg.

Since then I've needed my crutch to get around – I can shuffle around on my bottom of course, but I'd rather not. It's very slow and it makes me sore. It's not very dignified either. Everyone said at the time that I was lucky to be alive. But to be honest, I didn't feel that lucky. Anyway, I wasn't much use as a thief dog after that, only as a lookout. I couldn't thieve and make a run for it like the others. I couldn't even climb the rubbish tips to go scavenging with the pack. Emma and the other thief dogs, they looked after me as best they could. I managed to survive. Just.

I could still play my penny whistle, I could still beg. My leg – or perhaps my crutch I should say – helped a bit too. Some days, a few of the townspeople seemed to take pity on me as they passed me by, and I'd get quite a few coins dropped in my hat, enough sometimes to buy myself a bread roll and even a bit of cheese too, if I was really lucky. In spite of everything, I was all right.

But then came the rats – not just a few. No, this was a plague. Like locusts, they ate everything in their path, and there were hundreds of them, then before we knew it, thousands, then tens of thousands, even hundreds of thousands. The Mayor and his corporation did nothing about it, nothing whatsoever. It shouldn't have been a surprise to them, nor to any of us, not with the huge mountains of rubbish piling up around the town. I mean, rats and rubbish – they go together, don't they?

Of course we all knew that. We were used to rats. After all, we lived where they lived, in and around the rubbish tips. We ate what they did, and we ate them too – when we could catch them, that is. The trouble was that quite suddenly these rats weren't like normal rats any more. They were massive, as big as cats some of them, honestly. And they were everywhere, running all over us while we slept, eating up every scrap of food on the rubbish tips, so that there was scarcely a thing left for us. Worse still, these giant rats were beginning to attack us. A cornered rat will always go for you, but these were hunting now, in packs. They had a dangerous look in their eyes, and we knew what it meant. We knew that they would kill us if they could.

Soon they had chased us out of our shacks, out of our shanty town, and off the rubbish tips altogether. We had nowhere else to run to, but into Hamelin town itself, where the rich folk lived, and where we all knew we'd be very far from welcome. No one offered us food. No one offered us shelter from the winter cold. The rich children hurled abuse at us, threw stones at us whenever they saw us and the Mayor and his councillors set their dogs on us. At night-time we hid and huddled where we could, under bridges, under carriages and carts.

Emma became such a true and faithful friend to me in those hard times. Now that the plague of rats was eating all the town's scraps, there was precious little left for us. Only the best scavengers were eating at all. To be a good scavenger, you had to be quick on your feet – and I wasn't. Emma helped me all she could, sharing whatever food she found with me. She stuck by me, looked after me. We broke into houses together, hid down in cellars or up in attics, until we were discovered – as sooner or later we always were. Then people would drive us out with their cruel whips and their snarling dogs. The time came when there was no hiding place left and the two of us found ourselves with nowhere to shelter, almost always on the run. We were nearly starving and frozen half to death.

To begin with, while the rats swarmed over the rubbish tips on the other side of the river, the Mayor and his corporation saw them as an opportunity for a bit of fun. They made great sport of it, sending out hunting parties on horseback, seeing how many rats their dogs could kill in a day, and which of them could kill the biggest one. They killed hundreds and the more they killed the happier they were. It was just a lark for them – but not for long. Once the rats began to come into town, to find their way into larders, into shops, they realised they could soon be facing starvation in the face. At last they began to take the situation more seriously. Now they went out hunting in deadly earnest.

For days the Mayor and his corporation hunted down the rats and killed them. But then everything changed.

I remember the evening it happened. We were watching from the river bank, when we saw the Mayor's hunting party come galloping back over the bridge into town. Then we saw the rats coming after them, swarming across the bridge in their thousands. The horses had their ears back. They were running for their lives, the dogs in amongst them, baying in terror. I saw the look of panic and horror on the Mayor's face as he came riding by us. All over town, as the rats poured through the streets, people were barricading themselves in their houses. In the Market Square the vegetable and fruit stalls, the cheese and sausage stalls, were stripped bare. In through the drains they came, in under the eaves, in through even the smallest of holes.

In they came. It was an invasion, and within a few days it had become an occupation.

Everywhere you looked there were rats, in the streets, sitting watching you from window ledges, from the branches of trees. There wasn't a cat or dog to be seen in the streets. The rats were everywhere. These were angry rats. They'd bite you as soon as look at you. The Mayor and his councillors tried all they knew to get rid of them. They put down traps, but the rats took one look at them, and knew them for what they were. These rats were clever. They were super-rats! The Mayor gave instructions to put rat poison down all over the town. But the rats took one sniff and realised at once what it was. It didn't fool them. They didn't touch it.

So he sent his drummers out into the streets to try to frighten them away. This worked for a while, but as soon as the drummers stopped drumming, the rats came back. The Mayor ordered that fires should be lit in all their nesting holes. He was sure this would drive them away. And it did too, for a little while, but as soon as the fires went out, the rats came back. It was hopeless. There seemed to be nothing he could do to rid Hamelin town of the rats, nothing anyone could do. All they could think of was how to protect themselves and their children from the rats. As it turned out, it happened to be me that gave the Mayor the idea of how this might be done.

Sir Gawain and the Green Knight

*It is New Year's Eve and the Knights of the Round Table
are about to begin feasting when a terrible adversary
arrives. Camelot has been invaded by the
fearsome Green Knight…*

Think yourself back in years, my friends – not as far
as ancient Greece and the siege of Troy, nor as far
as Romulus and Remus and Rome, but to Britain after the
Romans had gone, a Britain in the early mystical mists of
her most turbulent times, striving always to keep the invader
at bay, and to make of herself a place where people could
live out their lives in peace and safety and prosperity. Many
kings came and went, many invaders and conquerors, and
as the battles raged throughout the land there was great
grief and suffering, and terrible hunger too.

Then, as the myth goes – and whether it is the myth of
the story or the myth of history is for you to decide – then
there came a king who would lead the people of Britain
out of the darkness of their misery and into the sunlight at
last. His name was Arthur. Never had there been a braver,
more noble king than this. Saved at birth, hidden away,

then plucked from obscurity and chosen to be High King by the magical powers of Merlin, he drew the sword from the famous stone and not long afterwards gathered about him at Camelot all those great Knights, who had goodness at heart, who shunned all greed and pride, the finest and fiercest Knights in the kingdom, who fought only for right and for the wellbeing of others and of their kingdom. You know their names as well as I do from stories that have come down to us through the ages: Sir Lancelot, Sir Percivale, Sir Galahad, Sir Tristram – dozens of them, too many to be listed here – and Sir Gawain, of course, who was the High King's nephew.

My story is of Gawain. Of all the tales of the Knights of the Round Table his is the most magical and the one I most love to tell. For Gawain, as you will shortly see, was as honest and true as a Knight of the Round Table should be, as kind and chivalrous and courteous, as brave as any other, and stronger in battle than any, except Lancelot. But Gawain was headstrong too, and more than a little vain; and as this story will show, sometimes not as honest or true as he would want himself to have been: much like many of us, I think.

So, to his story, the story of Sir Gawain and the Green Knight.

It was Christmas time at Camelot, that time of the year when all King Arthur's Knights gathered to celebrate the birth of their Lord and Saviour, Jesus Christ. For fifteen joyous days, after holy Mass each morning there was nothing but feasting and dancing and singing, and hunting and jousting too. Jousting was the favourite sport, each of them striving to unseat the mighty Sir Lancelot – but rarely succeeding of course. And all was done in fun, in a spirit of great comradeship, for they were happy to be together once more, at this blessed time. During the year these lords were so often parted from one another, and from their ladies, as they rode out through the kingdom on their dangerous missions. So this was a time when love and friendship was renewed, a time to celebrate with their young king all their achievements and their great and good purpose: to bring peace to the land, and make of it a kingdom as near to a heaven on earth as had never before been achieved in Britain, nor in any other land, come to that.

On New Year's Eve, after evening Mass had been said in the chapel and generous new year's gifts exchanged, the High King and Guinevere, his queen, came at last into the great hall where all the lords and ladies were waiting to dine. No one could begin the feasting until they came, of course, so as you can imagine they cheered them to the rafters when they saw them. Guinevere had never looked so gloriously beautiful as she did that evening, and there were gasps of admiration from around the hall, from lords and ladies alike.

With Arthur on one side of her and Gawain on the other, Guinevere sat down at the high table, which was set on a splendid dais draped all about with silk and richly hung with the finest tapestries from Toulouse and Turkestan. Then, with drummers drumming and pipers piping, the servants came in carrying the food on great silver plates, piling each table high with roasted meat, capons and venison and pork, and fish fresh-baked in sea salt, and baskets of crusty bread, and steaming soups. Truly there was enough to feed the five thousand, though there were only five hundred there to eat it. As they poured out the wine and ale, filling every goblet to the brim, the scents of the feast that lay before them filled the succulent air, and their nostrils too, so that, their appetites whetted, they were all longing now to begin. But the High King and his queen sat there, not touching their food nor their drink either. Everyone knew that if they did not begin, then out of respect nor could anyone else. And everyone knew also why it was that the king was refusing to let the feast begin.

The great hall fell silent as Arthur rose to his feet. "You know the custom," he began. "I will not take one mouthful, nor one sip of wine, until I am told of some new and stirring tale, some wonderfully outlandish adventure, some extraordinary feat of arms so far unheard of. And it must be true too. I don't want you to go making it up just

so you can get at the food – some of you are good at tall
stories." They laughed at that, but as they looked around it
became clear that none of them had a tale to tell. "What?"
cried the High King. "What? Not one of you? Well then I
see we must all go hungry. Such a pity. Isn't it strange how
food you cannot eat always smells so wonderful? It needn't
be a story, of course. It could be some new happening,
some weird and wondrous event. If I can't have a story,
then you'd better hope, as I do, that some stranger will
come striding in here right now and challenge us face to
face. That would do. I'd be happy with that. Then we could
all begin our feasting before the food gets cold." And with
that he sat down.

At that very same moment, just as the High King
had finished speaking, they heard a sudden roaring of
wind, the rattle of doors and windows shaking and then,
outside, the clatter of a horse's hooves on stone. The great
doors burst open, and into the hall rode the most awesome
stranger anyone there had ever set eyes on. For a start he
was a giant of a man, taller by two heads than any knight
there, but not lanky and long, not at all. No, shoulder to
shoulder he was as broad as any three men stood side by
side, and his legs were massive – like tree trunks, they were.
And you could see the man's arms were about as thick
and strong as his legs. But that wasn't all. This giant was
green: green from head to toe. Yes, bright green, I tell you,

as green as beech leaves in summer when the sun shines through. And when I say the man was green, I don't just mean his clothes. I mean him. His face. Green. His hands. Green. The hair that hung down to his shoulders. Green. Only his eyes, horror of horrors, glowed red, blood red and glaring from under his heavy eyebrows, which were as green as the rest of him. Everyone in that hall simply gaped at him, at his hugeness and his greenness, and at his grimness too, for the man had a thunderous scowl on his face that struck terror into every heart.

Grim he may have been, but the giant was gorgeous too – if such an apparition can ever be said to be gorgeous. He wore a tunic of green velvet with buttons of gleaming gold. Stirrups and spurs were all of gold, both encrusted with the brightest emeralds of the deepest green. And his horse! His warhorse was a monster of a creature – he had to be, just to carry this giant. The horse was green too, green from nose to hoof, from mane to tail. He was pawing at the ground, tossing his head, foaming at his bit; at least the foam was white. He looked every bit as bad-tempered as his master. They suited each other, those two.

Yet fierce though he seemed, the knight in green wore no war helmet and no armour either. He held no shield before him, and carried no spear, not even a sword at his side. Instead, the hand clutching the reins held a sprig of holly – green, naturally – which might have been laughable

had everyone not already noticed what he was carrying in
his other hand. It was an axe, but it was no ordinary battle-
axe. This weapon was a real head-cruncher. Yet the handle
was most delicately carved – bright green, of course, as
was the cord that looped about it and the tassels that hung
from it. Only the huge blade itself was not green. Curved
like a crescent moon at the cutting edge, it was made of
polished steel – a hideous widow-maker if ever there was
one. Even the dogs, usually so fierce with any stranger,
shrank back whining under the tables, their tails between
their legs.

HANSEL AND GRETEL

This well-known tale begins with the parents of Hansel and Gretel, a happy young couple who receive a visit from a most unwelcome stranger...

For Gabriel and Lisette, every day seemed fine and sunny. They loved one another deeply, and of course they hoped and believed, as all young couples do, that they would live happily ever after. Life seemed as perfect as it could be. Everyone called them Gabriel the Good and Lisette the Lovely. Very soon they were blessed with two wonderful children, Hansel, and Gretel, his little sister. They all lived together in a little thatched cottage on the edge of the forest. Here, they could easily gather enough firewood to cook their food, and to keep themselves warm through the winter. They could grow all the vegetables they needed in the field of sweet earth. They had eggs from the hens and milk from the cow that grazed on the lush grass in the meadow. They gathered fruit and berries and nuts. The river teemed with salmon and sea trout and sometimes, for feast days, Gabriel would bring back a deer from the forest. They were as happy as any family could ever hope to be. Truly it seemed that God must be smiling down on them.

Then, one fine and sunny day, all that changed. Something wicked came out of the forest, and she wasn't a wolf. She was worse than the worst wolf ever could be. She was a witch, a warty old witch, with gnarled skin like ancient treebark, a nose like a crabclaw, and her eyes glowed red, red as blood. Like all witches she was horribly cruel. Her greatest pleasure was to use her evil powers, all her wicked spells and enchantments, to cause as much mischief and suffering and grief as she possibly could. And this witch often didn't look like a witch at all. It was nothing for her to change herself into anything or anyone she wanted to be. But what she yearned for, as year by year she became older and uglier, as she ached more and more in her bones, as her eyesight grew dim and clouded with age, was to be young and beautiful. Above everything else, she longed to be loved.

When this gruesome old witch first happened to peep in through the cottage window and saw the family gathered inside, she came as a magpie, a cackling magpie, knocking on their windowpane. The children at once ran out and threw her some breadcrumbs, because they thought she might be hungry. And she *was* hungry too, but not for bread. She was hungry for something else entirely. Even as a magpie she could see only dimly. But that was enough.

From the moment she first set her eyes on Gabriel, she loved him – loved him completely and utterly. And from the moment she first saw Lisette, she hated her just as completely, just as utterly. This woman had everything she so desperately wanted. She was radiantly beautiful, and she was so obviously loved and adored by everyone around her.

It's quite simple, thought the witch. *I shall find a way to get rid of her. I shall take everything she has, her whole family. Then I shall have all I want. I shall be young and beautiful, even more beautiful than she is. I shall have Gabriel's love, and the love of his children too.*

And what this wicked old witch wanted she always had, and never by fair means, always foul, the foulest means imaginable. Cruelty was her special speciality.

The next day Hansel and Gretel were down by the rushing river, by the stepping stones, helping their mother with the washing, as they often did. "You've worked hard enough for one morning, children," said Lisette. "You go off and play now, but not in the forest, mind. You know I don't like you playing there. There are wolves in the forest. Stay close to the house." So Hansel and Gretel kissed their dear mother goodbye, and ran off to play. High above them in the great oak tree, a magpie sat on a branch, quite unnoticed, and watched, and waited.

It was so easy. Once the children had gone, the magpie

flew down and hopped silently towards Lisette who was still busy at her washing by the river's edge. It was nothing for the magpie to change herself, right there and then, into a beautiful young woman with green eyes and rose-red lips and chestnut-brown hair, nothing to cast a wicked spell on poor unsuspecting Lisette. "Be a tree," she whispered. "Be a tree, a weeping willow tree. Watch and weep. Watch and weep. All that you have, I will take. All that you are, I will be." And Lisette was turned, right there and then, into a weeping willow tree.

It was nothing for the witch, now this beautiful young woman, to throw herself into the river, to scream and shout, "Help me! Help me! She is drowning! She is drowning!" By the time Gabriel and the children came running, Lisette was gone, and instead they found a beautiful stranger, clambering exhausted and half drowned out of the water. "The river was too fast," she cried. "I did all I could, but I couldn't save her. She was swept away."

They searched and searched, but they could find no trace of Lisette, except the washing still left there on the river bank. They were all far too upset to notice that there was another weeping willow tree now growing near the very spot where Lisette had been washing their clothes. They did not hear it sighing for them in the breeze, crying for them in the wind. As for the beautiful stranger whom they all believed had nearly given her own life to try and save Lisette, Gabriel carried her home to their cottage and took her inside to look after her. She hardly had the strength to whisper her name. "Belladonna," she breathed. "I am Belladonna."

They gave her some dry clothes – Lisette's clothes seemed to fit her perfectly – and then Gabriel sat her down and gave her some piping hot soup. "Thank you," whispered Belladonna, and she looked deep into his eyes. Close to, she could see him a little better now, and he was even more handsome than she had thought. It seemed to good, kind Gabriel that she was still far too weak to leave, so he laid her down by the fire to rest. And there she slept (or pretended to sleep). She slept for days and days. And whilst she slept Gabriel looked down at her and, despite his grief for Lisette, he was soon completely enchanted. He thought she must be the bravest and, apart from Lisette of course, the most beautiful woman in the whole wide world.

Because of this, because of all she had done to try to save Lisette, and especially because she seemed so kind to the two children, it was only natural for Gabriel to ask her to stay on with them for a while. It was all turning out just as Belladonna had hoped and planned. And of course, the longer she stayed, the more bewitched Gabriel became. *She's so lovely*, he told himself. *We could be happy together. Hansel and Gretel would have a new mother, and I would have a new wife.*

When, a year or so later, he asked her to marry him, she was overjoyed. She threw her arms round his neck and kissed him. "I do love you so much," she said, "I'll make you the best wife. And I shall be the best mother to the children too. I love them so much – so much I could eat them."

On their wedding day, with everyone there, all their friends and family, with Hansel playing the flute and Gretel the fiddle, Gabriel and the beautiful Belladonna danced on the village green till the sun went down. There was hardly a whisper of wind that night, but still the weeping willow down by the river sighed and moaned all night long, so loud that neither Gabriel nor Belladonna could sleep.

"What's that strange noise?" Gabriel asked.

"I think it's that weeping willow tree," said Belladonna, and she was smiling to herself secretly in the darkness. "It sounds as if it's crying, don't you think? Almost as if it's in pain."

"You don't believe that trees have feelings, do you?" he said.

"Oh yes, they do," she replied. "Trees have feelings. And especially that one, I promise you."

BEOWULF

*In fifth-century Denmark, a murderous monster stalks
the night, and only the great prince of the Geats has the
strength and courage to defeat him...*

Hear, and listen well, my friends, and I will tell you
a tale that has been told for a thousand years and
more. It may be an old story, yet, as you will discover, it
troubles and terrifies us now as much as ever it did our
ancestors, for we still fear the evil that stalks out there in
the darkness and beyond. We know that each of us in our
time, in our own way, must confront our fears and grapple
with this monster of the night who, given a chance, would
invade our homes, and even our hearts, if he could.

So roll back the years now, back to the fifth century
after the birth of Christ, and come with me over the sea
to the Norse lands we now know as Sweden and Norway
and Denmark, to the ancient Viking lands of the Danes
and the Geats, the Angles and the Jutes. This will be our
here and now, as this tale of courage and cruelty unfolds,
as brave Beowulf battles with the forces of darkness, first
with that foul fiend Grendel, then with his sea-hag of a

mother, and last of all, with the death-dragon of the deep.

The story begins as all stories do, before it begins, for there is always a mother before a mother, and a king before a king. In Denmark all the great lords, those royal descendants of Scyld, that great and good king, followed in his footsteps and stayed strong against their foes and loyal to their friends. The kingdom prospered. From their conquests the land grew rich, so that the people flourished and were happy. Feared by their enemies, loved by their allies, the kingdom of the Danes became great and powerful in the world.

Then the lord Hrothgar came to the throne, son of the old King Healfdene, great grandson of Scyld, and he was to become the greatest warrior king of them all. Fierce in battle, he fetched back home more treasures from his conquests than had ever before been seen or even dreamt of in Denmark. But he was generous too and a good father to his people, so that they obeyed him always gladly. Hearing of his increasing glory in battles, more and more warriors came to join him. It seemed to them and to him that there could never be an end to all his power and wealth. The kingdom was safe from its enemies, the people warm at their hearths and well fed. Truly it was a land of sweet content.

To celebrate these years of prosperity and plenty, Hrothgar decided he would raise for his people a huge

mead-hall. It must, he declared, be larger and more
splendid than any mead-hall ever built. Only the best
timbers were used, only the finest craftsmen. At Hrothgar's
bidding they came from all over Denmark to construct it,
so that in no time at all the great hall was finished. It was
truly even more magnificent than he had ever imagined it
could be. Heorot he called it, and at the first banquet he
gave there, Hrothgar, by way of thanks, gave out to each
and every person rings and armbands of glowing gold.
No king could have been kinder, no people as proud and
as happy. Night after night they feasted in Heorot, and
listened to the music of the harp and song of the poet. And
every night the poet told them that story they most loved
to hear: how God had made the earth in all its beauty, its
mountains and meadows, seas and skies; how he had made
the sun and the moon to light it, the corn and the trees
to grow on it; how he gave life and being to every living
creature that crawls and creeps and moves on land or in
the sea or in the air. And man too he made to live in this
paradise. Around the warming hearth they listened to the
poet's story, enraptured, enthralled and entranced.

But there was another listener. Outside the walls of
Heorot, in the dim and the dark, there stalked an enemy
from hell itself, the monster Grendel, sworn enemy of
God and men alike, a beast born of evil and shame. He
heard that wondrous story of God's good creation, and

because it was good it was hateful to his ears. He heard the sweet music of the harp, and afterwards the joyous laughter echoing through the hall as the mead-horn was passed around. Nothing had ever so enraged this beast as night after night he had to listen to all this happiness and harmony. It was more than his evil heart could bear.

MICHAEL MORPURGO MBE is one of Britain's best-loved writers for children. He has written over 100 books and won many prizes, including the Smarties Prize, the Blue Peter Book Award and the Whitbread Award. His recent bestselling novels include *A Medal for Leroy*, *Shadow* and *Born to Run*.

His novel *War Horse* has been successfully adapted as a West End and Broadway theatre play and a major film by Steven Spielberg. A former Children's Laureate, Michael is also the co-founder, with his wife Clare, of the charity Farms for City Children.

PETER BAILEY was born in India and grew up in London. Since graduating from the Brighton School of Art, his extraordinary career has seen him illustrate over 100 books by some of Britain's best-known authors and poets, including Philip Pullman, Allan Ahlberg, Dick King Smith and Alexander McCall Smith. For twenty years he also taught illustration at the Liverpool School of Art and many of his students have gone on to great success.

CHRISTIAN BIRMINGHAM is one of the brightest stars of children's book illustration, known for the beauty, power and luminosity of his work.

Described by the *Guardian* as "a modern-day Degas", Christian has collaborated several times with Michael Morpurgo, on titles including *Shadow* and *Dear Olly*.

MICHAEL FOREMAN is one of the most successful and well-loved children's book illustrators of his generation. Among many other honours he has won the Kate Greenaway Award, the Smarties Prize (both for books which he wrote and illustrated) and the Children's Book Award. His friendship with Michael Morpurgo ("the other Michael") has led to many classic collaborations, including *Kaspar, Prince of Cats* and *Little Manfred*.

QUENTIN BLAKE CBE is one of the most iconic illustrators of our time, whose warm, spontaneous and witty style is both instantly recognisable and utterly inimitable. He is known for his collaboration with writers such as Russell Hoban, Joan Aiken, Michael Rosen, John Yeoman, David Walliams, and, most famously, Roald Dahl. He has also illustrated classic books, including *A Christmas Carol* and *Candide,* and created much-loved characters of his own, including Mister Magnolia and Mrs Armitage. In 1999 he was appointed the first ever Children's Laureate and in 2013 he received a knighthood for 'services to illustration' in the New Year's Honours.

EMMA CHICHESTER CLARK studied at Chelsea School of Art and the Royal College. As well as winning the Mother Goose Award, she has been nominated for the Kate Greenaway Medal, Kurt Maschler Award and Blue Peter Book Award. Emma has created many popular picture books including the *Melrose and Croc*, *Blue Kangaroo* and *Wagtail Town* series.

Bibliography of
Michael Morpurgo's Works

It Never Rained (1974)

Long Way Home (1975)

Thatcher Jones (1975)

Friend or Foe (1977)

Do All You Dare (1978)

What Shall We Do with It? (1978)

All Around the Year (with poems by Ted Hughes)
     (1979)

The Day I Took the Bull by the Horn (1979)

The Ghost-Fish (1979)

Love at First Sight (1979)

That's How It Is (1979)

The Marble Crusher and Other Stories (1980)

The Nine Lives of Montezuma (1980)

Miss Wirtles Revenge (1981)

War Horse (1982)

*The White Horse of Zennor and Other Stories
     from Below the Eagle's Nest* (1982)

Twist of Gold (1983)

Little Foxes (1984)

Snakes and Ladders (1994)

Stories from Mudpuddle Farm [1] (1994)

Blodin the Beast (1995)

Mum's the Word (1995)

Stories from Mudpuddle Farm [2] (1995)

The Wreck of the Zanzibar (1995)

The Butterfly Lion (1996)

The Ghost of Grania O'Malley (1996)

Robin of Sherwood (1996) republished as
    Outlaw (2012)

Sam's Duck (1996)

Farm Boy (1997)

Cockadoodle-doo, Mr Sultana! (1998)

Escape from Shangri-La (1998)

Joan of Arc (1998) republished as *Sparrow* (2012)

Red Eyes at Night (1998)

Wartman (1998)

Kensuke's Kingdom (1999)

The Rainbow Bear (1999)

Wombat Goes Walkabout (1999)

Billy the Kid (2000)

Running Wild (2009)
An Elephant in the Garden (2010)
It's a Dog's Life (2010)
Not Bad for a Bad Lad (2010)
Shadow (2010)
Little Manfred (2011)
The Pied Piper of Hamelin (2011)
Homecoming (2012)
Where My Wellies Take Me (with Clare Morpurgo) (2012)
A Medal for Leroy (2012)
Beauty and the Beast (2013)
Pinocchio by Pinocchio (2013)

Running Wild (2009)
An Elephant in the Garden (2010)
It's a Dog's Life (2010)
Not Bad for a Bad Lad (2010)
Shadow (2010)
Little Manfred (2011)
The Pied Piper of Hamelin (2011)
Homecoming (2012)
Where My Wellies Take Me (with Clare Morpurgo) (2012)
A Medal for Leroy (2012)
Beauty and the Beast (2013)
Pinocchio by Pinocchio (2013)